FORGOTTEN TREASURE

Ron,
  I hope you enjoy the
  story you are about
      to read.

        Peter W

PETER F. WARREN

outskirts
press

Outskirts Press, Inc.
http://www.outskirtspress.com

ISBN: 978-1-9772-4601-1

Library of Congress Control Number: 2021914733

Outskirts Press and the "OP" logo are trademarks belonging to Outskirts Press, Inc.

PRINTED IN THE UNITED STATES OF AMERICA

In most of my stories the majority of characters you have come to know are named after family, friends, and former co-workers. I do so as a means of honoring them for being such an important part of my life. As I was writing this story, Bobby Regan and I would occasionally catch up on what was taking place in the world, and in our own lives. On some of those occasions, we would spend time talking about South Carolina and many other issues.

I first met Bobby a few years back when he and his wife purchased the home my wife and I had come to love in South Carolina. During that process we learned how much we had in common, many of it from living most of our lives in New England. Over the course of the next few years, as we spent more and more time together the four of us became good friends. We may have become friends for many reasons, but the years we all spent living in Connecticut and Massachusetts certainly contributed to that friendship. Over dinners and visits, we learned of each other's love for South Carolina. I also learned his name was Bobby; not Robert.

During our many conversations over the past year, Bobby would always ask how my latest novel was progressing. Knowing there was a character in this story named after him, as an avid book reader he was looking forward to seeing what kind of a role he had been given.

As the editing phase of this project was taking place, my wife and I were devastated when we learned our friend had suddenly passed away. While he was not the first person to succumb to the COVID pandemic; Bobby's death has left so many of us shocked by how quickly this insidious virus claimed the life of a good friend. As I'm writing this, I find myself shaking my head in disbelief that he's no longer with us. I'm deeply troubled by the fact we'll never share another meal or a simple conversation together. I'm saddened he never had a chance to read this story.

Rest in peace, my friend.

Other books by Peter Warren

Confederate Gold and Silver

One Brother's Revenge

Murder in Murrells Inlet

The Horry County Murders

The Parliament Men

The Journey North
(Written with Roy McKinney and Edward Odom)

A Few of the Characters

Part One – The Civil War

Captain Noah Howard   A member of the Confederate Army.

Part Two – Modern Times

Paul Waring
> A reoccurring character in several of the author's stories; he is a retired state trooper. After retiring and moving to South Carolina, Paul continued his law enforcement career with a sheriff's department. He is a passionate, and distinguished, Civil War buff.

Donna Waring
> Paul's wife.

Bobby Ray Jenkins
> The undersheriff of Georgetown County; he is Paul's best friend. He is also a passionate Civil War buff.

Betty Repko
> A waitress. She is close friends with Paul, Donna, and Bobby Ray.

Phil Groski
> The owner of a construction company.

Simon Church
> Heavily involved in the gas and oil business; he is one of the world's richest men.

Genevieve Church
    She is married to Simon Church.

Robert Regan
    He is one of Simon Church's most-trusted employees.

Judge Howard Morgan
    A Federal Judge.

Many of the characters which appear in the beginning of this story are soldiers from the time of the Civil War. Like many people from that time period, they received little in the way of a formal education. Their coarse speech, and that of a few others, is intentional. It is not intended to be disrespectful or derogatory in any manner.

APRIL – MAY, 1865

1

Standing in the rear of the large spacious church, Sexton Granville Miller nervously scanned the rows of worshippers sitting inside St. Paul's Episcopal Church. While the mood inside was quiet and somber, outside the bustle of war-torn Richmond, Virginia, filtered in through the opened stained glass windows. Like their fellow Richmonders attending services in other nearby churches, those present had recently become acutely aware of how badly the war was progressing less than twenty-five miles away.

Having served the church for over thirty years as the person responsible for the care and upkeep of the grounds, and for responding to the occasional needs of those attending Sunday Mass, Miller knew almost every churchgoer by not only their first and last names, but by where their family pews were located. Many were some of the city's most influential citizens. Among them were members of the Confederate cabinet, local and state politicians, a variety of wealthy businessmen, and a number of high-ranking officers from the Confederate Army. Located directly across 9th Street from the Virginia state capital, the large stone structure, with its ornate steeple and massive exterior columns, was designed to replicate several churches built across Western Europe. It was every bit the Greek Revival building its architects had envisioned.

Approached moments earlier by Major Patrick Brophy, one of several military advisers serving the Confederate cabinet, Miller stood fidgeting as he waited for the right moment to honor Brophy's request. Having delivered a variety of messages in the past to politicians and others present during church services, from the panic clearly visible in Brophy's face Miller knew the message he was about to deliver was likely the most important, and most depressing, he would ever carry down the main aisle of the church he had grown to love. A widower for several years, Miller had often found solace sitting alone inside the large cathedral when it was not being used.

Slowly making his way towards the front of the church, Miller could not help noticing the concerned look displayed on the face of Reverend Charles Minnigerode as he finished his sermon. Born in Germany, Minnigerode, the rector at St. Paul's since 1856, was well respected across the city, and the entire Confederacy. Three years earlier, in 1862, he had baptized Jefferson Davis, the president of the rebellious states who were now struggling to keep their fight against the federal government alive. A year ago, Minnigerode had participated in General J.E.B. Stuart's funeral, one of the South's most-beloved figures.

Staring up at the pulpit as he passed row after row of some of Richmond's most respected citizens, Miller sensed their stares as he stopped next to the person he had been sent to find.

Bending down, he softly whispered in the distinguished church goer's left ear. As he fumbled for the right words, the person he was speaking to never flinched at the unexpected sound of Miller's voice. Instead, he remained focused on the sermon's last few words. Like Miller, this churchgoer had taken notice of the reverend's concerned look.

"Mr. President, I was told this is important. Your presence is needed immediately in the rear of the church."

As Miller finished speaking, the president of the Confederacy, Jefferson Davis, turned slightly in his seat to see who was waiting to escort him from his pew. Seeing two of his aides standing a few feet away, Davis sensed the bad news he was about to be told. Days of disappointing news had already served to warn him that this crisis would likely result in consequences too powerful for his government to overcome.

Patting his wife's hands as he stared into her eyes, Davis spoke to her in a hushed tone. As he spoke, the president tried his best to allay her concern. "I'm sure it's nothing, so don't worry. I'll meet you in the foyer when the service is over." Exiting his pew, the president, aware of the many faces staring in his direction, thanked Miller for his tact. Slowly striding towards the rear of the large ornate church, Davis, doing his best to present a poised and confident appearance, smiled at the many faces he recognized. Several feet away, two members of the Confederate cabinet followed the president to the rear of the church.

"How bad is it?" Davis asked, staring at the telegram he was being handed by one of his aides, Captain Isiah Avery. Born and raised in Mississippi, Avery, like many others across the South, had served in the Union Army prior to the hostilities the nation was currently engaged in. A few feet away, Captain Samuel Herndon, a native Virginian serving in several capacities on the president's staff, cautiously eyed Davis as he began to read the message he had been handed. As expected, despite the gravity of the situation confronting them both officers had saluted the president of the Confederacy. As the telegram was being read, Brophy updated the two cabinet members on its distressing news.

"Mr. President," Herndon replied, "I'm afraid the news is not what we had hoped for. This telegram confirms what we had suspected earlier this morning. I'm sorry to be the one who has to tell you this, but General Pickett has been driven from the field at Five Forks. By all accounts, he did everything possible to change the outcome, but Union troops under the command of General Sheridan overwhelmed our forces on nearly every front. Sir, the reports we're receiving indicate that we may have lost close to three thousand men."

Nodding his head over the news he was being told, Davis glanced at Herndon as he raised the telegram he was holding in his right hand. "Is this what this little meeting is all about or is there more bad news you need to tell me?"

With little choice, and with a great deal of sadness, Herndon answered Davis' question. "No, sir, there's more. All of it is just as bad; even worse, I suppose. We just received . . ."

Raising his left hand as a means of cutting Herndon off, Davis, hoping he had missed a morsel of good news, anxiously read the telegram a second time; slowly digesting every word. While overly confident in the fighting spirit possessed by the Army of Northern Virginia, over the past several weeks Davis had become too optimistic in its ability to turn back the advancing Union Army. The words he was reading for a second time were ones he and others had feared would soon come. *"I think it is absolutely necessary that we should abandon our position tonight."* With little food, dwindling amounts of ammunition, and the ranks of his army thinning out with each passing day due to desertions and deaths, in order to save his remaining resources one of Davis' most competent generals knew it was time to march west.

The disappointing words General Robert E. Lee had sent told Davis the two-hundred and ninety-two day siege of Petersburg was now a lost cause. While believing Lee had done everything possible to protect one of the Confederacy's vital supply lines and evacuation routes, Davis knew Petersburg and, most likely, the South Side Railroad had fallen. After months of arduous and bitter fighting in which his army was constantly being shelled and attacked by superior forces, Davis realized General Ulysses S. Grant and his men had won a strategic battle by sheer attrition. In less than twenty-four hours, the battles at Petersburg and Five Forks had been lost. By nightfall, with less than twenty-five miles separating the once vital railroad hub and the Confederate capitol, Davis feared Richmond would also fall to the relentless Union Army.

Watching as Davis seemed to age right in front of them, Avery updated the president with a few additional details. "Sir, the attack on Petersburg continued in earnest this morning; the reports we've received confirm the shelling intensified around seven a.m. The city's outer perimeter collapsed shortly afterwards . . . our boys did their best, but the news we're learning was there were just too many blue-bellies for them to stop." Outmanned and outmatched for the past several months, Lee's soldiers had done their best to defend Petersburg despite the squalid conditions inside their exposed trenches. With little support from Richmond and the army's Quartermaster Corps, Lee's soldiers had bravely persevered for longer than many had expected.

Turning to look back at where his wife was seated, Davis briefly listened to what his two advisors were telling him. Both were adamant that Richmond needed to be evacuated. Ignoring their comments, Davis' thoughts turned back to Petersburg. "What about the inner perimeter? Is it still in place or has General Lee already started withdrawing our troops?" Looking down at the telegram he was holding, Davis wished he had been sent more information.

Serving the president for as long as he had, Avery knew what Davis was thinking. "Mr. President, as far as we know some sections of Petersburg are still in our control. Sir, with your permission, I'd like to send General Lee a telegram suggesting he maintain the inner perimeter at all costs. This will buy us some time so we can start evacuating the capital. If he can hold out for a few more hours, it will allow us time to move the trains in position so we can transfer your office to another location."

With several thoughts running through his mind, and with a long history of being unable to get along with those he often disagreed with, Davis did his best at staying calm. "Isiah, do you expect me to send General Lee a telegraph telling him to hold the line at all costs? If that's what you expect me to do, then what I'm really asking is for General Lee to make the ultimate sacrifice so we can save our own lives. No matter how bleak the situation appears that's not an order I'll ever be prepared to issue."

Realizing he had misspoken, Avery clarified his position. "Sir, while that's what all good soldiers do for the cause their fighting for, I didn't mean to imply that General Lee should make such a sacrifice. I was simply suggesting that you might take this opportunity to express your concern about needing time to relocate your office, and those of your cabinet members. If we're to keep functioning . . . to keep supporting our armies, we can't do it with the Union Army on Richmond's doorsteps. If General Lee can hold the line for a few hours we should . . ."

"Isiah," Davis said, interrupting his aide's final thoughts, "send the telegram, but stress to General Lee that I want him to remove himself from the field as soon as possible. The news hasn't been good this morning, so let's not make it worse by losing our best general. I need General Lee to keep us in the fight over the coming weeks. If we lose him, surrender is inevitable." As he spoke, Davis recalled a prior discussion in which Lee had estimated it would take the better part of a week to remove the Army of Northern Virginia from Petersburg in the event of an emergency. Now he shuddered at the thought of Lee having to do so in less than a day.

"Thank you, Mr. President. Is there anything else you would like Captain Herndon and me to address this morning?"

Briefly conferring with his two cabinet members before sending them off to find their families, Davis then assigned his aides a set of tasks to complete. Much to his disappointment, each task was related to relocating the government of the Confederacy to another location.

Doing his best to appear as if he was undisturbed by the morning's unsettling news, Davis instructed Avery to locate the other members of the Confederate cabinet. Like Davis, most were attending morning services at two nearby churches, St. Peter's and the Baptist Church two streets over. "When you locate Secretary Breckinridge, tell him to have his family start packing, but I want him to meet me at my office in thirty minutes. Do the same when you locate Secretary Trenholm. Please advise him that we need our assets packed up and ready to be loaded on one of the trains later this afternoon. See to it that he has the assistance he needs. Tell him I also expect his staff to start packing up our records. That's to include any archives he feels are necessary so our government can continue to function, and any others pertinent to the creation of our cause. Anything he deems as useless is to be burned immediately."

"Yes, sir." Avery replied, acknowledging the order he had been given.

Looking at Brophy, Davis wasted little time before issuing his next order. "Major, make sure you assign one of our military aides to supervise that task as we can't afford anything being left behind for the Yankees to use to their advantage. Use as many soldiers as you need, but make sure they set fire to whatever we're not taking with us. Any cabinet members the three of you manage to locate are to report to my office in less than thirty minutes." In his comments, Davis had anxiously referred to two of his cabinet members; Major-General John C. Breckinridge, his Secretary of War, and George Trenholm, the Secretary of the Treasury.

"Yes, sir." As this small group of soldiers saluted their commanding officer, Avery asked, "Anything else, Mr. President?"

"Tell the cabinet members my train is leaving Richmond at eight p.m. There will be six seats reserved for each of their families. If there's anyone else at home beyond those six, well, I'm sorry, but they'll have to arrange their own transportation. And, Captain Avery, tell them to pack light. Now's not the time to be bringing along the family heirlooms. We've got a major crisis on our hands."

After sending Sexton Miller off to advise Reverend Minnigerode of his interest in addressing the congregation, Davis noticed the worried look on Herndon's face. Patting the young officer on the shoulder, he said, "Samuel, I'm just as worried as you are, but we're going to see this through. It's going to be difficult, but I need your help. Are you okay?"

Regaining his composure after realizing he had added to Davis' concerns, Herndon apologized. "I was just thinking about all of the hard work you've done to keep our cause on course. I . . . I just can't help thinking with Petersburg soon to be in the hands of the Yankees, all of your efforts may have been for naught." Looking at Davis as he prepared to move off, the young captain added, "Just as you are, Mr. President, I'm still holding out hope."

After smiling at Herndon's comments, Davis gave the young officer his final set of instructions. "Captain, you're in charge of the logistics concerning our move. I don't care how you do it, but I want two trains in place by four p.m. The first one is for the cabinet secretaries, their families, and for me and my family. See to it our bags are placed onboard, and make sure you save enough space in one of the baggage cars for our servants. You also need to save enough space for yourself and Captain Avery, and a small detachment of soldiers. Major Brophy will be in charge of the second train, so make sure you save seats for him and his family. If there's anyone else I've forgotten, find seats for them, as well. Make sure everyone knows the trains are leaving at eight p.m. If anyone is late, they can explain to the Yankees why they weren't there in time."

Davis' last comment caused Herndon a brief chuckle as he stared at the anxious faces staring his way from the pews in front of him. In several pews, a group of widows and orphaned children, all dressed in black, stared at the sudden frenzy taking place around the Confederate president. As Brophy and Avery moved off, Herndon asked, "Sir, what are your plans for the second train?"

"After I finish addressing the congregation, I'm going to have a private conversation with a few of the local bankers I see here. They'll be told to pack up their vaults, and to have their assets ready to be picked up by a military escort at three p.m. These bankers, their families, and the assets of each of their banks are to be assigned space on the second train. Those assets we have in our treasury will also be placed on this same train. Have a guard assigned to that train, as well. We can't afford for any of that money to fall into the hands of General Grant or any of his men."

With his instructions completed, President Jefferson Davis walked away to deliver the news that Petersburg would soon be in the hands of the Union Army. It was news many already suspected. What he would tell the congregation would cause them to lose any remaining hope of a Confederate victory.

2

By two p.m. panic filled the streets of Richmond as news of one of the last Confederate strongholds was about to fall. Like President Davis, many of the city's inhabitants were preparing to leave in advance of the expected arrival of Union forces. Within hours of hearing the frightening news, scenes of confusion, hopelessness, and the surge of an uncontrollable mob spread across the Confederate capital. Across the city tobacco warehouses, saloons, boarding homes, liquor and military warehouses, and other buildings were already burning; some by design and others by accident and acts of vandalism. Along the edge of the city near the James River, privately owned boats, as well as military vessels were either being scuttled or in the process of being burned. While Petersburg had been one of the vital railroad hubs the South depended on to move troops and supplies, the citizens of Richmond, like others across the rebellious states, had relied on the railroads for many other needs.

Later that evening, with a heavily armed company of soldiers clearing the blocked streets and intersections they encountered, Davis, accompanied by his family, Secretary of War John Breckinridge, Adjunct General Samuel Cooper, and several others, soon found safety inside a secure railroad car. It was now close to eleven p.m. Dealing with a variety of important issues since leaving St. Paul's, Davis' departure had been delayed for several hours. In and around the president's car, one hundred handpicked soldiers protected the only president the Confederate States of America would ever know.

Shortly after eleven, with acts of violence and intentionally set fires still raging out of control in almost every section of the city, Davis' train pulled out of the Richmond train station. Directly behind the president's train, another long line of assorted rail cars filled to near capacity with several prominent families prepared to leave the city. In the front, two wood burning engines and a tightly packed fuel car prepared to lead them to safety. With these families were high-ranking members of the Confederate Army, a handful of powerful politicians, and several influential bankers. In one of the tightly packed cars close to fifty soldiers guarded over $450,000.00 of gold coins that had been rescued from a handful of Richmond banks. Closer to the rear, in another crowded car under heavy guard sat the balance of the Confederate treasury. Composed primarily of gold and silver coins, as well as bullion and paper currency that were nearly worthless, the remaining funds totaled a paltry $500,000.00. By all accounts, the Confederacy, with its army close to being destroyed in the closing days of the war, teetered on the brink of bankruptcy. The last minute addition of two more cars to the president's train had also contributed to the delay in leaving the train station.

Twenty-four hours later, Davis arrived in Danville, Virginia, the Confederacy's new capital. On April 4th, in an attempt to ease fear among the local population, Treasury Secretary George Trenholm deposited a portion of the Confederate treasury in a local bank. Later, he began issuing silver coins in return for Confederate notes; issuing one silver dollar in return for seventy dollars of Confederate paper. It was another sign of the pending collapse of the Confederate government.

Days later, as Davis and the remnants of the once proud Confederate government fled further south, they arrived in Greensborough, North Carolina. Soon after arriving, the president, much to his dismay, learned General Robert E. Lee had surrendered the Army of Northern Virginia and other units to General Ulysses S. Grant. As expected, the citizens of Greensborough, upset over news from the front, failed to extend a warm greeting to their president. Hours later, in a last-ditch effort to keep the Confederacy alive, Davis met with Generals Joseph Johnston and Pierre G. T. Beauregard. Issued orders to continue fighting, Johnston, in an effort to prevent further and unnecessary bloodshed, refused to obey the orders Davis had given. Days later, Johnston surrendered the Army of Tennessee and the remaining Confederate forces operating across four Southern states. The war's largest surrender involved just over 89,000 Confederate soldiers. Upon learning of Johnston's surrender, Davis branded him a traitor.

On April 14th, with the events at Appomattox Court House completed days earlier, as Davis attempted to flee with his family and others towards Texas, he learned of the death of his bitter rival, President Abraham Lincoln. Discarding his authority after news of the collapse of his armies and Lincoln's assassination reached him, after a brief train stop in Charlotte, North Carolina,

Davis proceeded further south. Hours into this leg of his attempted escape, Trenholm and Attorney General George Davis broke ranks with their defeated president by resigning their posts. The situation now confronting Davis grew even more intense.

Days later, on May 5th, in Washington, Georgia, after conducting one final cabinet meeting with those still loyal to the Confederate cause, Davis dissolved the Confederacy. Hours later, the former president passed through the small hamlet of Milledgeville on his way towards Macon. In the wake of Johnston's surrender, the once powerful president of the Confederacy was told the federal government had posted a $100,000.00 reward for his capture.

In early May, Union troops assigned to the First Wisconsin Cavalry, under the command of Lieutenant Colonel Henry Harnden, scoured the countryside searching for the elusive Confederate president. Soon they obtained their first solid lead concerning Davis' whereabouts. Six days later, as they reach Irwinsville, Georgia, Harnden's troops learned Davis and his entourage were camped roughly one mile outside of town. At daylight, on the morning of May 10, 1865, Davis and his wife, Varina, were finally captured. With them were Postmaster General John Reagan and several Confederate officers. Caught with his wife and another woman as they attempted to flee; the former president was apprehended while wearing a cloak and mantle around his head. Both were designed to be worn by women.

In the days following his capture, it was later learned that as Davis fled south with the balance of the Confederate treasury, he and his followers, as they entered Washington, Georgia, had paid a sum of close to $108,000.00 to the troops charged with escorting the former president to safety. Later, Union troops documenting Davis' attempted escape learned another $40,000.00 had recently been spent on supplies. Those same troops also determined that during the final days of the Confederacy another large sum, roughly $86,000.00 in treasury funds, had been entrusted to a Confederate confidant in an attempt to smuggle that money to Great Britain. Like the story surrounding the legend of the lost Confederate treasury; that sum never arrived at its intended destination. Either lost or stolen in the days following the South's surrender, it has never been accounted for.

On May 24th, Union troops in possession of the gold that had once been the property of several Richmond banks were ambushed by a group of at least twenty men on horseback as the money was being escorted north. While close to $140,000.00 was later recovered, the rest of that money has never been accounted for. Years later, those missing funds were believed to have served as the basis for the wealth of several local families in the area where it had been stolen. The theft of this gold took place close to Danberg Crossroads in Lincoln County, Georgia. It has become part of the lore surrounding the missing Confederate treasury.

After his capture, President Davis, Alabama Senator Clement C. Clay, Jr., and A. H. Stephens, who had served as Davis' Vice-President, were escorted to Fortress Monroe in late May. Located in Hampton, Virginia, Davis was held there for two years despite never being tried or convicted of any crimes. He was later released on a $100,000.00 bond; the same amount of money that had been awarded to his captors.

******

While the legend of the lost Confederate treasury still excites almost everyone who learns its story, most people have little knowledge of the steps Davis and one of his former cabinet members, Treasury Secretary Christopher Memminger, had taken to protect the bulk of the funds possessed by the Confederate government after the South's demoralizing defeat at Gettysburg. In 2011, during the one hundred and fiftieth anniversary of the start of the American Civil War, a novel – *Confederate Gold and Silver* – documented the plan those two men had orchestrated.

This is another part of that same story.

3

Two years earlier, in the weeks following the bitter defeats suffered by the Confederate Army at Gettysburg and Vicksburg, President Davis and Treasury Secretary Memminger finalized plans to protect the bulk of the Confederate treasury. Advised by their spies of moves being made by the Union Army to march south in an attempt to destroy several Confederate strongholds, including Petersburg and Richmond, plans to protect the South's financial assets were quickly finalized.

After deciding to leave one million dollars in Memminger's control at two Richmond banks, Davis devised a plan to split the balance of the assets into three unequal portions. These assets totaled close to four million dollars; the bulk of it being in the form of gold and silver coins.

Less than three weeks after his army's demoralizing defeat at Gettysburg, Davis, with Memminger's full support, authorized the first shipment of gold and silver coins to leave Richmond. Entrusted to Captain William Bedford of the 1st Virginia Infantry

Battalion, this shipment would soon prove to be the smallest of the three the Confederacy planned on moving further south. With an estimated value of close to two hundred and fifty thousand dollars, the assets entrusted to Bedford and his troops were secreted inside wooden boxes, secret compartments, and barrels marked as containing gun powder, minie balls, liquor, and other supplies.

A Richmond native, Bedford, like a large number of soldiers in his battalion, had enlisted in 1861 as the unit was being formed. Consisting mainly of immigrants who had found their way south after making their way to the United States from Ireland, this group of battle-hardened soldiers had affectionately become known as the Irish Brigade.

After receiving his instructions to deliver the assets to Meridian, Mississippi, Bedford and his men set out by train with their precious cargo. Unbeknownst to them, they were being sent out in advance of two other groups of soldiers who would soon be charged with similar assignments. Willing to risk a certain amount of the treasury, Davis and Memminger sent Bedford and his men out as a way of determining how closely Union spies had been watching the activities taking place around the Richmond train station. It was not the only reason Bedford had been sent out before the others. Just as they would do in the closing days of the war, the Confederacy had begun to question the reliability of their rail system. Bedford's ability to complete his mission would answer that question. Unlike the other two shipments, Bedford's would soon prove to be the only one to reach its final destination.

Later that month, as Bedford and his men worked to complete their mission, the largest of the three shipments moved south out of Richmond. It was comprised of nearly three million dollars in gold and silver coins, as well as a small fortune in crudely-made gold and silver bars. Shipped by train on the first leg of its journey, the assets were being protected by a group of Confederate sergeants serving under the command of Captain Judiah Francis. Like their commanding officer, each of the sergeants had proven themselves in battle. Assigned to the Virginia Fourth Cavalry Regiment, Francis and his hand-picked sergeants had been selected by General Lee to assist Davis with this sensitive mission. With the exception of one particular state, Francis and his men represented each of the states still loyal to the Confederacy.

Unlike the shipment being protected by Bedford, the one Francis was responsible for was jinxed from the start. Hours after leaving the Richmond train station, Francis was greeted with the first of several significant problems. Extensively documented in the novel – *Confederate Gold and Silver* – Francis lost several men, horses, and wagons after being confronted by Union forces, sabotage, wrecked trains, and, most surprisingly, an attack accidently levelled against his men by injured Confederate soldiers. Unable to complete his assignment for several reasons, Francis took measures to protect the valuable assets by burying two large portions in different locations. Another portion, including jewelry and several gold and silver bars, were cleverly secreted inside Charleston, South Carolina. Those assets would not be found until 2011.

Another mystery involving the legend of the lost Confederate treasury involved the third shipment of gold and silver coins Davis and Memminger had shipped out of Richmond. This shipment left the city's train station nearly two years after Francis and his men moved out.

This story chronicles that failed mission, and the Confederate officer who led it.

4

Like Bedford and Captain Judiah Francis, Captain Noah Howard had been recommended for his assignment by his commanding officer, General James Longstreet. It was a selection ultimately approved by General Lee and, later, by President Davis. Assigned to the 1st Virginia Volunteer Infantry Regiment, the twenty-seven-year-old Howard had seen a fair amount of fighting since joining his regiment less than a month after the war had started.

At just over six-feet tall, Howard stood taller than almost every soldier assigned to his regiment. Committed to the Confederate cause, he, at times, was often not as friendly or as outgoing as his peer, Captain Judiah Francis. Determined to advance through the ranks, at the start of his mission Howard gave little thought to how his subordinates felt about him. Those feelings would change dramatically over the coming weeks.

In an attempt to conceal the purpose behind their mission, Howard and his men were disguised as Confederate soldiers being sent home to recuperate after recently being injured. In a further attempt to disguise the reason why they were being sent south, the train they were travelling on was decorated with red and white ribbons. It was done to deceive those still loyal to the federal government. Like the soldiers who would soon crowd the train, four hundred thousand dollars of gold and silver coins had also been disguised. Much of it had been secreted inside several large wooden containers and barrels. Among the other goods being transported were five crates of Spencer repeating rifles the Confederacy had seized from a Union supply train. Brand new, they were to be distributed to two Confederate cavalry units operating in Mississippi.

******

While Howard's train ride from Richmond to Danville, Virginia, had taken the better part of two days, unlike the one Captain Francis experienced, the ride went without a hitch. It did so until the train reached Danville. With the southern terminus of the rail line located at the site of an abandoned construction project where a new set of lines had been started, despite the extensive plans to extend the rail lines further south to Greensboro, North Carolina, the Confederacy had run out of money, men, and material to complete the project. Issued specific orders on how he and his men were to reach their final destination, complications soon caused Howard additional problems. With their departure having been delayed by several last minute logistical and equipment needs, Howard's train was now halted from travelling over a set of temporary tracks that had been damaged hours earlier by Union soldiers.

Aware of the scorched-earth policy the Confederate Army had initiated against several rail lines as the fighting intensified earlier that year, Howard and his men were forced to unload their precious cargo after arriving in Danville. Unable to transfer their cargo to any other railroad due to equipment failure and the lack of replacement parts needed to keep the trains in operation, Howard's precious cargo was packed inside a variety of different wagons. Along with their personal gear and food supplies, the crates of rifles were packed inside the same five wagons. In less than six hours, this hastily organized wagon train started making its way towards Greensboro.

Days later, after enduring long hours of travel under a relentless hot sun, Howard's men were relieved when they stumbled across another rail line. Unlike several others, this line was not displayed on Howard's map. Abandoned before the start of the war, the tracks had been owned by a company that had gone out of business due to fiscal mismanagement. It was now a set of tracks the Confederate Army occasionally used to deliver supplies to strategic locations inside the South Carolina border. After wasting several more hours reloading a supply train they had managed to flag down, Howard and his men began the next leg of their journey. This leg would take them to Columbia, South Carolina. Once there, they would change trains for the last leg of their journey. Issued less than an hour before boarding the train in Richmond, Howard's written orders had initially instructed him to deliver his cargo to Mississippi.

Crossing into South Carolina, the train Howard and his men had boarded was unexpectedly brought to a stop less than thirty minutes northeast of Columbia. Halted by a large bonfire burning on the tracks since early that afternoon, the intense fire had been set in place by Confederate soldiers.

Not sure who or what had caused the large smoky fire, Howard, anticipating trouble, readied his men as the train jerked and clacked to a long slow stop. Barking orders as his eyes studied the commotion taking place further down the tracks, the young captain directed a group of soldiers to stand with their weapons ready in the opened doorways of four boxcars. Calmly moving from car to car, he ordered several others to assume positions atop the cars containing their precious cargo. Between each car at least six soldiers fought to maintain their balance as they prepared to fire their weapons at the first threat they encountered. Finished moving his men into position, over the loud noise generated by the train's brakes Howard hollered a separate set of orders to Sergeant Seth Adams.

"Sergeant Adams, take six men and stand guard inside the boxcar carrying our special cargo. If anyone tries to open the doors after you're in there, drop them where they stand! No matter what takes place outside the train, don't open those doors unless I tell you it's safe."

Jumping off the train with four of his men as it rolled to a stop, Howard anxiously gripped his sidearm as he approached the lead engine. Unsure of what they were about to face, he quickly identified the four officers he wanted shot if trouble broke out. "I'll take the one wearing the saber; he looks to be the one in charge. The rest of you take out the three standing on either side of him; then do your best to defend yourselves." Realizing there was possibly another reason for why the train had been stopped; Howard issued one last set of instructions to his men. "On the chance these men were sent here to stop the train for a legitimate reason, don't fire until you see me raise my weapon."

Moving slowly as he walked past the front of the train, Howard quickly recognized two of the Confederate officers standing there. While unable to recall their names or the regiments they were assigned to, he had seen these men months earlier at previous engagements they had all fought in. Feeling relieved, Howard instructed his men to relax.

"Captain Howard, we've been expecting you!" The officer in charge stated as he tossed a half-smoked cigar into a bonfire comprised of old railroad ties and dry wood. Having been soaked in Creosote months earlier, the railroad ties contributed to the significant amount of smoke being given off. "My name is Captain Rufus Russell. I'm the commanding officer of the 4th South Carolina Cavalry Regiment. While I haven't been told the details of your assignment, I was instructed to stop this train before it reached Columbia." As he finished speaking, Russell removed one of his gauntlets before warmly extending his right hand in Howard's direction.

Still leery of the large number of armed soldiers standing close to Russell, Howard cautiously moved his sidearm to his other hand before shaking hands with someone he barely recognized. Unlike his counterpart, Howard did not remove his glove. "What's the purpose behind this greeting, captain? Yankees, perhaps? Or has the Confederate Army taken to stopping trains moving south on orders from the president?"

Howard's comment drew little in the way of any expression from the officer standing in front of him. "I assure you it's because of those damn Yankees. The war may be almost over, but there are no traitors standing here. My men and I are determined to see this war to the end."

"How bad?" Howard asked, his eyes focusing on Russell's facial features for any sign of a trap. For a brief moment, he allowed his stare to shift to Russell's saber. It was a weapon that he hoped would not be drawn in anger.

"Pretty bad." Russell replied, his head dropping in disgust against his chest as he thought about the recent events that had gone against the Confederacy. "The state capital is in ruins from all the fires Sherman's men set. With everything else that's happened here and in other parts of the South over the past several months, there's fear that Sherman's army might be headed back this way to do more damage. To me, that doesn't seem likely, but I've never claimed to know what General Sherman is thinking at any given moment. I'm just here following the orders I've been given, captain." Reaching inside his blouse, Russell produced a telegram he had been sent earlier in the day. Holding it up, he said, "I made sure your train was stopped just like this here telegram told me to. The way I see it, the war's almost over. There's no sense in anyone else getting hurt."

Ignoring Russell's opinion on the status of the war, as well as his obvious dislike for the assignment he had been given, Howard told his fellow captain a few brief details concerning the problems being encountered in Petersburg and Richmond.

While not surprised by what he was being told, Russell sought to learn more about the situation inside the Confederate capital. "What about the rail lines leading in and out of both cities? What about Petersburg itself? I've got kin living there. Is it just as bad as you have said? How are we going to be resupplied if the trains aren't running? What about General Lee? Was he captured?" With each question being asked, the pitch in Russell's voice rose slightly.

While more worried about his own problems than Russell's questions, Howard gave the concerned young officer bits of information concerning the collapse of the Confederate capital. "The last I knew, and this is a few days old by now, General Lee was safe. After he sent word to President Davis about the situation in Petersburg, the general and what was left of his army started moving west towards Farmville and Lynchburg. Maybe things have changed since we got on this train, but that's what I knew at the time."

"Thank God!" Russell replied, pleased to learn Lee was safe.

"As far as what I know about our railroads, it's not that good. I'm sure that bastard Grant and his men are either in control of most of the lines by now or they've destroyed them. How we plan on supplying what's left of our armies, well . . . I guess General Lee and a few others will have to figure that out pretty quick." Having been out of contact after being forced to march over land for several days, like Russell, Howard had yet to learn of Lee's surrender several days earlier.

"Damn blue-bellies!" Russell yelled, slapping his hand in disgust with his gauntlet.

Looking at the large fire straddling the tracks, Howard tried figuring out the rest of the news Russell had yet to reveal. "If my route to Columbia has been cut off, did that telegram contain any further instructions that I should know about? Because if it doesn't, I'm not sure how I'm supposed to make it to Mississippi if the trains aren't running." As he finished speaking, Howard instructed two of his men to return to the train so the others had some idea of why their progress had been halted. "Make sure Sergeant Adams knows there's no danger."

"Captain, besides my orders to stop your advance towards Columbia, my only other order was to tell you your new destination is Savannah. According to an earlier telegram my commanding officer received, your new orders are pretty explicit. You are to proceed to Savannah with the utmost haste. Once you arrive, you will receive further orders from one of President Davis' aides. In the meantime, Secretary Trenholm . . . or whoever else is in charge these days, is making arrangements for reinforcements to meet up with you somewhere between here and Charleston." Noticing the confused look on Howard's face, Russell simply added, "I'm sorry, but that's all I was told."

Staring back at the idling train packed full of gold and silver, Howard, confused by the sudden change of plans, smirked at the news he had been given. Being ordered to steer away from one large city and then head in a completely different direction was never a contingency that had been discussed.

"Are you sure about this?" Howard asked as he reached for the telegram Russell was holding. "When I was issued my orders, I was given a precise route to follow. Savannah was never an option."

"If that's the case, maybe you're not the reason they had me stop the train. Maybe it's the train they were concerned about. It could be the president or General Lee himself was afraid of that valuable piece of equipment falling into the hands of the Union Army." Russell said, referring to whoever had changed Howard's orders. "Or maybe it's what's on the train they care about?" Russell was grabbing at straws as he followed Howard's stare in the direction of the train.

Turning to look at Russell as he returned the telegram he had been handed, Howard realized his fellow officer was doing his best to figure out what the precious cargo was that he was escorting. Pulling a map from his blouse, Howard soon realized he had more than one-hundred and fifty miles to travel before reaching the city General James Oglethorpe had founded in

1733. Checking the map's topographical details caused Howard to pause and think about how he was going to navigate such a distance with a slow moving wagon train weighed down with a significant amount of gold and silver. He also realized it meant being confronted by terrain that would further slow his progress. With his route of travel now changed, Howard knew his chances of being confronted by Union troops had increased significantly.

Folding his map, Howard stared at the officers and soldiers standing near the growing bonfire. Like Russell, they were veterans who had experienced years of fighting with too few resources. From their emaciated looks, it looked as though most had barely managed to survive the last few months as rations and supplies continued to dwindle across the Confederacy. Like his own men, Howard knew the soldiers he was staring at had likely witnessed a number of friends and family members being sacrificed for a cause most Southerners barely understood.

Calling to one of his sergeants, Howard ordered him to make arrangements for some of their provisions to be shared with the gaunt figures standing around the fire. Turning to Russell, he said, "We don't have much, but whatever we can spare we're glad to share with our fellow soldiers."

"Thank you. My men and I will never forget this." Russell said, quickly realizing most of his men had not eaten for nearly two days. Like those worn by his men, Russell's uniform no longer fit as it once had. It was now far too big due to the amount of weight he had recently lost. As was the case with many of those still serving the Confederacy, it had been several weeks since he had eaten his last decent meal.

Nodding his head as he acknowledged the thanks he had been given, Howard said, "Captain Russell, you seem to speak with a distinct accent. It sounds very similar to one spoken by some of my friends. By chance, do you hail from the Roanoke area?"

Finally allowing himself to relax after another long day, Russell smiled as he answered Howard's question. "Well, I guess the best way to describe it is for me to say that I live a hard day's ride west of Roanoke. Same holds true for most of my men; we all hail from that section of Old Virginny. We started out with just over two hundred men; as of this morning we're down to fifty-four. From some accounts I've heard, I suppose I should be grateful to still have that many men with me. I've been told some pretty sad stories of entire regiments being wiped out in a single afternoon; in some cases, in less than an hour. We've recently had a few men added to our ranks to replace those who've been killed, but we could use a bunch more if we're gonna stay in this fight." As he finished speaking, Russell's face grew sad as he recalled the friends and neighbors he had seen killed.

"I guess we've all seen far too many of our friends killed over the past few years." Howard replied, reflecting back on the number of friends he had lost.

Nodding his head, Russell added, "Just like any regiment, we've also had our share of deserters and those who were sent home to recuperate. Those deserters who've left us, my men and I won't forget what they've done. Once this war is over with and we're back home, we've got a score to settle with those bastards." Watching as a handful of Howard's men drew closer to the bonfire carrying crates of food, Russell asked one more question before taking a sip from his canteen. "What about you? Where are you from?"

"I've moved around too much to call any one place my home, but whatever family I've got left lives outside of Grundy. You likely have never heard of it as it's a small village on the western edge of the state. That may have changed over the past few years as I've been kind of busy to check on them, but I'm sure a few of them still call it home. Both of my parents died of the fever when I was only two, so I have no recollection of them. After they died, my older sister was sent to live with my mother's sister. I haven't seen her in years, and because of our time apart I feel as if I barely know her. Before the war we exchanged a few letters from time to time, but we haven't written to each other for at least four or five years. For all I know, she could be married by now. After both sides either get tired of killing each other or one side gives up, I'm going to make it a point to go find her as she's the only real family I've got left. Besides those friends I told you about, I recognized your accent from passing through Roanoke several times when I was younger."

After several minutes of small talk, Russell, an experienced soldier who was wiser than most people thought, asked the other obvious question that had been bothering him. As he did, the veteran officer paid particular attention to how Howard and some of his men were dressed.

"No disrespect intended, but you and your men are moving pretty well for soldiers dressed up as being injured in the war. You going to tell me about these disguises y'all are wearing?"

Having forgotten about the roles he and his men had assumed, Howard laughed at Russell's question. While realizing their torn and tattered uniforms were made to look as if they were stained in blood, Howard refused to divulge any further information regarding his assignment. "Your powers of observation are very good, captain, and while these disguises weren't our idea, I'll say nothing more about our mission or the clothes we're wearing."

As Russell tried to push the issue, Howard cut him off. "Captain, while I appreciate your tenacity, you need to realize my assignment doesn't involve you. I'm not going to say anything else about it. I'm not being rude, but I have my orders."

Suspecting he had been ordered to stop a train carrying goods vital to the Confederate cause, Russell was disappointed by the stand Howard had taken.

Noticing Russell's frustration, Howard tried minimizing the angst his fellow officer was experiencing. "Rufus, you have completed your assignment very well. I'm grateful to you for protecting my men from any harm. But now I need another favor."

"Tell me how I can be of assistance." Russell offered, still hopeful of learning more about Howard's assignment.

Needing to unload the train of its precious cargo, but wanting to do so without Russell's men being too close to the boxcars, Howard told his fellow officer what he needed done. "Just in the event our enemy has any plans of attacking the train, it would be helpful if you could set up a perimeter around the cars as they're unloaded. I can't tell you what's in them, but know it's important. While I'd prefer it if you would stay with me during the unloading, I'd appreciate your men being posted roughly one hundred yards away. That will at least give us a bit of a warning if any unwanted visitors show up."

Moments later, as Russell's men were being posted a short distance from the train Howard knew the real reason behind this deployment. It was to keep unwanted eyes from seeing what was now being loaded inside the wagons.

5

As the perimeter around the train was being secured, and with Russell seated on his horse next to him, Howard watched intently as the railcars were being unloaded. Slowly lowered down a series of steep wooden ramps by way of sturdy ropes, Howard's men carefully loaded the wagons with an assortment of crates, boxes, and heavy wooden barrels. Once loaded, each wagon was moved to a safe position several yards away. Minutes after being parked, three other soldiers made sure the teams of horses were properly hitched to each of the wagons. Above them, four sharpshooters stood guard watching the activity taking place.

Watching intently as his men hustled to accomplish what needed to be done, Howard noticed Russell staring as two of the largest wagons were moved as close as possible to one of the rail car's opened set of doors. Moments later, Russell began paying even closer attention as five heavy wooden crates were slid to the edge of the doorway before being lowered inside the wagons. Moving his horse closer to the activity taking place, the inquisitive young officer noticed the crates had been marked on all four sides with the words *Property of the U.S. Army.*

As the crates were carefully loaded inside the two wagons, Russell turned and looked at Howard. "Those crates your men are in the process of loading into the wagons . . . are the markings real or have they been put there to deceive others like the uniforms y'all are wearing?" As he asked his question, Russell, for a brief moment, turned his attention back to the markings he had seen.

"They're the real deal. These crates, along with others like them and some gun-making equipment, were seized from the Union Army several months ago. The crates you're looking at represent what's left." Playing a bluff, Howard added, "Well, now that you've seen what's being unloaded, I guess you know what we've been tasked with delivering."

Alternating stares at the wagons and at Howard, Russell became confused. "If Petersburg and Richmond have fallen as you say they have, what's the purpose of moving these crates to Mississippi? If it hasn't already ended, it sounds like the war might be over within a few days. If that's the case, why go to the trouble of moving these crates? That's unless you boys plan on selling them back to the United States government."

Pleased Russell had fallen for the ruse, Howard let it play out by adding, "With all the problems we're facing these days, meaning how poorly the war is going for our side when it comes to the railroads we all depend on, there's likely only one other train you are going to encounter. Do you have any idea who the passengers might be?"

"Maybe President Davis and some of his cabinet members, I suppose? But what's that have to do with these crates?" To

Howard's surprise, Russell had answered his question without hesitating.

"Rufus, while the president has every intention of keeping the cause alive, more than anyone else he realizes the position we're in. With General Lee's army just a shell of what it was, and with Grant and that son of a bitch Sherman nipping away at us from every direction there is, for the time being President Davis is making plans to relocate the capital to either Texas or Mexico."

While having been skeptical of the South's chances of winning the war since the day he enlisted, Russell believed in everything the Confederacy stood for. Now he tried anticipating what the future would bring for Davis, Lee, and the Confederacy. What he said next proved he was a far better at taking orders than he was in predicting what the future held for his way of life.

"So, if the president is going to be making his way to Texas or to some God-forsaken place in Mexico as you say he is that must be why General Lee is moving west from Petersburg. They must have a plan to meet along the way so Lee can rally our armies to keep the fighting going. I'll bet he plans on hooking up with General Johnston and his troops in North Carolina. From there they'll likely head west to meet up with the president."

Briefly nodding at Russell's last statement, Howard caught sight of the signal Sergeant Adam's had given him. It told him the process of unloading the train had been completed.

"Captain Russell," Howard said as a small smile crossed his face, "I appreciate the help you and your men have given us. With a long journey in front of us, I plan on heading out as soon as the men are ready. Please know I'm grateful for all you've done."

"Good luck to you, captain," Russell said, extending his right hand as a way of saying goodbye.

As the two officers shook hands, Howard urged Russell to keep to himself what he had seen being loaded inside the wagons. "Just tell your men the president and General Lee plan on fighting until we win, but there's no reason for any of them to know what's inside our wagons. Until they finalize their plans, there's no need for soldiers like you and me to give away any secrets."

"There's nothing to worry about, Noah. I'll go to the grave before I tell anyone about what I've seen and heard." Waving as he moved away from the train, Russell headed back towards his men so they could return to Columbia and their next assignment.

As he walked to where Adams was waiting, Howard noticed the smirk displayed on his sergeant's face.

"No disrespect, captain, but that story you just told that fella, that's about the best line of crap I've ever heard. You really think he believes that nonsense you fed him?"

Without looking back as Russell rode away, Howard shot his sergeant a friendly wink. "As long as he believes it until we're out of sight, that's all that matters. Let's move out, sergeant."

Less than a week later, the young cavalry officer would honor his promise. Sent to protect the right flank of a large group of unarmed Confederate soldiers who had been paroled only days earlier, Russell was killed after being struck by a stray round fired by a Union soldier making his way home. While the young officer was not the last Confederate soldier to lose his life serving the cause he believed in, his death was one of the most senseless. Unlike most of their fellow combatants, the Union soldiers Russell and his men encountered had not yet learned Lee and Grant had met to begin the process of ending the deadliest war ever fought on United States soil.

6

Like Captain Bedford and Captain Francis who experienced similar problems during their assignments, Captain Noah Howard was also confronted with a variety of challenges while moving towards Savannah with his slow moving wagons.

Although the first few days of travel since leaving the train had caused Howard and his men to move over difficult terrain largely untouched by European settlers, the days had passed with relatively few problems. With two of the wagons carrying adequate supplies of food, they enjoyed meals far better than what most soldiers were currently experiencing. From the long hours they endured each day, this small group of weary soldiers somehow managed to enjoy several nights of sleep without being disturbed. But unbeknownst to Howard, the difficult days were about to begin.

As Howard and his men prepared to start a new day on the trail roughly sixty miles southeast of where they had left the train, Gordy Battle, a twenty-year-old soldier rode up to where Howard was enjoying his morning coffee. Dismounting his horse, the young soldier, already a veteran of three years of fighting against the powerful Union Army, used his hat to knock a significant amount of trail dust off his uniform. Like others his age, he had already been involved in far too many fights. With two of his fellow soldiers, Battle spent most of the night performing picket duty while Howard and the others had slept comfortably inside their tents. After dusting himself off, he stood for a few brief moments looking out at the ground he and the others had crisscrossed over the past several hours.

Paying close attention to Battle as he approached the small table where he was seated, somewhat out of character Howard acknowledged the young soldier with a simple wave as he sipped his coffee. Still fairly early, it was not quite six as Battle paused to brush more dust from his dirty uniform. Aware of his commanding officer's pet peeve when it came to soldiers and sergeants not saluting those holding the rank of lieutenant or higher the first time they crossed paths each morning, Battle paused, raised his right hand to his forehead, and saluted before placing his hat back on top of his head.

"How's the morning coffee, sir?" Battle asked, moving closer to where Howard had risen from the chair he had been sitting on. "Not nearly as good as it tastes back home, I suspect." Unlike many other soldiers his age, Battle was outgoing and friendly to most people he met. He was neither impressed nor intimidated by his commanding officer's rank.

"That about sums it up, private." While Howard often went days without speaking with those who had little rank, if any, he had grown fond of Battle after observing how well the young Virginian had conducted himself since joining the regiment. "By the looks of it, I'm guessing you spent another long night doing some hard riding. Anything unusual to report or was it another quiet night?"

"Mind if I get a swallow, captain?" Battle asked, nodding at the coffee pot sitting next to a small smoldering fire. At another nearby campfire, one slightly larger than the one keeping the coffee warm, two soldiers were beginning the task of preparing the camp's morning meal. "My mouth is kind of dry from swallowing dust all night. It's way too dry in these parts. We could use some rain to knock the dust down a bit."

Nodding his head, Howard pointed at two tin cups. "Help yourself." Nearby two of Howard's officers, having seen the young soldier ride up from just outside their tent, slowly approached the campfire. Expecting Howard to explode in anger as Battle picked up the coffee pot, Lieutenants David Radcliff and Paul Brown were surprised, and relieved, when their commanding officer and Battle resumed talking. As was the case in most camps, soldiers normally did not share pots of coffee with their commanding officer.

"Much obliged, captain." Battle offered, raising his cup in Howard's direction after taking his first sip.

"My pleasure," Howard replied, taking notice of Radcliff and Brown for the first time that morning. Returning their salutes, he again focused his attention on Battle. "Well? Did you see or hear anything unusual last night?"

With his back facing the large field he had ridden across several minutes earlier, Battle looked anxiously in Howard's direction. Standing there with his coffee cup in his left hand, he spoke to his commanding officer as the other two officers listened in.

"Captain, if the three of you could do this without being too conspicuous, look over my right shoulder at the woods on the other side of the clearing."

Focusing on the thick growth of trees nearly three hundred yards away, like the other two officers with him Howard strained to catch sight of anything unusual. Seconds later, unsure of what it was that he was supposed to be seeing, a frustrated Howard asked, "Am I supposed to be seeing anything unusual or is this some kind of a game you have us playing?" Like their commanding officer, Radcliff and Brown, at first, failed to see anything except trees, rocks, and a variety of native shrubs. Without turning around, Battle told the others exactly where to look.

"Focus your eyes on that small stand of white birch trees to the right of them other trees; you'll see what I'm talking about." Battle said, his thick Virginia accent making its presence known as he waited for the others to locate the target they were searching for.

Close to chewing Battle out for wasting his time trying to see something that did not exist, Howard suddenly saw the morning sun reflect off a metallic object just inside the tree line. Moments later, he mistakenly asked, "How many blue-bellies we looking at?"

"That's the problem, captain, I'm not sure they're blue-bellies." As he had answered Howard's question, Battle slowly turned to look back in the direction of where the men he first encountered a few hours earlier were now gathered. "Whoever they are, there's about twenty of them. From the tracks I seen in the ground out there, I'm thinking they be marauders more than soldiers as each time I managed to catch a glimpse of them all I saw was torn clothing, not Yankee blue."

"How long have they been out there?" Brown asked, interrupting his stare to look at Battle.

"Five . . . maybe six hours. Me and the boys first caught wind of them right around midnight. The two boys who were with me are still out there keepin' an eye on them fellas. They'll sound the alarm if them marauders head this way." As Battle had excitedly spoken about this group of strangers, his thick Southern accent would have made it difficult for folks from other parts of the country to understand the warning he was delivering. For Howard and the two others with him, Battle's speech was easy to follow.

Looking at Radcliff and Brown, Howard told them what he wanted done. "Lieutenant Brown, for now, let's proceed as normal. Get the men ready to move out. We can't stay here as that would be too suspicious. By now, I'm sure whoever's out there knows we're aware of their presence. Don't tell the men about the threat we're facing, but make sure they're ready to fight if I sound the alarm. If we're attacked, I want you to setup our defensive position like we've discussed. Circle the wagons so we can protect the gold and silver better than we could if the wagons were scattered to all creation. There's strength in numbers, so make sure we use the wagons to our advantage." To his credit, Howard had spent several hours over the past few days discussing defensive strategies with his lieutenants.

"Yes, sir." Brown replied, casting one last furtive glance at the woods off to his left.

"Lieutenant Radcliff, take Battle and two others with you. I want you to circle around those men out there and get behind them. Your job is to birddog them until we know what their intentions are. I shouldn't have to tell you this, but you can't let them see you. If they do, any tactical advantage we have will be lost."

"Sir, I understand. If they start anything, do you want us to attack them from the rear or rejoin you?"

Without hesitating, Howard replied. His simple response told Radcliff what he wanted done. *"Attack, attack, attack!"*

* * * * * *

Two hours after breaking camp, while doing his best to make it appear as if he and the others were blind to the threat facing them, Howard kept a watchful eye on the last wagon in line. But then, as the wagons slowed to cross a shallow, but wide stream, the sound of gunfire from off to Howard's right broke the otherwise calm morning air. In seconds, a dozen minie balls pierced the canvass tops of each of his wagons.

As Brown tried rallying the wagons on the far side of the stream, two of Howard's soldiers fell dead in the slow moving water as they prepared to return fire. By now, Howard's attackers had quickly reduced the distance between the two groups. Forming a haphazard line of defense behind whatever protection they could find, Brown and the soldiers with him took out four of the riders leading the attack with a barrage of well-aimed shots. Having gone undetected, Radcliff and his men quickly dispatched four others.

Twenty minutes later, the brief, but deadly exchange of gunfire cost the lives of six of Howard's men. On the other side, eleven marauders failed to rejoin their group. As the attackers called off their raid, Battle, one of the best shots in Howard's regiment, took one last shot. Moments later, one last attacker fell from his horse. Badly injured by the well placed shot, the attacker's body was pushed downstream by the slow moving current.

7

Pleased to learn the attackers had failed to reach any of the wagons, Howard seethed over the loss of six of his men. They were soldiers he could not afford to lose. As he spoke to two of his men being treated for minor gunshot wounds, the attacker Battle had shot was brusquely dragged from the water. Stained in blood, his torn shirt revealed the presence of a single bullet hole just above his right lung.

Glaring at the marauder screaming in pain, Howard saw the remnants of the uniform the former soldier was wearing. It was the uniform of a Confederate soldier. Immediately, the young officer sought to learn who this soldier was, and who the others were that he had been riding with.

"It don't make no difference what my name is, captain, but me and the fellas I was with were just plain ordinary soldiers. We weren't no important officers like y'all are pretending to be." Gasping for air after being punched in the face by Adams for insulting his commanding officer, the injured soldier did what he could to stem the steady flow of blood coming from the wound in his chest. "We all just got tired of fighting, of not being paid like we was promised, and having to beg for food while the officers we was serving under . . . those no-good rotten bastards who called themselves our leaders, ate right good every night. Piss on them bastards, they're the ones who caused us to desert," the soldier said angrily, spitting a mouthful of blood on the ground next to him.

Looking down, Howard scoffed at the soldier's comments. "So that conduct gives you the right to desert the army, or to attack us? We're all on the same side . . . at least, I thought we were."

"Captain, I'm sorry for what I've done," the soldier replied, panting for air as he looked up at Howard. "I know this don't mean much, but . . . I was just desperate. Look at me, I'm not only starving to death, but I'm as broke as all get out. I ain't seen home for nearly three years."

Ignoring the former soldier's pleas, Howard called for Sergeant Adams. As he waited, the young soldier, a tall emaciated figure of less than twenty years of age, pleaded for a sip of water. "Please, captain, can I bother you for a drink."

Paying little attention to his request, Howard glanced at the soldier lying there in his wet, tattered uniform. "You didn't know this at the time, but you had your last drink back in the stream."

As Adams arrived, Howard instructed him on what he wanted done. "Have a hole dug, and then gather the men around it. When you're ready, order a firing squad to send this man to Hell!" Angry and upset over the loss of his men during the senseless attack on his wagons, Howard walked away as the soldier repeatedly begged for his life. Less than twenty minutes later, the men Adam's had assigned to the firing squad began shoveling dirt on the body of a young deserter. Like the others he had been riding with, the soldier had turned his back on the cause he agreed to fight for just three years earlier. The lack of food, coupled with poor sanitary conditions and little pay, had wiped out what little fight the soldier had left to protect his way of life. Across the South, misery had begun to settle within the ranks of the Confederacy.

* * * * * *

Later that evening, after making sure those who had been wounded were being taken care of, Howard ate his evening meal as the sun began to set. Often dining alone or with one or two of his officers, on this occasion he sat with the others who had helped to defend the assets they were travelling with. As he enjoyed his meal, Howard, occasionally adding to the conversation taking place, listened as his subordinates described the intense fight they had somehow managed to survive.

Politely excusing himself after finishing his meal, with his haversack slung over his right shoulder Howard walked several feet away after speaking with the sergeant in charge of the evening's picket duty. Moments later, sitting with his back resting against a stately sycamore tree, Howard removed a journal from the cloth bag he had been carrying. As the young officer thought about the day's events, he used a small pocket knife to sharpen the blunt ends of two pencils.

Educated in Boston, Massachusetts, Howard had been teaching school in New England in early 1861 until it became clear that war was about to envelop the entire nation. Returning to Virginia shortly after the fighting had started; Howard joined the army to defend the state where he was born. A prolific writer of several short stories that had largely gone unnoticed, he had already filled six journals with details regarding camp life, his travels across the South, of the people he met, and, most importantly, of the battles he survived. Interested in writing a novel about his experiences in the war, Howard had sent each of his completed journals to his sister for safekeeping. He had also done so for one other reason. Howard wanted her to know what he was experiencing in the event he did not survive the war.

Collecting his thoughts as he opened his journal, Howard started the day's entry with the date and a general description of the ground he had covered. His first few sentences also included a brief description of the weather and an evaluation of the morale inside his camp. Then, in neat precise handwriting, the young officer wrote about first learning of the marauders' presence, of later being attacked by these deserters during their hunt for food and supplies, and of how his men had responded. Howard finished the day's entry by describing how concerned he was of being attacked again by these same deserters. In describing his concerns, he questioned whether he and his men would be successful in protecting the precious cargo they were travelling with.

His final entry identified the names of the nine men he had left.

8

Pushing further south over the next two days, Howard and his men remained vigilant as their wagon train was kept under constant surveillance by those men who had already attacked them. Occasionally showing themselves, the marauders used a variety of probes and feints to keep Howard's men on edge. Briefly challenged on two other occasions, including an attack during the middle of the night which had caught them off guard, Howard's pickets managed to beat back the remaining marauders as the former soldiers probed the area around the wagons. The two failed attempts had caused this loosely organized band of deserters to sustain four additional casualties. The probes and feints had also caused Howard to realize that Battle's earlier estimate of their numbers was lower than it actually was.

Within days of the first attack, as their slow moving wagon train found its way across the northern end of the Santee River, Battle rode to where Howard was watching the first two wagons being ferried across the river.

"You come to tell me good news or bad news, private?" Howard asked, casting a look in the direction of where the marauders had last been seen.

Gazing in the same direction, Battle wished he had more time to confirm the news he was about to pass on. "Good news this time, captain. Not sure if losing four more men is the reason behind this or not, but that group that's been doggin' us for the past few days rode off about an hour ago. It's anyone's guess as to what they're up to, but for the time being they ain't doggin' us like they have been. Could be they're trying to catch us off guard, but me and the boys will keep an eye out for any tricks them fellas plan on playing."

"They're gone?" Howard asked, unprepared for the news Battle had given him. "Are you sure of that? They've hit us three times so far . . . the first being the worse, so why would they ride off? They have to know our losses have weakened our ability to defend the wagons. We're certainly not as strong as we were a few days ago." As he finished speaking, Howard raised his binoculars to scan the horizon for any signs of trouble.

Spitting a mouthful of warm water on the ground, Battle nodded at Howard's comments as he rested his canteen on top of his saddle. "All I can tell you, captain, is me and the boys followed them for nearly twenty minutes after they got finished with some type of pow-wow. Don't know why they left, but I guess they realized they was messing with the wrong group of soldiers. But like I said, we'll keep our eyes peeled."

"Maybe . . . maybe." Howard replied, wary of some sort of trick being played. Still using his binoculars to look for any signs of trouble, he said, "Just to play it safe, I want you and the others with you to stay behind us for a spell. Just in case those men have something else planned, you'll be able to give us some type of a warning."

"We knew you'd want us to do that, captain." Battle said, proudly anticipating what his commanding officer had planned for him and the others. "I'm just gonna fill our canteens and grab some grub from the chuck wagon over yonder before I head out. We'll keep our eyes peeled for any signs of trouble as y'all cross the river, but don't worry, nothing's gonna happen. Once we see you've made camp for the night, after it gets dark we'll come in one at a time and grab some chow."

Pointing down river, Howard told Battle what his plans were. In doing so, he described how he planned to use the river to their advantage. "From what my map is telling me, as the river winds its way further east it appears its banks become much steeper. That old man we ran across the other day told me the current along that stretch is generally too strong for a horse to navigate, so we'll have to use the ferries that are operating there to get the teams across. If they decide to attack us again, those men will either try commandeering one or two of those ferries or they'll cross right here where it's shallow."

"Yes, sir." Saluting Howard, Battle rode off to fill six canteens with cool water. Before heading back to join the others on picket duty, the young soldier filled his saddlebags with beef jerky and three small cakes that had somehow gone uneaten from the camp's morning meal. Fried in bacon fat, the cornbread cakes had become a morning staple for Battle and his fellow soldiers. While not enough to fill the bellies of the men he was riding with, Battle knew the cakes were more than what their attackers had recently eaten.

******

As Battle made his way back to the two locations where his fellow soldiers planned on taking positions so they could observe anyone approaching, the young soldier munched on one of the cakes he had liberated from the chuck wagon.

Making his way to a section of woods blanketed with thick mature trees and small boulders lining the side of a large steep hill, Battle scanned the area for signs of Private Alfred Hatch. Barely nineteen-years-old, Hatch, whose family grew acres of tobacco less than thirty-five miles outside of Richmond, had told Battle he would use the boulders as cover while keeping a lookout in the event the marauders returned to resume their attacks.

Moving through the thick tree line after carefully making his way across a small section of uneven ground washed out by rainstorms, Battle looked for any signs Hatch had left. After spotting tracks left by Hatch's horse, he noticed blood had stained the rocky surface in several locations. Calling out as he followed the drops of blood for several hundred yards, Battle hoped his friend would identify his hiding spot. Listening for some kind of response, he noticed the tracks left by Hatch's horse had suddenly become mixed with those of several others. Further down the old trail, broken tree branches stained in blood, as well as the telltale signs of an intense struggle, told Battle something terrible had happened. Immediately, a cold chill ran down his spine as the sound of a falling tree branch caused him to swivel defensively in his saddle.

Minutes later, as he continued to ride along the side of the old Indian path, Battle saw what had caused the trail of blood. Tied to a large tree, his hands and ankles bound together with lengths of rope, Hatch's badly beaten body revealed he had endured a severe beating. The young soldier's bloody face had taken the brunt of his attackers' rage. Repeated blows from fists and kicks had left his boyish face a bloody pulp. Barely alive, his attackers had also broken several of his ribs and inflicted two deep puncture wounds on one side of his chest; both made breathing very difficult. With his own rifle ready to respond to any signs of trouble, Battle cautiously spoke to his friend as a steady stream of blood flowed from Hatch's mouth and nose.

Believing Hatch's attackers fled after taking the young soldier's horse, Battle slowly lowered his friend to the ground after cutting away the ropes that had pinned him to the tree. Hatch's badly broken body spasmed uncontrollably for several seconds as the young soldier was gently placed on the ground. "Alfred . . . my God, what happened? Who did this? Was it the same men who have been attacking us?"

Unable to speak due to a badly broken jaw, Hatch winced in pain as he nodded in response to Battle's question. Seconds later, two broken teeth tumbled from the young soldier's mouth.

Pouring water from his canteen, Battle soaked an old bandana he had taken from around his neck. Like most soldiers, Battle wore the bandana as a way of catching some of the sweat running down his neck on hot days. It was also something he sometimes wore as a mask on windy days to keep dirt and insects from entering his mouth and nose. As he soaked the cloth, Battle heard his friend moan as he took his last breath. Private Alfred Hatch had just become another senseless casualty of a war that had already claimed the lives of far too many men.

Grieving as he wrapped his friend's body in a blanket that had seen many other uses, Battle struggled as he fastened Hatch's body behind his saddle. Finishing his task, he thought, "I ain't about to leave him out here by himself. Someone needs to say some words over him before he's buried."

Hoping the other soldier in this loosely organized picket line was safe, Battle rode off to find him. What he would soon find would cause Howard to be confronted with a new set of problems.

9

Cautiously covering the distance between the two observation posts manned by Hatch and Private George Newcomb, Battle made sure he paid close attention to the thick line of shrubs and trees around him. Standing nearly five feet in height, the dense shrubs were the perfect hiding spots for men determined to get their way. Pushing forward at a slow, but steady pace, Battle alternated stares at the shrubs and trees, and at the many spaces around him where men could hide. Twice he froze, nearly scared out of his saddle by small flocks of crows who had watched his every move from the tops of two nearby trees. Believing the crows had been scared off by the sounds of feet running through the woods; Battle raised his musket after hearing their angry cries.

With his musket held firmly in his left hand, Battle slowly slid off his saddle as he neared the location where Newcomb had told him he would be waiting. Holding the reins to his horse in his right hand, Battle walked slowly as he did his best to avoid making any noise. Unlike the trail he followed several minutes earlier, this time he saw no blood as he drew closer to his friend's position.

Moving off the trail in an attempt to avoid being ambushed by any of the marauders, as Battle made his way through a thicket of pricker bushes; he paused after locating Newcomb's horse. Tied to a young sapling, the black mare was oblivious to Battle's presence as she munched on a small patch of grass amongst the many rocks and boulders that were present. Minutes later, startled by a small rock Battle had thrown in her direction, Newcomb's horse anxiously moved its feet; unaware that it had been thrown in an attempt to see if trouble was lurking nearby.

Unable to see where Newcomb was hidden, and too afraid of revealing his own position, Battle prayed his friend had not been harmed. Tossing another rock from the position he had taken less than fifty feet away from where Newcomb's horse was tethered, Battle again hoped to invoke some kind of a response from either Newcomb or the marauders.

After waiting to see if his efforts had drawn any attention or movements in the area around his friend's horse, with his own horse secured to a neighboring cedar tree, Battle kept Newcomb's horse between him and where he expected his friend to be hiding. Creeping closer, he saw his friend's legs awkwardly resting on top of a fallen tree. Scanning the area for any signs of trouble as he inched closer, with his musket levelled at waist-high height Battle slowly moved it from left to right several times.

Quietly whispering his friend's name, Battle noticed part of Newcomb's face had been grossly disfigured by a bullet fired from close range. Around the left side of Newcomb's face, powder burns and flecks of burnt skin gave every indication the fatal round had been fired only inches away from where his body now rested. While younger than most of the soldiers he was serving with, Battle knew the severe damage to Newcomb's face was meant as a warning to whoever found his body.

Bending down to see if Newcomb was still alive, three Minie balls whizzed inches over Battle's head; barely missing their intended target. Blindly returning fire, Battle fled in the direction of where he had left his horse. Reaching the animal, he cut the reins with a large knife he kept sheathed inside his right boot. Seconds later, straining to pull his friend's large black horse closer to his, Battle cut a second set of leather reins. Digging his heels hard into the belly of his horse, the young soldier tugged forcefully on both sets of reins as he urged them forward. As the large animals reacted to his commands, Battle anxiously glanced over his shoulders to see if anyone was gaining ground. Nervously scanning the ground he had covered only minutes earlier, loud angry words flew in his direction from two marauders set on doing him harm. To Battle's surprise, he recognized the faces as being among those who had attacked the wagons days earlier. Moments later, two more shots sailed over the young soldier's right shoulder before splintering the bark of a pine tree less than thirty feet in from of him.

Blessed with an amazing amount of good luck, Private Gordy Battle, outnumbered by an angry group of former soldiers who had every intention of viciously killing him just as they had done to his two friends, somehow managed to flee to safety. As he fled, Battle checked twice to make sure his friend's body had not fallen off. Nearing the camp Howard's men had setup, Battle's loud cries for help told his fellow soldiers trouble was headed their way.

Responding to the approaching threat, six of Howard's men, soon followed by their commanding officer and Sergeant Adams, raced to head off those who had senselessly killed two of their fellow soldiers. Taking up defensive positions behind several trees and a pile of large boulders that nature had conveniently set in place years earlier, Battle's fellow Confederates quickly cut down three of the marauders. They did so less than fifty yards away from their own tents. In the brief exchange of gunfire, Howard would lose one more soldier.

*****

Trembling from his close brush with death, with the marauders driven off Battle described how he had found the badly mutilated bodies of Privates Hatch and Newcomb. Incensed over the loss of three of his men, Howard's eyes glazed over from the anger burning inside his body.

While fuming for several minutes over the vicious manner in which two of his men had been murdered, unlike Adams and several others, Howard managed to keep his wits. Amongst the angry rants and raves of his subordinates came questions as to when the pursuit for those responsible for their friends' deaths would commence. The response they soon heard from their commanding officer, while doing little to temper their anger, caused them to realize one of the Confederate Army's most vindictive officers was about to unleash his fury on those responsible for murdering their friends.

Even though he expected trouble to occur during this mission, Howard had not expected it to come from soldiers who had once been proud of the uniform they wore.

<u>10</u>

Later that night, after most of his men had fallen asleep Howard mounted his horse and rode through his picket line in search of those responsible for the murders of two of his men. With his horse stripped of its saddle as a way of minimizing any unwanted noise, Howard carried only a repeating rifle and his pistol. Loaded with six shots, the pistol had been purchased years earlier by his father. Kept safe by his uncle in the years following his father's death, the pistol had been given to Howard as a means of keeping him safe during what would prove to be four long years of brutal fighting.

As a young boy, Howard had spent parts of seven summers working with one of his distant relatives as an apprentice surveyor in and around western Virginia. Doing so had taught him a wide variety of survival skills; among them were how to move quietly through the woods while avoiding unfriendly Indians and wild animals. On this particular night, he prayed his skills had not abandoned him.

After leaving his horse next to the mouth of a small stream, Howard set off on foot in search of those he was hunting. Hours earlier, he had sent two of his soldiers out to locate any signs of where the marauders were camped. Walking for nearly an hour in a wet uniform after hiking over unfriendly terrain during a brief, but intense rainstorm, Howard heard the skittish sounds made by several nervous horses. While the storm had passed as quickly as it had risen, off in the distance the sound of thunder and flashes of brief lightening continued to light up an otherwise dark sky. With the loud noise and bright light making the animals uneasy, it helped mask the small amount of noise being made by someone intent on retribution. Moving cautiously in the direction of where the marauders had made their camp, Howard eyed the woods around him as he caught sight of a large campfire being tended to by three men.

Fifteen minutes later, as he finished surveying the woods for those determined to harm anyone entering their camp, Howard, believing he was not being watched, moved closer to the fire. Squatting behind a decaying pile of firewood that had been stacked there years earlier, he watched as the men took turns roasting a deer on a series of large poles. Scanning the area around the fire and seeing no one performing picket duty like his own men were doing, the young officer theorized most of the marauders had taken refuge from the recent storm inside the remains of a small cabin. With the large fire illuminating a section of the old one-room frontier home, from where he knelt Howard could see one side of the dilapidated structure had fallen in years earlier. Despite the sheer darkness inside the woods, Howard also managed to notice the roof of the old home appeared as if it was ready to collapse at any moment. Doing what he could to survey the ground around the old cabin, his ears listened intently for the sounds of anyone attempting to do him harm. Spending several minutes obtaining an accurate count of the number of men making their way back and forth from the cabin to where the deer was being roasted, Howard was pleased moments later when his count of the number of horses tied up outside the cabin matched the number of men he had counted.

After taking in several other details, including what he could see of the terrain around the cabin, Howard carefully extricated himself from where he had been hiding. Too busy feasting on their late evening meal and too drunk from consuming several bottles of stolen whiskey, the marauders were unaware that someone had been watching them.

It was a mistake they would soon regret.

******

Safely making his way back inside his picket lines after retrieving his horse, Howard rode the short distance back to camp. Dismounting close to where the other horses had been placed inside a small makeshift corral, Howard noticed Adams making his way to where he was wiping down his horse. Unlike those sleeping less than sixty feet away, Howard and his sergeant were running on pure adrenalin.

"Find them?" Adams asked, curious over his commanding officer's success at finding those who had repeatedly attacked them over the past several days.

"*Ignorant fools* . . . they've hunkered down for the night. The entire time I was watching them there was never a guard posted outside this old cabin where they've taken refuge. Because of that, they never knew I was there. They're holed up inside this cabin eating venison and drinking whiskey." Pointing in the direction he had come from, Howard added, "They're about an hour away from this very spot. By now they're all asleep; passed out from too much booze and full bellies." Looking at Adams, Howard gave the sergeant his instructions. "I have everything planned, so wake the men. Leave two of them behind to guard the wagons. We'll take the others with us; including the men on picket duty." As he went over his plans, Howard's clothes gave off the aroma of the deer he had seen being roasted. "The smell of that venison has made me realize how hungry I am. I'm going to grab something to eat for the ride. Have the men saddle me a fresh horse; we're leaving in twenty minutes."

"Yes, sir!"

As Adams prepared to wake those sleeping comfortably inside their tents, his thoughts of what they were about to undertake caused his anxious mind to generate several questions. Realizing they were issues that would likely be addressed when Howard briefed the men before setting out, he held off on finding the answers to his questions. However, he did advise his commanding officer of one new problem. Not particularly fond of Lieutenant Brown, Adams hoped to hear a few choice words directed in Brown's direction for the untimely injuries the young officer had sustained.

"Sir, there's one more thing before we leave. Yesterday you sent Lieutenant Radcliff off to scout the area out in front of us. I suspect it's going to be a day or two before he's back; maybe even longer if he runs into any trouble."

Growing irritated by the delay Adams was causing, Howard urged his sergeant to get to the point he was trying to make.

"Sir, I'm afraid Lieutenant Brown is not going to be much use to us if you plan on taking him with us. While you were gone he was thrown from that no-good pain in the ass horse of his. He landed pretty hard . . . his right ankle is likely broken and his collarbone ain't much better. That part of him is likely fractured pretty badly." Like many of his men who received little in the way of a formal education, Adams speech was rather rough.

"Wonderful!" Howard replied, knocking the dust off his hat as he banged it against his right leg. "What the hell was he thinking? Instead of being out there on his damn horse, he should have been getting some rest. Where is he?" While having every right to berate Brown for what had happened, Howard elected not to do so in front of one of his enlisted men. Out of respect to another officer, he would wait to do so until he and Brown were alone.

"Resting inside his tent," Adams replied, doing his best to hide the smirk breaking out across his face. With it pitch-black inside the camp; Adams was lucky Howard had no way of seeing his expression. While upset over Brown's poor judgement, Howard would not have tolerated one of his officers being disrespected. "For what it's worth, the good lieutenant is expecting an ass chewing, sir. This is just my own humble opinion, but if I were you I wouldn't disappoint him."

Less than twenty minutes later, as his collective group of tired soldiers wiped the few hours of sleep from their eyes, Howard, his face freshly washed from the cool waters of a nearby stream, strode to where his horse was waiting. In his hands, he held the remnants of a small loaf of bread. As Howard polished off the remainder of his late night meal, Adams and the rest of the men assembled around him.

After issuing his orders, Howard pushed his men to cover as much ground as possible before the sun made its presence known. An hour later, as they made their way to the small structure the marauders had holed up in, he urged them to be as quiet as possible as they moved to the positions they had been assigned. As they prepared to move off, Howard gave Adams his last set of instructions. As he spoke, his dark brown eyes stared directly into the eyes of his young sergeant.

"If we don't take these bastards out with our first volley, whoever is left is going to try and make a run for it. They're smart enough not to use the front door, so they'll probably try to make their escape by smashing a hole in one of the cabin walls. Whether they decide to flee on foot or try to make it to their horses, you can't allow them to escape. Have one of your men make sure all of those critters belonging to those bastards are tied up real good. I'm going to give the men a few minutes to get into position and then all hell is going to bust loose. Have those with you ready to pick off whoever attempts to make a run for it." Finished saying what had to be said; Howard shook hands with one of the few sergeants he had ever completely trusted. Wishing each other good luck, Howard gave one last look in the direction of the cabin before moving closer to the front of the dilapidated structure.

"How am I going to know you've started the attack, captain?" Adams asked, whispering softly so as not to wake anyone sleeping inside the cabin.

"Believe me, you'll know. I don't intend on being quiet."

After making contact with Private Lester Norris, a twenty-one-year-old from just outside of Richmond who had taken up a position less than forty feet away from the cabin's right front corner, Howard set his plan in motion. With Norris' musket slung over his shoulder, Howard cautiously scanned the ground around them as they walked towards the structure's front door. In his hands, Norris carried the ends of two logs. Both glowed brightly after being brought back to life from inside the smoldering campfire. As Howard aimed his pistol at the rickety front door, Norris did what he could to fan the logs so they were as hot as they could be. Waiting for Norris to finish his task, Howard quietly enlarged a gaping hole that was present to the right of the door. Seconds later, the red hot logs were tossed inside the cabin where the unsuspecting marauders were fast asleep.

As the logs exploded after hitting the cabin's dirt floor, a shower of hot red embers caused dust, windblown leaves, blankets, and other dried material to quickly catch fire. In moments, the walls inside exploded in flames. As some of his men intentionally added confusion to the moment by throwing rocks against the cabin's siding, Howard and Norris began screaming at those inside the burning structure. Then, as the inebriated marauders struggled to their feet amongst the growing flames, both men repeatedly fired their weapons at the figures stumbling around inside. In less than three minutes, with little effort Howard and Norris shot and killed six men. Those who fell dead, men who had helped to kill soldiers still committed to defending the Confederacy, caused Howard to experience a sense of relief.

With the fire quickly spreading to all four walls, as several of their fellow traitors fell dead from well-placed shots fired from outside two others tried escaping by kicking a hole in the cabin's rear wall. As the former soldiers worked feverishly to escape the flames licking at their clothes, Adams, along with Private George Nester, took positions behind trees a short distance away. Off to their left, another of Howard's men took a similar position behind a small pile of rocks and dirt. Seconds later, the three aimed their weapons at the growing hole being made in the rear wall. As the two marauders managed to smash their way through the burning wall, red hot Minie balls fired from less than thirty feet away penetrated their upper torsos. Both had barely made it outside before falling dead. Like their friends inside the cabin, their bodies would become badly burned when the cabin finally collapsed.

Shouting to Adams and the others to hold their positions, Howard watched as a single figure inside the cabin frantically searched for an exit away from the intense smoke and growing heat. Moving about inside the structure, one already badly damaged from years of neglect, the last marauder recklessly fired a shot in Howard's direction. Moments later, as he desperately tried reloading his musket in an attempt to get off one last shot, a spark ignited a supply of black powder inside the cabin. Knocked off his feet by the small explosion and from a section of the roof collapsing on top of him, the marauder's musket was ripped from his hands.

Pulled from the burning ruins, Hobie Miller, a former sergeant in the Confederate Army, screamed in pain as he was gruffly tossed to the ground several feet away from where his men had roasted their last meal. Ignoring the questions he was being asked as some of Howard's men made sure his companions were dead, Miller screamed in pain from his searing wounds.

"What's your name, soldier? What regiment were you assigned to? What caused you to get busted?" Howard impatiently asked after noticing the faded outline of where a set of sergeant's stripes had once been sewn on the former soldier's shirt. None of Howard's questions were asked in a compassionate tone.

Taking note of his badly burned legs and left arm, Miller, at first, refused to answer. *"Not till you give me some help for these damn burns y'all caused. I ain't tellin' ya nothing!"* Upset at being badly injured, Miller's tone was just as loud and abrasive as Howard's.

Angrily staring at the former soldier lying near his feet, Howard sternly dictated how things were going to happen. What he was about to say was not entirely truthful. "I'll see to it that you receive some help, soldier, but first I need some answers. To start with, I want to know your name, regiment, why you deserted, and why you've been attacking us." Despite the seriousness of Miller's injuries, the tone in Howard's voice reflected the absence of any compassion.

Realizing he had little to bargain with, Miller told Howard what he wanted to know. "Sergeant Hobie Miller. Most of us fought with the 17th Virginia Infantry Regiment. I stayed with that outfit long enough to see two of my brothers killed in fights we had no business being in. I seen three other kin of mine killed as well. Me and the others ya dun killed; we all got fed up with the fightin' going on in Petersburg. The small amount of grub we was being given weren't fit for pigs. All them trenches we dug, all that sickness and bad weather we was forced to endure, that was bad enough, but when them bastards who call themselves officers couldn't find a way to feed us decent like, we just got fed up and left one night. Besides all of them other things, I got tired of too many piss-head officers making piss-poor decisions on whether us soldiers lived or died."

"When did you and the others desert?" Howard asked, glancing off to his right at the burning cabin.

"Me and two of them boys inside the cabin been gone about a month; we come across them other fellas in there two or three days later. Just like us, they ain't been fed too much. We's all tired of being mistreated; all we care about is getting back home. But seeing there ain't much left in Virginia these days on account of what them no good blue-bellies have done, for the time being we all decided we'd make our way further south."

Nodding his head over a story he had already heard far too many times, Howard glanced in Adams' direction. Like the devastating defeats the Confederate Army had recently begun to experience, the resources of their government had also slowly dwindled to next to nothing. Incompetent clerks, problems with the rail lines, and General Ulysses S. Grant's large army had contributed to the diminished number of supplies being received by the Confederate Army during the siege of Petersburg. All contributed to the large number of desertions that were occurring on a daily basis across the South.

Having little compassion for the tale of woe he was listening to, Howard tricked Milled into believing him. As a professional soldier, he had little tolerance for complainers and deserters. Asking Adams for his canteen, Howard poured most of the contents on the ground next to his feet. Leaving just enough to wet Miller's parched mouth; he tossed his prisoner the canteen. "Take that as a sign of my good faith. There's plenty more where that came from. Tell me why you and the others have been attacking us, and I'll see to it you get as much as you want. But, first, I want you to tell me what it is you think we have in our wagons. Answer me, and I'll have your injuries tended to."

Warily eyeing Howard and the others around him, Miller reluctantly explained the reasons behind the recent attacks. As he did, the former sergeant admitted he and his men had been responsible for killing Hatch and Newcomb. "Like I told ya, we ain't been fed too good for nearly a year. We was just hoping them wagons y'all got with ya were packed with food. Thought we'd run ya off fairly easily and have a few good meals, but you fellas ended up gettin' the best of us. Y'all killed more of us than we thought ya could. We still thought ya had plenty of grub with ya, but after we attacked the second time we started thinkin' ya must be protecting something pretty valuable by the way y'all fought back. Soldiers like you fellas can always find food, but whatever else ya got with ya . . . well, it must be pretty important."

Expressionless as Miller finished speaking; Howard paid little attention as the badly injured former soldier winced in pain for several seconds.

"Whatcha all got in them wagons, captain? Ya carrying payroll or something like that?"

Having been told as much as he expected, Howard nodded in Adams' direction. "That's enough, sergeant. See to it."

As one of his men flung a rope over a sturdy branch some twenty feet off the ground, two others picked Miller up and pinned him against the nearby tree. Knowing his men realized the role Miller had in the deaths of their two friends, Howard said nothing as his prisoner's face was pummeled by several angry blows. Barely able to stand after being severely beaten, the former soldier, now reduced to being a deserter to the cause he had sworn to defend, feebly tried kicking those who were tying his hands behind his back. Moments later, with a hastily tied noose in place around his neck, Miller was violently placed on the back of another marauder's horse. Around the tree's base, the other end of the rope had already been tied in place.

"Ya no-good son of a bitch," Miller screamed as spit and saliva flew from his mouth. *"Ya told me you were gonna get me some help for these burns I got."* Breathing heavily as his chest rose and fell with each breath, Miller spat in Howard's direction, missing his intended target. *"You're just like the rest of them pussies. Y'all call yourselves officers . . . but you're nothing but a bunch of no-good lying bastards!"*

Before Miller could utter another word, Adams slapped the backside of the animal the former Confederate soldier was sitting on. Scared by the commotion taking place, as the horse darted away the thick tree limb sagged as Miller violently bobbed in mid-air for several seconds. Kicking his legs, the brutal leader of a sadistic group of ex-soldiers fought to catch his breath as the noose quickly tightened around his sweaty neck. Moments later, as Miller took his last breath his neck snapped.

While pleased over the deaths of Miller and those responsible for murdering their fellow soldiers, Adams and the others with him did little celebrating as they picked through the saddlebags and gear found outside the smoldering cabin. With little need for the horses that had been tied up not far from where the cabin stood, two of Adams' soldiers ran them off. Nearby, Howard kept watch on the nearby woods.

Like most experienced soldiers, Howard never let his guard down.

******

With Battle leading the way after Howard decided they had accomplished everything there was to address concerning the marauders, the young captain and his men set out to recover the remains of Private George Newcomb. Unlike Private Hatch, Newcomb's body would soon be buried in a rocky grave not far from where he had been killed.

While the small pile of rocks on top of Newcomb's grave would mark the location of a fallen Confederate soldier for many years, the simple wooden cross Howard's men set in place fell apart in less than four years. Constructed of boards rescued from the log cabin they had set on fire, the weathered planks were held together by nails that had been pried from other pieces of wood. Battered by storms and fallen tree branches, the small cross finally came apart after being exposed to the elements for longer than it was built for.

Like many soldiers from both sides of the war, Newcomb's remains would rest in an unmarked grave for the rest of eternity.

11

Arriving safely back in camp after making sure plans had been made to protect the perimeter until the following morning, Howard prepared to grab some much-needed sleep after being awake for two long and demanding days. Heading towards his tent, he noticed one of his men down on his hands and knees close to where the wagons had been parked. Realizing something unusual was taking place; Howard paused to check on Private Norris.

"Norris, what's the problem? Are you not feeling well?"

"I'm not sure, captain. I've never felt like this before. This pain I'm feeling just came on as we were leaving that cabin back there." As he answered Howard's question, Norris used his right hand to point to where the pain had rapidly intensified near his lower abdomen. "I . . . I can't tell ya how bad I feel. I've been puking and crapping like crazy for the past hour or so. I'm also thirsty as hell, but each time I drink some water I have trouble keeping it down. Take a look at this," Norris said, pulling up his shirt as he again pointed to the area around his abdomen, "it looks as if my belly is swelling up."

Looking to his left after forcing Norris to lie down on his back as a way of trying to find some relief for the pain he was experiencing, Howard noticed Adams speaking with another soldier. *"Sergeant Adams! I need some help over here. Have Private Nester bring me a pail of water."*

After moving Norris to a position where he was comfortable taking a few sips of water, Howard, with virtually no medical training, did his best at evaluating the young soldier's condition. In doing so, he gingerly touched the right side of Norris' abdomen.

"Stop! Don't . . . don't do that, captain!" Norris shrieked as he fought the urge to puke from the intense pain Howard had unintentionally caused. Gasping for air as his pain slowly subsided; Norris tried apologizing for screaming at his commanding officer. His cries caused two of his fellow soldiers to run to his side. "I'm sorry, captain, but that pain I felt was . . ."

"No need to apologize, Norris. I probably shouldn't have done that, but I'm just trying to figure out what's making you feel this way. Do you have pain anywhere else besides your abdomen?"

Clenching his fists from the pain he was once again experiencing, Norris weakly responded by saying, "No, sir, just near my belly. It . . . it hurts real bad, even worse than it did a few minutes ago. Do ya think it's something I ate?"

"Unless you ate something different than the rest of us, I don't think so. I'm not sure what's causing this pain you're experiencing. I'd like to think it's just fatigue from the busy days we've all been through, but I'm afraid it's more than that. We've all been under a great deal of stress, but this seems to be some sort of a medical problem. It could be your body is telling you that you haven't been drinking enough water. Whatever it is, we'll figure it out." As he finished speaking, Howard took a moment to praise Norris' efforts back at the cabin. The words he heard brought a brief smile, and a moment of relief, to the young soldier's worried face.

After instructing Norris' fellow soldiers to find a comfortable place inside one of the wagons so their friend could rest, Howard spent several minutes talking with Adams about the symptoms Norris was experiencing. "Seen anything like this before?" Howard asked, watching as Norris was gently lifted inside one of the nearby wagons.

"Just once," Adams replied, recalling another soldier who had experienced similar symptoms three years earlier. "I'm afraid that outcome wasn't very good. The doctor who treated this soldier I'm thinking about had no idea what was causing the pain until it was too late. I later found out it was something related to a broken blood vessel that had burst inside of him."

Shaking his head over the upsetting news, Howard again stared at the wagon where Norris was resting. "What'd they call it? Seems doctors have a fancy name for just about every ailment there is."

Quiet for a few moments, Adams tried recalling the name that had been attributed to the soldier's death. "It's been a while, so I need a moment. But it had some strange sounding name I had only heard of once or twice before. Come to think of it, I haven't heard it since. I believe they called it appendicitis," Adams said, correctly pronouncing the medical condition Norris was experiencing. As he recalled the name assigned to the medical condition, Adams remembered one other important point. "They said it was his appendix that had ruptured. I don't believe too many folks have heard that term; maybe now they do, but back then they didn't. All I know is that's what killed that fine soldier a few years back."

Shaking his head as he started walking to his tent, Howard tried recalling if he had ever heard the name of the organ Adams had mentioned. He quickly realized it was one he had never heard. Entering his tent, Howard hoped a few hours of rest would cause Norris to feel better. After undressing and cleaning his face from a small pot of water sitting on a large wooden chest, Howard settled down on his cot. In less than five minutes, the exhausted young officer fell fast asleep. Over the next seven hours Howard would enjoy a peaceful few hours of rest. Nearby, Private Norris also drifted off to sleep.

While both soldiers fell fast asleep, the next morning only one of them would see the light of day.

12

As the morning sun began to show itself from off in the distance, Adams and Nester, often the first two soldiers awake each morning, brought the camp to life by tending to the campfires that had burned over night. One of them would soon warm a large pot of coffee for everyone to share. The dark brown liquid was one of the few pleasures which greeted the men each morning. With the recent deaths of several of the friends, one pot was more than enough for those still left. As they stoked the fires, one of their fellow soldiers saw to the needs of the horses. Before that chore could be finished, Adams had the pot of coffee warmed and ready to be shared.

Charged with making the camp's morning meal, Nester began preparing a thick porridge made from cornmeal, chunks of dried meat, flour, water, and a sprinkling of yellow grits. While the concoction proved to be hearty each time it had been made, it was quickly becoming one of the camp's least favorite meals. It was also one of the few meals Nester knew how to make. Much to his dismay, his fellow soldiers had recently dubbed it *Nester's Gruel.*

As the inexperienced cook carried the porridge towards one of the fires in order for it to be warmed up, another soldier, Charles Batten, hollered loud enough for everyone to hear. After climbing aboard the wagon where Norris had been sleeping, Batten had been startled by what he found. Barely nineteen-years-old, the pimply faced soldier had joined the regiment four months after it had been formed.

"Sergeant Adams... Sergeant Adams!" Batten screamed as he leaned out the back of the wagon after pushing aside the canvass shade. *"It's Norris! I think he's dead!"* Batten's loud cries caused Howard and the others to rush towards the wagon where Norris had been sleeping.

Climbing aboard, Howard listened as Batten told him what he had found. As he spoke, tears ran down the teenaged soldier's face. Like anyone his age, he was ill-prepared for the discovery he had just made. Like many others, Batten should have been home working on the family farm instead of fighting in a cruel war. Batten's lack of schooling was soon reflected in his speech. "Captain, sir, I just came to check on Norris here, and I . . . I found . . . I found him just as he's resting. I ain't no doctor, but I believe he's dead. I checked, but I couldn't feel no air coming out of his mouth or nose." Finished speaking, tears again started streaming down the face of a soldier who had yet to experience his first shave. Away from home for close to four years, Batten had developed a fondness for the soldier who was no longer breathing.

As Howard did his best to comfort the soldier kneeling next to him, Adams tore open Norris' shirt. Placing his left ear on the dead soldier's chest in the hopes of finding Norris still alive, he strained to hear even the faintest heartbeat. Seconds later, after placing his hand over Norris' mouth, he knew the soldier everyone had taken a liking to was dead. Pulling Norris' shirt up around his neck, Adams, then Howard, saw the bright red mark the burst appendix had left near the young soldier's abdomen.

Standing up inside the wagon, Howard realized he had lost another of his men. With only Adams, Battle, Nester, and Batten left in camp, and with Lieutenant Brown laid up from his recent fall, Howard began to question whether it was possible for he and his men to deliver their precious cargo to its final destination.

Already confronted by a handful of significant problems, Howard had no way of knowing his troubles were far from over.

******

Two hours after finding Norris dead, Howard gathered his men around the shallow grave that had been dug on a small knoll overlooking the nearby river. Roughly cut in the soft South Carolina soil, Norris' final resting place sat less than one hundred yards away from where the precious cargo was waiting to be moved further south. Perched thirty feet above the river's slow moving current, the impressive view was one the deceased soldier had recently commented on. Not far from the gravesite, long stretches of wide open fields were surrounded by abundant patches of colorful wildflowers. Off in the distance, small stands of maple and oak trees dotted the landscape with their lush green leaves. Further away, a steep line of hills wound further south for nearly a mile. They were the same hills Private Battle had climbed as he searched for Hatch and Newcomb two days earlier.

Upset over the loss of another of his men, someone who had died due to an unexpected medical condition and not as gloriously as he would have liked, Howard fumbled for the right words as he stood over Norris' blanket wrapped body. After several awkward moments, including two short periods of prolonged silence, the young Confederate officer delivered his first-ever sermon. Moments later, he gave the order for Norris' remains to be lowered inside the crudely-dug grave. As his lifeless body was being placed inside the grave, Norris was honored one last time as Howard called his men to attention. As a further tribute, Howard's crisp salute remained in place for several seconds.

After Norris was laid to rest, Howard and his men lingered near the freshly dug grave; each of them questioning what the condition was that had caused their friend's death. Knowing a couple of his men were still in a state of shock from the events no one could have predicted, Howard told them they had until noon to relax and get packed for the next leg of their journey. Like Adams and the others still in camp, Howard was in no mood to be climbing back on his horse.

With Lieutenant Radcliff off scouting the terrain in front of them for the past few days, and with Brown's nagging injuries keeping him from performing many of his duties, Howard's compliment of healthy soldiers was now down to four. Like their commanding officer, Adams and the others were now focused on matters far more important than their precious cargo. The sudden passing of a fellow soldier and a hastily arranged burial had caused them to think of little else.

It had also caused them to leave their muskets back in camp.

13

Hidden inside a thick stand of white birch trees that were being protected by several acres of chest-high grass, a Union cavalry officer stared through his binoculars as Howard's men finished tending to Norris' grave. Sitting atop his horse, a high-spirited animal still breathing heavily from the hilly terrain he and his rider had just covered, Lieutenant Alvin Anderson tried calming his mount as he studied the proceedings taking place around the small grave. Aware that he and his men had gone undetected, Anderson spent close to ten minutes watching the actions of the Confederate soldiers. With significant interest, he also took note of the wagons parked close to their tents.

Pushing south for the past several days out in front of his regiment, Anderson and his men had been living off the land for nearly two weeks. Tired of eating meals comprised of rancid meat, dried beans, moldy biscuits, and parts of animals he would have never eaten back home, the twenty-five-year-old West Point graduate saw the parked wagons as the means for ending the relentless hunger he and his men were experiencing.

Watching as the Confederate soldiers lazily began the short trek back to where they were camped; Anderson suddenly realized they were only armed with tools and not muskets. Rushing to where his men were hidden inside the tree line, he told them what he wanted done.

"There's only five Rebs out there that I could see, so the chances are pretty good that we can take them." Pointing to a line of trees off to his right as his men mounted their horses, Anderson continued with his instructions. "We'll use the trees to shade our movements for as long as possible. Once we clear them, we'll charge straight at them Johnny Rebs. When we're done with them, we'll see what's inside their wagons." Drawing his saber, Anderson cautiously spurred his horse forward. Moments later, it turned to the right in response to the command it had been given.

Clearing the protection the line of trees had afforded them, Anderson and his five men raced in Howard's direction, galloping undetected for several tense moments. Seconds later, panicked by the sight of several armed cavalry soldiers bearing down on them, Howard's men dropped the tools they had been carrying as they sprinted towards their tents and the muskets they had left there.

The loud anxious cries piercing the opened flaps of his tent, coupled with the unmistakable sound of several horses racing across the ground not far from where he was resting, caused Lieutenant Brown to gingerly sit up on his cot. Recognizing two of the voices to be those of Howard and Adams, Brown hobbled towards the opening of his tent. As he moved, the injured officer took the precaution of grabbing the pistol lying next to his cot. Stepping outside, Brown immediately saw the trouble confronting his fellow soldiers.

Awkwardly stepping back inside his tent, Brown grabbed the other pistol he always had ready in the event of trouble. Moments later, as he stood outside his small canvass tent the young officer took aim at the lead rider quickly gaining ground on Howard. Urging the others to make it back to camp, Howard fell behind after stopping to assist Nester who landed awkwardly after stepping into a small hole.

As Battle, and then Batten, made their way inside the safety of the camp, Brown fired three shots at the Union cavalry soldier who was less than twenty feet away from Howard. Struck in the right eye by Brown's second shot, the soldier immediately grabbed for his face as fell from his horse. Moments later, as he writhed in agony the soldier's chest was crushed by the weight of another horse.

With Battle and Batten soon kneeling alongside of him, as the two soldiers raised their muskets to fire their first shots, Brown fired the last two rounds from his first revolver. As he did, the soldiers next to him took out two more Union soldiers; both fell dead from well-placed shots to their chests.

"Come on, Howard! Hurry up for God's sake!" Brown hollered, dropping his empty revolver on the ground as he drew the next one from his waistband. *"Get your ass over here!"*

Ignoring Howard's rank, Brown urged his commanding officer and the others racing in front of him to cover the remaining fifty feet as quickly as they could. Taking a look to his right, Brown knew once Howard and the others made it past his position they would have access to their weapons. They would also be less exposed to being shot or slashed by a Union saber being swung in anger. Taking aim at the last Union soldier charging their position, Battle and Batten again sent two Minie balls racing towards their target. In seconds, the lead balls blew large holes in the soldier's left shoulder. Badly injured, but fighting to stay upright in his saddle, the soldier peeled away as the Union attack failed to achieve its objective. Seconds later, as Brown fired his last two shots at the Union officer directing the attack, one narrowly missed Anderson's left ear as the second tore open his horse's throat. Breathing hard after being shot, the horse's badly damaged throat began spewing rich frothy blood as its once fast gallop came to a painfully slow trot. Temporarily blinded by the blood that had been sprayed in his eyes, Anderson realized the advantage he had enjoyed minutes earlier now was lost. With four of his soldiers already dead and the other badly injured, Anderson called off the attack. More interested in living to see another day than he was in dying, the frightened officer retreated to a safer location.

As Howard and Adams finally stumbled to safety, the last of Anderson's soldiers took a moment to fire one last desperate shot. It was fired in retaliation for one of his friends being killed moments earlier. Galloping off to catch up to Anderson after firing his only shot that morning, Corporal Dennis Murphy never saw the damage it caused.

Catching his breath after making it past the position Brown had taken, Adams, after urging his men to reload their muskets as quickly as possible, turned to look back at the field he had just crossed. As he turned, Murphy's hastily fired shot struck Adams just above his left eyebrow. Falling backwards, his limp body crashed to the ground as Anderson crested a small rise two hundred yards away. Stunned by what had taken place, Howard, who was less than ten feet away from where Adams had been standing, failed to immediately comprehend the severity of this tragic sequence of events. As he stood there staring down at his sergeant's lifeless body, Nester confirmed that Adams was dead.

By way of one last shot that was fired with little hope of hitting anything important, Howard lost the one soldier he could not afford to lose. The young officer's problems had just become even more substantial.

14

After inspecting the bodies lying in the field to make sure they were dead, Howard had his men bury Sergeant Seth Adams in a simple grave not far from where Private Norris was laid to rest earlier that morning. In less than three hours, Howard had witnessed his dwindling compliment of men being reduced even more by the loss of two more soldiers. While the loss of any soldier impacted the ability of most commanders to accomplish their mission, the loss of two competent soldiers with the abilities they possessed was especially troublesome. With four wagons filled to near capacity with personal belongings, supplies, rifles, and, most importantly, the gold and silver they were escorting, Howard now had only three healthy soldiers to drive them.

While proud of Brown for making it possible for he and the others to make it safely back to camp, Howard knew the lieutenant's injuries would significantly impact his ability to drive a wagon filled to near capacity with a portion of the Confederacy's most-precious assets.

As he thought about how he was going to address this dilemma, Howard, unsure if he was giving himself or his men some extra time to grieve over Adams' sudden passing, left Brown in charge as he rode off to collect his thoughts. Pausing for a second time to briefly inspect the bodies of the soldiers his men had killed, Howard liberated two small packages of hardtack from a haversack he found lying on the ground. Climbing back on his horse, he gave little thought as to whether or not he was being watched by any Union soldiers.

Riding for close to an hour in the opposite direction of where he had located the marauders inside the dilapidated cabin, Howard's thoughts focused on the details of his mission and the tragic deaths of his men. Feeling as if the weight of the world had descended upon his shoulders, he paid little attention to the terrain around him as he struggled to figure out how he would cross the next one hundred miles with four wagons and only three healthy men. Moving along a narrow dusty trail that appeared as if it had not been visited for several years, Howard hoped Lieutenant Radcliff would soon return with good news. With the way his luck was going, it was not something he expected to happen.

Climbing down off his horse after passing through a large field dotted with thick weeds and patches of bright green grass, Howard noticed a stone wall running for close to one hundred yards not far from where he was standing. Built with a variety of different shaped rocks and stones, the wall looked as if it had been constructed years earlier from the heavy bulky objects tilled during several growing seasons.

Standing there as he admired the effort someone had toiled over as they made sure how straight the wall ran and how high it stood, Howard thought, "Whoever built it seemed to have given a great deal of thought to how high and wide they wanted some sections as it rises and falls in certain spots." Realizing he had not passed any homes or farms for the past hour, or foundations where barns had once stood, Howard scanned the horizon for any signs of life or crops. Nothing he saw gave any indication that the land around him had ever been settled. Confused, the young officer stared at the long line of neatly stacked rocks as a few new thoughts crossed his mind. "If there's nothing here, who built this stone wall? All of these rocks weren't put there by Mother Nature. Some farmer built it, but that must have been years ago. And what caused this narrow trail to be created? While it looks as if it hasn't been used for some time, someone had to travel over it at one point."

✶✶✶✶✶✶

Riding back to where his men were camped, Howard was far more composed than he had been a few hours earlier. The peaceful ride had given him time to clear his head of many unpleasant thoughts. Having spent a few minutes eating some wild berries, he had not only planned his next move but had temporarily pushed aside any further thoughts of the men he lost. While their deaths would continue to haunt him over the coming weeks, Howard forced himself to concentrate on the needs of the next few days. Like his solitary ride, the precious few minutes he spent writing in his journal had also helped to clear his head.

Taking a different route back to camp, Howard came across a small patch of ground that looked as if it had recently been disturbed. After climbing off his horse and scanning the trampled ground for footprints or other signs of trouble, the young officer found himself kneeling next to a small pile of rocks. Arranged in a crude circle, the rocks had recently been the site of a small campfire. Several yards away, another group of blackened rocks also showed signs of having contained a similar fire.

Leafing through the remnants of the two fires, Howard found several charred bones and the lids of two cans. The remains of several burnt logs, as well as other bits of debris, gave the impression the fires had burned for several hours. Holding two of the logs in his hands, Howard casually inspected them as he scanned the area for signs of anyone watching him. Looking down at the pile of bones resting inside the first campfire, he thought, "They're probably from a couple of quails or pigeons that were eaten by two or three people not too long ago." Picking up one of the lids, Howard suspected soldiers, either Anderson's men or those marauders he helped to kill, had likely warmed up cans of beans that originated up North as the few canning plants located inside the Confederacy had already been destroyed during the war. Briefly inspecting what remained inside the scene of the second campfire, Howard found a smaller number of bones and bits of charred wood. Unlike the first location, he also found shards of burnt glass.

Looking for signs of who might have camped there, Howard found nothing to indicate who had built the two fires. Growing concerned that his men may still be under the watchful eye of those intent on doing them harm, Howard mounted his horse and started making his way back.

Arriving back in camp, Howard had hoped to see that Lieutenant Radcliff had returned from his scouting mission. He was greatly disappointed when he learned Radcliff had yet to return. While still upset over the recent attacks he and his men had endured, and by his subordinate's prolonged absence, Howard managed to stay focused. Issuing his orders for the rest of the day, he directed his men to be ready to move out early the following morning.

Then, as he had done at least twice each day, Howard inspected the wagons containing his precious cargo. Minutes later, he was pleased to see nothing had been tampered with.

******

With a good part of the day already gone and his men still grieving over the loss of two of their fellow soldiers, Howard made his way towards his tent after making sure his orders had been understood. Before entering his tent, he stopped to check on Brown's injuries.

Sitting on the edge of his cot as Howard arrived, Brown went to stand but his commanding officer motioned for him to remain seated. It was quickly followed by a verbal order. "As you were, lieutenant, remain seated." Looking over Brown's injuries, Howard noticed the heavy bandage in place around his subordinate's right ankle. As expected, Howard asked the appropriate question the situation called for. "How's the collarbone and ankle feeling?"

"I'm doing better than I was," Brown replied, lying about the significant amount of pain he was still feeling from the injuries he had accidently sustained a few days earlier. "From the pain I'm experiencing, I'm afraid my ankle is broken, but I'll manage. My collarbone is also broken, but there's not too much we can do about that. It'll feel better in another few days or so." As he spoke, Brown did his best to hide his broken collarbone by hiking his shirt slightly higher than it was when Howard had stopped to see him. Embarrassed over being laid up, he had little interest in his commanding officer seeing how badly hurt he actually was.

Sitting down on a collapsible wooden stool, Howard wiped a fair amount of sweat from his brow as a slight breeze caused the flaps of Brown's tent to briefly rustle in the warm air. Close to 4 p.m., the day's temperature had caused the air inside the small tent to become quite warm. "You did a fine job earlier this morning, Paul," Howard said, extending his right hand in Brown's direction as he offered a rare compliment to his young officer. "I feel horrible about what happened to Sergeant Adams, but, by acting as quickly as you did, you likely kept another one or two of us from being shot, or even captured."

The fact that Howard had called him by his first name surprised Brown as his commanding officer almost never addressed his subordinates in such a personal manner. As someone who preferred addressing others by their last names or by their rank when the situation warranted, Howard had rarely reduced any conversation to a personal level.

"Thank you, sir." Brown replied, believing this to be only the second occasion in three long years that his commanding officer had addressed him by his first name. Much to his surprise, he was shocked Howard had remembered his first name.

"I've noted your actions in my journal. When we arrive at our destination, my official report will reflect your gallantry. Despite these injuries you've been dealing with, the fact that you performed as well as you did makes your actions even more impressive."

Nodding his head in appreciation, Brown acknowledged his commanding officer's recognition. In doing so, he also attempted to apologize for his unfortunate injuries. As he began speaking, Howard abruptly cut him off.

"Paul, while neither of us can be sure if my report will ever be read by those in charge, your injuries, and how they occurred, are nothing more than an unfortunate accident. They happen. I'm just grateful you responded as you did."

Never one to socialize much with his subordinates, as Howard finished speaking he stood, adjusted the saber affixed to his gun belt, and excused himself. Before Brown could stand, Howard was gone.

15

Like many officers on both sides of the war, Captain Noah Howard had learned to travel with as few personal necessities as possible. Unlike the soldiers and sergeants who were several rungs below him in rank and who were forced to carry their belongings wherever the army took them, as Howard and his men marched from one battle to another his rank afforded him the luxury of having his belongings being cared for by others. His belongings were often transported in wagons, trains, or by teams of mules being driven by teamsters travelling with the army. Often busy addressing a variety of operational needs; Howard's belongings were usually waiting for him inside his tent when the army arrived at its next encampment. On brief stops that often lasted for only one or two nights, his personal effects, like those of others, remained in place inside a cramped dusty wagon or baggage car. Outside of two wooden chests packed with uniforms, spare clothing he seldom wore, and a few personal items, Howard had only one other piece of property that accompanied him as his regiment travelled across the battle-weary states along the mid-Atlantic.

Approaching his large tent, one far more spacious and better designed than the square thin pieces of canvass usually shared by at least two ordinary foot soldiers, Howard noticed someone had already drawn open the front flaps. Held in place by two thin pieces of rope, the opened flaps allowed the tent to be far cooler than it would have been if the flaps had been left in the closed position. For this simple kind act, he was most appreciative. Over the tent's wide opening, a separate piece of canvass was held in place by rope. With one end secured directly to the tent and the other rigged to two tent poles, the canvass awning served to keep rain and bright sunlight from interfering with business Howard often conducted inside his quarters. On this particular occasion it provided just enough shade for him to relax under.

Removing his gun belt and then his uniform blouse, Howard splashed several handfuls of fresh clean water on his face from a small tin bowl resting on a rickety nightstand next to his cot. The battered and wobbly piece of furniture was one he had taken possession of after learning of a close friend's death. Along with several others he had served with, his friend had been killed during the brutal fighting that had taken place in Spotsylvania County during the Battle of the Wilderness. Soaking part of his towel, Howard wiped his face and the back of his neck as another means of cooling off. The simple act of washing his face, coupled with his heavy blouse no longer being strapped to his body, caused him to suddenly feel more energized. Glancing down at his blouse, one adorned with hand-sewn insignias indicating its wearer's rank, Howard knew the heavy cotton material was far too hot to wear during the spring and summer months, and not warm enough to ward off the chill of the winter months he would soon be facing.

Finished wiping his face and neck, Howard hung his blouse from a nail on one of the wooden posts inside his tent. Along with several others, the post helped to support the weight of the tent's heavy canvass shell. As was the case with his pants and several other articles of clothing, the butternut-colored blouse had not received a proper cleaning for several months. Stained in sweat, the heavy garment displayed a variety of other stains from weeks of hard work. Among them were droplets of blood shed by his men and by those he had recently helped to dispatch. Drying his face, Howard stared at his blouse as the sweat-stained material slowly began to dry in the warm air inside his tent.

Sitting on the edge of his cot, Howard thought, "My clothes stink nearly as much as I do." Like his men, the young officer, for a variety of reasons, had not found time to bathe in more than a week.

Reaching for the journal he had set near the foot of his cot, Howard then strode to the front of his tent and pulled the flaps closed. Besides minimizing the amount of light and noise filtering inside his tent, the closed flaps told others he was not to be disturbed. It was a message he conveyed to his men months earlier.

Sitting inside his tent nearly spent from his lack of sleep, Howard knew the details of the past few days had to be recorded while they were still fresh in his mind. Afraid of falling asleep as he had done on other occasions before recording the details surrounding a few skirmishes, with his quill and a small bottle of ink sitting next to him, Howard opened his journal and began writing.

April 17, 1865

For the past several days my men and I have been attacked by a group of former soldiers. Quite sadly, these marauders had once sworn an oath to protect the Confederacy. After several unsuccessful attacks, the marauders brutally killed two of my men who had been tracking them. Out of fear that these former soldiers were after the assets I have been assigned to protect, my men and I attacked them while they were holed up inside the remains of a small cabin. This cabin was located not far from our own camp. After surrounding this structure, all of these men were shot and killed. The only person who escaped that fate was their leader. Unrepentant for deserting the army in its time of need and for the attacks he had led against my men, I had no choice but to order him hung after I was finished questioning him.

After making it back to camp, one of my men (Private Norris) became seriously ill. He later died from what I believe was a ruptured appendix. Later, as my men and I were returning from a burial detail, we were again attacked; this time by a small group of Union cavalry. Near the end of this attack, Sergeant Adams was shot and killed. His death has saddened me greatly. It has also caused me to feel uneasy about the outcome of my mission. Tomorrow I will decide on my next course of action. I have become very weary of war as it seems to bring nothing but heartache. As I sit here, I am utterly exhausted from the events of the past few days. As I prepare to finish this entry, I am not certain if the words I have written accurately portray how difficult the past few days have been. Perhaps, like many others, I fear what the future will confront us with.

Whatever the future brings, I am confident that I shall never look back on these days with any degree of fondness.'

Placing his journal at the foot of his cot, Howard, drenched in sweat from both the temperature inside his tent and from his own fear, cautiously placed his quill and the remaining ink on the ground inside his tent. The small amount of grass that was present, no longer soft and green, was now wilted. Damaged by the number of boots passing over it, the oppressive humidity inside Howard's temporary home had also contributed to its unhealthy condition. Sitting there, he took note of the wooden chest he had placed on a small chair. Along with two other wooden chests, this smaller version held the majority of the few personal items he had packed weeks earlier as the fighting escalated around the Confederate capital. Among the items inside the chest were two other journals; one completely full of his notes and observations, and the other waiting for its first entry to be recorded. Resting near the bottom was another bottle of ink, the stubs of two pencils, and a handful of quills. Like his journals, Howard considered his writing utensils among his most-prized possessions.

Staring at the small chest, one he paid a skilled craftsman a hefty sum to construct from one of his own drawings, Howard stood up and walked to where it sat. Opening the top, he smiled as he looked inside the dark space. As his smile slowly grew in size, he thought, *"This secret you possess will someday be found by someone else. I can only hope that person appreciates what they have found."*

Forcing himself to lie down after reopening the flaps to his tent to allow fresh air to replace the stale humid air, Howard tried figuring out what his best course of action was for the following morning. But being far too tired, his mind soon shut down. In less than two minutes, he was fast asleep. With his thoughts neatly captured inside his journal, the young officer slept undisturbed until early the following morning.

16

Sleeping comfortably in his cot as the sun slowly pushed its way through a sky full of white pillowy clouds, Howard's senses gradually became aware of footsteps rushing towards his tent. With his eyes still closed, he realized something was taking place outside his tent. Slowly gaining his senses, Howard prayed someone else would address the situation taking place. Even with nearly eight hours of interrupted sleep under his belt, Howard was still exhausted from the long days he had recently experienced.

"Sir, beggin' your pardon," Private Nester offered, respectfully touching the brim of his hat as he threw open the flaps to Howard's tent. While far from being the proper salute Howard expected each morning, the simple gesture served to acknowledge his rank. Moments later, Nester repeated his greeting while doing his best at waking Howard from the deep sleep he had been enjoying. *"Sir, beggin' your pardon."* Seeing Howard's eyes starting to flutter, but still not getting the response he wanted, Nester shook the long set of legs extending over the end of the cot. A

moment later, out of frustration Nester banged a tin drinking cup against a tent pole in a further attempt to wake the person he had been sent to find. Before speaking again, Nester shot a mouthful of warm tobacco juice on the ground off to his left. *"Captain, Lieutenant Brown sent me to fetch ya. We got riders approaching."*

"Riders?" Howard mumbled, slowly freeing himself from a thin blanket that somehow had managed to snake its way around his lower extremities. Disappointed in being disturbed, Howard frowned at Nester as he shook the few remaining cobwebs from his head. Rubbing his eyes, he said, *"I wish you hadn't woken me. That's the best sleep I've had in days."*

"Sorry, sir, but Brownie, I . . . I mean Lieutenant Brown, sir, he wants you to meet him near the top of the bluff." Pointing off to his right, Nester added, "The one over yonder."

"What's this about riders, Private Nester? Has someone seen something?" Howard asked, mistakenly trying to put his left boot on his right foot as his eyes did their best at keeping the bright sunlight from blinding the tent's sleepy occupant.

"Yes, sir. Batten seen them when he was out riding the perimeter; he seen them coming from nearly a mile away. There's four of them headed this way."

"Riding the perimeter? I didn't tell anyone to do that." Howard replied as he tried recalling any last minute orders he had issued before falling asleep.

"No, sir. Brownie . . . I'm sorry, sir, Lieutenant Brown assigned Batten to do that. He knew how tired you were, and seeing how much trouble he's already in over them injuries he sustained, I'm guessing he sent Batten out there so we didn't get surprised by anyone." Turning to look in Brown's direction from where he stood near the opening to Howard's tent, as his commanding officer finished putting his boots on the correct feet, Nester, anxious to see what was taking place, gave his commanding officer a gentle nudge. "You coming, sir?"

"Lead the way, private," Howard replied, stomping the ground with his right foot in an attempt to get his foot in a more comfortable position inside his boot. Two more stomps and Howard's right foot slid into its normal position. Exiting his tent, Howard paused briefly before stepping back inside to retrieve something he felt might come in handy. Walking outside, the young officer stuck his revolver inside his waistband as he hustled to join Brown.

Handing Howard a pair of binoculars, Brown updated his commanding officer on the situation at hand. "Look off to your left . . . focus your attention on the area near those four dead pine trees out there." As he spoke, Brown used his right index finger to point in the direction of where he wanted Howard to focus his attention. "The riders Batten notified me about have just crossed the river. Just wait . . . they'll come back in view any second now. It's hard to tell which direction they're headed, but the way our luck has been they'll probably be headed our way in no time at all."

Focusing his binoculars, Howard saw the riders as they cleared the trees Brown had pointed out. Without saying a word, Howard stood still for several moments as he watched the riders draw closer to where he and Brown were standing. Hidden nearby inside a small stand of trees, Howard's three remaining soldiers talked in hushed tones as they watched the riders approach. Easily noticing the Confederate flag one of the riders displayed at the end of a short staff, Howard's men were far more relaxed than their commanding officer.

"What's the second flag I see flying, Lieutenant Brown?" Howard asked, unable to identify the flag's markings or the state it represented.

As Howard was handed his own binoculars that had been retrieved from his tent, Brown strained to identify the colors being displayed. "I'm not sure what regiment that flag is from, but it kind of resembles one I saw a year ago or so. At that time it was being carried by an outfit from Georgia. But with the war seeming as if it's a lost cause, I'm not sure why soldiers from that neck of the woods would be passing through here."

"Exactly." Howard replied, holding his binoculars steady as his eyes focused on the strange flag for another few seconds. Looking at Brown as he lowered his field glasses, Howard's face grew worried as he issued his next order.

"Have the men help you back to camp. I'm not taking any chances, so do what's necessary to protect the wagons. I'll stay here and keep an eye on these riders we've been watching. Once I know for certain where they're headed, then I'll join you."

"Yes, sir." Brown replied, turning gingerly on his broken ankle as he motioned towards the tree line for the others to assist him. Then Howard issued his lieutenant one last order.

"Lieutenant, you do what's necessary, but make sure the gold and silver is protected. Understood?"

"Understood, sir." Offering Howard a weak salute as he moved off, Brown and the others with him began making their way back to where the wagons were parked.

Ten minutes later, convinced the riders were headed in his direction, Howard quickly made his way back to camp. He had barely had time to issue his next set of orders when the four riders announced their presence as they briefly paused before riding to where Howard and Brown were talking.

"Howdy, friends! OK if we dismount? We've been in the saddle since early this morning, so we'd like to stretch our legs for a few minutes. We could sure use a cup of coffee if you'd be so kind." Like Howard and Brown, the lieutenant standing there in his Confederate uniform was as nervous as the two officers he was speaking with. Behind him, the lieutenant's three companions eyed, among other things, a coffee pot sitting on the ground next to a smoldering campfire.

"Sure, no problem." Brown replied, doing his best to hide his growing concerns over the riders who were less than eight feet away from where he stood. As he walked closer to where their unexpected visitors stood holding the reins of their horses, Brown fought the urge to shoot a look in the direction of the nearby wagons packed with gold and silver. Spying the state flag being displayed by one of the men, Brown added, "Anyone from Georgia is a friend of ours. *Welcome!"*

Holding onto the reins of his horse, Lieutenant Phillip Johnston shot a furtive glance at the others with him. It was something Howard took notice of. Like Johnston's ill-fitting uniform, his glance caused the hair on the back of Howard's neck to stand up.

"Come on, boys, let's grab some coffee. Tie your horses up over yonder by those wagons. We'll sit a spell with our new friends before we head out." Trying to appear as if he was more relaxed than he actually was, Johnston smiled as he looked in Howard's direction.

"Have your men tie up their horses over there, lieutenant." Howard said firmly, countermanding Johnston's order as he pointed to two trees on the opposite side of the camp. Both were located a few hundred feet away from where the wagons were parked. Not wanting Johnston's men to have the opportunity of seeing inside the wagons, Howard steered them as far away as possible without making his directive seem suspicious. "When you're done tying up your horse, lieutenant, I'll expect that salute my rank deserves." Always a stickler for details, Howard's last comment was meant to show Johnston who was in command inside the camp. It was also meant as a strong warning, to both Johnston and his own men.

"Sorry, sir, no harm meant; I apologize." Raising his right hand as he clutched the reins to his horse with the fingers of his other hand, Johnston rendered Howard the salute he deserved. The salute he was offered caught Howard's eye. It also caught the attention of two others.

Greeting their unexpected guests with hot coffee and small talk about the war, Howard, like Brown, grew more suspicious of their fellow patriots. It came from not only the questions these strangers asked, but from their interest in the nearby wagons.

"Where are the rest of your men?" Johnston asked, noting the number of horses Howard's men had tied up in another part of the camp. "They out rounding up some food? Maybe resting a bit inside one or two of them tents over yonder?" As he asked his questions, Johnston nodded in the direction of where Howard and Brown's tents had been setup.

"They're out hunting up some food." Howard replied, shooting Brown a quick look. "You and your men are welcome to join us for supper tonight. I'm sure my men won't mind sharing our meager supplies."

"Thank you, captain." Johnston replied, doffing his hat in response to Howard's offer of a hot meal. "We just might take you up on that. It's one that's very much appreciated." As Johnston finished speaking, Howard took note of the boots the lieutenant and two of his men were wearing. He took similar note of the firearms they possessed.

"Those horses I see tied up over there, and those wagons you fellas are travelling with, well . . . it seems like you should have more men with you than you do. I'm not sure how three men can drive those four wagons I see sitting there . . . not unless you or the good lieutenant plans on driving one. Begging your pardon, but I don't see that happening." Johnston's tone, like the words he used, caused Howard to feel for the revolver he had hidden inside his waistband.

Without announcing his intentions, Johnston quickly nodded at one of his men as he drew his saber from a scabbard on his right hip. As he did, another of his men, the short, but well-built sergeant who had been holding the Georgia flag, drew his revolver. In seconds, the flag, a poor representation of the real version carried throughout the war by many Georgia regiments, fell to the ground.

"What's this all about?" Howard asked, picking up the flag but not letting on that he had recognized it for what it was. Trying to diffuse the tension that had suddenly risen, he said, "Here, sergeant, take your flag back. Don't disrespect your colors by letting it fall to the ground. Brave men from across your state have died defending what this flag represents."

Holding his ground, Sergeant Russell Adkins kept his revolver aimed at Brown's chest for another few seconds until Johnston ordered it holstered.

"I'm sorry, captain, but my men and I are a bit edgy these days. We've been told about spies dressing up as Confederate soldiers and, well . . . I guess Sergeant Adkins and I just got spooked a bit. There's bad things going on inside the Confederacy these days; we just wanted to make sure you were who you said you were, that's all." Dropping his saber against his leg, Johnston glanced in Adkins' direction as his sergeant finished holstering his weapon.

Taking a deep breath, Howard said, "I share your concerns, lieutenant, but you had us scared there for a minute." As a wide smile appeared on his face, Howard attempted to show Johnston and his men that he was not a threat to their safety.

Continuing to hold his sword against his right thigh, Johnston nodded to his men as he spoke to Howard. "Captain, again I offer you an apology. However, just to make sure you boys are fighting for the right side, I'm going to have my men search your wagons."

As Johnston's men started moving towards the wagons, Howard's next few words caused them to stop in their tracks. "Sergeant, I've always admired the Georgia flag. It's very colorful and well designed. Where's your outfit from?"

"Woonsocket. I . . . I mean Augusta, up near the South Carolina border." Mistakenly identifying where his regiment had been formed caused Adkins' face to suddenly turn bright red.

"I've had the pleasure of visiting Augusta several times." Howard replied, ignoring the sergeant's grievous error. "In fact, I have family living just north of there in Monroe. Even been there?"

"Afraid I haven't, sir." Adkins nervously replied as an embarrassed look stayed in place across his ruddy unshaven face.

As Adkins and the two soldiers following him started moving towards the wagons packed with gold and silver, Brown hollered in their direction. *"Sergeant, if I were you, I'd stay away from those wagons. They're bad luck to anyone who gets too close to them."*

Giving Brown an ugly, disdainful look, Adkins began climbing onto the front seat of the first wagon he came to. His two men, both privates with hopes of finding something valuable inside the wagons they were about to search, moved closer to the other wagons.

"Sergeant," Brown yelled, hollering even louder than he had a few seconds earlier, *"if I were you I'd listen to what I'm telling you. You and your men need to stay off those wagons. There's a host of problems associated with them."*

Ignoring Brown's warning, Adkins barely had time to look inside the wagon when Private George Nester rose from his hiding spot and fired his musket at point-blank range. Unable to react to what he saw, Adkins fell dead; his face and jaw savagely torn apart from the round Nester had fired. Hitting the ground hard, Adkins' body convulsed for a few brief moments in response to the fatal wound.

Hearing Nester's shot, Privates Battle and Batten, both hidden inside the other two wagons, fired shots from close range at Johnston's other men. In seconds, both were dead from well-placed shots fired by two experienced soldiers.

"My lieutenant told your men not to approach the wagons." Howard said, pointing his revolver at Johnston's face as the stunned Union lieutenant turned to look back at him. "If you and your men had the intention of passing yourselves off as Confederate soldiers, you should have taken the time to learn a few things. The salute you gave me earlier was your first mistake, and the way you speak, well . . . let's just say folks in these parts don't speak like you and your men. Your next mistakes were the boots you're wearing and this ill-fitting uniform you've got on. Officers in the Confederate Army aren't in the habit of wearing uniforms that are two or three sizes too small for them." As he finished speaking, Howard shook his head over the number of mistakes Johnston and his men had made.

Reaching over to collect Johnston's saber, Brown added, "*Woonsocket?* Your late sergeant, was he really that stupid? If all of you are from Rhode Island, that flag he was carrying is a piss-poor representation of the real thing." Brown's comments caused Howard and the others to enjoy a hearty laugh at Johnston's expense.

After interrogating Johnston for close to an hour, Howard collected enough information to confirm the four riders who had entered his camp were Union spies. Thirty minutes after his interrogation was completed, Johnston's bullet-ridden body was unceremoniously placed in the same pile as the men he had ridden with. The four spies had been part of a failed attempt to capture President Jefferson Davis and members of the Confederate cabinet.

Later that evening, with Howard and his men having moved out, raccoons and other scavengers started feasting on the remains of the Union soldiers. Their ill-advised mission had caused them to perish several days after peace had been negotiated between Generals Ulysses S. Grant and Robert E. Lee.

In the days after their tragic deaths, time, like a variety of other more important issues, would cause most people to forget about the mission Johnston had been assigned. The only record of his death would come in the form of a brief entry Howard scribbled inside his journal.

It would be an entry no one would read or know about for over one hundred and fifty years.

17

The loud annoying noise generated by a flock of crows caused the young captain to wake earlier than he had planned. Sitting near the top of a small group of trees close to Howard's tent, the raucous birds had sat cawing for close to ten minutes. Turning over several times in his cot, Howard tried falling back asleep until the incessant noise told him his efforts were futile. Having made camp later than normal, he had endured a restless night after finally settling down.

Donning his boots after slipping on his trousers, Howard switched his revolver from his left hand to his right as he struggled with his suspenders. Angry over being woken up, after locating the noisy birds several yards away from his tent Howard recklessly fired two shots skyward in an attempt to drive away the source of his irritation.

"Stupid, damn birds!" As the crows flew off, Howard fired one last angry round in their direction.

"Them birds can be annoying, can't they, captain?" Standing a safe distance away, Brown smirked at the sight of his commanding officer firing his weapon at the group of creatures responsible for disturbing their sleep. Having experienced his own restless night of sleep, Brown stood there holding his pistol in his right hand. Much to his amusement, he had not had time to fire a shot.

"This is not how I care to be remembered, Lieutenant Brown, standing out here dressed as I am while firing away at a group of crows like some mad man. I may look foolish, but those noisy sons-of-bitches woke me up." Turning to look back at the birds as they sat cawing in another set of trees a short distance away, Howard, still upset over being woken up, added, "I hope I hit one of those bastards."

His comment drew another brief chuckle from Brown.

After briefly scanning the camp for the person he was looking for, Howard asked the same question he had asked several times over the past few days. "Still no sign of Lieutenant Radcliff?"

"No, sir." Brown replied, stretching his neck in hopes of seeing Radcliff returning. "I'm afraid something's happened to him. He should have been back by now."

"I'm afraid you're right. Maybe he had the unfortunate pleasure of running into that same group of blue-bellies we dealt with yesterday. If he did, I think we both know what the outcome was." Realizing Radcliff's chances of surviving an encounter with four spies were slim, Howard knew his lieutenant's demise could have occurred in a number of different ways.

Ignoring Brown's last comment, Howard inquired about the readiness of his men. "How close are we to breaking camp?"

Anxious to get the day started, Howard noticed two of his men already at work striking their tents.

"It won't be long, captain. As soon as the men finish their duties and have something to eat, they'll address the last few details that need to be taken care of. After that, they'll start packing your belongings. Once that's done, then they'll strike your tent and we'll be ready to go."

Nodding at the response he had been given, Howard started making his way back to his tent. As he moved off, Brown called out to him. Pointing off to his right at a small fire still smoldering from the previous evening, Brown said, "The coffee is still warm, so I told the men they could have another cup while you finish dressing. There's no sense wasting it. I'll make sure they save you a cup." The area around the fire that Brown had pointed to had previously served as the scene of the camp's late night dinner.

"Sounds good. Tell the men they can start tearing down my tent in ten minutes." Walking inside his tent, Howard donned his heavy cotton blouse. Like his wet towel, his sweaty blouse had dried overnight in the hot, humid air.

******

Pushing southeast over the next several days, Howard and his men made their way safely across the Santee River just north of Lee County, South Carolina. Fording the river at one of its shallowest points had allowed the wagons laden down with their precious cargo to cross with little difficulty. As each of the wagons passed through the slow moving water, Howard paid close attention as they crossed one of the river's widest points.

After setting up camp outside the small town of Bishopville late one afternoon, Howard allowed his men a few extra hours of rest after pushing them hard for the past four days. As his men made plans to roast three young turkeys they had shot earlier that afternoon, Howard rode off to see if he could locate anyone who had seen any signs of Lieutenant Radcliff.

After making his way across stretches of open land for nearly twenty minutes, Howard entered a small virgin forest littered with patches of thick brush. Riding out of the woods a short time later, the young officer followed what appeared to be a narrow trail for a short distance until it strangely disappeared near the outskirts of the small town. In the distance, near the intersection of the community's two hardscrabble roads, Howard spied an old two-story structure that had seen little, if any, care over the past several years. From a faded sign mounted on the shed-style roof, he saw a small tavern occupied the entire first floor. Situated alongside the intersection of a narrow road and a dusty trail that locals referred to as the Mecklenburg Road, Howard soon tied his horse to a badly rotted fence post. Nailed to another nearby post, a weather-beaten sign identified the wider of the two roads as being the McCallum Ferry Road. Like the one above the tavern, it was easy to tell this wooden road sign had been in place for many years. Walking towards the tavern, one of five businesses located inside a cluster of small buildings that had seen better days, Howard noticed two other structures. Both were smaller than any of the others inside the non-descript town. At first glance, believing them to be nothing more than a storage shed and an outhouse, much to Howard's surprise he heard children playing outside one of the dilapidated buildings. Laughing and screaming as they chased after each other, their mother busied herself hanging wash from a thin piece of rope tied from one corner of their home to a large tree in the backyard. Like their mother, the children were oblivious to Howard's presence. Seeing them playing in their tattered clothes caused Howard to realize he had been looking at the home of a young family struggling to make ends meet. Staring at the children's mother, a young woman whose tired looks belied her age, he thought, "I bet her husband is off fighting the war someplace. That's if he's still alive." For the children's sake, Howard quietly hoped their father was alive and well. Like the small shed-style structure the children called home, the tree holding one end of the clothesline had also seen better days.

Pushing open the tavern's rickety front door, Howard paused after stepping inside the dark, foul-smelling building. Behind him, the flimsy door creaked as it swung back and forth on several rusty hinges. Comprised of nothing more than four thin narrow boards, the door hung in such a way that each two-piece panel swung in or out depending on whether a visitor was either entering or leaving. Several feet away, on the far side of the small rectangular-shaped building sat the tavern's wooden bar. Comprised of rough hand-hewn planks, the bar was as rustic as they came. Next to it, a large wooden barrel containing empty whiskey bottles and food scraps sat covered with flies and other insects. Last emptied several days earlier, it was the source of most of the tavern's unpleasant smell.

First taking notice of two men dressed in threadbare uniforms standing at one end of the bar, Howard then spied an old man playing solitaire at a small table located next to a fieldstone fireplace. Having received little care since the day they were set in place, the large stones bordering the wide hearth were caked in rich black soot. It was a condition that was hard to miss. Barely turning his head as Howard had stepped inside, the old man quickly returned his attention to the worn deck of cards he was playing with. On the other side of the room, the two men dressed in badly torn Confederate uniforms warily eyed the young officer as he approached.

"Afternoon," Howard offered politely as he gazed at the meager furnishings inside the small tavern. Always aware of his surroundings, Howard took a moment to make sure he had not missed anyone, or any signs of trouble.

"Afternoon, captain." The younger of the two men offered, lightly touching his cap after noticing Howard's rank. To his right, his partner said nothing as he leaned against the bar nursing a drink. Instead, he simply chose to give the stranger who had invaded their space a casual, but curt nod. Howard took the gesture as being offered rather rudely.

Nodding his head at the two men, Howard took notice of a long thick scar prominently displayed on the second soldier's face. Running from the right side of his forehead, the old wound crossed the soldier's nose before ending near the left side of his mouth. While appearing to be completely healed, Howard thought the ugly pink scar looked just as painful as it must have felt when the soldier's face had first been sliced open.

Sitting on the bar directly in front of the soldiers was a bottle of cheap liquor. Half-empty, the bottle sat waiting to be polished off. As Howard moved closer to where they stood, the soldier whose face had been slashed open a year earlier by a Yankee saber drew a revolver from his waistband before loudly setting it down on the bar. As this took place, Howard noticed the right sleeve of the soldier's shirt was pinned in three places.

"Where'd you lose your arm, soldier?" Howard asked, trying not to stare at the shirt sleeve that had once held the soldier's arm.

Taking a swig of the potent clear liquid he was drinking, the one-armed soldier answered Howard's question in a threatening and unfriendly manner. *"Second Manassas, that's where. Got shot around dinner time, but there wasn't no one eatin' dinner that day. The date was August 30, 1862; remember it like it was yesterday. Got shot near the Old Warrenton Road, at least that's what I was told it was called."* Looking down at where his arm had once been, the soldier grew angrier and angrier as he continued speaking. *"Some Billy Yank son of a bitch got me good. Ruined my freakin' life with one lucky-ass shot."* Ignoring the glass he had been drinking from, the soldier drained a healthy portion of the bottle's remaining liquid.

"I'm sorry, captain," the one-armed soldier's friend said as he looked in Howard's direction. "Jeb here, well . . . Jeb's an angry man these days. Hope you understand and all. He don't mean no disrespect by how he talks." Like most people who had never been taught the correct way to speak, the soldier's speech was rather rough.

Stoic as he could be, Howard glared at the injured soldier before turning his attention back to the soldier he had been speaking with. It was then that Howard noticed this soldier's face also displayed a similar scar. Not as visible or as long as the first scar, this one was partially hidden under a thick layer of dirt and facial hair. Much to Howard's disgust, the nearby garbage barrel was not the only source of the foul smell that was present. From their looks and the condition of their clothes, he knew neither of the men had bathed for some time. "What about you? Where'd that happen?" Howard asked, pointing at the soldier's scar.

"Got mine two days before Jeb was injured," the soldier said, proudly rubbing his fingers across his old wound before exposing as much as he could for Howard to see. "Got sliced open at Thoroughfare Gap; back then we was riding with Old Pete himself. Ya know, with General Longstreet's cavalry. From the looks of my face, you wouldn't know we won that fight, but we did. We drove them blue-bellies off and then destroyed a bunch of their supplies. I weren't there when Jeb got wounded, but I would have liked to have been in the middle of that fight. When he got hurt, some sawbones was sewing my face back together. Dun a right good job; don't ya think?" As he finished speaking, Aaron Bothers, an eighteen-year-old deserter who had been raised outside of Chattanooga, Tennessee, touched his left cheek before running his left index finger down the entire length of his scar.

Nodding at what he had been told, Howard then thanked the soldiers for the sacrifices they had made. Trying to gather as much information as possible, Howard sought to learn even more as he attempted to determine the reasons behind the former soldiers' desertions. What he soon learned did not please him.

"Me and Aaron are done fightin', captain." The one-armed soldier snarled, moving his left hand closer to the revolver he had placed on the bar. "We quit fightin' a year back or so. We got tired of not being fed, and more tired of getting our asses hollered at by officers who had no idea what this God-forsaken war was all about. After I got hurt, not one of them worthless mama's boys came to see me in the hospital." To reinforce the sacrifices he had made, the former soldier angrily held up his empty right sleeve.

As Howard looked at Bothers, the young soldier, wearing torn and ripped clothes that were far dirtier than what any man should be forced to wear, stared back at him before speaking. "Like Jeb dun said, captain, we're both dun with this here war. We ain't seen our regiment fer a spell now, and we don't care if we ever see them fellas again. As long as my buddy and I got a bottle in front of us, we're okay. We ain't marchin' or fightin' no more." Lifting the dented tin cup he was drinking from, Bothers took a sip of the rotgut liquor he and his friend drank on a regular basis. With several grievances confronting them on a daily basis, the two former soldiers drank to excess with each passing day.

Bothers had barely set his cup back down on the bar when his friend made a desperate, and ill-advised, move to grab the revolver he had placed on the bar. Standing up as the soldier's left hand grabbed the heavy weapon, Howard crushed his adversary's face with a powerful blow. Far too drunk and weak from having eaten little over the past two days, the one-armed soldier was no match for the well-built officer he had challenged. Moments after being punched, the unconscious soldier's face bounced hard after striking the tavern's wooden floor. Seconds later, a steady stream of blood began flowing from the soldier's mouth where two teeth had once stood.

Unsure of what to expect and believing he was about to be attacked by Bothers, Howard raised his right fist as he took up a defensive position several feet away from where the soldiers had been standing. Seconds later, after seeing Bothers standing there with his hands raised high above his head, Howard relaxed his fist.

"I ain't lookin' fer no trouble, captain." Bothers said, clearly less interested in causing any trouble than his friend had been. "I'm sorry for what that lame brain did, but like I told ya, Jeb's an angry man these days. This ain't the first time he's gone and got his ass kicked fer doin' something stupid. I'm afraid all of this whiskey we've been drinkin' has gotten hold of Jeb's senses in a bad way."

Patting Bothers down for any hidden weapons, Howard then picked up the revolver that had been knocked out of the one-armed soldier's hand. Placing the weapon in his right hand, Howard sensed a deformity in the wooden grips. Almost immediately, he believed he had held the same revolver in the recent past. A quick inspection of the deformity, as well as noticing a long familiar scratch on the left side of the barrel, told him he was correct. Concerned over what he was holding, Howard anxiously began interrogating Bothers. As he did, he angrily grabbed the drunken soldier's filthy shirt. *"This . . . this revolver, where'd your friend get it? And, who did he get it from?"*

"I'm not sure where he got it, captain," Bothers nervously protested as he stared at his unconscious friend fast asleep on the tavern floor.

"Bullshit! Tell me where you two got this revolver!" Growing even angrier than he already was, Howard slapped Bothers across the face so hard he knocked the young soldier off balance. *"Where'd you get it?"*

Clutching a face already disfigured by the slash of a Union saber, as he regained his balance Bothers gently rubbed the spot Howard had slapped. "We took it from a Union soldier we ran across a couple of days ago. He weren't gonna be needin' it any longer, so Jeb took it from him."

Realizing the meaning behind Bothers' comment, Howard sought to learn more about the confrontation that had taken place between the two soldiers and their Union counterpart. *"Where'd you kill that soldier? Where's his body now?"*

Pulling his hand away from his unshaven face, Bothers checked for any signs of blood after being slapped. Seeing none, he then glanced at his unconscious friend after hearing the first of several soft moans. "Jeb, you ok, son? Jeb?"

"Don't worry about Jeb; worry about me!" Howard said, his anger growing even stronger after spending a few more moments

inspecting the revolver. Grabbing the front of Bothers' badly torn shirt for a second time, one he had torn even more after manhandling its wearer, Howard yelled, *"Answer my questions, damn it!"*

"That Billy Yank son of a bitch who had that gun and two of his friends were riding east of here two or three days ago when we first seen them. Me and Jeb were out in the woods getting drunk when we seen them coming our way. We just hid and waited for them to ride a bit closer . . . when they did, we shot their sorry asses. We're in the middle of a war, captain, that's what soldiers like us are supposed to do to those we's fightin' against. Shoot their sorry asses before they shoot us, ain't that right? That's how we come across that there revolver you're so fired up about." Bothers said before taking another healthy sip of the cheap liquor he was drinking.

Rising to his knees, the one-armed soldier spat a small amount of blood on the tavern's dirty floor as he gasped for air. A moment later, he spat another broken tooth out of his mouth. Looking up at Howard, the soldier tried standing as he threatened the person who had briefly knocked him cold. *"Ya shouldn't have dun that, captain. I may not be as strong as I once was, but I'm strong enough to kick your ass."* Pointing at the insignias on Howard's uniform, the soldier added, *"And, one more thing. I don't give a rat's ass about them things you're wearing. They don't mean nothin' to me. I'm just gonna give you a beating for punching me out."*

Barely making it to his feet, the one-armed soldier wobbled for a brief moment before Howard's fist violently collided with his mouth and nose. The strong right handed punch caused the injured soldier to bounce off the rickety bar before landing face first on the wooden floor. Nearly unconscious as his bloody nose and mouth continued to leak more blood, the one-armed soldier barely felt the next punch that broke his jaw.

"The next time you threaten an officer in the Confederate Army, make sure you're able to back your words up, you piece of crap." Kneeling over the unconscious soldier, Howard wiped the small amount of blood that had collected near his knuckles by dragging his hand across the soldier's filthy shirt. On the other side of the tavern, the old man playing cards barely paid attention to the action taking place less than thirty feet away.

"You were saying?" Howard said, moving closer to Bothers as he flexed his sore right hand.

"After we shot them Billy Yanks, we dragged their bodies inside a small cave that was about a hundred feet away. There's three of them there . . . caves, I mean. I'm not sure why Jeb wanted this done, but we dragged their bodies to the back of that middle cave." Looking wearily at the angry officer standing less than an arm's length away from his face, Bothers told Howard one other piece of information he believed to be important. "Captain, them caves I'm tellin' ya about, they're on the side of a steep rocky hill."

"That's where most caves are located, imbecile," Howard replied, his angry voiced laced with contempt for the person he was speaking with. Holding the revolver in his left hand, Howard flashed the weapon at Bothers as he added, "I don't suppose those Billy Yanks told you where they obtained this, did they?" As he finished asking this question, Howard hoped to hear an answer that was different than the one he expected.

"One of them Billy Yanks was somehow holding on even after we had shot him a couple of times. When we was draggin' his ass inside the cave, Jeb done asked him if it was his revolver, but . . ." Scared of being punched like his friend had been, Bothers, who was neither educated nor the best speaker, struggled to find the right words as he described the last few seconds of their encounter with the Union soldiers.

"Speak you, idiot! Where did that soldier tell you he got this revolver?" Already afraid of knowing the answer to his question, Howard angrily lashed out at Bothers as he waited to learn how the Union soldier had come to possess the weapon he was holding.

Staring at the weapon being pointed at his chest, Bothers gave Howard the answer he had hoped not to hear. "The only thing he said, and I swear this is the truth, that Billy Yank said he dun got it from some Confederate officer he had killed a few days earlier."

"What else did that soldier tell you before he died?" Howard asked, his voice growing softer as he stared at the weapon one of his officers had once owned. "Did this Billy Yank tell you or your asshole friend what happened to Lieutenant Radcliff's horse?"

Blinking excitedly over Howard's last question, Bothers finally grasped the meaning behind the young officer's questions. "Captain, by the sounds of it, you must have known the officer who owned that revolver, right?"

Upset by the news he had learned, Howard sat down on a wooden stool several feet away from the bar. As he thought of how Radcliff had died, the only noise inside the tavern was the sound of a worn out deck of cards being shuffled on the other side of the room. Old and hard of hearing, the card player had heard little of what had been said.

"Just like those Union soldiers you and your friend killed, the officer who owned this weapon was likely savagely murdered for little reason. He was one of my men. He was also someone I considered a friend." As Howard spoke, the tone in his voice gradually rose as he thought of the three Union soldiers who had been murdered during an already violent war. It was a war he suspected that may have already ended. While they were his adversaries, their senseless deaths upset him.

"Captain, I'm real sorry . . ."

Before Bothers could finish his thought, Howard angrily cut him off. *"Don't say another word! I don't care to hear what you have to say. Any contrived thoughts of sympathy you might be able to muster, mean nothing."* Standing up, Howard glared at Bothers before glancing in the direction of the deserter's unconscious friend.

"Captain, I'm . . ."

With one powerful blow to Bothers' face, Howard caused the young soldier's neck to snap backwards. Crashing into two chairs sitting next to what had once been a fancy poker table, Bothers fell to the floor. Stunned by the punch he had not seen coming, he quickly did his best to stem the steady flow of blood running from his broken nose.

"I told you not to say another word," Howard screamed, briefly inspecting Bothers' injury from where he stood. "You and your buddy should be glad I'm focused on something far more important than you two traitors. If I wasn't, you'd be tied up in the back of one of my wagons waiting for the provost marshal to come collect your sorry asses." Turning to look at the old man engrossed in his card game on the other side of the tavern, Howard then walked outside without saying another word. Reaching his horse, he placed Radcliff's revolver inside one of his saddlebags. Moments later, Howard rode back to where his men were camped.

******

Later that evening, Howard would make another entry in his journal. It would prove to be one of the most upsetting entries he would ever write. Next to it, he sketched a drawing of the revolver that had been involved in the deaths of at least four soldiers.

What Howard had no way of knowing was that he was only days away from writing one of his last entries. It would prove to be one of the most upsetting entries he would ever record.

18

Already confronted with the deaths of several of his men, as well as a host of other problems he had not anticipated, as Howard rode along the northern bank of the Santee River after learning of Radcliff's tragic death he was unaware that he was about to face his most significant problem. Off in the distance, the dark clouds filling the afternoon sky served as a sign of impending trouble.

Still stunned by the upsetting news he had learned, as Howard rode back into camp he gave a casual, but disinterested nod in Nester's direction. Riding towards his tent, he briefly stared as the young soldier tended to the needs of several horses. Not far away, Battle sat slumped against a tree. As he often did during periods of rest, Battle was whittling away on a small piece of wood. A talented woodcarver, he had already carved a series of small trinkets for those he was serving with.

"See anything, captain?" Brown asked, hobbling up to where Howard had just dismounted.

"Saw and learned more than I cared to." Pulling Radcliff's revolver from one of his saddlebags, Howard handed the weapon over for Brown to inspect. "Unfortunately, I also came across this."

As he inspected the revolver, Brown easily noticed the chip of wood that was missing from the grips. "This is Radcliff's revolver. Where'd you find this?" As Howard started to respond, Brown interrupted his commanding officer. In doing so, he cast a glance in the direction of where Howard had come from. "If this is Radcliff's revolver, where's David?"

"He's dead; at least it sounds that way." Howard replied rather bluntly. Before speaking again, Howard took a few sips of water from a canteen Nester handed him. "I came across this small town . . . if that's what you call it. It's called Bishopville, but I'm not sure how it came to be called that. Maybe it was named after the first person who settled there or the first postmaster or even the town's first mayor, but whoever that person was I guess his last name must have been Bishop. There's not much there except for a few old shacks, a small store which doubles as the local post office, and a few other rundown buildings. One of them houses a small tavern that's not much bigger, or better, than a rat hole; that's where I came across that revolver you're holding. It was in the possession of two traitors. I'm afraid this story I'm telling you is going to get worse as I continue, but, to start with, those bastards I'm referring to once served in the same army you and I belong to. One of the parts that makes me sick is they just decided one day that it was acceptable for them to simply stop fighting. Their decision to abandon the war was based on a variety of problems they had encountered; none were different than what many other soldiers have experienced over the past few years. I'll admit that one of them sustained two serious injuries, but they should have asked to be mustered out of the army instead of walking away. Even though they're nothing more than drunks these days, they're still deserters."

"You should have shot them." Brown uttered, his own anger growing as he waited to hear the rest of Howard's story.

"I certainly had every right to do that, but I was too upset after learning about Radcliff's death to do more than I did. I left one of them with a broken jaw, and the other with what I believe was a broken nose. They got off far easier than Radcliff did, but I kicked their asses pretty good." As he finished speaking, Howard showed Brown the bruised knuckles he sustained from the beatings he had given the two former soldiers.

Stunned by what he was being told, Brown sought to learn more about his friend's death. "Those deserters you're telling me about, are they responsible for Radcliff's death?"

Finished taking another sip of water, Howard described in detail what had taken place between he and the deserters. As he spoke, Private Nester, who had known Radcliff for several years prior to the war, did his best to listen in to what was being said between the two officers.

"They told you all of this?" Brown asked, stunned by the upsetting news he was being told. "I mean what caused them to tell you about killing those Union soldiers? Why would they do that? And, why would you believe their story about these Union soldiers being responsible for Radcliff's death? Besides being a couple of liars, they're traitors to our cause."

"First of all, they knew I would have kicked their asses even more than I did if I caught them lying to me. And, once they knew I had identified who the owner of the revolver was, they had no chance of bullshitting me. After I kicked the crap out of the soldier who tried pulling the revolver on me, they knew I had every reason to kill them. The soldier with the smaller scar clearly didn't want any trouble, so even though I wasn't pleased by the news he was telling me I did find out what happened to David. They both know I plan on heading to where the caves are located. If we don't find the bodies where they said they'd be, then we'll go back and find those two bastards. I'll have them hung from the highest tree we find." After collecting himself, Howard added one more comment. "From the directions I was given, it shouldn't be too hard to find those caves."

"Geez, I can't believe David is dead. His father is going to take the news of his son's death pretty hard. The two of them were very close." Nester muttered, letting out a loud sigh as he moved closer to where Howard and Brown were talking.

"Do you know where they hid the bodies?" Brown asked, slightly irritated by Nester's breach of military etiquette.

Nodding his head as he answered Brown's question, Howard looked off to the east in the direction of where the caves where located. It was the direction he and his men would head the following morning. "Not all of them, but I have a pretty good idea where three of them have been left. The other part of this story that upsets me is Radcliff's body isn't one of those that have been placed inside the caves. We'll have to start searching for his remains after we find the other bodies, but I'm afraid there's a pretty good chance we'll never find him."

"Damn it!" Nester muttered loud enough for Howard and Brown to hear.

"You're dismissed, private." Brown said sternly, embarrassed by the profanity Nester had used.

Aware of the long friendship Nester had shared with the Radcliff family, Howard countermanded Brown's order. "He's fine, lieutenant, Nester can stay. Just like us, he's upset over the news we've learned."

Regaining his focus, Howard scanned the grounds of the camp his men had set up in his absence. Taking note of where everything had been placed, he noticed Battle was still slumped against the same tree. Around his feet, the small pile of wood chips had increased in size as the young soldier continued to tinker with his newest carving. Realizing he had not seen Batten since returning to camp, Howard asked about the soldier's whereabouts.

"Holy shit!" Nester suddenly uttered, giving little thought to his choice of words. Swearing in front of the two officers for a second time, a touch of panic was now apparent in the young soldier's voice. Concerned over the newest problem Howard was about to be confronted with, Nester anxiously tried putting distance between he and the conversation taking place. *"By-your-leave, sir!"* Turning on his heels without waiting to be admonished for the second time, Nester left Brown to explain the circumstances surrounding Batten's absence. Surprised by Nester's hasty retreat, Howard turned to Brown for an explanation.

"Captain, Batten's not here. He apparently slipped out of camp shortly after you left." Not knowing how Howard was going to react to this news, Brown anxiously waited for his commanding officer's legendary temper to erupt. The calm response he soon heard was partially due to the stress and fatigue Howard was experiencing.

"Where is he then?" Howard asked as his right eyebrow raised high on his forehead. While similar to a nervous tic, Howard's eyebrow often fluttered when he was irritated or confused.

"Right after you left, Batten suddenly grew sullen and depressed. It was something I've never seen the likes of. Several minutes later, he started ranting and raving about the problems we've been facing, about how poorly the war has been going for us, and then he began yelling even louder about President Lincoln and the Union Army. I've . . . I've never heard him or, for that matter, anyone use so much profanity in such a short amount of time. It was as if the devil himself had climbed inside Batten's skin." As Brown spoke, he used his hands to emphasize the points he was trying to make. It was something he seldom did.

Caught off-guard by Brown's story, Howard stared incredulously at his aide for several long moments. "So, he didn't actually slip out of camp then, did he, lieutenant? The way you're describing the situation, it sounds like he rode out of here like a man gone crazy. Is that a fair way of putting it?"

"Yes, sir. You've described the situation much better than I had; my apologies." Brown replied, regretting his earlier choice of words.

"Did you or anyone else try stopping him?"

"We all tried, captain, but to no avail." As he answered Howard's question, Brown looked to where Nester and Battle were sitting. Pointing in their direction, he described the unsuccessful attempts the three of them had made in trying to prevent Batten from leaving. "Those two over there, they did their best but Batten's got a couple of inches on each of them, and he's also a lot stronger. They each landed a punch or two once the fighting started, but Battle, well . . . he was out of the fight after receiving a well-placed kick to the family jewels. Nester did his best at trying to wrestle the reins away from Batten while I was holding onto one of his legs, but then I got kicked in the jaw and Nester gave up after taking a punch to the face. As crazed as Batten was, there was just no way we were going to stop him. I gave thought to chasing after him, but I didn't want anyone else getting hurt."

Perhaps due to the fatigue he was experiencing, Howard chuckled over Battle's unpleasant injury. His reaction, while understandable, was completely out of character. Casting a look in the direction of where his last two soldiers were seated, he said, "Now I understand why Nester was rubbing his face a few minutes ago."

"Hate to admit it, sir, but that's the reason. Batten threw quite a few haymakers as we were fighting. Unfortunately for Private Nester, one of them ran smack into his jaw. From the way he's rubbing it, it must still hurt."

Quiet for several moments after learning how his AWOL soldier had ridden off, Howard soon got back to the business at hand. As he did, what had been a beautiful sunny day suddenly turned very dark. With the humidity level already high, thick grey clouds quickly threatened Howard and his men with the likelihood of having to endure a long night of heavy rain. Off in the distance, streaks of lightning danced across the sky as the familiar sounds of a fast approaching storm grew even more intense. In moments, large drops of rain began pelting the parched ground.

Holding onto his hat as a means of preventing it from flying away, Howard took note of the storm's intensity. "I was thinking of moving out, lieutenant, but seeing what's about to hit us I guess we're better off staying where we are. Have Battle and Nester spend the night in two of the wagons; you sleep in one of the others. Seeing what kind of day we've had, I'm not taking any chances. I'll sleep better knowing the three of you are staying dry while you're protecting the gold and silver."

"Yes, sir," Brown replied, less than pleased about having to spend the next several hours curled up inside an uncomfortable wagon.

Ignoring the storm's increasing intensity, Howard gave Brown the rest of his marching orders. "First thing tomorrow, have the men consolidate everything into two wagons. Along with everything else we don't need, we'll leave the other wagons behind. After we get started, I plan on finding the cave where the bodies of those Union soldiers were placed. If we can find them, maybe we'll learn where Radcliff's body was left. I'm not sure that's going to happen, but we'll give it a try as I'm not too keen on leaving his body out there for the animals to enjoy. If we manage to find him, then we'll take the time to give him a decent burial before we start making our way towards Savannah."

"What are the chances of finding those caves or Radcliff's body?" Brown asked as he glanced at the ominous clouds overhead. Nearby, close to where the wagons were parked, two pine trees toppled to the ground; victims of the storm's increasing wind.

"I'm afraid our chances of getting soaked in the next minute or two are far better than our chances of finding either the caves or our friend's body." Howard replied as he watched two bolts of lightning touch down a short distance away. "We'll find those caves alright, but not tonight. I'm headed to my tent to stay dry. I'll see you at first light."

Pleased to see the ground inside his tent had stayed dry as the rain beat steadily against the canvass exterior, Howard shook as much water off his blouse as possible before hanging it up to dry. As he undressed, it pleased him to know the gold and silver was being protected by his three remaining men. While they would sleep soundly for most of the night, he knew they would somehow sound the alarm if something went wrong. As he spent the night inside his dry tent, Howard penned the longest entry he had ever written inside one of his journals.

The number of entries Howard had left to record had just been reduced by one.

19

By the following afternoon, Howard and his men finally arrived alongside a steep rocky hillside. Along with the wagons packed with gold and silver were four extra horses and two large oxen. Like the wagons, the animals carried supplies and other equipment needed for the rest of their mission. Spread out along the base of the hillside was three caves; to Howard's surprise each of the openings was slightly larger than the one standing next to it. Nearby two similar looking hills ran south and east; off to the west a long narrow ridge rose to a height of close to three hundred feet. While most of the area surrounding the caves was filled with acres of rich fertile soil, the war no longer allowed the property owner time to plant crops for both his family and the Confederate Army. Like the area around the rocky hills, the neglected fields were now filled with tall invasive plants that satisfied no one's appetite.

After making his way to the entrance of the cave Bothers had described as being the one where the bodies of the Union soldiers had been left, Howard, seeing his first real cave, marveled at the work Mother Nature and years of shifting rocks had created. The three caves being located in close proximity to each other was something he had never thought was possible. Of the three, the cave he was standing in front of had the widest opening. Over twelve feet wide and nearly eight feet high at its tallest point, to Howard it also appeared to be the deepest. As Brown and the others walked to where their commanding officer stood some sixty feet away from the cave's opening, they watched in disgust as a flock of turkey vultures hopped, pranced, and, on occasion, flew in and out of the dark, rocky entrance.

Knowing quite well what he was seeing, as Nester turned to look at Brown he hoped his lieutenant had another explanation for what was taking place. "Lieutenant, you don't think those ugly ass birds are eatin' them Yankees, do ya?"

"They're considered vultures, right? What else would they be eating?" Brown replied, not bothering to take his eyes off the troublesome sight he was seeing.

"Well, if them Yankee boys were dragged in there like them fellas told the captain, then I guess we know what them birds is feastin' on, don't we. I'm sure glad it ain't me they're eatin'. Yankees or not, what I'm seeing ain't right." Not as educated or as proficient with the English language as Brown was, Nester's comments reflected his lack of schooling.

Walking back to the wagon he had been driving, Nester soon returned to where the others were still standing. Proficient with almost every type of firearm the Confederate Army possessed, the young soldier slowly loaded the rifle he had retrieved from the back of his wagon. Attached to the barrel was a telescopic sight that had been made shortly before the start of the war.

"Want me to scare these ugly birds away, captain? We ain't gettin' inside that cave with those bastards in the way."

Just as Howard gave Nester permission to fire, the hillside in front of them let out a loud moan. For close to a minute, Howard, along with his men, struggled to stay upright as the ground shook violently. Off to their right, two of their horses thrashed about on the ground after being knocked off their feet. Moving further away from the caves, they watched as rocks of all sizes tumbled down the rocky hillside. In several locations, including the entrances to each of the caves, thick swirling clouds of dust were expelled from deep inside the hillside. As they dodged several small rocks tumbling down the hill, Howard told his men what was happening.

"It's some kind of a tremor . . . maybe a small earthquake. It should be over within a few moments, but keep an eye out for any rocks headed our way." As he spoke, Howard kept an eye on a small cluster of trees located to the rear of where they were standing. Watching as they shook violently for several seconds, the trees suddenly began shedding a large number of leaves. Across the cluster of trees, branches that were either dead or weakened by previous storms fell to the ground. Watching them fall, Howard knew a good sized branch could wipe out he and his men just as easily as a heavy cascading rock.

Moments after Howard had issued his warning, the violent tremor suddenly stopped. As the area around them settled down, he checked to make sure his men, as well as the horses and wagons, had escaped injury. Much to his relief, everyone had. Turning to look back at the caves, Howard noticed while rocks, dirt, and other debris had closed part of the opening to the smallest cave, the tremor had only dumped a small amount of debris around the openings to the other two. For several long minutes, he and the others watched as dust and dirt continued to spew from the three caves. For now, it was the middle cave they all focused their attention on.

"Damn!" Battle said, still nervous over what he and the others had experienced. Of the small group standing there, he had been surprised the most by the tremor's magnitude and how violent the ground around them had shook. Like the others, he had never experienced the raw power associated with a natural phenomenon.

Pointing to the small stand of trees Howard had been watching, Nester showed the others where most of the turkey vultures had sought safety during the violent tremor. Raising his rifle, the expert marksman made a couple of minor adjustments to his scope before taking aim at one particular target. As he prepared to fire, Nester identified his target to the others. *"Second branch from the top, fellas. Third one in from the left."* Seconds later, a red hot bullet struck Nester's target high in the chest. Falling to the ground, the large carnivorous bird made the afternoon's third loudest noise upon impact. Spooked by what had taken place, several of the bird's companions settled on branches further away as they stared down at their dead comrade. Moments later, they turned and watched in silence as Howard's men approached the cave where some of their friends still dined on the remains of three Union soldiers.

Looking in Battle's direction as they inched closer towards the middle cave, Howard instructed him to fetch one of the long ropes stored in the back of the wagon the young soldier had been driving. Approaching the cave's entrance, Howard and the others detected the unmistakable smell of rotted flesh. The horrific stench was eerily similar to the putrid smells they had encountered on a variety of different battlefields while searching for survivors. At those locations, the mutilated and eviscerated bodies of hundreds of dead soldiers had often become bloated and foul-smelling. The strong smell making its way out of the cave's dark confines was not only overwhelming, but also confirmed something or someone was dead inside. Backing away from the cave's wide rocky mouth, which continued to spew fine particles of dust long after the tremor had ended, Howard told Brown what he wanted done with the rope. After hearing what their commanding officer had planned, Nester and Battle walked to where their horses were tied up.

Moments later, as the two soldiers moved Nester's horse in place in front of the cave, Brown tied one end of the rope into a lasso. As they worked to get everything ready, Howard, having spied several dead tree branches lying nearby, collected as many as he could carry. Dropping the branches close to the where the wagons had been parked, he then used his saber to hack away at the tall, thin stalks of several large pampas plants growing nearby. Trimming the stalks into rough, but equal lengths, and using pieces of rope Nester retrieved from his wagon, Howard fastened them to the ends of six branches. Minutes later, he carried his crudely-made torches to where the others were waiting.

With a handful of other tasks already completed, including Nester's task of fastening the lasso end of the rope to the horn of his saddle, Howard handed the torches to Brown. Then, as Howard finished going over his instructions, Brown, Nester, and Battle finished securing bandanas over their mouths. Besides offering a thin layer of protection over their nose and mouth against any lingering dust particles, the bandanas would help to reduce the foul smell they were about to inhale from the decaying corpses.

"This is going to be rather unpleasant, but it's the right thing to be doing." Howard said as he helped Nester fasten his bandana. "Somewhere in this cave are the bodies of those Union soldiers we've been talking about. I think we all agree the presence of these turkey vultures confirms that fact. Besides being bloated and foul smelling, I'm sure these vultures, and maybe some other animals, have done some pretty serious damage to those remains." While accustomed to giving orders, Howard was less than pleased over the one he was giving to his men.

Pulling Brown off to the side, Howard showed a side of him that he rarely let others see. As the two spoke, Nester and Battle did their best to listen in. "Lieutenant, I know your ankle is still causing you a great deal of pain, but I don't have anyone else I can count on. Just lead the way with one or two of these torches and let the men do the rest of the work. Find those bodies and then get the heck out of there."

Not particularly fond of the assignment he was about to undertake, Nester shuffled his feet as he anxiously glanced in Howard's direction. "Captain, sir, I'm asking this in a most respectful manner and all, but if we ain't burying the Yankees we shoot and kill on the battlefield then why are we fixin' to do so with these poor souls?"

"Soldiers accept the fact that they may die in battle, but most don't expect to be murdered during the war. That's what happened to those three in there," Howard replied as he pointed towards the rear of the cave. "The men who killed these Yankees, well, I guess they've lost their way in life. They may have been fine soldiers at one time, but now they're nothing more than a couple of drunks who like to murder people whenever the opportunity arises. Unlike those two traitors, I'd like to think the rest of us haven't lost our way. Those soldiers in there may have been fighting for the other side, but they didn't deserve to die like they did. I'd like to think they'll be at peace once they learn some Johnny Rebs like us saw to it they received a proper burial."

"For their sake, I hope that happens, captain. Who knows what the good Lord has in store for us, but if you think this is somehow gonna make a difference, then count me in. The only time I got anything against them blue-bellies is when they're trying to kill me. Right now, that ain't the case, is it?" As he finished speaking, Nester tried peering deeper inside the cave, but the sheer darkness prevented him from seeing past the first few feet.

After lighting two of the torches and handing them to Brown, Howard handed Nester and Battle the others. Moments later, two more were brought to life; their bright flames illuminating what moments earlier had been complete darkness. Cautiously stepping foot inside the cave's wide opening, Brown turned to make sure his two companions had not run off. Moving forward, he was pleased to see them only a few feet away. As they moved deeper inside the cave, all three were forced to walk hunched over as the available space gradually diminished. In his left hand, Nester held the other end of the rope that had been fastened to his saddle. As he walked, the rope slowly uncoiled as it was dragged further inside the dark confines. Moving towards the rear of the cave, the stench that been present moments earlier now grew more intense. Nauseated by the horrific smell, Brown and the others gagged repeatedly.

With the torches lighting their way, as the cave began to narrow Brown was the first to see the two sets of red eyes staring back at them. First believing them to be those of the dead soldiers, Brown froze in his tracks as soon as he saw them blink. Realizing the eyes watching them were reflecting the light being given off by the torches, he suddenly saw both sets of eyes move in his direction. Just as Nester and Battle realized what was moving towards them, Brown screamed a loud warning. *"Get down, get down!"*

As the three soldiers dove to the ground, the loud noise made by two ungainly turkey vultures passed over them. Like the soldiers watching them, the vultures had become scared of those who had invaded their dark, musty space. Hearing Brown's frantic screams from where he stood near the cave's entrance, Howard ducked just in time to avoid being struck by the large birds.

"You okay in there?" Howard yelled, dusting himself off as he stared inside the dark confines in front of him. The commotion caused by the bird's brief flight caused Howard to catch a wisp of the strong, putrid smell confronting his men.

"We're alright!" Brown answered rather loudly as he composed himself after barely avoiding being struck by one of the birds. "I think one of these guys may have soiled himself, but we're okay." Brown's comments caused one of the soldiers with him to let out a nervous laugh.

Moving cautiously towards the rear of the cave, Brown found what he had been sent to find. Halting their slow march, he saw the soldiers' remains as they came into view after being illuminated by the light thrown off from the torches. Lying side by side on their backs, the soldiers' boots were the first thing Brown recognized. Despite the cooler temperature inside the cave, the smell being given off by the decaying bodies was horrific.

Purposely holding the torches far enough away so the light did not illuminate the damage the vultures had inflicted on the soldiers' faces, Brown turned towards the cave's entrance as Battle and Nester hurriedly fastened the rope around the three sets of legs. As they worked, Brown shouted an update in Howard's direction.

"Captain, we found them. They're here, but those birds have done some serious damage to these bodies; especially to the areas with any exposed flesh. We'll be finished with the rope in a couple of minutes. Are you all set on your end?" Brown asked, just as anxious as his men for this detail to be over with.

As Howard answered, a loud groan emanated from deep inside the hillside. While similar in sound to the one they had heard several minutes earlier, this noise was far louder. In seconds, the cave rocked violently as dust and small rocks began dropping from the low ceiling.

"Captain, we got us a problem here!" Brown frantically yelled as his gaze looked back towards the cave's opening. *"We're done here. We need you to start hauling these bodies out of here. Get that damn horse moving!"*

Smacking the backside of Nester's horse as he yelled and screamed for it to move out, Howard anxiously watched as the rope tightened as the large animal slowly moved away from the cave's entrance. Losing its footing twice on the rocky ground outside the cave, the frightened horse strained under the weight it was being asked to pull. As the remains of the Union soldiers were slowly being pulled from where they had been unceremoniously dumped, Howard watched as the amount of dust being expelled quickly grew in volume. Seconds later, as the moans from deep inside the hillside grew louder, the unstable cave began spitting rocks larger than pumpkins through the air.

Then, with their escape from the dark confines less than fifteen feet away, Brown, surrounded by a cloud of thick choking dust, watched as a wall of dirt and rocks raced towards him from deep inside the collapsing cave. Frantically trying to make their way past the bodies of the Union soldiers, Brown and his men were instantly crushed under the weight of tons of rocks and dirt.

Outside the cave, Howard watched in horror as the cave quickly filled with debris from the hill above it. In seconds, the entrance no longer existed. Stunned by how quickly the hillside had collapsed, the young officer watched as the rope that had been tied around the legs of the Union soldiers flew past him. Shocked by what he was seeing, Howard realized the fallen debris had torn the soldiers' remains in half. Looking at what remained attached to the rope; Howard was mortified to see only three pairs of boots and six severed legs. Like the bodies of his men, the soldiers' upper torsos were now entombed inside the cave.

Rushing to where the mouth of the cave had stood, Howard screamed as loud as he could as the tremor slowly quieted; anxiously calling out for Brown and his men. While having seen several disasters play out on the battlefield, Howard was stunned by the cave's sudden collapse. Acutely aware of the fate of his men, but still holding out hope that they were still alive, Howard hollered for someone to answer him as the thick choking dust began to dissipate.

After climbing over several rocks close to where the entrance had stood, Howard, on the verge of going into shock, realized his men had perished. With most of the rocks and boulders far too heavy to move, Howard stumbled back to where the wagons had been parked. Holding himself accountable for the deaths of his men, the distraught young officer held his head in his hands as he tried comprehending what had taken place. Sitting down, Howard sobbed as he rested against one of the large wagon wheels.

"I just wanted to do the right thing," Howard said softly as he looked towards a sky filled with white puffy clouds. As someone who believed in the Almighty, Howard tried speaking to the Lord as he wrestled with his emotions. *"Lord, I was just trying to give those soldiers a decent burial. I . . . I didn't mean for my own men to die like that."* Through his tears, he pleaded for forgiveness for sending his men to their death. *"Lord, please know I would gladly change places with my men if you would let me."*

Except for an occasional glance at the hillside which continued to groan and spew dust from a handful of different locations, as Howard sought absolution for the order he had given, he remained fixed in the same position. For nearly four hours, the emotionally distraught officer sat quietly as he gazed at the heavens above him.

<u>20</u>

Caked with dust and dried sweat, as Howard remained seated with his back against the wagon wheel, a wide range of thoughts raced through his mind as he replayed the tragic sequence of events that had taken place. As his thoughts played out, he realized for the first time that he was all alone. Disembarking from the train a few weeks earlier with a full complement of men, he now reflected on the decision to send his men inside the cave. It was a move that robbed him of his most precious resource.

Flooded with a wide range of thoughts, Howard realized he was still responsible for delivering the gold and silver he had been assigned to protect. To do so, he would have to navigate the daunting terrain still in front of him. Remaining in the same position he had occupied for the past several hours, his eyes moved from staring skyward to staring at the horses still hitched to the wagons. Moments later, they focused on the Conestoga wagons. But despite his efforts to regain his composure, Howard grew more and more depressed. Devastated over the loss of his men, he began staring at the revolver he had taken away from the traitors inside the old tavern. Holding the weapon in his hands for almost the entire time he was sitting there, he became convinced it had been the cause of everything that had gone wrong.

Later that afternoon as he pushed aside the issues surrounding Radcliff's revolver, Howard thought, "There's no way I can drive two wagons, and there's even a lesser chance that one of them can carry all of the gold and silver. The weight alone would cause the axles or wheels to collapse if I tried moving it in one wagon. Besides, that amount of weight would be too much for the horses and oxen to pull. They'd be dead in less than two days."

Forcing himself to stand up, Howard opened a small wooden barrel filled with dried beef. Eating several pieces as he ran a series of thoughts through his worried mind, the young officer took notice of something he had missed in the wake of everything that had taken place. Scanning the hillside as he sipped from his canteen, he noticed while two of the caves had completely collapsed, the third, the one furthest to the right, appeared to be partially intact.

Situated close to where he and his men stood before starting their fateful assignment, Howard listened for sounds similar to the ones he had heard earlier that morning. Pausing twice as he made his way towards the last cave, Howard heard nothing that indicated trouble was still lurking inside the hillside. As he listened, all around him the cracks and crevices which had groaned as they sent clouds of dust into the air now sat quiet.

Standing in front of the partially collapsed entrance, Howard soon negotiated his way inside the tight opening. Stopping less than fifteen feet inside, he questioned how structurally sound the cave remained. Minutes later, after extracting himself Howard gathered his remaining courage as he hastily went to work constructing several torches. Each would prove cruder than the ones issued to his men. Completing his work, Howard thought about the cave's interior as he glanced at the nearby wagons. Putting the finishing touches on the torches, he thought, "From what little I saw while I was standing there, this may work. If I can muster the courage to make my way inside, these torches should allow me to make my final decision." As he repeatedly went over his thoughts, all around the hillside small amounts of stone dust once again began venting from deep inside the collapsed caves.

Twenty minutes after mustering enough courage to explore the partially collapsed cave, Howard moved the first wagon as close as possible to the narrow entrance. Soaked in perspiration and hungry from the demanding work he had already performed, Howard unloaded the wagon of its precious contents. When that was done, he repeated the process with the second wagon.

Taking a few moments to recover his strength after working steadily for close to three hours, Howard enjoyed some much-needed water. Quenching his thirst as he stared at the small mountain of crates and broken barrels he had stacked near the cave's entrance, he then began the process of unloading each of the barrels containing the gold and silver. Too heavy for one person to carry, most had been damaged after being rolled off or dropped from the back of the wagons.

Over the next two hours, Howard sidestepped fallen rocks and a host of other obstacles as he carried the bags of coins to the rear of the cave. Moving them inside, he carefully navigated his way past the torches lighting the caves short, but dark interior. Reaching the rear of the cave, Howard stacked the heavier bags in a neat circular pile before piling the smaller bags on top. Once finished, he stacked the precious gold and silver bars behind the waist-high pile of coins. Heavier than the bags of coins, the individual bars were neatly stacked in five rows. Stacked five bars high, each row held an assortment of twenty-five gold and silver bars.

Finishing his work under the light given off from a fresh set of torches, Howard knelt down to admire his work. In front of the cave's rear wall, a sturdy boundary comprised of granite and other types of sedimentary rock, the valuable mound of assets stood nearly four feet high. Centered in the middle was the large pile of coins. To their left, Howard had stacked the wooden crates containing the repeating rifles. Unlike the barrels that had held the valuable coins, the crates had not been damaged. While heavy and cumbersome, Howard had managed to drag them to the rear of the cave before willing them into place. Then, in an attempt to further hide the precious assets from view, in front of everything he piled a collection of splintered wood. Most had been gathered from the damaged barrels, while other pieces came from food crates stored inside the wagons.

Mentally and physically exhausted as he exited the cave, and with little interest in preparing a hot meal, Howard sat down inside the wagon containing his personal belongings. Drinking the little water that was left, Howard gazed at the cave as he cooled down. Two hours later, under the light of two small candles, he began writing in his journal. Like the hard work he completed that afternoon, memorializing what had taken place helped to reduce the anguish he was still experiencing. While his writing helped to dull his pain, it did little to diminish his thoughts of being responsible for the deaths of his men. Pausing on a couple of occasions to rest his eyes, as he sat there the young officer thought of another means of hiding the assets he had placed inside the cave. Far too tired, and far more interested in writing down his thoughts, Howard decided he would complete this last task the following morning. Shaking sleep from his eyes as he took his last sip of water, he put the finishing touches on the most important entry he would ever record.

May 5, 1865

'As I write this, I will always remember this particular day as being the most horrific time of my life. I shall never forget what has taken place.

Early this morning I ordered Lt. Brown and my two remaining men to retrieve the remains of three Union soldiers from a small cave. The previous day I experienced an encounter with two Confederate soldiers; both had abandoned their regiment more than a year ago. These traitors not only told me where the remains of the Union soldiers were located, but also admitted to murdering them. During this encounter, I found them to be in the possession of a revolver that had been owned by another of my men. That officer, Lt. David Radcliff, was apparently killed by these Union soldiers. Like the location of his remains, the circumstances surrounding Lt. Radcliff's death are unknown to me at this time.

As my men were retrieving the remains of these Union soldiers from this small cave, the hillside above them collapsed. Much to my regret, my men were instantly killed by the massive amount of weight which fell upon them. As a result of this collapse, two of the three caves that were present no longer exist.

After spending most of the day praying for the souls of my departed men, I have asked my Lord for forgiveness. As I was praying, I realized another cave, one to the right of where my men lie buried, had only partially collapsed. Realizing I am now alone and likely unable to complete the assignment I have been given, I have hidden the precious assets I was escorting inside this remaining cave. With them are several unopened crates of repeating rifles.

Tomorrow morning I plan on hiding everything even more by stacking several layers of tree branches on top of these assets. After I finish, if my pain allows this to happen, I will move out in hopes of finding some men to help me recover these assets. If I'm successful, I shall endeavor to complete my mission.

The area where the cave is located is surrounded by pine trees and what I assume were once fertile fields. Strangely, the hillside where the three caves are located is one of the few hilly areas I have seen.

If I should fail to retrieve these precious assets, or if I should somehow perish, I pray that the souls of my men have been blessed with a place in Heaven. If forgiven for my many faults and sins, I hope to be blessed with a place alongside them. I pray to Jesus that will happen.

I also hope what I am about to do, will also be forgiven.'

Under his entry, Captain Noah Howard, as a way of taking responsibility for the deaths of his men, signed his name as neatly as his shaky hand allowed. It was the only time he signed his name after making an entry in any of his journals.

*****

The following morning, ignoring his intense hunger, Howard spent the better part of a warm spring day cutting and trimming tree branches. Most of what he cut was taken from the same pine trees where the turkey vultures had landed after being spooked by the first warning the hillside had given. After stacking the branches on and around the assets he had hidden near the rear of the cave, Howard, with his work finally completed, sat down and ate his first real meal in nearly three days.

Later, after consolidating everything he was taking with him into one wagon; Howard moved out to find the next town south of where the caves were located. Unlike many of his previous moves, the deep depression that had settled inside his mind caused him to ignore the maps he normally consulted. As his wagon slowly made its way across open fields and shallow streams, a small team of horses and oxen followed close behind. Each had been tethered to the rear of the wagon. As he pushed south, it was in Moncks Corner, South Carolina, where Howard hoped to find the resources needed to finish his mission.

Two days later, as he continued to push south the dark cloud which had settled in Howard's mind shortly after the death of his men caused him to do the unthinkable. Wracked with guilt over the decision which had caused his men to perish, and too afraid of having to relive that tragic moment for the rest of his life, Captain Howard placed his friend's pistol against his right temple and committed suicide. Three days later, not far from where his body was found, on the wagon's front seat was a small wooden chest. On the front panel, the initials N. H. had been neatly engraved.

Like many others from both sides of the war, officers who often had no other options than to order soldiers to advance in the face of a withering attack, Howard had seen his men perish only yards from where he stood. While others before him had somehow managed to justify their decisions, and their losses, Howard had not. Whether it was due to the small number of men at his disposal or because of the manner in which they perished, Howard knew he could never forgive himself for the order he had given. With the war seemingly over, and with a sister back home that he barely knew, he took the only means available to silence his pain. His death was another tragedy inflicted upon this nation by a senseless war.

Soon after Howard was laid to rest, the family who found his remains opened the young captain's wooden chest. In doing so, they divided the contents amongst themselves. Among the contents was a small amount of Confederate currency, two gold coins, a bible, a blank journal, and a simple gold ring.

Three years earlier, needing another chest to hold some of his personal belongings, Howard commissioned one of Richmond's most-talented cabinetmakers to build a small wooden chest. Concerned his belongings would often be stored out of sight for prolonged periods, Howard made sure the chest was outfitted with a secure lock. While never intending to store money or other valuables inside it, Howard had the cabinetmaker create one special feature. Along the back wall, a hidden compartment was built inside the chest.

It was one no one had ever known about.

******

Nearly one hundred and sixty years after his death, Howard's wooden chest, handed down from generation to generation inside the family who found his remains, was put up for sale. With the current owner no longer interested in its historic value, the chest was sent to an auction house in Ohio to be sold with several other Civil War artifacts.

A week after taking possession of the chest, a rich, but eccentric student of the Civil War accidently discovered the hidden compartment the previous owners had never found. Inside the hiding spot the new owner found one item.

It was something the chest's original owner had spent hours filling with his thoughts and experiences.

SPRING, 2020

21

After being seriously wounded three months earlier during a running gun battle inside a sprawling commercial parking lot in Southbury, Connecticut, Paul Waring spent the better part of a month recuperating back home before returning to Murrells Inlet, South Carolina.

A retired Connecticut state trooper, Paul had spent the better part of his thirty-year career managing a variety of criminal investigative units before being transferred to an administrative position. Like doctors and nurses who thrive from the pressure generated by working in life and death situations inside busy emergency rooms, Paul had been at his best when working difficult and stressful investigations. Trained to be a leader the state police could count on, the administrative assignment he was given was one he despised. His transfer was the result of an assignment performed too well. Months earlier, he had been assigned a sensitive internal affairs investigation to conduct. It was an assignment he wanted no part of. Later, after the findings of his investigation had been released, Paul became involved in a bitter dispute with the state police commissioner over a transfer he never saw coming. Weeks later, fed up with politics and with a commissioner who refused to reassign him to his former command, Paul reluctantly retired from a career that had once been a natural fit.

Within weeks of his retirement, Paul and his wife, Donna, a retired bank manager, moved to Murrells Inlet. Years earlier, they had fallen in love with South Carolina's comfortable climate after spending several summers vacationing in North Myrtle Beach. With the prospect of enjoying warmer temperatures and sandy beaches throughout the year, as well as having two close friends living in the area, Paul convinced his wife the time was right to move south. While selling their home and moving away from family and friends had created a host of issues, Paul and Donna never looked back as they escaped Connecticut's cold winters and high cost of living.

During his time with the state police, Paul had earned the reputation as being one of the state's most talented investigators. In the high-profile posts he held during the latter half of his career, Paul and his detectives had investigated a number of gruesome murders, violent and deadly bank robberies, and several kidnappings. Among the murders were several in which irate spouses, after learning of their partner's adulterous acts, had brutally killed them in fits of rage.

While Connecticut had always had its share of talented criminal investigators, from the ranks of both the state police and several local departments, a unique talent Paul possessed caused him to stand out from the others. On many occasions this talent allowed him to connect evidence, previously dismissed by other investigators as being either insignificant or unrelated, to other more important evidence. By doing so, those innocuous bits of evidence often allowed him to identify those responsible for committing the acts he was investigating. While another of Paul's talents sometimes caused him to become embroiled in jurisdictional issues with a handful of local departments, members of the States Attorney's Office often called for his assistance at some of the state's most heinous crime scenes. Working scenes often littered with blood and drugs had caused Paul to conduct a wide range of interviews with victims, witnesses, and with those accused of a number of sadistic crimes. He had also had the opportunity to sit in on a number of confessions involving every kind of criminal there was. In doing so, much to the dismay of several high-priced defense attorneys, the Connecticut courts had recognized Paul as an expert when it came to dissecting oral and written statements. This had made him a legend with the cops and prosecutors he worked with. Quiet and unassuming, his reputation as being one of Connecticut's best investigators was something he never exploited.

Shortly after retiring to South Carolina, one of Paul's closest friends, Bobby Ray Jenkins, the undersheriff of Georgetown County, along with his boss, Sheriff LeRoy Renda, had asked for help in solving a series of brutal murders. Committed in Myrtle Beach and other locations along the Grand Strand, each had taken place during the time leading up to Paul and Donna's move to Murrells Inlet. Quite strangely, while each of the victims had been murdered several miles away, their bodies were dumped along Front Street in the small fishing village of Georgetown, South Carolina.

Working with a team of detectives from several state and local law enforcement agencies, Paul, as he had done on many occasions back home, began focusing on the evidence that had been collected at each of the scenes. That was especially true with the evidence collected from the locations where the bodies had been dumped. In doing so, and from his review of each of the case files he spent hours poring over, Paul noticed a particular pattern – a modus operandi – being used by the killer. Two weeks after signing on, and after participating in a number of stakeouts and witness interviews, Paul's team not only solved the murders they had been working on but two others that had gone unreported. Both had involved victims with no immediate relatives living in the area.

As months went by, Paul was also asked to assist the Georgetown County Sheriff's Office with several other nefarious crimes. Each had involved a significant degree of random violence. It was during one of these investigations when Bobby Ray had been promoted to his current position. From his role as a part-time investigator, Paul was asked to assume his friend's former position as the commanding officer of the department's Major Case Squad. With no one else in the department possessing the skills and experience of its newest employee, Paul's appointment was one no one could fault. Endorsed by Solicitor Joseph Pascento, it was a position Paul reluctantly accepted. For now, retirement would have to wait.

Shortly after assuming his new position, Paul had unknowingly become the target of Diego Medina, a notorious member of one of Mexico's most vicious drug cartels. Convinced for years Paul was responsible for the death of one of his younger brothers during a buy-bust operation that had gone horribly wrong, after escaping from a federal prison in Mexico with several members of his gang Medina sought to avenge his brother's death.

Entering the United States illegally in Texas, Medina and his gang began a cross country crime spree by conducting a series of violent and deadly assaults on armored cars. Using several stolen cars, a variety of automatic weapons, and tactics developed during their years of being ruthless killers, Medina's crew quickly came into possession of a large sum of money. Headed east after using a portion of the stolen money to learn where Paul was living, Medina and his crew continued to commit a number of armed robberies to further help finance their trip. Along the way, they left a wake of dead prostitutes; many who had satisfied a variety of Medina's perverse sexual pleasures.

Hiding out in rural North Carolina for several days after committing their third armored car heist, Medina sent one of his brothers and a longtime associate to South Carolina after learning of Paul and Donna's recent move. Sent to keep Medina's younger brother out of trouble, Diego's associate was someone he always turned to when violence needed to be meted out. Wanting to impress his older and far more experienced brother, Juan Medina foolishly chose to ignore the orders he had been given. Electing to attack Paul's home without gathering any intelligence or consulting his brother not only resulted in their target's home being badly shot up, but led to Juan and his partner being shot to death. It also resulted in several of Paul's law enforcement friends becoming seriously pissed off after one of their partners was badly wounded during the exchange of gunfire. Already obsessed with killing Paul, the five thousand dollars Medina paid to informants in an effort to locate his target's whereabouts was money he considered well spent. With two of his brothers now dead, the expenditure intensified Medina's need for revenge.

At the time of this vicious attack, the veteran investigator and his wife were in Connecticut visiting his elderly mother and their new granddaughter. Born two weeks earlier, Paul and Donna were excited at the thought of spending several days with their first grandchild. While keenly aware that he was now the target of Medina's revenge, it was during this visit Paul first took notice of the men who had been paid to follow him. A day later, along with several undercover officers who were working to keep him safe, Paul was viciously attacked by Medina and his gang.

In a wild shootout which slowly unfolded inside a large parking lot crowded with shoppers, pedestrians, and a host of different vehicles, hundreds of gunshots were exchanged between the two factions. As the shootout moved from one section of the parking lot to another, parked cars, storefronts, and an armored car were repeatedly struck by gunfire.

As the chaotic scene inside the parking lot came to an end, Medina and nearly every member of his gang had been killed. Among the law enforcement personnel present, Paul sustained the most serious injury. Shot in the chest and left shoulder, but saved from further injury by the bullet-proof vest he had been wearing, his wounds were both painful and extensive. Thought to be life threatening at first, after undergoing three operations in the span of less than two days, Paul managed to survive.

After recuperating in Connecticut for several weeks, Paul returned to his home in South Carolina. Still upset by what had happened there and by the deaths that occurred inside her home, Donna, at first, refused to return to South Carolina. Staying in Connecticut, she helped her son and daughter-in-law with a variety of needs associated with a new baby. Despite assurances that her home no longer bore any signs of the deadly shooting, Donna had sent her husband back to South Carolina with orders to sell their home.

But then, less than a month later, after giving it a great deal of thought and from a touching phone call she received from a special friend, Donna called her husband to tell them they were staying. They were staying, she told him, as long as Paul agreed to find a new home for them to live in.

It was a condition her husband readily agreed to.

<u>**22**</u>

After finding a new home inside *The Seasons at Prince Creek West*, an active retirement community located in Murrells Inlet, and with Donna back to work at the bank she managed in Garden City, Paul returned to his practice of enjoying breakfast at the Waccamaw Diner. No longer employed by the Georgetown County Sheriff's Office due to the injuries he was still recovering from, Paul had plenty of time to do whatever suited him.

Located in a small strip mall off Highway 17 in Murrells Inlet, the small family-run diner had become one of Paul's favorite haunts. Featuring the simple, but delicious kind of food one of his favorite television shows - *Diners, Drive-Ins and Dives* - often showcased, Paul had become a frequent visitor to the not-so-trendy restaurant. On most occasions, he took pleasure in sitting inside his favorite booth enjoying a hearty breakfast while reading one of the morning newspapers that always seemed to be available. While better known for its version of a tasty Low Country favorite, She-crab soup, the diner's freshly made blueberry pancakes had become Paul's favorite morning meal. Topped with a light dusting of powdered sugar and three slices of thick maple-roasted bacon, and generally paired with a glass of OJ and two or three cups of coffee, it was the only meal he ordered on a regular basis.

On this particularly pleasant morning as he sat waiting for his breakfast, Paul's peaceful morning was interrupted several times as he scanned the local newspaper for anything interesting to read. A baseball junkie for nearly his whole life, he routinely followed the exploits of his favorite team, the New York Yankees. However, on this occasion, each attempt at reading the Major League box scores was interrupted by a few well-meaning visitors. Just as always, after becoming somewhat of a local celebrity after finding a portion of the lost Confederate treasury, whenever a fellow patron stopped to wish him well in his recovery Paul smiled and responded with a few kind words of his own. Most of the encouragement was from folks he had never met. While it had its tedious moments, life in the south was proving to be far friendlier than it had been on many occasions back home.

Prior to resuming his law enforcement career in South Carolina, Paul purchased a used pontoon boat from a new found friend. Seizing an opportunity to satisfy an urge he had wrestled with for years, he purchased the boat for a fair price after learning his friend had just wanted it gone. Like his vehicles, Paul soon had the neglected and slightly damaged vessel looking far better than it had in years. While his remarkable discovery of the millions of dollars in gold and silver had evaded a countless number of other searchers during the years following the Civil War, the news stories of Paul's boat being used in this adventure had contributed to his meals being interrupted on a regular basis.

It was during Paul's first ride on his *new* boat out on the Waccamaw River that a simple observation had caused him to start searching for the missing Confederate treasury. Like many other passionate Civil War enthusiasts, he was aware of the various myths surrounding the missing treasury. After tying his boat up alongside a long sandbar, Paul had walked inside the nearby woods to answer the call of Mother Nature. Taking notice of the pristine surroundings during this unexpected stop, he spotted an object reflecting the sun's afternoon rays. That simple observation soon led to his discovery of the remains of a Confederate soldier who had died inside a massive Live Oak tree nearly one hundred and fifty years earlier.

Days later, with the support of Bobby Ray Jenkins and two other friends, Chick Mann and Jayne Ewald, Paul started working the clues he uncovered near the soldier's remains. Over the course of several weeks, he worked them just as hard as he had done with the clues he and his detectives uncovered during their many labor-intensive investigations.

Within the span of a few short weeks, Paul Waring, an intense investigator who never took his foot off the throttle once he started working a particular issue, discovered several million dollars of gold and silver coins that had once been part of the Confederate treasury. Lost since the end of the Civil War, the coins had been the focus of treasure hunters and fortune seekers for decades. While possessing a nearly insatiable thirst for anything related to the war, Paul laughed on several occasions when others had joked about the mystery of the lost treasury being solved by a Yankee.

With his remarkable discovery documented by a countless number of newspapers and magazines, as well as by a novel entitled *Confederate Gold and Silver*, Paul, much to his dismay, had become a celebrity; not only inside the Waccamaw Diner and Murrells Inlet, but across the country. This status, which lasted far longer than he cared for, was something he neither sought nor enjoyed. A private person in both his personal and professional lives, Paul somehow managed to tolerate the attention that came his way. While pestered for several months after his discovery had been made public, he was pleased when the reporters and writers finally shifted their attention to other matters.

Unaware of what was about to be asked of him, Paul enjoyed his morning pancakes as he thumbed through the newspaper. He was also unaware that his quiet morning was about to be interrupted by a close friend.

Later, it would again be interrupted by a total stranger.

23

Looking up from the newspaper he was reading, Paul smiled as he watched Betty Repko approach his booth carrying his breakfast. Setting down the two plates next to a small glass of OJ and the coffee he was nursing, Betty started ribbing her friend over his morning meal choice.

"I ain't gonna ask ya about grits no more as the last time I brought them up ya damn near chewed my head off," the short, stocky waitress offered, chuckling as she acknowledged another customer's friendly wave. "I know ya don't like that creamy delicacy all us true Southerners enjoy, but ya need to order something different once in a while besides them pancakes ya like so much."

In her mid-sixties, slightly overweight, and doing her best at fighting a nicotine habit she first acquired at the ripe old age of fourteen, Betty had met Paul several years earlier during his first visit to the diner. Enduring three difficult divorces and a handful of other separations from men who promised her everything but delivered on very little, for several reasons Betty had developed a special fondness for Paul. Most importantly, she appreciated the respect he showed her and the other hard-working waitresses who did their best at accommodating the many different requests they fielded during their long shifts. Forgoing school after turning sixteen, Betty's use of the English language often reflected the lazy manner in which she spoke. It also reflected how little she had paid attention while attending school. But, to Paul, of the thousands of people he had met from all walks of life, she was one of the kindest and most sincere. It was because of a simple phone call Betty had made that caused Paul and Donna to still call South Carolina their home.

Weeks earlier, Betty had been devastated after hearing the news that Paul had nearly died after being seriously wounded in Connecticut. During his first visit back to the diner as he recovered from his injuries, her tears reflected how emotional she had become after seeing Paul limp inside the front door. While shot in the left shoulder and near the middle of his chest, a round that had ricocheted off a light stanchion had done serious damage to Paul's right ankle. Later, during that same visit, Betty became even more upset after learning Paul and Donna were planning on moving back home. Having already lost several men in her life who had meant something special, the news of someone else planning to leave her, someone she considered a special friend, was one of the biggest disappointments Betty had ever experienced.

Two weeks after her friend's return, and against Paul's wishes, Betty had called Donna back in Connecticut. While not as close to her as she was to Paul, Betty was fond of Donna, and of the financial guidance she had given her. With Donna's help, Betty had finally begun to set aside funds for her retirement.

During a long teary phone call, Betty spoke to Donna about the friendship they each shared, and how Paul had taken to his new life in South Carolina. Between their tears, Betty sprinkled the conversation with thoughts about Paul's boat, with comments regarding his discovery of the lost Confederate treasury, and, most importantly, about antics involving Paul and Donna's mutual friend, Bobby Ray Jenkins. A natural-born comedian who often thought he was just as good a cop as Paul, Bobby Ray and Betty had known each other for years.

In the days following their poignant phone conversation, Donna wrestled with her decision about never returning to South Carolina. Pushing aside the thought that she and her husband had been the actual targets of the men who invaded their home, Donna spent time thinking of the many good times they shared with old and new friends. Like Betty, her thoughts also included those of her husband and of how happy he had become after moving to the Palmetto state.

After struggling with her thoughts for a few more days, Donna decided to rescind the demand she had placed upon her husband. While never giving any thought to returning to their home in the Blue Dunes community of Murrells Inlet, a home she believed she could no longer be happy in, Donna soon realized she had been very content in the new life she and her husband had created for themselves. While never admitting that Betty's phone call had convinced her to stay, in the end it had proven to have a great deal of influence on her decision to return to their adopted home in South Carolina.

"I'm not sure what I disliked more, Betty," Paul said, taking notice of Bobby Ray walking towards his booth. "The grits themselves or the fact you brought them up every time I was here. Thank God we got that mess straightened out."

Noticing Paul's stare, Betty turned to see Bobby Ray speaking with two elderly customers seated at the lunch counter. Like a few others on the other side of the diner, those currently occupying Bobby Ray's attention were folks he had gotten to know from his career with the Georgetown County Sheriff's Office.

"There goes the morning," Betty quipped, shaking her head in mock disgust as she placed a placemat, silverware, and a cup and saucer across from where Paul was seated. Like the versions found in many other diners, the paper placemat was adorned with a variety of ads from local businesses. On the other side, a large cartoon sat waiting to be colored by a young child. Jerking her thumb in Bobby Ray's direction, Betty asked "Were you expecting him?"

"Nope." Paul replied, stabbing three warm pieces of pancakes with his fork before stuffing them inside his mouth.

Staring in the direction of the lunch counter, Betty watched as Bobby Ray delivered friendly pats to the backs of those he was speaking with. Moments earlier, he had deftly delivered the punchline of an old, but funny joke. "Me neither. Don't get me wrong, I love that boy to death, but he's one of those folks I wish someone had called me about before he showed up. You know, like a two-minute warning or a heads-up . . . that's not much to ask for, is it? God knows that boy can stir up trouble like no one else I've ever known." Walking away, Betty left to fetch a fresh pot of coffee. As she did, two coffee cups sat waiting to be filled with the diner's special blend of hot roasted coffee.

Seconds later, Bobby Ray slid inside the booth where Paul was seated. Like life in general, there were unwritten rules concerning the seating arrangements inside the booth. As the one who had designated the booth as his, Paul always sat with his back against the diner's rear wall. Like most cops, he always felt more comfortable seeing who was approaching the booth than he did while seated on the other side. Being aware of a number of unprovoked attacks on police officers as they relaxed while enjoying a meal between calls, Paul had never felt comfortable being blind to anyone intent on harming him. It was a feeling many who had never worn the badge could ever understand. While having the same feeling about being caught off-guard, Bobby Ray often deferred to his friend's seniority by sitting across from him. When others joined them, no matter if it was only for a cup of coffee or a full meal, protocol required their guests to occupy the seats facing the rear wall. As someone who always carried a sidearm near his right hip, and with Bobby Ray being left-handed and carrying his pistol on his left hip, the seating arrangement worked well in the event they were forced to stand and draw their weapons. While such an event was unlikely, both would be able to address the person invading their space without having to draw their weapons across their bodies. It was a tactical advantage they both appreciated.

Smiling as he got settled inside the booth, Bobby Ray looked down at the breakfast his friend was eating. "Ya can't stop eatin' them pancakes, can ya?" Unlike Betty, after graduating from high school, Bobby Ray had attended college for four years, receiving his B.S. in Criminal Justice Administration. But just like Betty, Bobby Ray's lazy Southern drawl often caused his words to run together.

"There's not much of a difference between these pancakes and the grits I see you and others eating here on most occasions, is there?" As he asked his question, Paul used his fork to point at the remaining pancakes on his plate. As a way of making Paul's meal appear even more attractive than it was, Betty had placed a slice from an orange and several blueberries off to the side. The presentation had not gone unnoticed.

"There's a big difference, one's Yankee food and the other's country food. Best ya remember that, Billy Yank." Bobby Ray joked, nearly knocking over his coffee cup with the sleeve of his sports coat. A fervent Civil War buff like Paul, the undersheriff enjoyed antagonizing his Northern friend on what section of the country he had abandoned in order to live in a much friendlier climate.

"Leave my customers alone, Bobby Ray!" Betty said, displaying a small scowl as she poured Paul a fresh cup of coffee. "And never mind that smack you're dishing out about grits. I can't recall the last time I seen you eatin' them." As she finished speaking, Paul's favorite waitress filled her newest customer's coffee cup close to the brim.

"Had some earlier today, Miss Betty," Bobby Ray replied, feigning a disgusted look in her direction. Seconds later, he shot Paul a friendly wink. "Care to know where I had them?"

"No, not really, but I'm sure I'm about to find out. Just do me one favor, Lord, please make this quick!" Betty's brief, but sarcastic response caused Paul to laugh at the look she shot Bobby Ray.

"Had them across town at Bud's Kitchen; ya know, up on 501. Real tasty they were; nice and smooth going down. They were nothing like the chunky stuff y'all serve here." While he did his best, Bobby Ray failed to hold back the serious look on his face.

"Bet that poor gal who waited on ya was real happy when she found that fifty cent tip ya left her." Betty replied, cringing over the small tip she believed Bobby Ray had likely left. "Where's she going with that kind of money, Disney World?" While not the worst tipper in the world, Bobby Ray was not as generous as his friend when it came to leaving a tip.

"Was that supposed to be funny?"

"Y'all eatin' or just drinkin', Bobby Ray? I've got other customers to be tending to." Waiting for a response, Betty switched the hot coffee pot from one hand to the other as she stood at the end of the booth.

"Just drinkin'." Pointing across the table at his friend, Bobby Ray added, "I saw this guy's truck out front, so I thought I'd stop and chew the fat for a few minutes. Seeing your smiling face is just an added blessing, darling." Bobby Ray smiled at the frustrated look he saw in Betty's face as she turned to walk away.

"Great," Betty replied, ignoring Bobby Ray's attempt at getting on her good side. "That's two of us you've screwed today. At least, the first gal went home with fifty cents. I'll probably get a quarter for this wonderful service I'm providing you."

As Bobby Ray and Betty ended the bantering between them, Paul noticed someone he had never seen inside the diner. While the retired state trooper usually took note of the many strangers who came and went during his morning meals, this person, or at least the way he was dressed, was not the kind of customer the diner normally hosted. Situated a short distance away from the county courthouse and a number of small stores that were located inside three nearby strip malls, the diner's clientele tended to wear work clothes, tee shirts, hunting and fishing gear, or similar attire while stopping in for a quick meal. Men in expensive suits were rarely seen inside the greasy spoon that Paul and his friends generally referred to as their home away from home.

Dressed in an expensive-looking black suit, the stranger's presence was accentuated by a white long sleeve dress shirt and a pair of freshly polished dress shoes. After noticing the stranger's collar had been left unbuttoned, Paul took note of the gold cuff links being worn. Trained to notice relevant details, the veteran investigator also noticed the stylish black valise that was being carried. With neatly cropped black hair which looked far too dark for the stranger's age, Paul guessed the person he was staring at was doing his best to disguise his actual age. Briefly glancing around the diner at those eating their morning meals, the stranger soon glanced in Paul's direction before turning his attention to those seated in neighboring booths.

"Paul, you boys need anything else this morning?" Betty asked as Paul watched the stranger momentarily disappear from view. Walking the length of the lunch counter, the stranger continued with his efforts at locating the person he was sent to find.

"No, thanks. Bobby Ray and I are going to sit here for a few more minutes. I'll take the check whenever you have it."

Looking up from where he was seated, Bobby Ray, always looking to be the one who received the last laugh, directed one more comment in Betty's direction. Winking at her, he said, "Same place, same time this Friday night?" While she would have slapped most men who talked to her that way, Bobby Ray's comment was part of a running joke he and Betty had shared over the past several months.

Having clobbered her share of drunks, perverts, and lonely men who had asked that same question more times than she could remember, with barely an expression showing on her tired face, Betty responded to her friend's comment. "Sounds good. Let's make it ten p.m. behind the funeral home. If I'm not there, start without me."

The response Betty offered caused Paul to burst out laughing. On the other side of the booth, Bobby Ray was at a loss for what to say. On this occasion, it was Betty who managed to get the last laugh.

24

As he always did when listening to a discussion involving a new approach being taken in a particularly complex criminal investigation, Paul had been too focused on what Bobby Ray was telling him to notice Betty approaching their booth. He also failed to notice her worried look. Sliding inside the booth, something she never did, Betty cast a worried look in the direction of the lunch counter. Nervously speaking in a hushed tone, she said, *"You can't see him from here, but there's a guy sitting at the counter asking questions about you. When he asked me if I knew you, I tried telling him that I didn't have any idea who you were, but I'm not so sure how convincing I was."* Concerned over the questions being asked, Betty briefly fidgeted with her uniform as she prayed the stranger would not see her sitting there.

"Did he say what he wanted?" Paul asked, curious over the stranger's presence, but unfazed by the questions being asked. Since discovering the lost Confederate treasury, Paul had routinely been stopped at gas stations, grocery stores, while shopping at the mall, and even in his own driveway by people curious about the details of his adventure.

"No, he didn't. Do you want me to go ask him why he's looking for you? Maybe he's a bill collector or something?"

"Is that him?" Slightly amused by Betty's last comment, Paul pointed to where the well-dressed stranger was standing near the diner's only cash register. As he pointed, Paul watched as the stranger smiled and offered a friendly wave in his direction. Waiting for his change, the diner's newest customer held a large Styrofoam cup in his left hand. Moments later, as he pocketed his change the well-dressed male took a brief sip of his drink before bending down to retrieve his valise.

"Yep, that's him. Think he's a snake in the grass?" Screwed over in each of her divorces, Betty had developed a significant dislike for most attorneys. Watching as the stranger approached Paul's booth, someone she was already convinced she disliked as much as any man who had ever mistreated her, Betty looked across the diner as she pretended not to see him walking in their direction. Seconds later, afraid of what was taking place, Betty's heart began racing as the stranger paused next to her.

"Mr. Waring?"

"That's me." Paul replied, casually giving the person standing next to his booth the once-over. "Can I help you?" As the stranger answered Paul's question, Betty decided it was time for her to leave. Awkwardly standing up due to a minor knee injury she had recently sustained, Betty slowly made her way back to the kitchen as the pain subsided. Walking towards the front of the diner, she cast a concerned look back in Paul's direction.

"Mr. Waring, my name is Robert Regan. My employer sent me here to find you so we could have a talk regarding a matter he considers very important. Do you mind if I sit down?" As Regan finished speaking, Bobby Ray, suspicious of what was taking place and fully aware of the recent attempt on his friend's life, slowly slid out of the booth. As he stood up, the veteran cop kept a close eye on Regan's hands and the valise he was holding.

"Have a seat where I was sitting, Robert." Bobby Ray said, pointing to the bench style seat inside Paul's booth. "I'll grab a chair for myself." Not sure of what to make of the person seeking some of Paul's time, Bobby Ray refused to address their unexpected guest by his last name.

Staring at Bobby Ray as he slid inside the booth, Regan spoke to Paul's friend. Speaking civilly despite Bobby Ray's curt reception, Regan announced the reason for his visit. "I was hoping to speak with Mr. Waring in private for a few minutes, if you don't mind."

"Actually I do." Before Bobby Ray could say anything else, Paul politely cut him off.

"Mr. Regan, I'm not sure why you're interested in speaking with me or, for that matter, why you've been asking questions about me, but this guy right here is my closest friend. If you're interested in speaking with me, he stays. If that doesn't suit you, I wish you a good day."

Eyeing Paul closely before glancing at Bobby Ray, Regan smiled as he finished introducing himself. As the three men shook hands, Regan said, "I see the waitress who told me you weren't here suddenly found you. Either that or you appeared out of thin air. I take it she's the one who told you I was asking questions about your whereabouts."

Returning Regan's smile, Paul responded by defending Betty's actions. "I'm sure your friends protect you whenever they feel it's necessary, Mr. Regan. She was just doing what she thought was right. There's no need to be upset with her."

"Not at all. I just found it amusing when I saw her sitting next to you after she had told me she didn't know you." Regan offered, using a napkin to make sure his side of the table was free of moisture before pulling any documents from his valise. "It's nice to know your friends are looking out for you, especially after that unfortunate incident in Connecticut. I trust you're feeling better with each passing day."

Surprised to some degree over Regan knowing of the recent attempt on his life, Paul did his best at hiding his emotions. To his right, Bobby Ray was not as successful.

"Is that why you're here, Robert? To talk about that ambush which nearly cost Paul his life? If that's the case, he's not interested in speaking about it." Sliding forward in his chair, Bobby Ray glared at the person he had taken an immediate disliking to.

"Actually, that's not the reason behind my visit," Regan replied, moving his hands closer to the two locking mechanisms near the top of his valise. "I came to speak to him about this."

Concerned over what Regan might be reaching for, Bobby Ray moved his left hand closer to where his Sig Sauer was holstered on his hip. A dark brown belt firmly held the Sig's pancake-style holster in place. Opening his sports coat, Bobby Ray made sure Regan saw what was hidden behind it. "If I were you, I'd open that fancy briefcase real slow. My friend and I, and I'm not referring to this pistol I'm carrying, we don't take kindly to surprises. Especially when they're sprung on us by someone we don't know."

Realizing he may have acted too quickly in the wake of the incident he had referred to, after listening to the warning he was given

Regan slowly moved his hands away from the valise sitting at the edge of the table. "Gentlemen, I apologize. That was foolish on my part. Please accept my apology." Nodding at Bobby Ray in an attempt to diffuse the slight amount of tension existing between them, Regan then continued. "Mr. Waring, I can assure you I mean no harm to either you or your friend. My reasons for being here are related to a legitimate business proposition." Noticing the two men he was sitting with continued to focus their attention on his hands, Regan carefully slid his valise off the table and placed it on the seat next to him. "I'll tell you what, for now let's forget about my valise. Let's talk for a few minutes. After you hear me out, then I'll show you why my employer is seeking your assistance."

"That's a good idea, Mr. Regan. We're both anxious to hear what you have to say. Isn't that right, Bobby Ray?" While Paul was anxious to hear what Regan had to say, his comment was meant as a way of putting some distance between his friend's left hand and the pistol displayed on his belt. It was the same weapon Bobby Ray had worn to work each day for the past ten years. Having used it on several occasions to maintain his status as one of the department's firearms instructors, he had become extremely proficient with this weapon and several others.

Ignoring the suspicious look on Bobby Ray's face, Regan said, "Mr. Waring, my employer is a rather wealthy, but eccentric billionaire. For now, at his request his name will go unmentioned. Please know that despite his advanced age, he's quite healthy and very much in control of his affairs."

"Just how old is this boss of yours?" Bobby Ray asked, still wondering if Regan was there to harm the person sitting next to him. "And just how rich is this old coot?"

"He's eighty-nine." Regan replied curtly, clearly irritated over the reference Bobby Ray had made about his employer's wealth. "A very young eighty-nine, might I add. He's also rich enough to be a billionaire several times over. If you don't know how to spell that, it starts with a b, not an m." Paul smiled at the sarcastic remark Regan directed at Bobby Ray.

"Mr. Waring, I was . . ."

"My friend and I are both regular folks, so while we appreciate the respect you're showing us, he's Bobby Ray and I'm Paul. There's no need for any sirs or misters in this conversation, ok?" Never one for formalities, Paul again tried to reduce the amount of tension still lingering inside the booth.

"That's fine, thank you. I'm the same way; I'd much prefer it if we used our first names. Now that that's been decided, and so we all get started on the same page, let me begin by saying my employer has a deep interest in American history; especially when it comes to the Civil War. He's told me on several occasions his fascination with the war is something he can't describe, but it's something he's been passionate about for many years. From the notoriety you've gained from your remarkable discovery of the lost Confederate treasury a few years back, my employer has spent a great deal of time, and money, delving into your background. From what he's learned, he's of the opinion you share the same passion."

"I guess I do. So does your new best friend." Paul said, pointing at Bobby Ray.

"Is that why you're here?" Bobby Ray asked, motioning for Betty to refresh their coffee cups.

Directing his comments in Paul's direction, Regan answered Bobby Ray's question. "Yes, it is. My employer was amazed by the remarkable discovery you and your friends made. In fact, I think he's probably read every newspaper article and magazine story that's been written about this discovery. He'd probably get ticked at me for telling you this, but you actually had a brief conversation with him after one of your talks. As part of my marching orders I can't tell you where that took place, but I know you left him with a very favorable impression. He's watched the documentary film you and your friends produced more times than I can count."

"That's nice to hear. If he doesn't already have one, I'll have to send you home with a copy of my favorite novel, *Confederate Gold and Silver*. It's a story about the steps we took to uncover the lost treasury. If he's as passionate about the Civil War as you say he is, I'm sure he'll enjoy reading it."

"Thank you, but that's not necessary. He already has two or three copies. He pulls one out each time he watches that documentary."

"So what's the real reason you've come to see me, Robert? You haven't travelled all this way just to rehash the story about the Confederate treasury, or have you?" Paul asked, glancing at the black valise sitting next to Regan.

"Actually, I have." Looking at Bobby Ray, Regan asked if he was good with him opening his valise. As he asked the question, Regan took the liberty of placing the valise on his lap. "Am I correct in thinking it's safe to open this now?"

"You're good." Focused on his valise, Regan failed to notice Bobby Ray's left hand slowly making its way closer to his Sig.

As the valise was being opened, Regan told Paul and Bobby Ray one more interesting piece of information about his employer. "While he's visited many of the more significant Civil War battlefields at least five or six times, watched the movie *Gettysburg* a dozen times or more, and read at least several hundred books on the war, his pride and joy is his collection of Civil War artifacts. Without a hint of embellishment on my part, it's probably the best private collection of Civil War memorabilia in the entire country, if not the world. There are many museums whose collections aren't nearly as good as his."

"What's he own besides a bunch of muskets and some canteens?" Paul asked, growing more and more curious about Regan's employer. "Let me put it this way, what's he consider to be his five best pieces?" What he was told caused Paul to become even more curious about the reason behind Regan's visit.

"As Civil War buffs, I expect the two of you are going to be extremely envious of the artifacts in his collection. On the other hand, you might be disappointed to learn these pieces are in a private collection and not in a museum for others to see." As he answered Paul's question, Regan rested his arms on top of his valise. It was done to convey the importance of the contents inside his valise. "His pride and joy is an early draft of President Lincoln's Gettysburg Address. It's not the version we're all familiar with, but it's pretty damn close. When it was purchased at an auction a few years ago, my employer was told Lincoln had written that version during his train ride from Washington to Gettysburg. However, if you know anything about the five versions of his speech that Lincoln wrote, the one my employer owns was likely written in Washington, D.C. before the president set foot on any train."

"I'm glad you clarified that point," Paul said, well aware of the poignant, but inaccurate story concerning Lincoln working on his speech as he travelled to Gettysburg for the dedication ceremony. "Most of the original versions which still exist are worded slightly differently than the one we were taught. Which version does your employer own?"

"It's a version which is identical to the one most people refer to as the Hay Copy. The only thing that's not well known is that Lincoln gave John Hay two identical copies for some reason. I'm sure you know this, but Mr. Hay served as Lincoln's personal secretary; he was a trusted assistant for many years. He later went on to serve as Secretary of State under Presidents William McKinley and Theodore Roosevelt."

Stunned by the story Regan was telling them, Paul and Bobby Ray sat quiet as they waited for him to continue.

"Because it was penned by Lincoln himself, when you read this early draft it's easy to see the words that were scratched out and the ones he inserted in their place. Even though it's not the final version, it's a pretty impressive piece. While we all know the significance this document has in American history, and while my employer purchased it knowing it was not the version we've all studied in school, he purchased it because at the very end it bears a simple signature. That signature reads, *A. Lincoln*."

"*What!*" Paul shrieked, oblivious to the diner's other customers. "How much did he pay for that?" A fervent admirer of Lincoln's presidency, Paul was surprised to learn such an important document existed in someone's private collection.

"It was purchased at an auction in New York City back in 2018. It's not as valuable as the version on display inside the White House, but it still cost my employer a bunch of money. The purchase price ended up being higher than anyone expected, but he was bidding against three other wealthy individuals who collect everything there is that's associated with President Lincoln. Each of them was determined to outbid the competition."

"How much?"

"Three point eight million."

"That's crazy," Bobby Ray said, looking to see how his friend had reacted after hearing the price of the winning bid. "I'm hoping he had someone verify its authenticity before forking over that kind of dough."

"It came with its own set of papers, but my employer had his own experts inspect the document before the sale went through. They verified Lincoln's signature, the age of the paper it was written on, and several other details. In the end, it's a version President Lincoln wrote as he fine-tuned his speech. Believe me, it's real."

"Have you seen it yourself?" Bobby Ray asked, nearly as excited as his friend after learning of this historic document.

Nodding his head as he looked at the smiles displayed on the faces of his companions, Regan said, "I've not only seen it, but I've been fortunate enough to have held it; several times, in fact. You can't help feeling the excitement that comes over you as you hold this single sheet of paper. It's a piece of American history that cannot be replaced."

"You've told us the purchase price, so what's it worth?"

"I'm sorry, Bobby Ray, I'm not allowed to discuss that. The fact that this artifact was authored by one of the nation's most revered presidents as a means of honoring those brave men who perished during one of the war's most epic battles makes it worth a great deal of money. While some people consider it nothing more than a working copy, it's a working copy signed by President Lincoln. I'm sorry, but that's all I can say about it."

Impressed by what he heard, Bobby Ray let out a long soft whistle.

"Another exquisite piece my employer owns is one of General JEB Stuart's saddles. It's not the one he was sitting in when he was mortally wounded at Yellow Tavern, but it's one he owned. Just like the artifact we've been speaking about, it's been inspected, examined, and looked at by people far more knowledgeable about the war than my employer. Believe me; if he purchased it, it's real."

"Impressive." Paul offered.

"I'd have to say the other three pieces he's fond of are a piece of furniture from the parlor of Wilmer McLean, a pistol once owned by Major General Phillip Sheridan, and a pair of uniform pants which belonged to General George Custer. My employer has never been able to verify that Custer ever wore them into battle, but they were his. From the name stitched inside the waistband, there's no doubt they were his."

"He owns a piece of furniture from the parlor where General Ulysses S. Grant and General Robert E. Lee met to work out the terms of Lee's surrender? You're telling us he owns an actual piece of furniture from McLean's home in Appomattox? What . . . what kind of piece is it?" Paul asked, stunned that an ordinary citizen was the owner of a piece of McLean's furniture. While knowing most Civil War buffs knew that a great deal of furniture had been purchased from Wilmer McLean in the wake of this historic event, Paul never expected to learn that Regan's employer owned such a piece.

"A wooden table. A small non-descript end table that was in the parlor when the surrender was signed. It's not in the best condition, but the fact it was present when the surrender took place causes it to be worth a great deal of money. I'm sure you know this, but many of Grant's staff realized the significance of the moment and wanted to own a piece of history. History has recorded the fact that a few of those Union officers paid McLean a good deal of money to own a piece of furniture from that historic meeting. I have to assume many of those pieces were handed down to the generations that followed." From their excited looks, Regan knew he had gotten Paul and Bobby Ray's attention.

"Being Civil War buffs, I'm sure you know the story about Wilmer McLean, correct?" Regan asked, testing Paul and Bobby Ray's knowledge of a rather obscure figure from the war.

"Sure do," Paul responded. "It ranks right up there with the circumstances involving General Robert Anderson. At the start of the war, Anderson was the Union officer in command at Fort Sumter. He was also the one who lowered the flag when the fort surrendered in 1861. Years later, in April, 1865, he was the officer who raised the American flag after the South surrendered. The fascinating story involving Wilmer McLean begins with the war basically starting on his property in Manassas, Virginia, and then ending on his property in Appomattox, Virginia, where he and his family had moved. That story is just as captivating as Anderson's; maybe even more so because of the players involved at Appomattox Court House. The fact that McLean tried protecting his family by moving away from the war's theater to having it end a few years later on the property where they had moved is quite remarkable."

"Very good," Regan said, nodding his head as Paul added a few more bits of information to his comments. While aware of another historical artifact his employer had in his collection, one nearly as valuable as the document containing Lincoln's signature,

Regan, for now, choose to ignore its existence. "Those pieces we just spoke about represent some of my employer's finest artifacts. However, a recent piece he's just purchased at an auction has now gotten his full attention."

"What's that?" Bobby Ray asked, already impressed by the artifacts he and Paul had been told about.

Opening his valise, Regan, someone who also dabbled in Civil War artifacts, showed Paul a photograph of the artifact his employer had recently purchased. As Bobby Ray slid into the booth next to him, Paul began studying a photograph of an old wooden chest. As he did, his investigative instincts took over. Taking his time, he carefully inspected the image by adjusting its angle as he held it up to the light inside his booth. Several minutes went by before Paul handed the photograph to Bobby Ray so his friend could have a better look. As Bobby Ray stared at the photograph, Paul asked Regan several questions.

"Photographs don't always tell you everything you need to know, but from what little I can tell this chest appears to be a nice piece. Did this belong to anyone famous?"

"Not in the normal context, but once you learn more about it you'll likely agree it was owned by someone famous. By no means was he a general or a well-known officer or even a politician who history remembers for his role in the war, but, if I present my case well enough, this person will soon be talked about for years to come. For now, there's a pretty good chance neither of you have ever heard his name being mentioned."

"You're alluding to the fact that this chest was owned by someone who served in the Civil War. Has anyone verified who the owner was?" Paul asked as he took another brief look at the photograph Bobby Ray had set down.

"Like I said earlier, my employer is very rich. It's an authentic Civil War piece; that's not the issue."

"I understand that point," Paul replied, "but often times an artifact's value has more to do with who the person was that owned it than it has to do with the time period it came from. In the case of certain inventions, say a repeating rifle . . . its value comes from the name of the person who invented it." Remaining silent for several moments as Bobby Ray continued to study the photograph, Paul processed what he had seen and what little he had been told about the chest. What he said next caused Regan to realize his employer had selected the right person.

"My guess is while this chest is obviously worth a few bucks, what was in it is likely worth a whole lot more." As he finished speaking, Paul noticed the smile forming in the corners of Regan's mouth. "If that's the case, what was it that your employer found?"

Reaching inside his valise, Regan pulled out a large manila envelope; one large enough to hold a full sheet of paper without it having to be folded. "Before I show you this, inside the lid of this chest the date 1861 has been burned into the wood. It was likely done by whoever made it. This piece of paper I'm about to show you is one of several that were discovered inside the chest less than four months ago. We have no way of knowing how many people have owned this chest, but we do know two things. We're fairly certain we know who the first owner was and now we know who the current owner is. This piece of paper, while it's not absolute proof of who the first owner was it pretty much tells us that person's name." What Regan told them intrigued Paul and Bobby Ray. It also lowered Bobby

Ray's concerns about Regan being interested in harming his friend.

"Is that person the same individual who owned the chest? If he was, he's probably the one who wrote whatever's on that piece of paper you keep referring to. The one you've yet to show us." Bobby Ray said, his mind busy performing some quick calculations.

"That's correct. We believe the first owner was the same person who authored what I'm about to show you."

"Does that piece of paper have a date on it? And, if it does, what is it?"

"1865."

Trying his best to comprehend what Regan was telling them, Bobby Ray briefly struggled with the sequence of events they had been told about. Moments later, pointing to the envelope Regan was holding, he sought a degree of confirmation. "You're telling us the person who owned this chest is likely the same person who wrote whatever's on the piece of paper inside that envelope you're holding? You're also telling us you believe he's the one who placed it inside the chest sometime in 1865. And, despite the number of times the chest has likely been looked through, over what . . . the past one hundred and fifty-four years or so, that sheet of paper . . . and maybe some others like it have just been found. How could that be?"

"Because they were hidden inside a secret compartment." Paul said, his eyes staring intently at Regan as he waited for his response.

Shifting his focus from Bobby Ray to Paul, Regan smiled after hearing what Paul had said. "Mr. Waring, you've lived up to your reputation quite nicely. I'm rather impressed as that's a very good guess."

"I never guess, Robert." Paul said matter-of-factly as his stare shifted to the envelope his guest was holding. "Are you going to show us what was found inside the chest or are we going to sit here all morning testing each other's knowledge on the Civil War?"

"Before you see what's inside this envelope, let me ask you one last question." Regan said, prolonging Paul and Bobby Ray's interest in inspecting the item he had pulled from his valise. "Does the name Captain Noah Howard mean anything to you?"

Leaning against the back of his seat, Paul's eyes blinked twice as he heard Howard's name being mentioned. Looking at Bobby Ray, he could see the wheels turning inside his friend's head as they both tried recalling what they had learned about Howard. Having done more research than Bobby Ray during their hunt for the Confederate treasury, Paul easily recalled a name most Civil War buffs had never heard or even read about. It was also a name few historians had spent much time researching.

"While Captain Judiah Francis has remained the focus of most of my efforts as I continue to research the legend surrounding the Confederate treasury, Captain Howard's name has also been linked with that same legend."

"Very good," Regan replied, taking his first sip of coffee. "Please, go on."

"I haven't spent much time digging into his background, but the story goes that Howard, who I believe was an officer assigned to the 1st Virginia Volunteer Infantry Regiment, had been selected to escort some of the Confederate treasury out of Richmond around the time President Davis and his cabinet were fleeing south. That part of the treasury, while not as large as the amount Francis was travelling with, was still fairly significant. From the records I've looked at, as Howard and his men were escorting that portion of the treasury they used the same rail line Davis had used."

"I'm impressed," Regan offered, softly clapping his hands as a way of applauding Paul's knowledge of a Civil War figure most people had never heard of.

Ignoring Regan's praise, Paul continued on with what he had learned. "Like I said, I haven't finished my research, but I believe Howard and one other officer had been charged with moving smaller portions of the treasury than Francis. While my friends and I found the bulk of it, we don't believe the gold and silver Howard was escorting has ever been found. From what I've learned, the first shipment likely made it to its destination, but the other two wound up being lost due to problems that confronted the men protecting the money. That's why my research is still an on-going project. I refuse to give up until it's all been found."

"Is that what this piece of paper is all about?" Bobby Ray asked as his eyes locked on the envelope Regan was holding.

"Precisely." Regan replied, handing the envelope to Paul to open.

While making sure his hands were clean, Paul paused before removing the single sheet of paper the envelope contained. "I'm sure you would have said something if this wasn't the case, but this is a copy, correct?" Not wanting to damage anything of historical significance, Paul sought Regan's assurance on what the envelope contained.

"It's a copy of a copy. Thank you for your concern, but it's just a copy." Regan replied, closing his valise so neither Paul nor Bobby Ray could see inside it.

Setting the sheet of paper on the table in front of him so Bobby Ray could view it at the same time, Paul carefully began examining the document Regan's employer had recently discovered. Unlike Bobby Ray, Paul studied the copy itself for any clues or defects before reading what had been written. The first detail he took notice of was the date and location where it had been written. Both caused him to pay particular attention to the words that followed.

"Do you and your boss really believe Howard was the person responsible for what's been written?" Bobby Ray asked, looking at Regan for a brief moment before returning his attention to the document Paul was slowly reading. "And, if you do, why do you believe he was the one who authored it?"

"I appreciate your questions, Bobby Ray, but seeing it was found inside a hidden compartment of a chest bearing the same initials as the person who we've been speaking about, I think it's safe to assume Howard was the person who wrote it. I'm not sure if you missed it or not, and I'm not being a wise guy by bringing this up, but it appears when Howard finished he even signed his name to it. The bottom of the page is not as clear as the rest of the document, but if you take a closer look you'll see he signed his name after making this entry. From our review, it's the only entry he ever signed."

Regan's accidental slip of the tongue did not go unnoticed as Paul finished reading the document for the second time. "Robert, Bobby Ray and I don't operate under assumptions. The initials engraved on the front of the chest, while they match the person we've been speaking about, neither they nor the fact that someone signed this document using Howard's name verifies he actually wrote this or, for that matter, even signed it."

"From your former line of work, I guess that's a fair assumption to make." Aware that Paul had raised several valid points, Regan slumped against his side of the booth as he mulled them over.

"From what you've told us, it sounds as if you and your boss haven't taken anything for granted when it comes to authenticating the history of the artifacts in his collection. However, with that being said, I still believe there's some work left to do with this document. That may also hold true for the chest."

"Perhaps you're right." Regan admitted, taking another sip of coffee.

Taking note of Regan's unexpected response, Paul continued with a few other thoughts. "The fact that this document was allegedly signed by Howard and that it was found inside a hidden compartment inside a chest bearing the same initials as the person who wrote it, those are what Bobby Ray and I call clues. They're all associated with the smoking gun; in this case, a wooden chest dating back to the time of the Civil War."

Nodding his head, Regan remained silent as Paul continued.

"Robert," Paul said, noticing Regan's right hand resting on top of his valise, "before we talk about the contents of this document, it's my opinion this wasn't the only sheet of paper your employer found inside that chest. After seeing how this document was written, which, in my opinion, offers a fair amount of proof that Howard had been escorting a portion of the Confederate treasury, I believe this secret compartment likely held his journal or his diary. From what little you've told us, I also believe this may have been one of his last entries. In fact, I wouldn't be surprised if you told us this had been his final entry."

Sitting quietly, Paul waited for Regan to respond to his comment about the possibility of a journal being hidden inside the secret compartment.

Opening his valise with a small degree of fanfare after donning a pair of white cloth gloves he removed from inside his jacket, Regan held up a large clear plastic bag. It was very similar to the type Paul and Bobby Ray had used when seizing evidence from the many crime scenes they had worked. Sealed shut by way of a double seal running across the top of the bag, both cops easily noticed the item it held. Inside was a brownish leather-bound journal. Frayed around three of its corners, and with a spine that age had caused to peel apart in several locations, Howard's journal had been the artifact hidden inside the secret compartment. Hidden for nearly one hundred and sixty years, it had been there since the time of Howard's death. Holding up the plastic bag even higher, Regan said, "This represents another remarkable guess on your part, Mr. Waring."

Smiling as he and Bobby Ray were handed gloves similar to the kind Regan had donned, Paul carefully took hold of the frayed journal. Setting the journal down after removing it from the layer of protection Regan had placed it in, he said, "As I mentioned before, I never guess when it comes to matters like this."

As he had done minutes earlier with the single sheet of paper, Paul gave the journal a brief visual inspection. As his friend carefully inspected the journal's exterior, Bobby Ray shook his head as he looked at Regan. "You'll soon learn that this here friend of mine is a pretty amazing guy. I can't explain it, and on most occasions neither can he, but he's never wrong. There's something about this guy that just lets him see things that you and I can't." As Bobby Ray had spoken, he did so in a far friendlier manner than he displayed several minutes earlier. Like Paul, he began to feel far more at ease with their unexpected guest.

"I'm beginning to see that." Regan said, concurring with Bobby Ray's statement concerning Paul's unusual talent.

As Paul carefully inspected a few of the other entries Howard had written, Bobby Ray asked Regan about the contents of the entry they had been shown. In doing so, he spoke far less eloquently than Regan. "You and your boss, you both believe Howard wrote this entry about that cave in?"

"Yes, we do. My employer has had some preliminary work done on Captain Howard's background. That investigative work, as brief as it may be, points to Howard being in Richmond during the time Petersburg fell to the Union Army. This investigation has also documented the fact that he and several other soldiers had boarded a train which appeared to have been headed to Columbia, South Carolina. The manifest that was found showed he was listed as being responsible for several crates, barrels, and wagons that were on the train. From what little I know about your Captain Francis, he was responsible for pretty much the same type of goods when he and his men left Richmond."

"What about these rifles he wrote about?" Bobby Ray asked, searching the document Howard had written for the reference regarding the rifles.

"When the manifest was reviewed it showed several crates of rifles had been loaded on the same train we know Howard was on. Where these rifles came from, or if Howard was the person responsible for them, those are questions I don't have the answers to at this time. But seeing where they ended up, I believe it's a safe bet to assume he was the person responsible for moving them further south."

"How much gold and silver do you think was on that train?" Bobby Ray asked, continuing with a series of questions he was peppering Regan with. While this was taking place, Paul continued with his inspection of the exterior of Howard's journal. As he often did when confronted with an unexpected piece of evidence, Paul took his time examining the artifact he was now holding.

"Neither my employer nor I have any idea how much gold was on that train. But knowing the state of the Confederate economy near the end of the war, I would doubt it was anywhere near what you and Paul have already found. If Howard was escorting a portion of the treasury like we believe, I'm guessing the train may have been carrying somewhere in the neighborhood of a few hundred thousand dollars of precious assets . . . maybe close to a million, but not much more than that."

Like he had done earlier, Bobby Ray let out a soft whistle over the amount of money Regan had mentioned. "If his train was headed south like you believe, do you have any thoughts on where that money was supposed to end up?"

"Not really," Regan admitted. "What I have in my head is nothing more than speculation on my part, but I admit that may be influenced by some of the reading I've recently been doing regarding the legend of the missing treasury."

Looking up from the journal he had been inspecting, Paul chimed in with his own thoughts on where Howard's part of the treasury had likely been headed. "When Richmond was evacuated, all hope was lost for the Confederacy. To this day, there are still a few die-hard Confederate sympathizers who can't accept the fact that the war was over, but they're just kidding themselves. The last few days of the war were nothing more than two exhausted armies senselessly losing more men as the armies clashed across the Virginia countryside. If this train was headed south like you believe, and if President Davis and members of his cabinet were on a similar train around the same time period, I'm thinking Davis, Treasury Secretary George Trenholm, and maybe a few others, planned on using whatever money was available to form a new Confederate government in Texas . . . or maybe Mexico. They may have been headed south, but I believe Davis wasn't interested in surrendering. Unlike General Lee, he wanted the fighting to continue, so maybe his plan was to fund a form of guerilla warfare. Lee, however, knew it was time for the country to start healing, so he refused to prolong the hostilities. As we know, Davis didn't subscribe to that position."

Paul's answer surprised Regan. "You really think that's what they had planned on using it for?"

"Yes, I do. And so do a lot of historians and Civil War experts who are far more knowledgeable about the war than I am. There's quite a bit of documentation that exists to support my interpretation of what this money was going to be used for."

As Paul and Regan briefly traded some ideas and thoughts regarding a few other entries Howard had written, Bobby Ray suddenly realized the purpose behind Regan's visit. It was something his friend had already figured out. After running that thought through his head for several minutes, Bobby Ray raised the issue surrounding Regan's visit.

194 | PETER WARREN

"Besides your unexpected visit, Robert, from the way you've phrased a few points, especially the part about the incomplete investigation into Howard's background that your boss paid to have done, I believe I know the purpose of your visit. The way you've presented that page from Howard's journal, as well as the journal itself, tells me my hunch is probably correct."

Smiling in Bobby Ray's direction, Regan said, "Well, let's see if you're as good as your friend. Let's hear it."

"Not so fast . . . let's hold on a minute." Bobby Ray said, still putting some of the pieces together for why Regan had travelled as far as he had when he could have simply spoken to Paul over the phone. "I have one other reason for what's behind your visit."

"What's that?" Regan asked, adjusting how he was seated inside the booth so he faced Bobby Ray.

"The fact that you haven't really spoken much about the gold and silver Howard supposedly placed inside that cave is rather odd. Seeing how far you've travelled, I thought you would have talked more about it. I'm not sure how Paul feels about this, but I find that rather odd. The absence of any conversation on your part also seems to indicate you have no idea of where that cave is located. If Howard was telling the truth when he wrote about his men being killed when that cave collapsed, it's caused me to believe you have no idea what's buried under all that rock and dirt. That's if anything of value was ever inside either of those caves." As Bobby Ray had spoken, Paul listened attentively as his friend connected all of the bits of information behind Regan's visit. While his face reflected his appreciation for what Bobby Ray had put together, Regan's remained rather stoic.

"I have one more question. I mean no disrespect when I ask this, but each time you refer to your boss you use the term employer. He's your boss; why not simply call him that?" Bobby Ray asked.

"Mr. Church . . ." Regan said, immediately regretting the unintentional release of his employer's name. Quickly recovering, he tried covering up his gaffe by adding, "My employer is someone I have the utmost respect for. He's a wealthy, intelligent person who I admire a great deal. Over the ten years that I've worked for him, he's treated me like a son so that's why I refer to him as my employer. The term *boss* seems less respectful than the one I use. And until we conclude our conversation, I've been instructed to protect his identity."

Quickly recognizing the name he heard, Bobby Ray excitedly asked, "You work for Simon Church . . . *the Simon Church?* The owner of Church Industries in Texas? What's he, the richest man on the entire planet?" As he spoke, a wide and astonished look appeared across the veteran cop's face.

"Yes, I do." Regan replied. As he answered Bobby Ray's question, a look of embarrassment creased Regan's face as he knew he had accidently revealed his employer's name.

25

After answering a few additional questions regarding Simon Church's background, including how it felt to be working for one of the richest men in the world, Regan managed to return the conversation to why he had sought Paul out. He had barely started to speak when Paul interrupted him.

"Robert, the questions and answers I've been listening to regarding Mr. Church's background are all interesting bits of information, but let's get down to why you're here. What is it that he wants from us?"

"Well, he thought . . ."

"Correct me if I'm wrong, but you're here because Mr. Church wants to know if we might be interested in locating this other portion of the Confederate treasury. That's why you've come to see us, isn't it?"

Frustrated over the conversation not going as he had planned, Regan spoke softly as he answered Paul's question. "Yes. That's part of the reason behind my visit." Staring at the person he was speaking with, Regan waited to see if Paul had figured out the rest of the reason for his visit.

Sliding Howard's journal towards Bobby Ray, the expression on Paul's face gave little indication that he had already surmised the purpose behind Regan's visit. "I'm not someone who really bets on things like this, but I think it's safe to assume Mr. Church wants to hire us because he knows we're not like a lot of other people; meaning we're not going to cheat him out of anything we find. I'm also of the opinion he sent you here due to the success we had in finding the millions of dollars in gold and silver Captain Francis had been escorting."

"Correct on both accounts." Regan said succinctly.

"Besides expecting us to hunt for the gold and silver Howard was responsible for, Mr. Church likely wants us to learn as much as we can about Howard's career in the Confederate Army, correct?"

"Correct, again."

Nodding his head at the answer he was given, Paul smiled as he glanced at Bobby Ray. What the retired state trooper said next was even a surprise to his friend.

"Seeing that I'm pretty much retired from police work these days, I may be interested in working with Mr. Church if he agrees to some of my requests. I guess it also comes down to whether or not he, or you, will answer a few of my questions."

"Fair enough," Regan replied, having already expected a response similar to the one he received.

"First question, Robert. Say my friends and I get lucky, what . . ."

"Your friends?" Bobby Ray said, interrupting the question Paul was asking. "Are you expecting me to help you again?"

"Absolutely," Paul replied, smiling at his friend as he continued with his first question. "What does Mr. Church plan on doing with this part of the treasury if we get lucky enough to find it?"

Producing a notarized letter from his valise, Regan handed it to Paul. "Just as you and your friends have done with the gold and silver you found, that letter you're reading informs you Mr. Church has no intention of keeping anything more than a few coins. He just wants a few of them for his collection. Whatever else you recover he intends on donating to schools or museums or to whomever the authorities suggest."

"That's reassuring," Bobby Ray admitted, setting Howard's journal on the seat next to him. "He's got enough dough already, so I'm pleased to learn he's not planning on hoarding it for himself."

"Once you meet him, you'll see he's not that type of person, Bobby Ray. You may find this hard to believe, but he's really down-to-earth; he knows how well off he is, so he's not the type to sit around all day counting his money. He's also someone who keeps himself busy by serving on the boards of several charities. And, as you just heard me say, if you get lucky enough to find some of this missing money, Mr. Church will be donating the majority of it to schools and museums across the country."

Hearing Simon Church, a billionaire several times over, being described as a down-to-earth person caused Paul to chuckle over that description. It was not how he pictured people with that kind of money.

"The majority of it?" Bobby Ray asked.

"Mr. Church may be a Civil War enthusiast, but he's also an astute businessman. Based on the amount of money he expects to spend in financing this search, Mr. Church believes he's entitled to some kind of a return on his investment. It may mean some of the artifacts will end up being sold so he can recoup a portion of the costs, or it may come in the form of a tax break, but I know he's looking forward to adding a few coins to his collection of Civil War memorabilia. You may not agree with this, but I believe his expectations are far different than most investors. He's certainly not looking to increase his wealth from anything that's found. If this helps with your decision as to whether you decide to work for Mr. Church or not, he's already made plans to donate his entire collection to the University of South Carolina and the Confederate Relic Room in Columbia, South Carolina, after he passes. If you need to see those documents, I can show them to you at another time."

"Please." Paul replied rather coolly, his response clearly indicating the need to see some form of documentation to support Regan's statement. He hoped the documentation would also reveal what the actual motive was for Simon Church to be willing to assume the cost of financing this search. For now, Paul believed there was more to Regan's statement than just his employer's interest in adding a few old coins to his collection of Civil War artifacts.

"So where do you and Mr. Church believe this money was hidden?" Bobby Ray asked, interjecting himself back into the conversation. "A couple of entries in Howard's journal seem to refer to a few rivers he crossed before the incident at the cave, but that's not much to go on if you're trying to pinpoint the exact location of this set of caves you and Mr. Church seem to be interested in. Howard also wrote about travelling in and around the area near Moncks Corner, but that was another reference that was very vague. Like several other locations he wrote about, the reference to Moncks Corner needs to be looked at very closely."

"We believe it's hidden here in South Carolina. With the exception of some of those entries you've referred to, Mr. Church doesn't have much to base his feelings on. However, he fervently believes this part of the treasury has been hidden not far from Moncks Corner." Prepared to address any issue that was raised, Regan's response was given with little hesitation.

"I'm not trying to be rude, but Mr. Church's opinion as to where this money has been hidden isn't enough for anyone to start searching for whatever Howard may have had in his possession. If it was me, I wouldn't necessarily need absolute proof of where it was, but I'd need more than someone's hunch before I committed my resources." As he finished speaking, Paul rested his back against the seat he was sitting on. In continuing, he broke his own rule about being too formal in how he and the others addressed each other. "Mr. Regan, let's say we narrow down the places where this money might be hidden. To move this conversation along, let's say we eliminate all but one or two locations. If that happens, then we'd have to take your plan a step further. What makes you think whoever owns that property is going to be willing to let us do any digging there? Bobby Ray and I got lucky in North Carolina when we were looking for the first part of the missing treasury. I say that because we met this nice fella by the name of Duke Johnson who allowed us to do whatever it took to find what we were looking for. We may not be so lucky this time." As he waited for Regan to answer his question, Paul noticed Bobby Ray taking a long sip of the soft drink Betty had brought him. It was the first of several he drank nearly every day.

"As I've mentioned, Mr. Church is a very wealthy individual. No matter what the cost is to get us on that piece of property, he will gladly pay it. I certainly have no intention of portraying him as a bully, but Mr. Church always gets what he wants. He doesn't have the kind of money he has from being a poor negotiator. And, just so you two law enforcement professionals know, he's *always* honest in his dealings with others. Whether it's the owner of this piece of property we're talking about or either of you, he's always fair with the people he's working with."

"Let's hope so, because Bobby Ray and I will have no problem reminding you of that statement if Mr. Church tries pulling a fast one."

After several minutes of discussing the need to conduct as much research as possible, as well as the possibility of having to secure historical and work permits before planting any shovels in the ground, Bobby Ray asked Regan one last question. He did so after realizing how badly Simon Church wanted this part of the Confederate treasury to be found.

"Robert, your rich boss, he isn't expecting this work to be done for free, is he? While Paul and I are big time into the Civil War as much as Mr. Church is, neither of us work for free."

Smiling at Bobby Ray's expectation of a big payday, Regan chose to look at the person he had come to see as he answered the question. "Paul, my employer intends to compensate you quite nicely for your efforts. As he does with most independent contractors he hires, he'll require you to sign a non-disclosure agreement. Basically that means you can't tell anyone about this project; nor can you identify in any way the name of the person who's providing the funding. That's especially true when it comes to dealing with the media. This agreement will prohibit you from talking about this project for ten years. A separate personal services agreement will also stipulate that during the time of your employment you will not be allowed to work on any other historical projects without Mr. Church's written consent. If he should pass away during your period of employment, the non-disclosure agreement and the personal services agreement both go away. As you have likely figured out, he's a person who enjoys his privacy; hence the two agreements I've been referring to. For now, he'll insist you sign both of them before conducting any work."

As someone who disliked dealing with the media, the part Regan mentioned about not being able to comment on any work he was conducting was one Paul had no issue with.

"I'm not going to give you my final commitment today, Robert, but I'm intrigued enough to discuss it further with Bobby Ray and my wife. Put your proposal down on paper and once I've had a chance to meet with Mr. Church I'm sure we can come to some sort of an agreement on a compensation package. Fair enough?"

"Paul, as far as I'm concerned that's fair enough." Regan replied, reaching across the booth to shake hands with one of Simon Church's future employees.

"Wait a minute! Not so fast there, Robert!" Bobby Ray exclaimed, upset at what Paul had suggested. "Let's talk compensation for a minute or two. What's Church paying us?"

Laughing at Bobby Ray's vested interest, Regan chuckled as he answered the question. "Well, to start with, at this time *you* aren't getting a dime. I was sent here to meet with Paul so I could determine his level of interest. But seeing that you two are a team, I'm sure Mr. Church will compensate you accordingly."

"What's *accordingly* worth these days?"

"Mr. Church has authorized me to offer Paul a salary of one hundred thousand dollars for the balance of the year. That's a fair amount of money for roughly six months of work."

"That's not bad," Bobby Ray admitted, nodding his head in Paul's direction.

"He's told me that if it becomes necessary he would be willing to extend these agreements for another six months. After that, he and I would have to sit down and decide whether it's to his benefit to continue with this project. However, as an added bonus, if the gold and silver is found within the first year of Paul's contract, Mr. Church will pay him a finder's fee of five percent for everything he recovers. That fee will be based on the value placed on the recovered artifacts by two or three experts he hires."

Regan's comments caused Paul to smile at how the offer had been structured. "That's a generous offer, so don't take this the wrong way but I have no way of knowing how Mr. Church operates. I'm somewhat embarrassed about saying this as money really means very little to me. Ask anyone who knows me, I'm not impressed by how much or how little anyone has; that's just how I'm wired. However, if he's willing to pay me an additional bonus based on what I find, then one of those experts is going to be someone I select. Again, don't get upset over this, but I need to protect my interest in this matter."

Not expecting the person he was talking with to be as savvy as he was, Regan was momentarily caught off-guard by the demand Paul had made. "Well . . . I'll have to talk with Mr. Church about that before I can agree to it, but I'm sure he'll understand your point. I'll have to get back to you on that in a day or two."

"Sounds fair. But just to be clear, that fee does include the value of those rifles you've talked about?" Bobby Ray asked, testing Church's generosity.

"Gold, silver, rifles . . . it doesn't matter. As long as it's Civil War related, the bonus will be paid. I'll just have to obtain Mr. Church's permission regarding Paul's request."

"Again, I'm not trying to come across as being greedy, but it's not a request. Whether it's referred to as a condition or a demand or simply as a request, I'm selecting one of the three appraisers or there's no deal." Without flinching, Paul stood his ground regarding how many appraisers would be examining whatever artifacts he and his team recovered.

"You still haven't answered my question. What's *accordingly* worth these days?"

Staring straight ahead as he thought about Bobby Ray's question, Regan, as he placed Howard's journal back inside this valise, answered the veteran investigator's question. "As I said, I'm quite sure Mr. Church would be willing to compensate you for your services. When I get back to Texas, I'll recommend he pay you a salary of seventy-five thousand dollars for the same period of time as Paul's contract calls for. I'll work out the details, but Mr. Church will certainly cover any expenses you both incur."

"What kind of bonus would he be inclined to pay Paul's right-hand man?" Nearing retirement, Bobby Ray was looking to be compensated for his skills and talents, and for being Paul's best friend.

"One percent. No more, no less. Take it or leave it. Just do yourself a favor when you meet Mr. Church, don't bring up the issue of money and bonuses. You may find this hard to believe, but he finds that kind of talk rather displeasing."

Briefly giving thought to Regan's offer, Bobby Ray, without consulting Paul, told their guest how he felt. "OK, Robert, setup a meeting with Mr. Church. Tell us when and where, and we'll be there. On Mr. Church's dime, of course, but we'll be there."

With their business soon concluded, Robert Regan left to get word to his employer that Paul had agreed in principle to start the search for another portion of the Confederate treasury.

At least in Bobby Ray's opinion he had.

<u>26</u>

Four days after meeting at the Waccamaw Diner, Robert Regan called Paul to work out a convenient time to meet with Simon Church. Two days earlier, after some frank discussions with Donna, Paul advised Regan he was willing to go to work to try and find the valuable assets Captain Howard had hidden inside a cave not far from Moncks Corner.

"Mr. Church has business in Savannah next Tuesday with two of his partners regarding a rather large acquisition they're about to close on. After his meeting he'll be flying into Hilton Head to see one of his cousins, and to play some golf for a few days. Any chance you and Bobby Ray can get down there on Wednesday; he'd like to have a day or two to talk business with you."

"Shouldn't be a problem for me, but I'll have to check with Bobby Ray on that." Paul said, checking the calendar on his phone to make sure he had not forgotten about any previous commitments.

"That's great," Regan replied, pleased by Paul's answer. "From the brief conversation we had at the diner last week, I know both of you play some golf so bring your clubs with you. Mr. Church has asked me to setup a tee time so the three of you can get to know each other. Along with members of his security team, I'll be there as well, but as a non-golfer. I'm good at many things, but golf isn't one of them."

"Tell your boss to make sure he stands behind me when I'm swinging," Paul said, joking about his golfing skills. "I'm actually not that bad, but my ball sometimes seems to find a tree or two during each round. I don't want Mr. Church getting hurt due to my lack of talent."

Paul's comments made Regan laugh. "Listen, I'll deny I ever told you this, but make sure you do the same when the old fella pulls out his sticks. He loves the game, but he's pretty horrible."

Just as Regan had done, Paul laughed at the warning he was given. "Good to know, thanks."

"Mr. Church is a member of the Port Royal Golf Club. It's right there on the island. He'll be fairly busy on Wednesday after he arrives, so I'll setup a tee time for around 10:00 the following morning. I'll also reserve a suite for you and Bobby Ray at the Westin Hilton; it's a four-star resort that's less than five minutes from the golf course."

"Sounds fancy." Paul said.

"It's a very nice hotel. Mr. Church does a fair amount of business there when he's in town, so you'll be well taken care of by the staff. I'll make the reservation under your name. I'll reserve the suite until the end of the week in case you decide to stay an extra day or two."

"I've never stayed there, but I know where the hotel is located. Bobby Ray and I visited the island a couple of years ago with our wives."

Paul's comment caused Regan to realize he had forgotten to address one important detail. "Both of you are welcome to bring your wives along if you wish. In fact, Mr. Church asked me to make sure I mentioned that to you. When you arrive, ask for Andre . . . he's one of the managers. He'll see to it that your needs are taken care of."

"Will do. Thanks for arranging all of this." Paul said, growing more impressed with the arrangements Regan was addressing.

"Incidentals, food, drinks . . . whatever you need, just charge them to your room. I'll take care of the bill after your visit is over with."

"Sounds good. See you next week."

"Paul, just one more thing. After you finish playing golf, Mr. Church would like you and Bobby Ray to join him for a working lunch right there at the club. I can't tell you how long it will last, but he tends to spend a great deal of time going over the logistics of anything he's involved in. I'm just telling you this so you have time to plan some type of activity to keep your wives busy."

"Understood. Thanks."

"Later that evening, Mr. Church would like you and your wives to join him for dinner at his home."

"Will Mrs. Church be joining us?" Paul asked.

After being quiet for several seconds, Regan answered Paul's question. "I'm not sure about that as he hasn't told me. I probably shouldn't be saying this, but Mrs. Regan . . . well, she's a lot younger than he is. He hasn't said anything to me, but I've recently noticed there's some tension brewing between them. No arguments or anything like that, but they've had their share of good days and bad days over the past few weeks. Perhaps it's because Mr. Church hasn't been feeling that well for the past two weeks or so, but somehow they'll manage to get through it. I just thought you should know about this in the event the evening has a few strange twists to it."

"Got it. Please tell Mr. Church we accept his invitation. I'm sure our wives will look forward to meeting him."

As he finished his call, Paul picked up on something Regan had said about Simon Church's health. Sitting down in his kitchen, a thought ran through his mind. "Last week Regan mentioned Church was in good health for someone his age, but today he described him as being under the weather for the past two weeks. What would cause him to describe his health in two different ways?"

Like always, Paul never failed to pick up on a detail that had previously been mentioned. That was especially true when two of Regan's statements conflicted with each other.

27

Arriving early at the Port Royal Golf Club on the morning they were to meet with Simon Church, Paul and Bobby stood in the parking lot admiring the views of the nearby golf course when a golf cart pulled up next to them. The small electric vehicle had barely come to a stop when Bobby Ray opened the trunk to his Chevy Impala.

"Mr. Waring . . . Mr. Jenkins?"

"Yes, that's us." Bobby Ray groaned as he lifted his golf bag out of the trunk. Unlike Paul's, the large cart bag was stuffed with far too many golf balls, tees, and, not surprisingly, an opened bottle of Jack Daniels. Each contributed to the bag being far heavier than it should have been.

"Good morning, I'm Jamir Wallace," the neatly dressed black male said as he shook hands with the two men he had been told to expect. Placing the bags on the back of the golf cart, Wallace directed his guests to have a seat inside the cart. Unlike a traditional golf cart, this version had room for six passengers and just as many golf bags. Often used for a variety of different needs, for the moment it was being used to transport Simon Church's guests back to the clubhouse. Climbing into the cart, Wallace spoke to his passengers. "I work for Mr. Church when he's in town. He and Mr. Regan are inside the clubhouse waiting for you to join them."

"Here's something for your help, Jamir. Thanks for taking care of our bags."

Looking across the front seat as he pulled up to the curb in front of the clubhouse, Jamir waved off the ten dollar bill Bobby Ray held in his hand. "That's not necessary, but I appreciate the gesture. Mr. Church pays very well, so he frowns on me accepting gratuities from his guests."

"Yeah, well, screw him. We both appreciate the help. Have a beer on us." Without another word being said, Bobby Ray slid the bill under the clip located on the steering well. It was normally used to hold a scorecard or other paperwork.

Always early for whatever appointment he had, Paul was not accustomed to others arriving before him. It was a pleasant surprise, and one that set the tone for the rest of the day after learning Simon Church and Regan were already inside the clubhouse.

Reaching out to shake Jamir's hand, Bobby Ray's large hand was swallowed up by one that was even larger. A passionate Civil War buff, Bobby Ray was an even bigger college football fan. Moments later, he watched as Jamir loaded their bags onto the rear of a rather fancy golf cart. "You the same Jamir Wallace that folks in Texas call Big J?"

"That's me," Jamir replied, a wide toothy smile breaking out across his face as he finished securing the two golf bags. Like always, Jamir was pleased at being recognized. Years earlier, his football career had suddenly ended after playing at the University of Texas from 2013 to 2017.

Finishing second in the Heisman Trophy voting in 2016 and 2017, the following season Big J had blown out his knee in only his second start in the National Football League while playing for the Houston Texans. After three surgical procedures failed to stabilize his knee, Big J's promising professional football career had tragically ended before it ever got started.

"Jamir, that was one helluva senior year you had." Bobby Ray said, shaking Jamir's hand for the second time. "What'd you have . . . fifteen hundred or sixteen hundred yards rushing that season and maybe close to eleven hundred receiving yards?" As someone who was often not impressed by most of the celebrities he met during his career, Bobby Ray was taken back by a football player whose career he had closely followed several years earlier.

"Eleven hundred and sixty-six receiving yards to be precise, Mr. Jenkins. I also scored sixteen touchdowns, but most folks don't remember that. My stats were better than the guy who won the Heisman during my senior year, but his Athletic Director used his media staff a lot better than mine did. The guy who beat me out, Cliff Johnson from Auburn, what's he . . . maybe a third-string running back for the Chargers these days. He had a decent college career, but he's not an NFL running back folks are gonna remember." As Jamir spoke, a touch of regret was clearly present in his voice.

Walking back to the golf cart he had been driving, Big J stopped to shake hands with Paul. "I didn't mean to ignore you, Mr.

Waring, but once your friend got hold of me I didn't want to be rude by walking away."

"No problem, Jamir. My friend is a huge college football fan, so I understand his excitement in meeting you. When we get home, he's going to tell everyone he knows that he shook your hand. If he wasn't already one of your biggest fans, he will be from now on."

As Paul and Jamir spent a few minutes talking, Bobby Ray joined them. Curious over Jamir's duties with Simon Church, as someone who was never afraid of asking any question that crossed his mind, Bobby Ray said, "If you don't mind me asking, how'd you get hooked up with Simon?" Bobby Ray's question made it sound as if he was on a first-name basis with one of the world's richest men.

"At the time I got hurt, Mr. Church was a minority owner in the Houston Texans. He's the real deal, if you know what I mean. Besides being the only one with a stake in the team who was kind enough to come see me after each of my surgeries, he made sure my contract was honored even though I was washed up as a player. After I retired, which still sounds funny because I only played in two games, Mr. Church offered me a job. So, here we are. My home's in South Carolina, but I usually travel wherever he goes; mostly doing odd jobs and all, but he's a pleasure to work for. He's even teaching me about the oil business, so who knows where that might take me. For an old white dude who grew up in the Deep South when things were way different than they are today, he's a pretty special guy." From his comments, Paul could tell how much the former football star respected the person he was working for.

After saying their goodbyes to Big J, as Paul and Bobby Ray walked inside the clubhouse they spied Regan standing several feet away. As he spoke with one of Mr. Church's clients, Regan, at first, failed to make eye contact with either Paul or Bobby Ray. Further away, Simon Church stood talking with two members of the club's staff. Easily recognizable from his frequent appearances on nightly news shows and from recently appearing on the covers of several national business publications due to the recent fluctuations of global oil prices, Church was suitably dressed for his round of golf.

Attracting Bobby Ray's attention as they waited for Regan to finish his call, Paul spoke softly as he made sure his friend knew who their host was. "That's Mr. Church standing there in the red golf shirt."

"From what I've read about him, that's pretty typical," Bobby Ray replied, watching as Simon Church continued with his conversation with members of the club's staff. While barely making ends meet as a result of the minimum wage positions they each held, the employees were all smiles as they listened to one of the world's richest men complain about his golf game. "From what I've read about him, he'll stop and have a conversation at the drop of a hat with just about anyone; bag drop attendants, waiters, waitresses, flunkies like you and me, and just about anyone else he comes in contact with. He's supposedly a very easy guy to talk with."

******

Having managed to play fifteen holes of golf before being caught in the middle of a brief, but intense rainstorm, Simon Church and the other members of his foursome elected to finish the afternoon by sitting at a large table inside the club's dining room. Made of solid oak, the heavy round table was one of fifteen tables and matching chairs occupying most of the room.

Sitting near the back of the room, Simon Church and his guests were comfortably out of earshot of the other guests enjoying a mid-afternoon meal. At another nearby table, two members of Church's security team did their best at being as inconspicuous as possible. Like their employer, they had changed their clothes after being caught in the unexpected storm.

Tastefully decorated with thick white tablecloths and fine china that most households in the country could not afford, and with silverware whose weight reflected the expense associated with each place setting, the club's dining room was by far the nicest restaurant Paul and Bobby Ray had visited inside a golf course. Along two walls, large floor to ceiling sliding glass doors allowed visitors to enjoy scenic views of both the course's challenging finishing hole and the Atlantic Ocean as they ate their meals and lied about their golf scores.

"Here's to both of you, welcome to our wonderful hideaway here at Port Royal," Simon Church said as he raised his chilled vodka martini. "I hope you both enjoyed our round of golf before we were chased off the course by that unexpected storm."

"It's a very nice course, very challenging to the average golfer, but well-laid out." Paul graciously replied after acknowledging the toast his host had offered. As was normal, Paul's beverage choice was a Jack and Coke. The tall, cold beverage was neatly dressed with a small garnish, a specialty of the house. Allowing his eyes time to take in the portraits and golf memorabilia tastefully decorating the walls around them, Paul added, "This dining room is just as nice as the golf course."

"I play several rounds a year at some of the finest courses the country has to offer, but this setting makes Port Royal my favorite. I've been a member for years at two of the finest courses back home, Colonial Country Club in Fort Worth and TPC San Antonio, but I just love this track. It's close to the ocean on an island I believe God himself created, and it's no more than a three minute drive to my house. What more could I ask for?" Pointing towards a bank of sliding glass doors, Church directed Paul's attention to where his house was located on nearby Fort Walker Drive. "You'll see it up close tonight when we meet for dinner. I'm not saying this to impress you, but outside of my home in Texas the one I have here on Hilton Head is probably my favorite."

"How many homes do you own, Mr. Church?" Bobby Ray asked from the other side of the table.

"Six that I know of," Church replied, laughing at his own little joke. "That's probably one or two too many, but the various businesses I'm involved in require me to do a great deal of travelling. It's not always possible, but whenever I can I prefer staying in one of my homes than in some fancy hotel. At my age, it's the small things in life which please me the most. I'm not sure how Paul or you feel about this, but there's nothing better than sleeping in your own bed."

Having pictured their host as being someone who enjoyed his financial status more than he enjoyed sleeping in his own bed, the billionaire's statement about enjoying the simpler things in life nearly caused Bobby Ray to choke on the cracker he was eating.

"This home I have here is smaller than a few of the others, but my wife has transformed it into a special place for us to enjoy. She's had some help from Robert and from an amazing group of designers I do a great deal of business with, but she's done a wonderful job making it feel like we've always lived here. This home holds some special memories." As he finished describing several of the upgrades his wife and others had made to his home since purchasing it six years earlier, Church coughed several times rather violently. The last two brought up a small amount of blood which he unsuccessfully tried hiding inside his gold-colored napkin. It was something Paul took notice of.

Handing Church a glass of water to help sooth his throat, Paul asked their host if he needed any further assistance.

"No, I'm fine, I'll be alright. I'm more embarrassed than anything, so please excuse me for this unpleasant interruption. My throat has been rather scratchy for the past few weeks. Robert has been bugging me get it looked at, but my schedule has been rather crazy lately. After I return to Texas next week I'll have more time to have it looked at." As he finished speaking, Church placed his soiled napkin in his lap. Moments later, it was discreetly replaced by one of the waitresses assigned to take care of the club's wealthiest member. Like one of her fellow employees, she witnessed the violent coughing spell Simon Church had endured.

Ordering their second round of drinks as lunch was being served; with his throat feeling slightly better, Church finally raised the issue of why he had asked Paul and Bobby Ray to join him. It was a topic he barely broached while on the golf course. Starting off by discussing his passion for learning everything there was to know about the Civil War and then explaining how he had gotten started collecting military artifacts from that turbulent conflict, Church then summarized the events surrounding the purchase of the latest addition to his collection. As he spoke, the elderly billionaire explained how he had come across Howard's journal.

"As I do with almost every piece I purchase, when they finally arrive at my home I spend a great deal of time inspecting them. This may surprise you, but with pieces like this extraordinary wooden chest I personally clean each one after they arrive. It's my way of getting familiar with these artifacts, and with the dings, dents, and scratches that, in most cases, date back to the war. That's how I found this hidden compartment that's held this remarkable journal since the end of the war."

Setting down his fork, Regan chuckled as he recalled the moment his employer let out a loud cry after finding the hidden compartment. As he did, Regan looked at Church to confirm the story he was telling. "I think you were more stunned than anything, Mr. Church. We may have been in different rooms, but the cry you let out scared the heck out of me."

"I believe you're right, Robert. I'm afraid I was rather loud, wasn't I." Church smiled as he recalled the moment being discussed. Seconds later, a long sip of his martini made Church's throat feel better for a few brief moments.

Pausing as their waiter stopped to refill their water glasses, Church then continued. "Paul, I know you and Bobby Ray haven't seen this chest Robert and I have been referring to, or, for that matter, most of what's been written in Howard's journal. While you both will have time to inspect everything there is over the next couple of days, I'd like to hear your thoughts on how you propose to start searching for this mysterious set of caves Howard has told us about."

"Well, first of all we need to see this chest you and Robert have talked about so much. Then we'd like to have a few days to review the contents of Howard's journal. Just as we can't go charging off into the woods without having some kind of sense as to where he may have hidden a portion of the Confederate treasury, we can't formulate a plan without knowing as many of the details as possible. I'd like to know some more information about Howard, what the last few days of his life were like, and how he coped with the loss of his men. Reading his journal will hopefully tell us some of that information. Not only is it important for us to read what he wrote, but I'd appreciate having the opportunity to see what his style of writing was like. How he described his feelings is just as important as what he left behind in those caves. I'm not sure if that's the answer you were looking for, but that's how Bobby Ray and I would like to get started."

"That sounds like a wise move. It's just the kind of response I expected to hear from someone with your experience. Like you've said, starting off half-cocked certainly wouldn't be the way to begin a search as labor intensive as ours is going to be." Church offered, complimenting Paul on the approach he had offered." Off to the left of where Simon Church was sitting, Regan nodded his head in response to the comments he was hearing. "I've already taken the necessary steps for you to inspect the chest. You'll have your first opportunity to see it tonight before dinner, and you'll have as much time as you need after we have breakfast tomorrow morning. To illustrate just how important this project is to me, I've assumed the expense of having the chest flown here from Texas on one of my private planes. If that wasn't enough, to further assist you with your needs Robert has personally photocopied the contents of Howard's journal. You'll each receive a complete set tomorrow morning. If you would like to inspect the journal itself, you may do so in my study after you complete your inspection of the chest. Please don't be offended, but for obvious reasons both will remain in my custody during your period of employment. Should you need to inspect them at a later time, I'll have Robert make them available."

"Thank you. We're looking forward to spending a fair amount of time with those two artifacts." After taking another sip of his Jack and Coke, Paul then asked for some additional details on how the hidden compartment had been found.

"As I've already mentioned, I was giving the interior a thorough cleaning when I apparently moved my right hand in an upward direction against one of the interior walls. This hiding space was constructed so well that it wasn't possible to see it with the naked eye. Even if I told you where it's located you wouldn't be able to find it. There isn't a seam, a joint, or anything else like that to suggest there's a hidden compartment inside this chest. Whoever built it, I'd like to hire that talented son of a bitch to do some work for me." Church's colorful comment caused the others sitting with him to not only laugh, but to have an appreciation for the talents the cabinetmaker displayed many years earlier.

"The hidden compartment is located against the back wall. It slides up and down on two wooden rails. The way it's been designed only allows the hidden compartment to reveal itself if you apply a significant amount of pressure to one specific location as obviously there are no handles or holes for your fingers to grab. It's the damnedest thing I've ever seen." Realizing he had become overly excited as he spoke about his remarkable discovery, Church glanced at the few people eating lunch on the other side of the room. Seeing them engaged in their own conversations caused him to realize neither they nor any of the wait staff had overheard his comments.

"Mr. Church," Bobby Ray said, jumping into the conversation before Paul had time to comment on the story their host had told, "I know this isn't your favorite topic to discuss, but the personal service agreements you expect us to sign, well . . . I'm afraid this search may not be as easy, or as inexpensive, as the previous one we conducted. To start with, there's still a bunch of research which needs to be conducted on Captain Howard; including the ancillary details associated with his train ride. All of that is going to take several weeks to complete. Because of that, we need to bring in two or three of the folks who've worked with us during our previous search for the missing treasury."

Somewhat annoyed with his friend for raising this concern during their first meeting, Paul had no choice but to take it a bit further. As he did, he shot Bobby Ray an irritated look. "Mr. Church, besides the concerns Bobby Ray has just raised, unless we somehow manage to get lucky and find this gold and silver sooner than we expect, we may have to spend some money on a helicopter. With the terrain around Moncks Corner not only being steep and fairly rural, it's comprised of hundreds of acres of virgin timber. Having a helicopter available will allow us to conduct our search in a more efficient manner. There's certainly a large expense associated with a piece of equipment like a helicopter, but in the end I believe the results will justify its use. We're also going to incur some costs in having to secure permission to search for these caves as there's a good chance they're on private property. Then there's the likelihood of EPA costs, title searches, historical costs involving permits and other matters, costs related to renting construction equipment, and so on. And, as Bobby Ray has mentioned, he and I can't undertake all of this on our own. I would like to bring in a couple of friends who have worked with us in the past. Doing so would eliminate any type of a learning curve we might run into if we had to bring in some help with no experience. If we bring them in, our friends can hit the ground running. We also need to reinforce to you that not only is the research going to take a few weeks to complete, but it's also going to take just as long for us to wrap our heads around this problem. To do that, it's going to cost you some money, but I expect you knew that."

Nodding his head, Church was silent as he stared out one of the nearby sliders while processing the information Paul had told him. As he did, Bobby Ray took the opportunity to eat the last few French fries remaining on his plate.

"Paul, I'm keenly aware of what this may cost, but I'm determined to find this missing part of the Confederate treasury. If you think you'll need a helicopter, Robert will arrange for one of my pilots to fly one up here. If we have to, we'll use more than one." Reaching over, Church grabbed Paul's left arm to reinforce what he was about to say. "Any heavy equipment we need, any money needed to pay for permits, property acquisition, hotels, food, tools . . . you'll have whatever you need. If you need to bring those friends of yours on board so we have a few extra sets of hands helping us find what we're looking for, then you do what you think is right. Tell Robert what you think they're worth and I'll OK it. You won't hear me squawking about spending a few extra bucks."

"Thank you, Mr. Church," Paul said, shooting a surprised look at Bobby Ray.

Turning in his chair, Church explained to his trusted aide what his role in this project was going to be. "Robert, Paul's in charge of this search, but you're the person responsible for keeping this project moving in the right direction. If he needs something, you make sure he gets it. I want you working with Paul and Bobby Ray as much as your schedule allows. Give them whatever they need, but call me with any questions. I'm depending on the three of you to manage this dream of mine, understood?" As he finished speaking, without warning Church suddenly experienced another violent coughing spell. Like before, his napkin was soon full of blood.

"You OK, Mr. Church?" Regan asked, concerned over his employer's health. Like Paul, Regan noticed Church had hardly touched his lunch.

"Yes, I'm fine." Church replied, lying about how he was feeling. "It doesn't seem like a sore throat, but my throat feels like it's on fire. I'll be fine after a few sips of water." As he sat sipping a glass of ice water, the skin on Church's face and neck turned deep red. To those sitting with him, it was obvious Simon Church was experiencing something more than an irritated throat.

Busy jotting down some notes on the discussion that had taken place as he gave the elderly billionaire a few minutes to compose himself, Regan then asked Church how he intended to finance the search for the missing treasury.

"Tomorrow morning I'll have five hundred thousand dollars transferred to the account we use for special projects. That will be enough to get us started. The thought that's been nagging me is I expect there will be times when you'll be back in Texas or someplace else taking care of another problem while Paul is tracking down this treasure we're looking for. To play it safe, after that transfer takes place have a check cut for twenty-five thousand. Have it made out to Paul so he can open an account at a local bank close to where he'll be working. That way if you're not around he'll have some cash in the event he needs it. A couple of debit cards will also make life easier for both of these gentlemen." As he finished pointing in Paul's direction, Simon Church began munching on small chunks of ice in an attempt to sooth the intense pain inside his throat.

* * * * * *

Thirty minutes later, with their business meeting concluded Paul and Bobby Ray headed back to their suite at the Westin Hilton. As they drove, the only topic being discussed was their concern for Simon Church's health.

"Think the old guy's got cancer?" Bobby Ray asked.

"Whatever his problem is, he needs to see a doctor sooner than later." Like Bobby Ray, the amount of blood Church had spit up caused Paul to become alarmed.

It had also caused him to become very suspicious.

Several minutes later, as they walked through the hotel lobby the only other comment Bobby Ray raised was in regards to the amount of money Church had committed to his special project. With years of service to two large government agencies which operated with a host of rules and regulations involving layers of mindless bureaucracy when it came to spending even a few meager dollars on an investigation, neither Paul nor Bobby Ray had ever seen a project, or that amount of money, moved into position that fast.

28

Once inside their hotel suite, after cleaning up from a day that included a wet round of golf and their first meeting with Simon Church, Paul started working the phones. Needing some additional help from people he could trust, his first call was to a friend he and Bobby Ray had worked with in the past. As he made his call, Bobby Ray, far more computer literate than he had been during their first search for the missing Confederate treasury, began searching for more information on Captain Noah Howard.

Sitting inside his office at the University of South Carolina, Chick Mann, a tenured American history professor, was reviewing applications for a vacant teaching position when a phone call interrupted his work. A friend of Paul's for the past few years after being introduced to each other through a mutual friend, Chick, like a few others, had played an important role in his friend's success. Most of which had come after a series of clues had been deciphered. Those cryptic clues had been found in letters written by Captain Francis. Found with his remains, each contained bits of information concerning the whereabouts of a portion of the Confederate treasury.

"Hey, Paul!" Chick said, answering the phone after seeing his friend's name displayed on the Caller ID. Resting his feet on one of the opened drawers of his desk, Chick smiled as he leaned back in his chair after hearing his friend's voice.

"Chick, how are things going these days? I miss seeing you."

Staring at the thick pile of applications sitting on his desk, Chick sounded far cheerier than he actually was. "Things are good, a little boring perhaps, but I have nothing to complain about. Life isn't nearly as exciting as it was when we were searching through old graveyards and rusty cannons for gold coins, but that's to be expected, I guess. On the other hand, if you're asking about my golf game then life is pretty lousy. I'm afraid a defibrillator couldn't resuscitate my game."

"Funny you should say that." Paul replied, ignoring Chick's comment regarding his golf game.

As Chick sat up in his chair, Paul took time to explain the circumstances surrounding his first meeting with Robert Regan. Minutes later, he summarized his subsequent meeting with Simon Church. As he spoke, Paul carefully described the journal Church had found inside Howard's old chest. As the conversation continued, Paul outlined the project he had been asked to undertake.

As someone who spent most of his career focusing on the Civil War, Chick, at first, ignored his friend's comments regarding the project he had been asked to assume. Instead, Chick focused on the journal and the mysterious secret compartment inside Howard's wooden chest.

"From what little you've told me, I'm having trouble believing that a chest, which you admit has had several owners over the past one hundred and fifty some-odd years, has finally decided to reveal something that's been hidden inside it for as long as it has." Standing up from his desk, Chick tried comprehending the news his friend had told him as he strolled aimlessly around his office. Under his desk, Chick's boat shoes sat waiting for their owner to claim them.

Chuckling over Chick's response, Paul said, "I don't believe the chest decided anything. I think the journal was found by sheer accident. It's one of those things that can't be explained. For what it's worth, I've seen and touched the journal. Later tonight Bobby Ray and I will have our first chance to see the chest. Tomorrow morning we're having breakfast with Mr. Church, and then we'll have a second opportunity to inspect the journal and the chest. From the questions we've asked and the little bit of documentation we've been privy to, both of these artifacts appear to be real; they're not forgeries. I've even conducted a brief review of the appraisals they went through, and the credentials of the people who conducted them. We're going to be doing some more digging on our own regarding all of these issues, but, for now, everything appears to be legit. I'm thinking I'll have Jayne handle that task once we get up to speed with this project."

As the phone went quiet for what seemed to be several minutes, Paul broke the silence by checking on his friend. "Chick, you still there? Is everything OK?"

"Uh, yeah, sort of." Paul's friend said rather quietly.

"What's wrong?"

"Well, for one thing Jayne won't be assisting us with this project. She and I recently had a huge disagreement over a few professional matters we were working on. When all was said and done, I'm afraid it didn't end as well as we would have liked. Much to my regret, we both made some comments about things that were bothering us. When we finished saying what had to be said, she quit her job here, and took off. I've tried reaching out to her on several occasions, but she's not taking my calls. It pains me to say this, but it appears we're no longer the friends we once were."

"I . . . I can't believe that." Paul said, stunned by the news that two of his friends were no longer speaking to each other. "Should I give her a call to see if I can help work things out between you two?"

"That's up to you, but I'm done. I've done everything possible to make things right, but she's apparently moved on. For the time being I'm giving myself some time to cool down before I try calling her again. Listen, I'm not trying to change the subject, but tell me more about this project you're working on."

While disappointed over the news of his friends no longer being in contact with each other, Paul decided to do as Chick had asked. He then explained the reason behind his call. "Well, it appears that after his men were killed Captain Howard made a few entries in his journal about hiding some gold and silver inside a cave in South Carolina. Its money that was part of the Confederate treasury; the same gold and silver you, Bobby Ray, and I are already familiar with. Mr. Church seems to have made this his life's mission, so he's hired Bobby Ray and I to find it. I'm calling because I'm interested in having you and Jayne help us. I told Mr. Church I needed your help, so he's agreed to let me hire whoever

I want. For what it's worth, if you're interested Bobby Ray and I would love to have you join us."

As the two friends spoke at length regarding Howard's journal and what his assignment had likely entailed, Paul spent a few extra minutes explaining how Simon Church had accidently come across this journal. As they talked, Chick became more and more interested in his friend's newest adventure.

"OK, count me in," Chick said after hearing all of the details. As he and Paul were speaking, Chick was already jotting down some of the information his friend had mentioned. Those details included the background work Bobby Ray was working on regarding Captain Howard. "Where do we go from here? And what's the plan for getting started?"

Pleased to learn his friend had agreed to join them, Paul flashed Bobby Ray a thumbs-up. It was done to let him know Chick was on-board. What that gesture did not convey was that Jayne would not be joining them.

"Listen, for the time being I'm not going to mention her name again, but if Jayne is out of the picture we need someone else to help us. How about your buddy, Peter? Think he might be interested?" Paul asked, knowing he needed at least one more set of hands to assist with the project they were about to start. Just like Chick and Bobby Ray, Peter Cater possessed a variety of unique skills that would come in handy. In their first search for the missing treasury, Chick's colleague had signed on at the last minute after being convinced it was in his best interest to do so.

Almost sixty years of age, Peter had been working as an adjunct professor at Coastal Carolina University in Myrtle Beach, South Carolina, when Chick first asked him to be part of Paul's team.

With years of experience working as a cameraman for several local television stations, he was far more knowledgeable than most when it came to using cameras and other types of video equipment. With his acquired skills. Peter had been the person needed to document the search for the missing treasury. After the first part of the treasury was found, Peter had also been responsible for editing the documentary Paul's team produced. Impressive in many ways, this film won several awards for cinematography, and two others for how the story had been narrated by a small group of Civil War reenactors.

"I just saw him yesterday. I wish I knew about this then." Chick said, recalling his accidental meeting with their mutual friend.

"Go find him. Tell him we need his help. He needs to know he's going to get his hands dirty again, but tell him he's the one we want capturing our work. Also tell him this is a paying gig, that'll motivate him to come along." After addressing the need for Peter's help, Paul addressed one last issue. "Bobby Ray and I are headed home tomorrow, so let's get together at the diner for a late lunch. We'll see you there around 1:30. I'll bring a few photographs and some of the entries in Howard's journal for you to look at."

"See you there."

＊＊＊＊＊

While Bobby Ray had already scored a minor victory by finding Captain Howard's name listed on two Civil War websites by the time Paul finished his call, what he and his friend would learn over the next several weeks would prove to be just as interesting as the discoveries they made during their first search for the missing Confederate treasury.

29

Walking inside the Waccamaw Diner just before he was scheduled to meet with Chick and Bobby Ray, Paul gave a friendly wave to a married couple he had become friendly with during his brief tenure as a ranger at a local golf course in Pawleys Island. Owned by his good friend, Steve Alcott, who had sold him his first pontoon boat, *The Links at Pawleys Island* was one of the premier golf destinations for tourists visiting the Grand Strand. For a Saturday afternoon when most people were either off from work or winding down from a busy week, the diner was strangely free of its normal weekend crowd.

"Hey, stranger, I ain't seen ya for the past few days. Where ya been hiding? You ain't been cheating on me, have ya?" Betty asked, joking with Paul as she set a cup of coffee down in front of one of her favorite customers. Among her many positive traits was Betty's ability to always be upbeat and outgoing while dealing with her customers. That was especially true with Paul.

After a few brief comments back and forth in which Paul vaguely explained his recent absence, the retired state trooper commented on the light lunch crowd. "I saw Doc and Linda when I walked in, but outside of them and a few others, where's the usual Saturday crowd? On most weekends your customers generally have to wait in line for a place to sit, so why's today so different? Did the health department give you guys a bad rating or something?" Looking in the direction of where Doc and Linda Hoffman were sitting on the opposite end of the diner, Paul counted only four other customers having lunch. As was the case with many of Betty's customers, the Hoffman's were recent transplants from northern Maine. They had moved to the Grand Strand to escape Maine's high cost of living and to enjoy the warmer winter months. Like Paul and many others, they visited the diner two or three times a week to socialize while enjoying a good meal.

"Nope, it's nothing like that." Betty replied, laughing at Paul's comment regarding the health department. "We were busy earlier, but I guess folks are out enjoying the weather. It's the first nice weekend we've had for quite a spell; it's been cold and far too rainy to get outside." Turning from staring out the window, Betty asked her question for a second time. "Seeing that ya haven't answered me, I'll ask ya again. So where ya been? You ain't been cheating on me, have ya?"

"I would never do that to you, Miss Betty. Bobby Ray and I were down in Hilton Head with our wives for a couple of days, that's all. In fact, he and two of our friends will be here in a few minutes. We'll need four menus, please." Trying his best to limit the number of questions Betty was asking, Paul did what he could to refocus her attention on setting the table inside his booth before the others arrived. Like it was on most occasions, his subtle hint did not receive the attention he had hoped it would.

"Y'all here to talk about something special or ya just having lunch? Lord knows, y'all can't be talkin' about finding any more gold as ya done found that money a few years back."

While her rough language reflected the fact that she had dropped out of school far too early, Betty's comments caused Paul a brief laugh. Her lack of an education did little to impact her ability in sensing Paul's lunch meeting was more than just a group of friends getting together with no set purpose. To Paul's amazement, Betty's questions were often spot-on.

"Yeah, something like that, but mostly it's just friends having lunch." Looking towards the diner's front door, Paul was relieved to see Bobby Ray headed his way. Following close behind were Chick and Peter.

Noticing who was filing into the booth where Paul was seated, Betty smirked as Bobby Ray sat down. Handing Paul's lunch companions their menus, she snorted as the others got comfortable. "Looks like the gold and silver gang is at it again, I see. How much you fellas gonna find this time?" Shooting Bobby Ray a suspicious wink, Betty walked off to fill their drink orders.

"What the heck did you tell her?" Bobby Ray asked, jumping the gun as he often did before seeking the answer to his question in a more diplomatic manner. The concern in his face was quite apparent as he watched Betty walk away. Moments later, he turned to face his friend.

"I . . . I didn't tell her anything." Paul replied, less than pleased by the tone in Bobby Ray's voice. "I just told her the four of us were meeting here to have lunch. Somehow she assumed, quite correctly might I add, that we were here to talk about finding another stash of gold and silver. You know how she is. She likes to ding you with a million questions when she suspects something's up. It's her way of being nosy."

"Dude, that's amazing!" Bobby Ray said, unsure of whether to believe his friend or no.

"Bobby Ray, I'm an old man. I'm nearly sixty-seven years old, please don't *dude* me. I hate that." As he finished speaking, Paul thanked his two friends on the other side of the booth for joining him for lunch. Scanning the menus they each had been handed, Chick and Peter, at first, both acknowledged Paul's friendly greeting by simply nodding in his direction.

"I told you I was in, but I'm looking forward to seeing what you have sitting there in front of you before I make my final commitment." Chick said as he pointed to the contents sitting inside a fat file folder near Paul's left elbow. Resting on top of the already crowded table, the bulky folder took up most of the remaining space. "I assume those are copies of Howard's journal entries and perhaps a few photographs of this mysterious chest?"

Handing the folder across the table, Paul asked Peter if he was committed to the project. "I'm in. I wouldn't be here if I wasn't. If what you and Bobby Ray have seen convinces you that the documents are real, then I'm in. You amazed me enough during our first search that I'd be a fool not to tag along just to see if you can do it again. I still find myself shaking my head over your ability to connect so many of those clues we were dealing with to where the gold and silver was hidden. With that being said, I've got some vacation time accrued and I already live by the beach, so where am I going to go? I'm all packed. Just tell me when and where we're headed." After answering Paul's question regarding his level of commitment, Peter's eyes focused on the menu's many offerings. Having spent a good part of the morning working out in preparation for a local road race he was participating in the following weekend, he was ready to enjoy a good meal.

"I'm pleased to hear that, Peter. I really am." As he thanked his cinematographer for being there, Paul noticed Peter had suddenly set down his menu. In moments, his attention turned from selecting his next meal to studying the photographs Chick was looking at. For a few brief moments, Paul questioned whether Peter was actually interested in the photographs of the wooden chest or if his training and experience was causing him to grade the quality of the photos he was looking at.

Doing his best to hide the photographs from Betty's prying eyes as she stopped to take their lunch orders, Peter waited until she was gone before expressing his thoughts on the information Chick had earlier shared with him. As Betty moved off, he asked Paul how his plans were coming for this newest adventure.

"To start with, Bobby Ray has been digging into Howard's background. He's found some useful information, but we need to see what else we can learn about him. We definitely need to find out as much as we can about his military career. To go along with what Bobby Ray is working on, I would like you to see what you can learn about this chest that's been found. Dig into the history of Richmond around the time of the war to see if you can determine if the name we have is actually the person who made this chest for Captain Howard. While maps from those days were not as detailed as they are today, they sometimes listed the person's name and occupation when they identified the locations of their homes or businesses. Perhaps you'll come across one like that. Then I'd like you to find out as much as you can about the people who appraised this chest for Mr. Church."

Writing down a few notes on a yellow legal pad as Betty placed their lunch orders in front of them; after waiting for her to leave Peter asked his friend a question about the assignment he had been given. "Your thought is that the more we know about these people, the better understanding we might have on how qualified they were to make these appraisals, correct?"

As Peter took the first bite of his chicken sandwich, Paul momentarily ignored his own meal as he responded to his friend's question. "Precisely. If those appraisers don't have a proven track record that might influence our thoughts on being committed to this project. It would also mean we would have to have the journal and the chest appraised by one or two others before we proceed any further. I'm not interested in wasting our time if this chest isn't the real McCoy. The same holds true for the journal."

"Got it," Peter mumbled, covering his mouth as he continued to enjoy his lunch. "I'll focus most of my efforts on finding out what I can about the person who made this chest." As he finished his response, Peter pointed to the name of the cabinetmaker displayed in one of the photographs. Many years earlier, as a means of promoting his skills, J. William Morse had burned his name inside the lid of Howard's wooden chest.

"Finding any information on this cabinetmaker would be huge. It might prove to be a big help with some of the other background work that still needs looking into. In the meantime, Bobby Ray is going to try and learn as much as he can about Howard's background and the assignment he was given. I'm not too optimistic that he'll find any letters written on his behalf like those we found for Judiah Francis, but we'll see what his search uncovers."

"What are you and Chick going to be working on while we're doing this research?" Bobby Ray asked, staring intently at the steak sandwich he had yet to taste.

Nodding at the folder Chick had been leafing through, Paul said, "Chick and I are going to start dissecting every entry Howard wrote. We'll collect as much useful information as we can . . . maybe going as far as creating a timeline to show where Howard had been and who he had met. Doing so might help us narrow our focus. If we decide to do that, we'll see where it takes us."

As the members of Paul's team sat eating their lunch, they bounced thoughts and ideas off each other just as they had done during their first search. It was their way of trying to make sense of what little information they had.

30

Making her way across the sun-drenched parking lot of the run-down apartment complex she called home, Isabella Vasquez suddenly paused as the sound of gunshots drifted in her direction. Believing the shots had been fired from between two buildings located at the far end of the courtyard where trouble seemed to occur on a daily basis, Isabella stared in that direction as she waited to hear the inevitable cries for help. Concerned over the welfare of those living close to where the shots had rung out, to Isabella those piercing cries always seemed to follow the daily discharge of weapons by immature young gangsters flexing their muscles. Like others their age, the wannabe gang bangers gave little thought to those they might hurt. While most of the residents inside the complex were either still asleep or out trying to find work as day laborers, the gunfire Isabella and others heard on the grounds of *The Gardens Apartment Complex* had rung out far earlier than it had on most days.

Comprised of six freestanding brick buildings, the four floors in each location housed close to three hundred low income residents of several different nationalities. Like those residing in other depressed neighborhoods, the tenants dealt with vandalism, graffiti covered doors and hallways, broken elevators, and a variety of rodents and bugs who somehow found their way inside every inch of space there was. For most, it was the only place they could afford. Like most urban housing developments, it was often the scene of all types of violent crime. Discontent, apathy, intolerance, drugs, and poverty were among the daily visitors greeting residents inside the complex located on Dallas' east side. Among the others who visited on a daily basis were police officers, ambulance personnel, and an endless number of parole and probation officers.

Standing in the middle of the parking lot exhausted from the double shift she had just worked, Isabella stood still for several moments as she waited to see if the first round of shots would be angrily answered by rival gang members living inside the apartment complex. Shaking her head in disgust as she stared at the metal carcasses of several abandoned vehicles and other trash littering the large parking lot, the twenty-five-year-old former resident of El Progreso, Guatemala, realized there was little difference between her former neighborhood and the place she now called home. Her new home, located inside an old dilapidated neighborhood commonly referred to as *El Barrio,* had previously been occupied by waves of other illegals who had fled Central America in hopes of finding a better life.

Resuming her slow march towards the front door of her tiny two-bedroom apartment after not hearing any additional gunfire, Isabella's arms ached under the weight of what she was carrying. Too tired to make more than one trip from her car to her apartment, she delicately balanced a cardboard tray of drinks from a local restaurant, her heavy pocketbook, and a coat. In her left hand, Isabella firmly clutched a bag of warm breakfast treats from the same fast-food restaurant. Hidden from view, in her other hand her fingers strained to select the correct key to her apartment. Looking over her shoulders as she approached her front door, Isabella prayed she would avoid becoming the next victim in a series of violent home invasions that had recently occurred inside the apartment complex. She was just as anxious to lighten the heavy load she was carrying.

Moments later, after successfully unlocking the apartment's front door the sound of it being pushed open caused Isabella's three children – Roberto, age 8; Maria, age 6; and Jacinto, age 3 – to squeal in delight at the sight of their mother. Jumping off the couch where they had sat huddled under two blankets while watching morning cartoons, her children waited patiently for their mother to shower them with hugs and kisses.

"Mommy, I heard you coming up the sidewalk, but you've told me not to unlock the door. I could have helped you carry something into the house, but I didn't want you getting mad at me." Roberto said, watching his mother as she placed her coat and the tray of drinks on the counter next to their stove. Several years old, the stove's broken heating element and problems with three of the four burners had rendered it nearly useless. Moments earlier, Isabella's oldest son had pushed the front door closed and turned the lock to firmly secure it in place.

"I would have appreciated your help, but you did just what I have asked you to do." Isabella replied, bending over to kiss her son's forehead. The victim of two recent muggings, Isabella, who was constantly afraid of her family becoming the victims of another home invasion inside their crime-infested apartment complex, had repeatedly instructed her children not to unlock the apartment door when they saw her coming home from work.

Exhausted from the long shift she had worked and from the hour-long commute she spent on the road each day, Isabella arrived home an hour later than normal. A devout Roman Catholic who made sure her children were neatly dressed for Mass each Sunday, she had spent close to forty minutes praying for guidance inside a nearby church before buying breakfast for her family.

Isabella's fatigue was soon forgotten as she and her children exchanged warm loving embraces inside the kitchen shortly after setting down the bag of food and the other items she had been carrying. Much closer to their mother than they were with their often-angry and verbally abusive father, Isabella's children had spent much of the time she was at work either on the sofa watching television or asleep in their small bedroom. With their father having little interest in making them dinner, the children had fixed themselves a late night meal of cold cereal.

"I'm so happy to see my babies. I've missed each of you so much while I've been at work," Isabella said, hugging her children before taking off her sweater. Slightly discolored from the number of times it had been washed, Isabella's green sweater had been purchased at a nearby thrift store two years earlier. Returning to the kitchen after turning off the television, Isabella frowned as she noticed the three empty cereal bowls in the sink. Without her children having to tell her, she knew her husband had done little to care for them while she was gone.

"Mama, we're hungry. Why are you so late coming home?" Roberto asked as he watched his mother move the tray of drinks and the bag of food from the counter to their tiny kitchen table.

Around the table, five wooden chairs were pushed tightly against each other making it impossible for more than two of Isabella's children to take their seats at the same time. Dinged, dented, and painted a variety of different colors, two of the chairs had been purchased at a local flea market, while the others had been handed down from other equally destitute families living nearby. Like the rest of her furniture, none of the chairs matched.

Ignoring the question her son had asked, Isabella smiled as her children took turns sitting down. After carefully setting down the small containers of milk in front of them, with nearly as much care as if she had made them herself, Isabella unwrapped the warm Egg McMuffin sandwiches before placing them in front of her children. After doing so, she closed the brown paper bag they had come in so the remaining sandwiches stayed warm. Purchased at a McDonald's Restaurant located not far from their apartment, the cost of the family's breakfast had been lessened slightly by the manager on duty. Living in the building next to Isabella's family, the Black female manager was well-aware of the daily struggle her neighbors experienced while doing their best to put food on the table at least twice a day. During their brief exchange of eye contact, Isabella had given the middle-aged manager a quick nod of thanks after realizing she had not been charged for three of the breakfast sandwiches.

Quickly accosted by her hungry children as she arrived home, Isabella had not had time to greet, or even locate, her husband. "Where's daddy?" She asked after finally noticing her husband's recliner was sitting unused. Like the other furniture inside the small apartment, the recliner had seen better days.

"He's in bed watching television. He's been there ever since you left, mama." Roberto replied, using the back of one of his hands to wipe his mouth after taking a long sip of milk from the container his mother had opened. Unlike his two siblings, following the examples set by some of the older children he went to school with, Roberto ignored the straw that had been placed in front of him. Looking eagerly at the food in front of him, Isabella's oldest child added one more comment before taking the first bite of his breakfast sandwich. "We told Daddy we were hungry last night, but he wouldn't fix us anything. We just had some cereal while we were watching television."

"I'm sorry he didn't make you any dinner." Isabella replied, stroking her daughter's long black hair as she sat watching her children enjoy their breakfast. Furious at the lack of attention her husband had given their children, Isabella did as much as she could to hide the anger brewing inside of her. "Daddy knows better than that. I'll talk with him in a few minutes so he knows to make you dinner when I'm at work."

Often nervous and confused around her father, Maria turned and looked at her mother as she toyed with her breakfast. "Mama, why is daddy so mean and angry all the time? He's not like you, you're never mean. You always smile and give us hugs. We don't like it when you have to go to work. We miss you when you're gone." Busy eating the treat their mother had bought them; Maria's siblings nodded their heads in agreement over the long hours their mother spent at work.

Wrapping her arms around her daughter, Isabella gave Maria a long tight hug as she fought back the tears forming in her eyes. Already upset over something that had occurred at work, her daughter's comments upset her even more. "Your father loves each of you, Maria. He's just not feeling that well these days since his accident. Give him some time; he'll be better soon, I promise."

"If daddy is mad because he was hurt at work, then why does he play soccer with his friends instead of playing with us? When you're not around he just lies in bed watching television. He . . . he must not like us anymore." Roberto said sadly as he pushed his empty plate away. A young and talented soccer player who inherited his parent's passion for the sport, his father had made little effort to attend his son's recent youth league matches.

Noticing the upset expressions on the three faces staring back at her, Isabella turned away from her children as she stared down the hallway in the direction of her bedroom. Already concerned over her husband's recent behavior towards her and their children, Isabella fought to control her emotions after hearing what her children had told her. Sitting at the table, she heard her husband's voice call out to her.

"Isabella, I'm hungry. Bring me my breakfast."

* * * * * *

Four months older than his wife, Carlos Martinez had crossed the border into the United States six months before her arrival. Unlike Isabella, he had neither a Visa nor any form of documentation allowing him to be in the country he had dreamed of living in for several years. Like others who failed to make it across the border on his own, Martinez had paid a *coyote* eight thousand dollars to smuggle him into Texas. Arriving in the United States after nearly suffocating in the back of a tractor-trailer packed with fifty other illegals, Martinez made it inside the Land of the Free on his third attempt.

Finding work as a field laborer at two different farms in southeast Texas, Martinez proved to be an industrious and dependable worker who spent what little free time he had playing soccer in loosely organized leagues in and around his newly adopted hometown. Playing against teams comprised primarily by Mexicans, Hispanics, and by a small number of talented players from Guatemala, Martinez spent many late night hours playing soccer at fields maintained by the local school system. With no money to pay for the lights to be turned on when the matches went deep into the night, many die-hard players and their fans took turns using their vehicles as light stanchions so play could continue. On most Sundays, Martinez and his friends, often the first to arrive and the last to leave, played on fields in far better condition. Two years after his arrival in the United States, Martinez grew tired of working long hot days in the blistering sun for little money. Deciding there was little to be made from spending six days a week picking fruit for someone other than himself; he accepted an offer from the brother of one of his soccer friends to become a crew leader for a local painting contractor. It was work he had never performed.

While given the responsibility of finding commercial projects for his crew to paint, and for making sure they arrived to work on time, despite his fancy new title Martinez was only paid a few dollars more each week than he had been making while picking fruit. While primarily hired to work inside large buildings, the paltry salary increase Martinez received was less than what several other crew leaders were being paid.

In spite of his low salary, Martinez appreciated the fact that he was no longer making a living toiling in the fields like so many of his friends. With a strong work ethic and a determination to improve his chances of finding a better paying job, he spent some of his time away from work learning to speak English at a local community center with other immigrants. He did so to not only improve his chances of obtaining a better job, but to realize his dream of becoming an American citizen.

Shortly after assuming his new position, Martinez married Isabella Vasquez in a simple ceremony. While happily married despite their austere lifestyle, their low paying jobs caused them to struggle to make ends meet. Committed to improving themselves and to starting a family of their own, Martinez and his new wife did what they could to put food on the table. Sometimes seeing very little of each other for days on end, neither of them turned down an opportunity at making a few extra dollars. With many of his friends staying out late and occasionally running afoul of the law, Martinez promised his wife he would avoid putting himself in trouble with the police. But then, as fate would have it, shortly after the birth of his youngest son Martinez was dealt a crushing blow.

Working late one night with two members of his crew to complete a large painting job inside a mall undergoing an extensive renovation, Martinez did what he could to beat the deadline set by his boss. Finishing ahead of schedule meant the crew leader and his men would share a cash bonus promised by the mall's owner. While his share would be less than a month's rent, for Martinez it was money Uncle Sam would never know about.

Perched on scaffolding close to forty-five feet above the mall's concrete floor as he and his men painted the façade of the last store on their list to paint, one of the welds supporting the planking Martinez was standing on gave way. Ignoring one of the safety mandates his boss had constantly preached, Martinez lost his balance as the scaffolding gave way. Frantically trying to grab the safety harness he should have been wearing, Martinez bounced off two other sections of metal planking before striking the floor with a loud thud. With his body awkwardly stretched out in an attempt to break his fall, he had little means of protecting himself.

While his head and neck had been saved from being seriously injured by a pile of drop cloths piled up near the base of the scaffolding, other parts of Martinez's body were not as lucky. Knocked unconscious when his head struck a section of metal planking, the crew leader was soon rushed to a nearby hospital. Less than twenty minutes after arriving, Martinez was being operated on.

Two weeks later, with Isabella refusing to allow her children to see their father in the condition he was in, Martinez was released from the hospital. With a series of titanium screws and a metal plate holding his surgically repaired left hip in place, and with his broken left arm secured inside a cast that looked far more painful than it actually was, Martinez's children were reduced to tears when they first saw how badly their father had been hurt. Three broken ribs and a fractured collarbone prevented the children from hugging their father as he left the hospital.

Over the course of the next few weeks, with the owner of the mall refusing to accept responsibility for the piece of scaffolding that had failed, Martinez's medical bills began to accumulate. To make matters worse, his employer, a convicted felon with little to no insurance, refused to pay his injured employee's medical bills and the bonus he had been promised. His refusal was based on Martinez's failure to wear the appropriate safety equipment. With little knowledge of how the Workers' Compensation Commission worked, Martinez and his family fell on the mercy of friends to help make ends meet.

In the months that followed, Martinez's injuries slowly began to heal. Angry and upset over how he and his family had been treated by his former boss, Martinez grew discontented. The hard-working crew leader who had once filled crate after crate with more fruit than any two or three men he worked with, now cared little about his marriage, his three precious children, and his future.

* * * * * *

"Isabella, why are you so late getting home? I'm hungry. You should have been here an hour ago." Upset over his morning meal being delayed, Martinez glared at his wife as she walked inside their bedroom. Stepping over a pile of dirty clothes her husband had carelessly tossed on the floor near the foot of their bed, Isabella placed the remaining breakfast sandwiches and a cup of Coca-Cola on the small nightstand next to her side of the bed. Sitting up, Martinez quickly spied the soft drink and breakfast sandwiches his wife had brought home. Changing his attitude in hopes of being handed his breakfast, Martinez added, "With me out of work, I didn't think we would afford a meal like this."

Kissing her husband's forehead, Isabella forced herself to smile as she watched her husband take the first bite of his sandwich. "Don't worry, we'll manage. Enjoy your breakfast." While irritated at her husband for the past two weeks over his refusal to find some sort of work, Isabella cared deeply about his health. Sitting down on the bed next to him after changing into a simple cotton nightgown, she gently rubbed one of the scars that served as a reminder of her husband's recent fall. Moments later, she asked how his broken ribs were feeling.

"They feel okay, but I'm sure after I rest for another few weeks they'll feel much better. This doesn't make sense, but they seem to hurt more when I'm lying in bed than when I'm up walking around." As he answered his wife's question, Martinez's hands searched inside the paper bag for the second breakfast sandwich. Unlike his work ethic, his appetite had not slowed down. Soon focused on removing the plastic lid from the top of his soft drink, Isabella's husband took a healthy swig of the cold drink after carelessly tossing the lid on the nightstand. As someone who seldom drank coffee or hot tea, the unemployed crew leader's preferred beverage was an icy cup of Coca-Cola during most meals. Addicted to the sweet taste, Martinez often drank two or three liter bottles of the sugary drink on a daily basis.

"I would have thought your ribs hurt more when you were playing soccer with your friends." Upset over her husband's recent lack of interest in their children's welfare, Isabella's biting comment was said as she stood staring at him in the mirror. The purpose behind her comment was to let him know she knew what he had been up to on several recent occasions while she was working.

"Are we really going to discuss how I spend my time when you're at work?" Martinez asked, angrily rolling the fast food wrappers into a ball. Disgusted by his wife's comment, he threw the rolled up wrappers against the small television located near the foot of their bed. Bouncing off the screen without inflicting any damage, the wrappers came to rest on the floor next to the sneakers Isabella had taken off moments earlier.

"Not now we aren't, but tomorrow we will." Isabella angrily replied, showing a side of her she seldom revealed. "I have to be at the grocery store in less than seven hours. They called me on my way to work yesterday afternoon and asked if I could come in for a few hours today. When I finish there, I'm going straight to my real job. In the event this means anything to you, I'm scheduled to work another double at the Church estate. That means I probably won't see you and kids much before noon tomorrow, so make sure you feed my babies. If you don't, there's going to be some serious trouble between us. Understood?" As she finished outlining her expectations and the details surrounding her work schedule, Isabella pulled the bed's top sheet and blanket over her.

Looking at his wife as she settled into bed, Martinez tried apologizing. "Don't worry about the kids; I'll take care of them. But, listen to me . . . you're working too much, Isabella. I'm afraid you're going to get hurt working all of these crazy hours. We . . . we need the money to keep us fed, but all the money in the world won't mean anything if you get hurt."

Patting his hand, Isabella smiled over her husband's concern. "I'll be alright, don't worry. Maybe when you get back to work I can cut back on my hours some, but, for now, we need every dime I can make." The conversation they were having caused Isabella to realize that over the next few days she would somehow have to come up with enough money to pay the next month's rent and two utility bills. Beginning to worry about her impending bills, Isabella suddenly sat up in bed. Reaching for the pants she had worn to work, Isabella reached inside one of the pockets before fishing out four fresh twenty-dollar bills. Their crisp condition was an indication they had recently been placed in circulation.

"Look, Carlos! We're rich!" Holding up the four new bills in her right hand, Isabella briefly smiled before a worried look took its place.

"Where did this money come from?" Martinez asked, gently freeing the unexpected windfall from his wife's hand. The eighty dollars was the most money the unemployed crew leader had seen in several weeks.

"I didn't find it. Mrs. Church gave me a hundred dollar bill last night before she went to bed. I . . . I used some of it this morning to buy breakfast for you and the kids."

"She just gave you a hundred dollar bill? Why would she do that? Is this something she owed you or is this some kind of a bonus?" As he asked his questions, Martinez tried recalling the few occasions he had actually handled a hundred dollar bill.

"It's nothing like that . . . it's more like . . ."

"It's more like *what*, Isabella?" Martinez asked impatiently, cutting his wife off before she had time to finish her explanation.

"Like hush money." Isabella softly replied.

"Hush money? What's that mean?"

Pulling the sheet tightly around her neck as she gave thought to ignoring her husband's last two questions, Isabella said, "We'll talk about it when I get home tomorrow. For the time being, I need to get some sleep." With his wife's back facing him and her face buried deep inside her pillow, Martinez failed to see the tears staining her side of the bed.

With his wife refusing to answer his questions, Martinez struggled to make sense of why the money Genevieve Church had given her had been referred to as hush money.

By refusing to answer, Isabella had not told her husband one other important point. She had not mentioned what she witnessed Genevieve Church doing inside the Church estate.

Nor had she told him about her visit inside a small Catholic church and the guidance she had sought.

31

A week after showing his friends the documents and photographs he had been given by Simon Church, Paul and Chick met at the Socastee Library just outside of Myrtle Beach. By now both had spent several long hours on their own poring over the entries Captain Howard had written as he moved across South Carolina near the end of the war.

Located in Horry County, South Carolina, the small modern library had been the setting years earlier for much of the research Paul conducted after finding a set of letters authored by another Confederate soldier. Believing his previous success was due in-part to the research he had conducted there, Paul reserved one of the library's small meeting rooms so he and Chick were not disturbed as they dissected the entries in Howard's journal. Normally used for a variety of activities by senior citizens and by a quilting club comprised of women from three area churches, on this occasion it was being used to locate a portion of the missing Confederate treasury.

As the two friends discussed what Howard had recorded, Chick raised several valid points involving a handful of different entries. They were ones Paul had also highlighted in his working copy of Howard's journal. Searching through some of the notes he had jotted down in a spiral notebook, Chick spoke about one important observation.

"I'm sure you took note of this, but Howard is someone we owe some thanks to. I found it interesting that for every entry he made, and this holds true no matter how insignificant some of them were, he started by jotting down the date. Without intending to do so, he's created a timeline for us to examine."

"I picked up on that after reading the first few entries in this particular journal," Paul said, pleased his friend had noticed the small detail Howard had given to each entry. "He also started many of his entries with what I would have to believe were the names and descriptions of the places where he was camped or resting. From what I've read, it appears Howard wrote most of his entries at the end of many long and difficult days. Some, like this entry here, only offered a vague reference to where he was, but in many cases it almost appears as if he wanted someone to know where his travels had taken him. In this case, that someone is us." As he had spoken, Paul pointed to where Howard had written the date at the beginning of one particular entry. It had been written on April 15, 1865. Unbeknownst to Howard, General Robert E. Lee had surrendered to General Ulysses S. Grant six days earlier.

"Or maybe he had thoughts about writing a story . . . or a book about his exploits. These entries we've been reading may have been his way of keeping track of everything he had seen and done. The first date he jotted down in this particular journal was in March, 1865. At this point we have no way of knowing this, but I have to believe this was not his only journal as some of his entries seem to reference certain events that had taken place prior to the ones we've been discussing. Who knows, maybe he mailed the others home so they didn't get lost or maybe they were thrown away after his body was found. If they somehow managed to survive his death, they could even be gathering dust in a library or museum someplace."

"I agree, Chick. This certainly isn't the only one, but, for now, there's no telling where the others might be. We know this was Howard's last journal . . ." Paul paused before somberly finishing his thought several seconds later. "I . . . I guess we know it's the last one based on his final entry."

"Yeah . . . I guess we do." Chick replied, turning to the last page of his working copy of Howard's journal. "That last entry must have been tough to write." Chick's comment was in reference to the entry Howard had written just before his suicide.

As the two friends continued to discuss a handful of entries Howard had written, including those describing President Davis' decision to abandon Richmond in the wake of the events surrounding the collapse of Petersburg, Chick spoke about one of the obvious points his review had raised. Again, it was one Paul concurred with.

"Right away, as he's writing these long descriptive entries, Howard's witnessing the collapse of the Confederacy. He's not only witnessing history as it's taking place, but he's right there with President Davis . . . a guy you either love or hate depending on which side of the war you were on. But, either way Davis is still someone who was one of the principal players inside this horrific four-year conflict. Howard is a freaking witness to something Civil War buffs like you and I would have paid a bunch of money to witness."

As a wistful smile creased Paul's face, without thinking he nodded at the comments his friend had offered. Digressing from the other points they had been speaking about, he said, "Not only would I have liked to witness certain events during the war, like those that took place at Gettysburg, Appomattox Court House, Fredericksburg, and other places history has taught us about, I've often found myself wondering what it must have been like to witness the ferocious fighting at the Alamo or to be at Yorktown as the Revolutionary War came to a close. I also sometimes find myself wondering what it must have been like to have been the first person to witness the beauty of Yellowstone or even the Rocky Mountains."

Barely giving any thought to Paul's comments, as Chick ran his fingers over the first few notes he had written he offered a comment on the most important issue at hand. "If we're operating on the theory that these entries are authentic, then I have to believe Howard was telling the truth when he described hiding a portion of the Confederate treasury inside a partially collapsed cave."

"I had my doubts at first, but there's too much detail in all of his entries for me to believe he made them up. Some of these details, like those that mention Davis or the fall of Richmond, are ones history has told us are true. Those related to the fall of Richmond or the trains which carried Davis and his family south as the war was ending are all issues we've read about. The same holds true for that one entry in which he describes how some of Davis' most trusted advisors were present when the trains headed south. Others, ones which include some of the war's more obscure details, are entries we can't dismiss; somehow we need to corroborate those details he's written about. I'm sure they all took place; we just need to verify Howard was there when they occurred."

After spending close to ninety minutes discussing their thoughts and ideas regarding points contained in some of Howard's other entries, Chick brought up the problems the young officer had encountered after being forced to abandon the train; specifically those involving the slow moving wagons. "In our previous adventure, we learned about similar problems Captain Francis experienced when he was travelling with a much larger portion of the treasury. While his trip covered more ground than Howard's and spanned a greater time period, from the number of men Howard lost to accidents and hostile attacks I'm not so sure he had it any easier. To lose that number of men must have made it a very difficult trip to endure; especially when you think of those who were killed when the cave collapsed."

Sitting back in his chair, Paul thought of another troubling issue Howard had faced on more than one occasion. "The part which bothers me a great deal is when he was describing the series of attacks that killed several of his men. While he described these attacks in great detail in several of his entries, including how he had ordered the attackers to be either shot or hung, he never really explained who they were. He described them as being traitors to the Confederate cause, but he never identified them by name or by what regiment they had served with. An example of that is the person who was hung after the incident at the small cabin; he never identified who that person was. I'm not sure if he was trying to protect them or if was embarrassed over the fact that he had been attacked by a group of men who had once fought for the Confederacy, but I would have thought he would have identified them in some manner; if not by name, then by their regiment or company. He also never really identified the reason behind these attacks. It could be those former soldiers were simply after the food in Howard's wagons. Perhaps they were starving and saw the wagons as the means of ending their hunger, but I find it strange he never explained or even speculated on the reason why he and his men had been attacked." As he thought about the points he had raised, Paul added one last comment. "It's also possible they had found out about the gold and silver Howard was transporting."

"I suppose those attacks could have occurred for a number of reasons, but I suspect those attackers were primarily looking for food. Near the end of the war many soldiers, especially those fighting for the South, were dying of hunger." Thumbing his way through several more pages of Howard's journal, Chick continued to nod at the points Paul had raised.

Sitting quietly as they went over their notes, Paul reflected back on Howard's entries regarding the collapsed caves and the description the young officer had left concerning the whereabouts of the various assets he had hidden. As his fingers busied themselves playing with the pen he had been writing with, Paul spoke to his friend. He did so to remove any lingering doubts regarding what Howard's assignment had involved.

"Correct me if I'm wrong, but I think we both agree Howard was escorting a portion of the Confederate treasury to some place south of Moncks Corner. Possibly to either Charleston or Savannah, correct?"

"Correct." Chick replied, curious as to why Paul had even asked this question.

"So, if that's the case, from his last couple of entries do you agree we need to start our search somewhere west of Moncks Corner?" Paul asked, referring to the last known location Howard had mentioned in his journal.

"I'd go along with that," Chick said slowly, agreeing with Paul's assessment of where their search should commence. "But how do you plan on starting and, better yet, where do you plan on starting?"

"Well, if he was west of Moncks Corner and south of a large body of water like we've read about in a few of his entries, let's start our search just south of Lake Moultrie." Unfolding a large map of South Carolina, Paul pointed to the area he was referring to. "I did a Google search of the area last night, and there are still huge tracts of land that have yet to be developed. Its land that's just as rural as it was during the war. As the map shows, four or five of these areas have hills and ridges running through them. I suggest we start there and work our way across this entire area. The one thing we need to keep in mind while we're searching for the location where these caves are located is Howard described the surrounding terrain as being fairly flat. If we find any areas that don't match his description, I suggest we ignore them for the time being as there's no sense searching there if the ground seems totally off."

"Are you thinking of using Church's helicopter to help with this search?" Chick asked as he continued to focus most of his attention on the area of the map Paul had been pointing to.

"Perhaps, but first I believe it's important for us to see what the ground looks like. To do that, we need to be on the ground, not in the air. Besides, if we can't see through the trees from that high up, there's no sense using the bird. For now, I'm thinking a drone might be a better way for us to cover some of the ground we're interested in, but just to play it safe we'll start our search on foot. Moncks Corner isn't that far of a drive from Murrells Inlet, so we'll get started after we speak with Bobby Ray and Peter. I'm interested in learning how much progress they've been able to make. Once we arrive in Moncks Corner, we'll talk to the folks who live and work there. We'll talk to the cops, firemen, a few park rangers, and maybe even a couple of hunters, to see if they can suggest a good spot for us to start. I'm all about getting as much help as we can."

What Paul and Chick had no way of knowing was that their search for this portion of the missing Confederate treasury would prove to be even harder and far more dangerous than their first adventure.

32

Determined not to interrupt the research his friends were conducting, Paul forced himself to keep busy as he waited to hear the results of Bobby Ray's and Peter's hard work.

Four days after meeting with Chick, while sitting at his desk concentrating on the last few entries Howard had written, Paul finally heard from Peter. Less than an hour after ending their call, Bobby Ray contacted his friend to give him an update on where he stood with Howard's background.

"That all sounds great, Bobby Ray," Paul said, setting his coffee cup down on the desk after listening to his friend for several minutes. "But before you go any further, let's stop right here. Can you be at my house around ten tomorrow morning?"

"Yeah, sure. I've got some time coming, so I'll blow the morning off and go into work after we finish."

"Sounds good. I'll reach out to Chick and Peter and see if they can make it. That way we can update each other on where we stand."

"Sounds like a plan. See you tomorrow."

Minutes later, after washing out his coffee cup in the kitchen sink, Paul called his other two friends. Like Bobby Ray, they both agreed to meet at Paul's home the following morning.

******

Knowing how punctual their host was, as Chick and Peter pulled into Paul's driveway the following morning ahead of their scheduled meeting time both were surprised to see Bobby Ray's unmarked police vehicle already there.

"Maybe he wanted to have the grand tour all to himself," Chick said, gathering up the documents he planned on referring to during their meeting. As was the case for Chick and Peter, it was also Bobby Ray's first visit to Paul's new home.

Located off of TPC Boulevard in Murrells Inlet, Paul and Donna's new four-bedroom home on Kiawah Loop sat inside a gated fifty-five and older community known as *The Seasons at Prince Creek West*. Surrounded by close to two hundred single family homes, the upscale community featured a wide variety of amenities and social clubs, as well as golfing privileges at a nearby golf course, TPC Myrtle Beach.

Walking inside the spacious home after being greeted by their host, one Donna was still in the midst of decorating, Peter waved to Bobby Ray after seeing him seated at the dining room table. One of the few items Donna had allowed to be moved into their new home from the one that had been damaged during the shootout months earlier, the wide modern table had been the scene of many dinners she and Paul had hosted over the past few years.

"Morning, Bobby Ray!" Peter cheerfully offered after seeing his friend sitting there.

With his mouth stuffed full of the fresh cinnamon covered coffeecake Donna had made earlier that morning, Bobby Ray barely managed to mumble a brief greeting in response to the one Peter had offered.

"You'll have to excuse him, Peter, his mouth has been busy since he got here." Paul said, shaking his head as he watched his friend slowly devour his second helping of Donna's coffeecake. "He called earlier to see if I wanted him to pick anything up for this meeting we're about to have, but when I told him Donna had gotten up early to fix a little treat for us to enjoy I was amazed at how fast he got here. He's been working that fork hard ever since he arrived." A prodigious eater, Bobby Ray's slim frame was in sharp contrast to the amount of food he consumed on a daily basis.

Leaving Bobby Ray seated at the table as he explained that Donna had already left for work, Paul gave Chick and Peter a brief tour of his new home. Joking with his guests as he showed them his study, he said, "We've only been here for a few weeks, but the good news is no one's tried to murder us inside our new home." Far too polite to laugh at the tragedy that had taken place at the home their host had previously owned, Paul's attempt at humor barely managed to arouse a weak response from either of his guests.

Returning to where Bobby Ray was still seated at Donna's dining room table, Chick noticed the healthy portion of the coffee cake his friend had consumed. "Save any for us?" His mouth stuffed full from his last bite of the sugary treat, Bobby Ray just smiled as he added a small amount of milk to the coffee Paul set down in front of him.

After taking a sip of the hot beverage, Bobby Ray answered Chick's friendly comment. "There are still a few bites left, but as you can see I did some serious damage to this wonderful treat Donna made for us. She's too good of a cook for me not to enjoy myself." As he sat there sipping his coffee, Bobby Ray slid what remained of one of Donna's favorite treats in front of where Chick was seated. From the two large pieces that were missing, it was apparent Bobby Ray had enjoyed his morning snack.

As Paul placed slices of Donna's coffee cake on plates for himself, Peter, and Chick, their host started the business part of the morning meeting. He did so by advising his guests of a recent conversation he had with Robert Regan. "When we were speaking, Robert told me that unless something popped up at the last minute he expected to arrive in South Carolina late Friday afternoon. If his plans go as he expects they will, he'll stay in Charleston overnight and arrive at our hotel the following morning. He's going to meet us before we start our search on Saturday."

"We're starting on Saturday?" Chick asked, somewhat surprised by the fact that Paul had arbitrarily made the decision to start their search without asking his partners if they had anything planned for the weekend.

"Unless that's a problem, that's when I'd like to start. We'll talk later about where and when we'll meet on Saturday morning, but that's when I plan on driving to Moncks Corner. Robert has some business to attend to when he first arrives, but he'll meet up with us for lunch that afternoon." As he answered Chick's question, Paul scanned the faces of his three friends for any signs of disappointment concerning the plans he had arranged. Seeing none, he then continued with some additional information.

"Robert wanted me to pass on one important point. While he's our direct connection to Mr. Church, he's really not that interested in calling the shots once work starts in the field. He understands the success we had in finding the other portion of the Confederate treasury, so he just wants it known that he's leaving the decision-making up to us." Waiting for a response from one of his friends, Paul took a sip of the hot coffee he had poured for himself moments earlier.

"What about getting his hands dirty? Is he going to pitch in or just be the money guy whenever we need something?" Chick asked, pushing his empty plate towards the center of the large dining room table.

"Guess we'll have to wait and see, won't we? We had the same thoughts last time when Peter signed on, and he ended up pitching in just as much as any of us. Let's hope for the same result from Robert." Paul replied, smiling across the table at Peter after acknowledging the variety of tasks his friend performed during their first search.

Opening one of his notebooks, Peter began speaking about some of the research he had conducted in an attempt to learn as much as possible about J. William Morse, the cabinetmaker responsible for crafting Howard's chest. "While I didn't find much, I did learn that our favorite cabinetmaker was born and raised in Richmond. In fact, like a number of people from that period of time who never travelled too far from their birthplace, he ended up dying there as well. According to the records I was able to find, he was born on June 23, 1832 to Lyman and Marion Morse. Those same records identified his father as being a carpenter. Our Mr. Morse died fifty-seven years later in 1889. Quite sadly, he died on his birthday. His remains are buried in Richmond inside Hollywood Cemetery."

Pausing a moment as a way of adding a tease to his presentation, Peter asked, "Care to guess who else is buried there?"

"Jefferson Davis, as well as Presidents James Monroe and John Tyler." Paul replied matter-of-factly as he waited for Peter to continue.

Somewhat stunned by the correct response Paul had given to what he thought was a question no one would have known the answer to, Peter turned and looked at their host. "How . . . how'd you know that?"

"Besides being a retired state trooper and a history buff, I somehow have the ability to retain a lot of useless information. While I can recite dates, times, and the names of people buried in the cemetery you just mentioned, don't ask me how long I've been married or the dates my two sons were born. I'm horrible when it comes to remembering details like that." A sheepish smile creased Paul's face as he shot a glance at the others seated around the table. A moment later, he tried explaining how he knew the answer to the question Peter had asked. "Back when Bobby Ray and I were attending the FBI National Academy, we spent a couple of weekends touring the sites in and around Richmond. Hollywood Cemetery was a place we spent time visiting one afternoon. That's how I knew the answer to the question."

"That's still pretty remarkable, Paul. You guys went there, what . . . twenty years ago or so? I'd have trouble just remembering the name of the cemetery, never mind trying to recall whose graves I visited."

"There's at least one other semi-famous person who's buried there that comes to mind," Paul said, recalling a name he had seen engraved on a tombstone.

"And?" Peter asked, impatiently waiting for his friend to mention the person's name he had seen.

"The Reverend Charles Minnigerode. For many years he served at St. Paul's Episcopal Church in Richmond. In fact, St. Paul's has often been referred to as the Cathedral of the Confederacy. He was someone who knew Jefferson Davis and Robert E. Lee very well."

"I'm glad you told us that, Paul, as my life is now complete knowing where the good reverend is buried." Peter's sarcastic response caused his friends to enjoy a good laugh.

"Learn anything else about Morse?" Paul asked before taking another sip of his coffee.

"While I plan on doing some more digging to see if I can come up with anything else, I did learn that Mr. Morse owned a woodworking shop just outside the shadows of the Confederate capital. From talking with a woman who works at the American Civil War Museum, she told me she's assisted others in the past when his name was mentioned. This lady considers Morse to have been a pretty talented cabinetmaker. Besides Howard's chest, some of his other work still survives to this day. Many of his pieces, such as desks, tables, and wall cabinets, are considered to be among the finest examples of Civil War era furniture on display in museums around Richmond. When I was speaking with this museum staff member, she recalled one collector paying close to fifteen thousand dollars for a desk Morse had crafted in 1863. Apparently this buyer also believes his name is synonymous with quality work."

"Any of those pieces have hidden compartments like the one Mr. Church found?" Bobby Ray asked, listening intently to what Peter was telling them.

"Not that I know of, but maybe that's an angle someone should start looking into. Who knows what someone else might haven hidden in one of his other pieces just to keep it from falling into the hands of the Union Army. Maybe we need to look into that after we're done with this project."

"That's not a bad idea, Peter." Paul offered as he thought about the possibility of other secrets being hidden inside furniture Morse had crafted. "What you've learned about the late Mr. Morse is very interesting. Thanks for the effort you put forth on learning as much as you have on such an obscure character. What about those folks who appraised Mr. Church's wooden chest and the journal he found. Were you able to learn anything about them?" Paul asked, more interested in this part of Peter's research than he was in the life of a lesser known figure from the time of the Civil War.

Wiping his mouth with a napkin after taking a sip of his coffee, Peter briefly referred to his notes before responding to Paul's question. "A simple answer would be, yes, I learned a great deal about them. However, when you think about it, I was looking for information on people who are still alive in this modern world where information is king. I mention that because I've finally realized you can't do anything these days without someone capturing your actions in some database. While the search for information on Mr. Morse was ultimately successful, it was much more intense. What I've been able to determine about the people Mr. Church hired to examine the chest was they're among the best of the best when it comes to appraising antiques. Their track records show they have examined hundreds of pieces; some dating back to when the country was first being settled. When I looked for any information on whether their appraisals had ever been questioned, or if anyone had challenged their credentials, I couldn't find any occasions when another so-called expert was called in to offer another opinion. I checked on their credentials and found each of these appraisers to be in good standing with the International Society of Appraisers, the American Society of Appraisers, and the Appraiser's Association of America. To be certified by one of these associations is an accomplishment in itself; to be certified by all three means you know what you're talking about when it comes to antiques. These appraisers Mr. Church hired are among a small number of people who currently possess certifications from all three associations."

"Impressive." Bobby Ray said, letting out a loud whistle as he looked across the table at the others sitting there.

"So it's safe to say they each gave Mr. Church a pretty accurate appraisal of not only what the chest and journal are worth, but they also confirmed the two pieces are from the time of the Civil War; meaning they're not forgeries or knock-offs."

"Correct. When I called Robert regarding these appraisals, he faxed me copies of the paperwork for both items. The documentation Mr. Church has . . . commonly referred to as provenance, is pretty remarkable. It will definitely come in handy if he ever decides to sell either piece."

"Good to know." Paul said, pleased by the information Peter had learned.

"There's one more thing," Peter said, chuckling about a topic that had nothing to do with the meeting they were having. "When I was talking with Robert, he asked me to pass on one more piece of information to all of you." Trying to keep from laughing, he said, "Paul, you and I call Robert by his formal name, while Bobby Ray simply calls him Bobby. He wants all of you to know that he hates being called Bobby. He wants all of us to call him Robert. While that piece of information is not as important as what I learned about Mr. Morse and the appraisers, if it keeps the guy happy please call him Robert whenever you're speaking with him."

"Whatever." Paul replied, rolling his eyes over this useless piece of information.

"Care to know what each piece has been appraised at?" Peter asked.

"Nope. I don't care. You know that kind of stuff doesn't interest me." As with the valuable Confederate assets he and his team recovered during their first search, Paul had little interest in knowing what Howard's journal or the wooden chest were worth. Far more interested in solving the current mystery of where the valuable assets had been hidden, he cared little about the value of the artifacts they had been discussing. Raised by parents who lived paycheck to paycheck, money was something that had never interested the retired state trooper.

Smiling as he put his notes away, Peter had expected Paul to answer his question just as he had. From working alongside Paul during their first search, he learned his friend had little interest in knowing the value of certain artifacts. The same had been true for the millions of dollars in gold and silver they recovered; Paul's interest had always been focused on solving the mystery surrounding the lost Confederate treasury. This intense focus, something Paul brought with him to every criminal investigation he worked, had been with him during his entire career. He had never been interested in being outwitted by those he was sworn to arrest.

Noticing Bobby Ray eyeing what was left of the coffeecake, Chick asked his friend what he had learned about Howard's background.

"Well, the good news is there really was a Captain Noah Howard who served in the Confederate Army during the Civil War." Looking across the table, Bobby Ray continued by saying, "Y'all know I'm a huge supporter of the National Park Service, so I started my search by using the Civil War Soldiers and Sailors System; the CWSS as it's often called. The Park Service, along with a few other agencies involved with preserving the history of the war, does a great job in maintaining this database."

"You found him that easy?" Chick asked, recalling some of the frustration he endured when trying to track down the backgrounds of soldiers he and the others had sought information on a few years earlier.

"Yep, sure did," Bobby Ray replied, nodding his head without giving Chick's question much thought. Looking at his notes, he added, "Here it is right here, Captain Noah Howard. He was a member of the 1st Virginia Volunteer Infantry Regiment. The records I found showed he enlisted in the Confederate Army on May 12, 1861. Those same records list him as being killed in May, 1865, but they don't say how or where he died."

Exchanging startled looks with each other, Paul responded to Bobby Ray's last comment before Chick could muster his thoughts. "If he was in the middle of nowhere where he committed suicide, how were you able to verify his death? Did the records indicate how the Confederacy learned of his death?"

"No, they didn't. As hard as I tried, I wasn't able to locate any supporting documents to show how the army or, for that matter, how anyone had learned about his death. From his last few entries, we're fairly certain Howard committed suicide shortly after the war had ended. Someone must have found his remains, but I doubt they went to the trouble of notifying anyone about his death. Besides, the Confederacy no longer existed, so who would they have reported his death to?"

"That's my point." As he thought about Howard's death being recorded, Paul wondered how the news of the young officer's passing had been determined.

Looking at a copy of the page which recorded Howard's enlistment and the information related to his death, Paul commented on the news Bobby Ray had presented. "If the journal turns out to be Howard's as we expect, perhaps we can fill in some of the missing information on how he died. If we have the means to update his service record as a result of this project we're about to start, I vote we do that."

"I agree." Chick offered, waiting to hear what other information Bobby Ray had to tell them.

"The records listed Howard as holding the rank of captain. They also show he was assigned to the regiment I've told you about. There was no mention of him sustaining any injuries or ever serving with another unit during the war. After I finished searching through the CWSS records, I searched some other sites and learned he was born in Grundy, Virginia. Those records, which I have copies of, list each of the engagements his regiment fought in. Those same records briefly list what role his regiment played in each of those engagements. In a few of them, his regiment had been held in reserve so it's likely they didn't see any action."

"What about this assignment he was given just as things started falling apart near the end of the war? Were you able to find any documents which showed President Davis personally ordered Howard to escort this portion of the treasury that he's written about?" Not allowing Bobby Ray time to answer, Paul asked his next question. "Besides the ones you've looked at, were there any other records which confirmed Howard had actually left Richmond with a portion of the treasury?" While pleased to learn Bobby Ray had managed to find some additional information regarding Howard's background, he doubted any records existed regarding who or what was being transported on the train mentioned in several of the captain's entries. Instead, Paul was hoping the documentation his friend had found would help prove Howard was telling the truth when he described the chaos that existed in Richmond as the Union Army drew closer.

"Just like Peter, I still have some work to do on what Howard's role was during the last few weeks of the war. But the good news is I was told there's a manifest that actually does exist which captured the names of some of the passengers on the train Howard took out of Richmond. I'm not sure if it lists the type of cargo that was put aboard, but I'm told it did list who the passengers were. With the Confederate rail system being in the shambles it was during the last couple years of the war, I'm surprised such a manifest exists. If it does, and if it lists President Davis' name as being the official who authorized its departure, there's a good chance Howard's name will be on it. As soon as I know more, so will all of you."

"That would be an amazing document to find, Bobby Ray." As the person sitting at the table with the most knowledge regarding the Civil War, even Chick was surprised by the news Bobby Ray had told them.

Sitting pensively as he digested the importance of the research being conducted, Paul barely paid attention as his friends talked about the information Peter and Bobby Ray had uncovered. Leaning forward in his chair several minutes later, he listened to a question Chick raised rather quietly. The calmness in Chick's voice told Paul his friend was still working out the details of some confusing issue. "So, for now, we just have to accept Howard's entries as being truthful, correct?"

"I don't see how we have any other choice," Paul said, jumping back into the conversation. "What little information we've been able to verify about some of the points he's raised shows, at least in my opinion it does, he wasn't embellishing any of the details or what his assignment actually entailed. Until we prove otherwise, we have to trust what he wrote to be the truth."

Still weighing the thought that had crossed his mind, Chick looked to Paul for his opinion on a related concern. "What's more important, sending Bobby Ray up to Richmond or taking him with us on Saturday?"

Blessed with the ability to make tough decisions during his career, Paul never hesitated as he answered his friend's question. "He's coming with us. I'm with Bobby Ray; my gut is telling me Howard was being truthful each time he made those entries in his journal. We'll start by looking for the place where he hid the gold and silver. If the search proves difficult or if we determine Howard wasn't being as honest as we're giving him credit for, then we'll reconsider the research option. For now, let's concentrate on finding those caves."

33

Early Saturday morning, a day which started off with periods of heavy rain and high winds pummeling the South Carolina coastline, Paul and Bobby Ray, followed by Chick and Peter, started south on Highway 17 towards the small town of McCellanville. Planning on being away from home for several days, Paul's pick-up, like Chick's van, was packed with food, extra clothing, maps, research material, several tools for digging, and other equipment. In Chick's van, Peter had carefully packed away his cameras and one video camera.

Enjoying cups of coffee they picked up at a local coffee shop in Pawleys Island, Paul and Bobby Ray exchanged thoughts and ideas on how they expected the next few days to unfold. As they talked, Bobby Ray spent several minutes casually studying the topography of the area they planned on searching. The partially unfolded map showed the area to be mostly flat, with only slight changes in the elevation further west of Lake Moultrie.

Stopping along Highway 17 roughly forty minutes later, in the small, rustic fishing village of McClellanville, Paul stretched his legs in the parking lot of a local diner. Unlike several others associated with the town's fishing industry in some manner or another, the McClellanville Diner was one of the few prosperous businesses in the historic community. As he waited outside, Paul's three companions walked inside to reload their cups with hot coffee.

Minutes later, after turning onto Highway 45, a two-lane road running through the heart of the Francis Marion National Forest, Paul and Bobby Ray spoke about the person the forest had been named for and his daring exploits against the British during the Revolutionary War. Fans of Marion's tactics, the two talked for close to ninety minutes on how the late Indian fighter and his men had tormented the British with a variety of different tactics and attacks. Nicknamed the *Swamp Fox,* the legendary fighter was still revered across South Carolina as one of the state's most favorite sons.

Early that afternoon, as he pulled into the parking lot of a Subway Restaurant on West Main Street in Moncks Corner, an area local residents referred to as being the hub of their small community, Paul spied Robert Regan leaning against the rear of his rental car. Like always, the retired state trooper was ten minutes early for their pre-arranged meeting.

"Morning, Paul! Morning, everyone!" Regan politely offered. Fatigued from a busy week of non-stop work which required him to travel back and forth across two different time zones on three separate occasions, Simon Church's right-hand man was still in need of some additional sleep. While the seven hours of uninterrupted sleep in a comfortable bed had been just what he needed, Regan was already

looking forward to another night of sound sleep. Casually dressed in a pair of freshly pressed blue Dockers and wearing a dark red golf shirt similar to the expensive versions worn on television by a host of PGA professionals, Regan's friendly greeting was nearly drowned out by the noise generated by the Jake brake of a passing logging truck. The loud noise caused Paul and Bobby Ray to briefly divert their attention to the large truck passing through town before acknowledging Regan's greeting.

"Afternoon, Robert! Welcome to Moncks Corner." Paul said, remembering to address Regan as he preferred.

Casting his eyes in several different directions before focusing his attention on Paul, Regan said, "This is my first time visiting the thriving metropolis of Moncks Corner. I did some research on the flight here and learned this small town of less than ten thousand souls started out as a trading post in the early 1720s. Despite its small size and rustic appearance, it looks like a nice place to raise a family. I grew up in a town not much bigger than this, so I'm starting to feel like I'm back home."

"Robert, you and I have something in common. It's my first time here as well." Paul said, shaking hands with Regan. "I've been living in South Carolina for close to seven years, but for some reason Donna and I have never made it down here."

Walking towards the restaurant's front door as Paul introduced Regan to his friends, the person Simon Church had designated as his point of contact listened intently as Chick and Peter's backgrounds and qualifications were being explained.

Inside the restaurant, as Paul and Regan ordered lunch for the five of them, Bobby Ray walked outside after spying a deputy from the Berkley County Sheriff's Department sitting inside his SUV. Fifteen minutes later, after introducing himself by way of showing the deputy his credentials, the undersheriff of Georgetown County sat down at the table where his friends were eating.

"Someone you know?" Paul asked, taking notice of the marked SUV as it drove out of the parking lot.

"No, not really," Bobby Ray replied, unwrapping his sandwich as he answered Paul's question. "I've seen him a few times at some training classes we've attended, but I've never spoken to him. Not until now, that is."

Putting down his sandwich, Paul realized why Bobby Ray had gone outside to speak with the deputy. "Looking for some local knowledge, huh? What did your new best friend have to say?"

Finishing the first bite of his sandwich, Bobby Ray took a moment to wipe his mouth before speaking. "Deputy Caterson told me he's lived in these parts for most of his life. He claims to have hunted and fished across most of Berkeley County for the past thirty years or so. He's also spent countless hours in the woods with his partners eradicating marijuana fields each summer. From the sounds of it, he knows these parts pretty well."

Putting down the soda he had been drinking, Peter briefly looked at Paul before directing a question at Bobby Ray. He did so just as Bobby Ray was about to take another bite of his thick sandwich. "While all of that is interesting, what did this colleague of yours have to say about the locations of any caves? Has he ever seen any?"

"Maybe, but not really." Bobby Ray replied, quickly taking another bite of his sandwich before being asked another question.

"What the hell kind of an answer is that?" Peter demanded, expecting a better response than the one they were all given. The barter that followed caused Regan to smile as he witnessed the exchange taking place.

"I don't like answering questions while I'm eating. It gives me indigestion." Bobby Ray's comment caused Peter to roll his eyes at the lame excuse his friend had offered.

"I'll buy you some Tums later this afternoon," Paul said sarcastically, jumping into the conversation as a way of keeping the discussion going. "Please answer the question, would you."

Smirking over Paul's comment, Bobby Ray told his friends what he learned from Deputy Caterson. "He told me not far from where we're sitting, maybe three miles tops, are two fairly long ridge lines. He claimed there's at least one cave in one of those ridge lines, but he couldn't recall seeing any others. It's not much, but it's a place for us start our search. Who knows, maybe the other two caves collapsed like Howard described. If they have, it's possible Caterson just didn't recognize what was hidden under the hillside."

"That's good news, isn't it?" Regan asked out loud to no one in particular.

"Maybe, maybe not," Paul replied, replaying the words his friend has used.

"Caterson told me one of these ridge lines is not far from a body of water that's known as the Tail Race Canal. The canal supposedly flows for several miles from Lake Moultrie to where it drains into what is called the West Branch of the Cooper River. I'm not so sure about the river, but it's possible Lake Moultrie or the canal may be the one Howard mentioned in his journal."

"Maybe." Paul replied, keeping his response short for the second time in less than a minute. "He didn't say anything about ever seeing something that may have resembled a collapsed cave, did he?"

"He sure didn't," Bobby Ray replied, taking another healthy bite of his sandwich. "Maybe they're out there, but I didn't want to let the cat out of the bag. If he figured out we were here to do some exploring for gold and silver that went missing at the end of the Civil War, Lord knows how many people might start searching for these caves."

******

Later that afternoon, Paul and his small caravan travelled to the upper part of the Tail Race Canal. Speaking with several fishermen on the banks of the canal, they narrowed down the location of the two ridge lines.

After hiking for several miles through woods populated with tall pine trees and sporadic patches of thick undergrowth, Paul and his team finally located the ridgelines they had been told about. The hilly and dense terrain had kept the ridgelines from view since starting their search.

With Regan joining Paul and Bobby Ray, the three treasure hunters continued to move west as they followed the larger ridgeline. As Paul and the others searched the ridgeline in one direction, Chick and Peter moved east, scouring the opposite end of the same ridgeline for the cave Howard described as holding a significant portion of the Confederate treasury. The ridgeline they were searching sat further away from the canal than the longer ridgeline running along the western edge of Lake Moultrie.

As the two groups moved off in different directions, Paul hollered a friendly warning to his friends in the other group. *"Watch out for*

snakes! We don't need anyone being bit. We'll meet back here in three hours.
Whatever is out there, it isn't going any place if we don't find it today."

******

Over the course of the next three hours, under a warm sun the two groups hiked the entire length of the first ridgeline, crisscrossing the rocky terrain from several different directions. Hiking up one slope that was significantly steeper than the others, Paul's team stopped to examine four different boulder-strewn sites that, at first glance, showed promise of being the site of the collapsed caves. Like three previous locations which attracted their attention, their hopes were dashed at this newest site when thick sheets of ledge were discovered under a layer of surface rocks.

With the terrain being slightly different in its appearance from the one described in Howard's journal, the search of the first ridgeline turned up little to give the two teams any hope of finding the caves.

It was the first of several disappointments Paul and his team would encounter.

<u>34</u>

Spending the next eight days doggedly searching the woods and fields around Moncks Corner for the caves Howard had supposedly filled with Confederate treasure, like his friends, Paul experienced a wide range of emotions as each day ended with their hopes being dashed. To make matters worse, during their fruitless days of searching Paul's team had endured a variety of different weather conditions; some pleasant and some which left them cursing Mother Nature.

Faced with periods of high winds, intermittent showers, and falling temperatures as they scoured the area over the last three days of their stay, the end of their visit was proving to be far less enjoyable than the first few days. Those last three days included searching a remote and steep section of terrain northwest of town. Searching for hours during periods of intermittent rain showers and cool temperatures had caused their clothes and boots to become soaking wet. In addition to the adverse weather conditions, they also dealt with fallen tree limbs, slippery terrain, and occasional torrents of water racing down sections of the rocky slopes they were hiking over. Fortunately, despite their wet clothes, they managed to navigate the wet ground without any serious injuries being incurred. While disappointed over the lack of any success, Paul was comforted by the positive attitude his friends continued to display.

Their resolve had stayed strong over the course of their search due to nightly pep talks from Simon Church and from a variety of good meals Regan had paid for at several nearby restaurants. It had also been fortified after learning Church had instructed Regan to purchase a set of new hiking boots and warmer clothing for each of them from a local Big Lots store. "I'm not having these folks doing my dirty work while wearing wet boots. Buy them each another pair of boots so one pair can be drying when they're not being worn. If they need anything else, make sure they get it." For now, Church was holding up his end of the bargain.

After a few nights of sitting in bars watching mindless television shows and drinking far too many Jack and Cokes, Paul spent the last couple of nights sitting in his hotel room reviewing his working copy of Howard's journal. As he read and reread a number of entries, Paul tried plotting the route Howard had taken on a large map. With Bobby Ray back home addressing a significant personnel matter within his department and with his map covered with notes and reference marks, as the others enjoyed themselves Paul spent hours looking for the one clue he believed he had overlooked.

Inside his neatly decorated room within the Carolina Inn, a three-story hotel built to look like an old Southern mansion, Paul did his best at absorbing every word Howard had written. As he had done with the letters discovered during his previous adventure, Paul hoped to uncover that one clue that would tell him where the caves were located. They were the same caves where Howard spent the final days of his life hiding the precious assets he had been charged with moving south.

Ignoring the loud noises penetrating the walls of his hotel room, Paul reread what Howard had written many years earlier. As he tried concentrating, he was forced to ignore the shrieks and laughter coming from one of the adjacent rooms. It had been rented by a young couple intent on making love to each other as many times as possible each night. Inside the other adjoining room, a television, its volume turned up far too loud, occasionally interrupted his thoughts as heavy bombers from the United States reduced Germany's munition plants to rubble on the History Channel. As the bombing runs took place, the room's elderly occupant dozed peacefully in a leather recliner.

Putting down Howard's journal on the last night of his stay, Paul called Donna to make sure she was enjoying her new home. Speaking on the phone for several minutes, he listened as his wife described how the past few days had gone. As they were speaking, Donna suddenly paused after hearing the sounds Paul had been forced to endure over the past few nights.

"Paul, what the heck is that racket I'm hearing? Are you and your friends having a party in your room?" Donna's ears strained to make out the sounds she was hearing.

Laughing at his wife's question, Paul said, "What racket are you referring to? The loud television being played in the room to the left of mine or, and pardon me for saying it this way, the occasional bang of my other neighbors' headboard against the wall we share? The way they've been going at it over the past few nights, they're either newlyweds experiencing sex for the first time or it's a couple whose spouses must be out of town."

"I'm hoping it's the television." Donna replied after running the scenarios Paul had described through her head. "Why haven't you complained about the noise? Have them move you to another room so you can get some rest from that God-awful racket I'm hearing."

"It has its moments, that's for sure." Paul said, staring at the common wall being shared with the romantic couple next door. "I tried asking for another room the other evening, but the hotel is booked solid. The local VFW has rented most of the rooms for a convention of some kind. This place and every hotel in the area are full for the next three nights. I'll call down to the Front Desk in a few minutes and ask them to ground the bombers for the next few hours."

"What?"

"Nothing, I was just making a joke, that's all."

"Geez, that's marvelous," Donna said, referring to the loud noises that continued to penetrate the walls of Paul's room. "Don't take this the wrong way, but I'm glad I'm not there. I think I'd go postal if I had to listen to that racket."

Snickering over his wife's comments, Paul said, "Care to guess the name of one of the other hotels in town?"

Blessed with a quick wit, one that often reflected the sarcasm she used so well, Donna did not miss a beat. "Knowing where you are, I'm sure it's something pretty swanky sounding. Maybe something like *The Dew Drop Inn?*"

"Pretty close . . . it's called *The Why Knot Inn*."

"*Marvelous!* I'll have to check the *Michelin Guide* to see how many stars they've been given." Donna's sarcastic sense of humor referred to the rating system the well-known publication often gave to hotels across the world.

Saying their goodbyes a few minutes later, Paul continued to chuckle over his wife's comments. Feeling refreshed after speaking to her, he returned to reading the entries Howard had written. In the background, Allied planes continued to annihilate Dresden, Germany.

Reading a few of the last entries Howard had written, Paul concentrated on the long descriptive entry the young Confederate officer wrote after first locating the caves. Setting down the pages he was reading, moments later, as Paul brushed his teeth he stared at the bathroom mirror while doing his best to flush out an important thought.

"*Turkey vultures?*"

35

Sitting inside the hotel restaurant the following morning, Paul paid little attention to a FOX news story being shown on a nearby television regarding the latest candidates to join an already lengthy list of Democratic presidential hopefuls. Sipping his first cup of coffee, and far more interested in the historical treasures he was attempting to locate than the flawed solutions to America's problems being offered by three inexperienced congressmen, Paul continued to focus on a small number of entries Howard had written in the days before his death. They were the same ones that had attracted his attention the previous evening.

While Howard had made a brief passing comment regarding a flock of turkey vultures in one of his entries, before falling asleep Paul managed to figure out why the Confederate officer had even bothered to mention them. Pulling out a small pad he always carried with him, he had just started jotting down a thought about the caves when Chick and Peter slid inside the booth he was sitting in.

Adjusting the left sleeve of his bulky sweatshirt, Peter offered a friendly smile as he wiped the remaining sleep from his eyes. Seconds later, he uttered his first words of the day. "Morning . . . how's the coffee?" Dressed for another day in the woods, Peter's attire looked as if he was modeling a set of warm outdoor clothing from L.L. Bean.

"It's not bad. Actually it's pretty good." Paul replied, nodding at the coffee cup sitting off to his left as he set his pen down after jotting down a brief reminder regarding one of Howard's entries. Unlike the small diner he often visited in Murrells Inlet, the hotel's dining room was not only decorated with nicer furniture, it was also much more spacious. Seated in a booth in the back corner of the room, Paul took note of the white linen napkins and shiny silverware placed in each of the twenty-four booths. In the center of the room, eight neatly dressed tables sat waiting for the day's breakfast crowd to arrive. As someone who had spent a great deal of time eating far too many meals inside more greasy spoons than he could remember, the fancy place settings seemed far too elegant for the morning meal he was about to order.

"We missed your company last night, Paul," Peter offered from across the table as their waitress filled two more cups with hot coffee before topping off the one she had poured minutes earlier. "You should have stayed. Unlike the past couple of nights, we kept the drinking to a minimum."

"Really?" Paul replied, questioning the redness in Chick's eyes as he pointed at his friend. "The look on this guy's face tells me one of you may have kept it to a minimum, but I'm not so sure about the other."

"Where's Robert?" Chick asked, less interested in revisiting the previous night's escapades than his two friends. Taking his first sip of coffee, Chick began eyeing the extensive breakfast buffet sitting less than fifteen feet away.

"I bumped into him in the lobby on my way in here. He was headed back to his room with a coffee and a bagel. He's going to join us after he speaks with his boss about the progress we're making."

"Or lack of." Chick retorted, pointing out the fact that he and his friends had yet to find the caves they were looking for.

After filling their plates from the well-stocked breakfast buffet that featured three different kinds of eggs, fresh cooked bacon and sausage, home fries, toast, several different kinds of sliced fruit, and much more, Paul and his friends resumed their conversation as they settled back inside their booth. Knowing lunch would likely consist of nothing more than a piece of fruit and one or two granola bars, they each filled their plates with more food than they would normally eat for breakfast.

Unlike Paul, Chick had yet to figure out what Howard had meant by his brief reference to the turkey vultures. "I know you've dissected his entries more than I have, so what's so important about those damn turkey vultures. He was rather vague or maybe even distracted when he mentioned them." Reaching across the table, Chick sprinkled a healthy dose of Frank's Hot Sauce on the pile of eggs sitting on his plate.

"From one of his previous entries, it's pretty obvious Howard was disgusted by the way those Union soldiers had been murdered. That's one of the reasons I believe he started searching for these caves we're looking for. From the manner in which he described those murders, I think Howard felt an obligation to not only find the body of one of his fellow soldiers, but to make sure those

Union soldiers received a proper burial. If I'm right, that makes Howard even more special than we believe he was."

Finished eating some of the fruit on his plate, Peter set his fork down as he looked across the table at Paul. "I'm starting to think you believe Howard was a compassionate person. That's despite the fact he had been fighting against the Union Army for nearly four years. There's an oxymoron built in there someplace, but what's his reason for feeling so sympathetic?"

Ignoring Peter's comment about which side of the war Howard had been fighting for, Paul took a moment to explain some of the feelings he believed the young officer had displayed. His own feelings were based on the last few entries Howard had written inside his journal. "Well, to start with, I don't believe it was just about those Union soldiers. In some of his entries Howard comes across as being a loner, someone far more interested in being promoted than he was in anything else. However, on this particular occasion I believe he went looking for those caves in the hopes of finding the remains of one of his men."

"You're referring to Lieutenant Ratcliff, correct?" Chick replied. His response pleased Paul as it indicated his friend had earnestly studied the contents of Howard's journal, instead of merely glossing over it.

"Correct. I don't mean to suggest Howard was not upset by how those soldiers had been murdered, but I think he was far more interested in recovering the remains of a fellow officer."

"So, what I still don't understand is the part about the turkey vultures?" Chick said, polishing off the last of his scrambled eggs.

"Turkey vultures aren't much different than you and Bobby Ray." Paul said, nodding at his friend's plate. "They like to eat."

Glancing down at his nearly empty plate, Chick finally understood what Howard's reference had meant. "You think those vultures were eating the remains of those Union soldiers?" Chick's question caused Peter to cover his mouth in disgust.

"Absolutely, that's why they're called vultures. They eat whatever is available, even the remains of dead soldiers."

"So maybe Howard wasn't planning on burying those soldiers, but when his men told him what those birds had done to their remains he felt compelled to do the right thing."

"Perhaps." Paul said, thinking of what it must have been like when Howard's men located the partially-eaten remains. "In the end, his compassion, if that's what it was, cost him dearly."

"That first cave, the one where the remains of the Union soldiers were found, it also contains the remains of some of Howard's men, doesn't it?" By now, Peter knew the answer to the question he had raised moments earlier.

"Afraid so," Paul replied, sipping his coffee as his breakfast grew cold. "If we get lucky and find these caves, we're going to have to figure out a way of excavating at least one of them. I consider the cave where Howard's men perished to be a grave. We'll have to make a decision on how to proceed once we find it." Having barely touched his breakfast, Paul pushed his plate away as he thought of how badly the bodies of several soldiers had been crushed when the cave and the adjoining hillside collapsed.

With a lifelong interest in American history, one far more advanced than Paul's or anyone else he was currently working with, Chick's other passion involved studying all there was to know about maritime disasters. Speaking rather emphatically, he said, "That cave you're talking about, that's no different than many other places where men have tragically lost their lives. Whether it's the U.S.S. Arizona, the Titanic, or whatever Civil War battlefield you care to talk about, those are graves that shouldn't be disturbed unless it's absolutely necessary. I agree with your statement about the cave being a gravesite that shouldn't be disturbed. If the National Park Service wants to undertake a project like that, so be it, but people like us should never disturb a grave just for the sake of recovering a hidden relic or someone's remains. If we find it, we need to have an archeologist with us before anything gets disturbed." While helping to recover the remains of several Confederate soldiers during their previous search for the missing treasury, Chick's opinion on whether it was appropriate for any unmarked graves to be disturbed had changed significantly. It would change again over the next few days.

"I agree," Peter said, echoing the position taken by his two friends.

It was a position that would soon become more complex than any of them could have imagined.

******

Later that morning, with Regan already on his way to the Charleston airport for his return trip back to Texas, Paul and the other members of his team ventured to another rocky setting not far from Lake Moultrie. Nine hot and dusty hours later, after another day of failing to find any signs of the collapsed caves, they ended their search for the elusive treasure. Returning to their hotel rooms, they packed their belongings, showered, and headed back to Murrells Inlet.

Over the course of the next several days, Paul conferred with Simon Church and Robert Regan during two long phone calls. During that time, just as he had done with the letters found during his first adventure, Paul studied Howard's journal entries several more times. Convinced he was close to solving the mystery regarding the disappearance of a significant amount of money, Paul read and reread Howard's journal every chance he could.

Doing so was his only hope of solving the mystery Simon Church had hired him to find.

36

After spending the better part of his first three days back home catching up with Donna, Paul spent several hours one afternoon cleaning his pontoon boat. Christened the *Donna Lynn* shortly after being gifted the boat by a group of admirers and friends, Paul's boat was a newer version of the one he had purchased from a friend, Steve Alcott. Like his vehicles, tools, and firearms, *Donna Lynn's* appearance reflected the care and attention Paul gave his boat.

Pushing eighty-nine years of age, Steve Alcott was one of the last remaining members of the first group of European families to settle the area around Murrells Inlet. From property left to him by his family, as well as from money setup in a trust fund by his wealthy parents, Steve had managed to parlay a series of successful business ventures into a sizeable fortune.

One of the first people they met after moving to the Inlet, the octogenarian had quickly become close friends with Paul and Donna Waring. His warm, friendly demeanor, coupled with his successful business acumen, had also caused him to become one of Paul's closest confidants.

Seated across from each other in Paul's favorite booth inside the Waccamaw Diner, the two friends engaged themselves in a friendly, lighthearted conversation as Betty took their orders. Having already eaten their mid-day meals hours earlier, both ordered a cup of coffee and a slice of apple pie to enjoy during one of their weekly talks.

"I'll have mine warm, Betty," Steve offered, tweaking his order after Betty finished filling his coffee cup for the second time. "I'd better play it safe, so please add a small scoop of vanilla ice cream on the side." Like most people, Steve had a sweet tooth which occasionally needed satisfying late in the day.

Spending several minutes speaking about the project he was working on and how one of the country's wealthiest individuals had approached him to lead it, Paul took his time describing the journal Simon Church had accidently come across. Like Bobby Ray, Chick, and several others, Steve had played a minor role in Paul's first discovery.

"That's a remarkable story, Paul. I can't believe no one else found it." Steve offered as he placed a spoonful of creamy vanilla ice cream in his mouth while waiting for his pie to cool down.

"I had the same thought when I first learned about the journal, but then I realized the chest had likely been owned by only a handful of people since Howard's death. If you think of what a chest is used for . . . obviously storing someone's belongings, then it's not so difficult to understand how it hadn't been found. It probably sat for extended periods of time without ever being touched."

Finishing the first bite of his warm afternoon treat, Steve concurred with his friend's thought. "I guess so. I know I have a few chests and bins that I store some of my belongings in. Some I may only open once or twice a year; others I may not open at all."

Having lost his interest in finishing his rare afternoon snack, Paul pushed his plate away as he listened to Steve's question regarding what his plans were for locating the still-to-be-found set of caves. As his friend asked his question, Betty stopped to check on the only two customers on her side of the diner. As it was on most afternoons, the hours leading up to when the dinner crowd started filtering in were often very quiet.

Refilling their coffee cups, Betty eyed the retired state trooper as a suspicious thought entered her mind. "Ya know, I can't help thinkin' that you two sitting here like ya are reminds me of the days when you and them other friends of yours were trying to find that Confederate treasury y'all were after." Stepping away from the booth, Betty added, "Y'all got anything to say?"

Without missing a beat, as Steve looked up from where he was seated, he said, "The pie's pretty tasty."

Biting her tongue, Betty walked away shaking her head as Paul snickered over Steve's comment.

"She's smarter than I give her credit for," Steve chuckled, watching Betty as she disappeared behind the lunch counter.

"She certainly is. I haven't told her anything as I don't have time to answer all the questions she'd be asking, so please don't say anything to her."

After assuring Paul he would honor his request, Steve asked his next set of questions. "So if you haven't been able to find these caves, what's your next step? And, how long do you plan on traipsing through the woods looking for something that may not exist any longer? After all this time, they could be hidden under rocks or shrubs or trees and you wouldn't know it."

Setting down his coffee cup, Paul sat quietly for a few moments before responding. Sitting in his usual spot, he briefly gave thought to something he had come across the night before while reading parts of Howard's journal. "To answer your question, yes, that's my intention. But before I do, I'm going to study my maps to see if they can steer me to where the caves might be . . . or were. The way I see it, we really don't have much of a choice. My team and I will just have to keep searching until we find them."

"*Maps?* What kind of maps? Maps show you roads, highways, and stuff like that." Steve said, licking his fork after eating the last of his pie. "They don't show you where caves are located; at least, not the kind of maps I sometimes look at." Mistakenly of the opinion that Paul was planning on consulting the kind of maps commonly sold over-the-counter, Steve had no idea why his friend would waste his time doing so.

"The kind I have does. Last week I ordered a set of topographical maps from the United States Army Corps of Engineers. The ones I ordered show the different elevations in and around the area where we've been looking. They just arrived yesterday afternoon, so I haven't had much of a chance to study them as yet, but what I saw was far better than the maps I've been working with. There's far more detail than the kind you're thinking about."

"So what happens if these maps don't lead you to the caves?"

Electing to keep a recent observation to himself, Paul simply shrugged his shoulders in response to his friend's question.

"You'll figure it out, I guess." Steve said, reaching across the table to pat his friend's left hand. "You're the smartest guy I've ever met. Others may have never found them, but my money is on you. You'll find those caves."

Walking towards the diner's front door after leaving enough money on the table to cover the cost of their afternoon treat and Betty's tip, Paul and Steve waved to her as she sat drinking a soft drink at the lunch counter. With only three hours to go in her shift, she was enjoying her first break since early that morning.

As they approached the door, Steve managed to attract Betty's attention by letting out a soft whistle. Trying not to laugh, he hollered, *"My friend and I are off to find the rest of the Confederate treasury!"*

Pooh-poohing Steve's friendly comment with a wave of her hand, Betty's sarcastic look told those who saw it that she believed her friends had been joking.

What their favorite waitress did not realize was that one of them was actively searching for a cache of goods a Civil War soldier had hidden deep inside a small cave.

37

The following evening, Paul and Donna sat talking at their kitchen table while enjoying a meal Donna had prepared the night before. Treated to a countless number of home-cooked meals during their nearly forty-two years of being together, Donna's lasagna, packed full of homemade pasta and small chunks of sausage, was one of her husband's favorites.

With her own life just as busy as her husband's due to the long hours she spent managing a branch of the Murrells Inlet National Savings and Loan, Donna always found time each week to be creative in the kitchen. While her husband was content just having a good meal in front of him, Donna preferred eating at home as often as possible. With several cookbooks chocked full of recipes handed down from her mother and grandmother, Donna's lasagna recipe was one she had tweaked over the years with the help of her husband and two sons. Tonight's meal was one Paul had placed in the oven just before his wife arrived home.

While keenly aware of the amount of time Paul had spent reading through Howard's journal, as they talked over dinner Donna asked her husband about his upcoming trip back to the hills surrounding Moncks Corner. "What's your plan for this trip? I've seen you studying the map that recently arrived, has it been any help?"

"It's definitely helped me define the next area I plan on searching," Paul replied, referring to the map he received from the United States Army Corps of Engineers. "It's still a crapshoot, but I'm fairly certain we'll find what we've been looking for. It may take longer than Mr. Church likes, but with everyone's help we'll figure it out."

After helping Donna clear off the table, Paul walked to the small office he had setup in one of the spare bedrooms. Returning to the kitchen table several minutes later, he set down a yellow legal pad, a pen, and the notebook containing Howard's journal. As Donna finished cleaning up, starting from the journal's first entry Paul began writing down a series of words Howard had circled. Written over the course of several weeks, the words were contained in thirty entries which spanned the journal's first thirty-five pages. While Paul's version showed the circles to be black, inside the original journal the words had been circled in what was now faded blue ink.

Noticing the circled words during his first review of the young officer's journal, Paul had given them little thought until earlier that day. Deliberately scanning each page so he did not miss any of the words Howard had circled, Paul carefully jotted down each one he came across. Thirty minutes later, after double-checking his work and counting the number of words he had jotted down, he realized Howard had circled a total of one hundred and nineteen words and numbers. Among them were six numbers that had not been spelled out; one of which was the number 18. As he studied the words on his pad, words such as treasury, Hidden Cove, turkey vultures, oak trees, paces, and others, Donna took a moment to scan her husband's work. She did so while looking over Paul's right shoulder.

Running one of her fingers down the list, she asked, "What's this you're working on?"

"I'm hoping they're a clue, but right now I'm not so sure." Paul replied, his focus remaining on the words in front of him.

Sitting down next to her husband, Donna said, "A clue? You mean like the ones Judiah Francis left in those other letters you found?"

Nodding his head as he continued to stare at the list in front of him, Paul knew Donna had been referring to the letters Captain Judiah Francis had written to his father and Confederate President Jefferson Davis. Years earlier, Paul had found a series of letters Francis had written when his remains were discovered in Murrells Inlet. Knowing he was dying from a severe infection, Francis had protected the letters from the elements by placing them inside two glass bottles. Like Howard, Francis, another officer charged with protecting part of the Confederate treasury, had failed to reach his final destination. As Donna turned the pages of Paul's working copy of Howard's journal, her eyes bounced from where the words had been circled to the yellow legal pad where her husband had jotted them down. They had each been written down in the same exact order as they appeared in Howard's journal.

"You think this list, which in its current form makes no sense to me, is his way of telling you where the caves are located?" Donna asked as she tried making sense of the words she was staring at.

"Like I said, I don't know. There has to be some reason they've been circled, but who knows." Frustrated over his lack of progress in determining what Howard's purpose had been for circling the words, Paul sat staring at his pad for several minutes.

As she continued to study what Paul had written down, Donna asked, "This Captain Howard you keep referring to . . . he's the same officer whose journal we're looking at, correct?" Having heard Paul mention a variety of names associated with his new project, Donna had done her best to remember the role they each played.

"Correct."

"He's the same one who committed suicide, right?" Donna asked, trying her best to keep all of the facts in order.

"So the story goes, but as far as I know there's no absolute proof that Captain Howard died that way. However, if I accept the other parts of his journal to be accurate then I have to accept the unpleasant part about the manner of his death. The confusing part is prior to his suicide, he never let on that he was depressed or had any interest in hurting himself. Because of that, I have to believe his suicide was a result of the guilt he was experiencing from that tragic order he issued. Just as there's no proof that he died by his own hands, there's also no account of where his remains have been buried. From what little we know at this time, mostly from a few entries Howard penned after his men had been killed, he experienced a tremendous amount of guilt after the cave collapsed." As he spoke, Paul's eyes stayed focused on his list of words.

"Let's just assume that Howard knew he was going to kill himself. If that was the case, then why didn't he just identify the cave's location in one of his last entries?"

Turning his head slightly, Paul looked into Donna's eyes as a look of frustration began to reveal itself. "Really? Do you really think that would have been a wise move on his part?"

Leaning back in her chair, Donna quietly processed her husband's curt response. "I . . . I guess not. That would have not only told whoever found his journal where the cave was located, but it would have also revealed the location where the gold and silver had been left."

"Very good," Paul offered, responding in a much friendlier manner than he had done moments earlier.

Standing up from the table, Donna patted her husband on the top of his head before kissing him goodnight. "Good luck with all of this, Sherlock Holmes. I hope it works out for you like you want. I'm doing my nails, and then I'm watching television in bed for an hour or so. I have a meeting early tomorrow morning, so I need my beauty rest. Don't stay up too late."

Ignoring his wife's friendly suggestion, Paul remained seated at their kitchen table until just after midnight. Working diligently as he nursed a hot cup of tea, the retired state trooper tried placing the random list of words in proper order.

With little success in doing so, Paul soon decided to call it a night. Words that had been written and later circled some one hundred and fifty years earlier would have to wait at least one more day before revealing the message Howard had cleverly hidden inside his journal.

<u>38</u>

Two days after creating his list from the words Howard had circled inside his journal, Paul sat at a round wooden table in the rear of the Waccamaw Library as he waited for his friends to join him. Looking out a panel of tall, fixed windows situated along the rear wall, he stared in the direction of Highway 707. Distracted for several moments, he watched as the steady stream of late morning traffic moving up and down the four-lane road began reacting to the heavy rain that was now falling. A light grey sky which had been present earlier had slowly become darker and much more ominous. In both directions, motorists responded to the reduced visibility by increasing the speed of their windshield wipers. The intelligent ones, Paul noticed, had also turned on their headlights.

Reaching inside a folder previously used for other needs, Paul placed single sheets of paper on the table in front of the three empty chairs sitting close to his. Each had been neatly set in place by the cleaning crew the previous evening. Next to each sheet,

304 | PETER WARREN

he placed a yellow pencil. Always concerned over the details of a meeting he called, before leaving home Paul had sharpened each pencil. Turned face down, each sheet contained the same list of words he had written down the previous evening. Until it was time, the lists would remain hidden from view. Minutes after finishing his tasks, Paul watched as his three friends made their way to where he was seated. Like their wet shoes, their jackets showed the effects of having trudged across the parking lot during a rainstorm which had grown even more intense over the past five minutes.

Glancing down at the sheets of paper as he removed his thin, wet jacket, which had done little to keep his shirt as dry as he would have liked, Bobby Ray smiled as he shot a glance in Paul's direction. Sarcastic as always, the undersheriff of Georgetown County addressed his friend by using a nickname he had tagged him with years earlier.

"Yankee Boy, y'all didn't tell us we were going to be taking a test today."

Laughing at Bobby Ray's comment as he placed his umbrella on an adjoining table, Peter stared at the sheet of paper that had been placed in front of his chair. Concerned over whether he was about to do something wrong, as he pointed down at the table, he asked, "Is it OK for me to turn this sheet of paper over?"

"Be my guest." Paul replied, nodding at Chick as his friend sat down in the chair next to him.

Allowing his friends a few moments to inspect the list of words he had jotted down and later copied, Paul watched as Peter withdrew a 3-ring binder from a canvass tote bag he often carried with him. While it served his needs, the generic bag was not as fancy as the valise Robert Regan often travelled with. Moments later, he noticed Peter's binder held a working copy of Howard's journal. It was one he had been given a few weeks earlier. As someone who had previously shown little interest in conducting any type of research, Peter's copy now displayed a large number of handwritten notes. Written in blue ink, the notes had been jotted down near the end of many of Howard's entries. Others adorned the top and bottom of nearly every page.

Watching as Peter's fingers flipped through several pages of Howard's journal, Paul noticed his friend paused at each entry containing a word that had been circled. As he did, Peter's eyes bounced back and forth from each of the words to those Paul had written down. Moments later, he withdrew a smaller notebook from the same bag. Flipping through several pages, Peter soon found the page he was looking for. Like Howard's journal, Peter's small notebook contained several notes he had jotted down.

Holding up his notebook, Peter pointed to the list of words Paul had supplied him with. "My list matches yours . . . they're even in the same order. Both contain the same words . . . the ones circled in Howard's journal." As Peter finished speaking, Chick stared in disbelief at the notebook his friend was holding.

As Peter had spoken about the two lists, a smile broke out across Paul's face. Of his three friends sitting around the table, Peter would not have been the one he would have picked to have made the same connection. Watching as Bobby Ray and Chick matched their lists to the words circled in Howard's journal, Paul held up another sheet of paper. Among the many notes he had jotted down was one sentence. Before reading what he had written, he said, "Tell me if this makes sense."

"How about *you* telling me if *this* makes sense," Peter replied, anxiously emphasizing two words as he prepared to read a sentence he had written down in his notebook. *"They were placed 18 paces inside the mouth of this small cave."* As he finished, Bobby Ray and Chick stared at the two separate lists their friends had comprised. Taking the piece of paper Paul was holding, Peter crossed off the words he had spoken. They were the same ones Paul had not had a chance to utter. Looking across the table after reading the sentence he and his friend had both constructed on their own, Peter smiled as he noticed the grin on Paul's face.

"So, by the looks of it I'm not the only crazy person sitting here," Peter said. "I spent most of the night depriving myself of sleep after jotting down this list of words Howard had circled. I became intrigued with them after realizing they may have been his way of leaving us a message." Turning to look at Paul, Peter added, "From what you've set down in front of us, I'm guessing you also believe these words form some sort of a message. Or, maybe it's a clue he's left us."

"Yes, that's right. That same thought came to me early yesterday morning." Paul replied, enjoying the confused looks on the faces of his other two friends.

Pleased by what he heard, Peter again pointed to the list Paul had composed. "Like I said, my thoughts about this message came to me late last night. I really haven't had much time to study these words, but how's this sound?" Searching his notes for a second entry he had jotted down, Peter finally read what he believed to be an important part of Howard's cryptic clue. Looking up, he said, *"So have several crates of rifles."*

As his eyes moved down his list, Paul placed a small checkmark next to the six words Peter had strung together. "Those are just as good as the other ones. Makes sense, that's for sure. We know from a few of Howard's entries that his wagons contained crates of rifles."

Just as Chick was doing, Bobby Ray ran a thin line through the words Paul and Peter had tried to make sense of. Still somewhat confused, he asked, "So you two geniuses believe that Howard . . . perhaps as he gathered the courage to commit suicide, circled these words as a way of telling whoever found his journal where he hid the gold and silver? That's if he really did commit suicide. And, why . . . why would he do that?" Bobby Ray's last comment questioned Howard's reason for circling this set of words. It was not meant to question why the Confederate officer had taken his own life.

"Because he wanted someone, certainly someone sympathetic to the Confederate cause, to figure out where he had hidden the gold and silver. Just as I explained to Donna last evening, if he simply left a note, anyone . . . including Union soldiers, could have found the cave." Picking up his copy of the list, Paul added, "It's a stretch, but I believe these words we're looking at tell us where the caves are located."

Sitting across from Bobby Ray, Chick was not as skeptical as his friend. "I agree it's a bit of a stretch, Bobby Ray, but I have to give our partners some credit, this idea of theirs could have some merit."

More focused on the words he was studying than on what Chick had said, Bobby Ray suddenly grew excited. Doing his best to contain his emotions so the other patrons sitting inside the library were not startled, he said, "What about this . . . *'has been hidden inside a cave alongside a river'* . . . that could be part of his clue, right?" Like the disarranged letters of a word featured inside a Jumble puzzle often do, the words Bobby Ray had spoken had jumped off the page at him.

"Sure could." Chick admitted, crossing off the words Bobby Ray put together.

"Too bad Howard didn't leave us a map." Peter joked as he jotted down the partial sentence Bobby Ray had crafted.

While Peter's comment intrigued him, Paul knew his own inspection of Howard's wooden chest had failed to turn up any additional hiding spots where a map may have been secreted. Still intrigued, he made a mental note to call Regan so the chest could carefully be gone over one more time.

After discussing a few more thoughts regarding the words he had written down, Paul explained how he intended to return to the same general area they had already spent several days exploring. His explanation also included the fact that Regan had taken the steps to secure hotel rooms for each of them. "I have a couple of things to clear up on the home front, but I'm headed back there in four days. Anyone coming with me?"

Rather quickly, three hands shot up in the air.

Putting his belongings away inside an old valise that was nicer than Peter's tote bag but not as nice as the one Regan occasionally carried, Paul noticed the three hands still raised high in the air. Smiling, he said, "I'm pleased to see you'll be joining me. In the meantime, see if you can make any more sense of this list I've given you. If you come up with anything over the next couple of days, give me a call. If not, I'll be in touch very soon. When we do head out, we'll meet at the diner that morning for a quick breakfast."

39

Four days after their meeting at the Socastee Library, with his belly full from a nice pancake breakfast at the Waccamaw Diner, Paul made the drive to Moncks Corner. With Bobby Ray set to testify in federal court in Charleston later that morning, and with Chick and Peter's schedules filled with a variety of teaching needs for most of the day, Paul was alone in his truck as he made his way towards his destination. Unlike his first trip to Moncks Corner, this one allowed him time to finish drafting his game plan for the next few days. It was a plan he would discuss with his friends when they arrived later that afternoon.

In the days following their meeting at the library, Paul and his partners exchanged a flurry of phone calls, emails, and text messages as they excitedly tried composing sentences from the list of words circled inside Howard's journal. After several heated arguments, including two occasions which resulted in Chick hanging up on Paul after his friend summarily dismissed two sentences he had crafted, the team Simon Church hired managed to construct most of the message Howard had cleverly hidden.

With the radio in his truck turned off just like it was on most occasions, Paul held a warm cup of coffee in his left hand as he passed through Pawleys Island. Sipping the dark liquid, he tried piecing together the remaining words he and the others had yet to make sense of. While most people enjoyed listening to the radio or to the songs on their playlists while driving, Paul often used the times he was alone to work out whatever issue it was that was confronting him. The peace and quiet inside his vehicle was time he routinely referred to as *"My alone time."*

After running the remaining words through his head, Paul thought, "He's telling us about those trees he used as reference points; that part I'm pretty confident about. But what do those two numbers refer to? Are they the number of steps he took as he walked away from the cave where his men had perished or are they the number of steps he took after hiding the gold and silver inside the other cave?" Frustrated by his thoughts, Paul slapped his steering wheel as he drove towards Georgetown on his way to Moncks Corner.

Briefly dismissing his thoughts regarding this stubborn group of words, Paul stopped to refresh his coffee at a small mini-mart south of Georgetown. Climbing back inside his truck after assisting a group of elderly motorists with directions to a nearby restaurant, Paul glanced at his list one more time before exiting the parking lot. Like his friends, once a group of words was used to create a sentence they all agreed upon, he crossed them off his list. Now as he stared at the remaining words, a small number of them suddenly made sense. Excited over the words he had put together, Paul called Chick's cell phone.

"Morning, Paul, everything OK?" Chick asked, still agitated to some degree over his friend's dismissal of the two sentences he had come up with. Sitting in a small conference room down the hall from his office, Chick was waiting with several other faculty members for a staff meeting to begin. With a great deal of work waiting for him outside of Moncks Corner, it was not where he wanted to be on this pleasant sunny morning.

"Yeah, all's good," Paul replied, detecting a touch of frustration in his friend's voice. "Listen, I just stopped outside of Georgetown and . . . well, I don't know how this happened, but I think I just solved another part of Howard's message. When I was looking at them, they . . . these words just jumped off the page at me. Just as you've been struggling, I've struggled for hours trying to make sense of what he was trying to tell us, but . . . *wow!*"

Nodding to another faculty member as she arrived for their meeting, Chick pulled his list from his shirt pocket. A small tear in one corner was an indication of the number of times it had been folded after being reviewed. "These magical words you're referring to, which ones are they?" While doing his best to dismiss his lingering frustration, Chick had doubts that what Paul was about to tell him would make any sense.

"Under these rocks rest the partial remains of three Union soldiers."

Stunned by what he heard, Chick sat quietly for several moments. Trying to contain his emotions as he recalled one particular entry Howard had written, he excitedly ran a finger up and down the list of remaining words. As he did, the words Paul had spoken were mentally checked off. Standing up from the chair he was sitting in, Chick walked out of the conference room into the adjacent hallway. Frantically searching for a few precious feet of privacy, he entered a small breakroom that was not being used. Moments later, he confirmed the words his friend had strung together.

Nearly out of breath from the sudden excitement, Chick said, "I'm with you, buddy! Those words make far more sense than anything else I've been working on this morning. As soon as you mentioned them, I recalled an entry Howard composed after his men had been killed. When he composed that particular entry, I'm sure he was feeling guilty for having his men search for the remains of those Union soldiers." Excited by this latest set of words Paul had pieced together, the anger and frustration Chick had experienced over the past few days was quickly brushed aside.

Pleased by his friend's response, Paul slowly crossed the words off his list. "Well, that helps, doesn't it? We just have to make sense of what the last few words mean. Once we do, then we'll have figured out what Howard was trying to tell us."

"We'll get it, don't worry." Chick said as his eyes began focusing on the few remaining words. "Hey, want me to tell Bobby Ray and Peter about this new sentence you put together?"

"Go ahead and tell Peter, but Bobby Ray can't be bothered right now. We'll fill him in at the hotel later tonight." Glancing at his watch, Paul realized he had just enough time to make it to a meeting he had scheduled with Regan. "Listen, Chick, I have to go. I'm meeting with Robert at the hotel so we can discuss our plans to use one of Simon's helicopters. We'll also be talking about some other equipment we need. I'll see you when you get there."

******

Forty minutes later, as Paul pulled into the hotel parking lot he realized his cell phone had just finished capturing a new message.

Questioning why he had not heard his phone ring, he recalled the area in and around Moncks Corner being known for having sporadic cell service. It was an issue he and his team had dealt with on several occasions during their recent stay. After parking his truck in a space near the front of the hotel, Paul listened to his new message.

"Paul, it's Bobby Ray. I know you're the brains of this outfit, but I've been obsessing over this list of words while I'm sitting here waiting to testify. I think I may have put a few of them together, so let me know what you think. *The tree on the left sits thirty-six paces away, while the other sits thirty-two paces away. Between them is a small pile of rocks.* Who knows if I have the numbers right as I may have transposed them, but the rest of the sentence makes sense, right? We'll talk about it when I get to the hotel later tonight. Later, Yankee Boy."

Gazing at his list as the message finished playing; Paul realized his friend had correctly pieced together the remaining words. Like the others, they had been part of several entries inside Howard's journal.

"Nice job, Bobby Ray! You've just completed this cryptic message Howard left us. Now we just have to find these caves he's written about." Paul said out loud as a wide smile crossed his face. Seconds later, he played Bobby Ray's message for a second time.

Folding up the small sheet of paper he had been referring to, Paul grabbed the two folders needed for his meeting with the one person Simon Church trusted more than anyone else. Walking towards the front of the hotel, he decided that for now he would not tell Regan about the exciting message he and his team had just unraveled.

40

The following morning as Paul and his friends met for breakfast in the restaurant located adjacent to the hotel lobby, he carefully went over the intricate clue that had been found inside Howard's journal. With the court case he was testifying in running later than expected, Bobby Ray had not arrived at the hotel until after ten the previous evening. It was well after the others had already called it a day. Waiting until after their coffee had been poured, Paul then explained his findings. As he did, Regan was handed a list of the words Howard had circled years earlier.

"What makes you think they have any connection to what we're looking for? Maybe the guy was sitting inside his tent one night with nothing else to do and decided to circle a few words out of sheer boredom." Regan said, playing the role of the devil's advocate. His comments had been made without the benefit of much thought.

Smiling as he placed his cup down on the table, Paul pulled out several sheets of paper from a folder he had placed on the seat next to him. For the moment, he elected to leave them face down.

"When you came to see me on Mr. Church's behalf, the reason for your visit wasn't because Howard decided to draw a few circles around some arbitrary words inside his journal. You came to see me because my friends and I are good at solving clues others have left behind. In fact, and excuse me for taking this moment to brag, but they're clues most other people would have never put together; yet alone solved. Isn't that correct?"

"Correct on all accounts." Regan replied, taking notice of the four sets of eyes staring at him from around the table. Picking up the list Paul had given him, he asked, "You really believe these words represent some kind of a convoluted clue?"

Handing everyone a new sheet of paper he had pulled from his folder, Paul answered Regan's question. "That's what we all thought when we first compiled the list, but when you read what's on that sheet of paper I just handed you I believe you'll see we've changed our position." As he finished speaking, Paul let everyone know of the last two sentences he and Bobby Ray had crafted from the remaining words.

Without another word being spoken, Paul's friends, including Regan who was still doubtful over what the list truly represented, read the clue Captain Noah Howard had cleverly hid inside his journal.

The treasury I've been charged with protecting is now hidden inside a cave not far from a river northeast of Moncks Corner. So have several crates of rifles. The cave is located close to a place the locals call Hidden Cove. The assets were placed 18 aces inside the mouth of this small cave. Look for turkey vultures who like to roost in two young oak trees adjacent to the cave. The tree on the left sits 36 paces away and the other sits 32 paces away. Between them is a small pile of rocks. They are ones I took from the mouth of one of the caves. Under these rocks rest the partial remains of three Union soldiers.'

"You have to be kidding me, right!" Regan said loudly after reading the clue Howard had left. Shocked by what he read, Regan quickly opened up his copy of Howard's journal as a means of verifying what Paul had written were the same words the young Confederate officer had circled. Soon convinced they were, he still remained skeptical of how much help this clue would be. "Kudos to all of you for figuring out what these words represent, but I still have my doubts. If you knew me better, you'd know that's just how I'm wired. I mean . . . you can't believe we're going to find these caves just because this guy made a reference to some turkey vultures who enjoyed sitting in a couple of trees over a hundred and fifty years ago, do you?"

"It sounds like you don't believe those turkey vultures will still be sitting there." Paul joked.

"No, I don't. And I hope you realize those trees are likely no longer there. I'm no expert on the life expectancy of oak trees, but in this case there's a good chance they've already died or been used for furniture." Regan quipped, his eyes bouncing from the list he was studying to the faces of those he was sitting with.

"I'll take the wait-and-see approach on the trees." Paul replied. "If they're still standing, there's a good chance they're massive by now. Just like the vultures, that pile of rocks Howard referred to may no longer exist.'

Jumping into the conversation, Chick said, "Robert, the turkey vultures, just like the trees and that pile of rocks, they were just observations or landmarks Captain Howard referred to at the time he was leaving this clue for someone to find. They're things for us to be aware of; not things we expect to find."

"Like Paul and Chick have just mentioned, those trees aren't as young as they used to be. If we get lucky and find them still standing, I suspect they would be pretty huge by now," Peter said, adding his opinion to the conversation taking place. "They were reference points Howard believed were important enough to mention."

Still skeptical of what he had read and was being told, Regan sat stunned over the clue Paul and the others had deciphered. Figuring out the meaning of a convoluted clue was not the way he and Simon Church normally did business. "You . . . the four of you figured all of this out on your own?"

"We're a whole lot smarter than we look," Bobby Ray said with a straight face as he stirred his coffee.

"We all had our moments of glory," Paul replied, responding to Regan's comment as he acknowledged the contributions his teammates had made. As he had done throughout his career, by a simple wave of his hand Paul deferred much of the credit to those who assisted him.

"Maybe so," Regan said, briefly glancing at the others seated around the table, "but you're the person Mr. Church hired to find this part of the missing treasury. That means you should receive most of the credit."

Regan's comment caused Paul to stiffen over the meaning behind it. "That's not how I operate, Robert. My friends and I work as a team, so I'm not interested in receiving any special attention." Standing up from the table, Paul made it known he was done talking about who deserved what degree of credit for solving Howard's clue.

"Are we still planning on using the helicopter?" Regan asked, waiting for their waitress to return with his credit card so he could finish paying the breakfast tab. The helicopter, the main issue they intended to discuss over breakfast, had taken a backseat to the important news Paul delivered.

"Yes, I think that's a wise move. After giving this some thought, there's a legitimate reason to be using the helicopter. Seeing we now have a better idea of where to search, I'm going to have Bobby Ray join you and the pilot. The rest of us will continue to serve as the ground team. I'd like to concentrate our search on that hilly area I showed you earlier on the map. It's as promising as any other area, so let's focus our attention on that location this morning."

* * * * * *

For two long and exhausting hot days, Paul and his team searched unsuccessfully for the caves Captain Howard had described in his journal. Covering nearly one hundred acres of steep rocky hillsides, some of which were surrounded by meadows that appeared as if they had never been walked on, Paul's team found little to support the cryptic clue Howard had left.

While crisscrossing several promising sites had dampened their spirits to some degree, the rocky hillsides had led to two minor, but painful injuries. Losing his footing while hiking up a steep grade, Chick sustained a badly sprained left ankle. Several minutes later, as he continued with the search, his ankle had swollen considerably. Rushing to help his friend, Peter suffered a nasty cut to his left elbow after slipping off a rock that had not been as stable as it appeared. Both injuries had occurred near the end of the second day when everyone was spent from their long and unsuccessful search.

Unlike his two friends, while completely exhausted from their arduous search Paul managed to avoid any serious injuries. With his body still healing from the gunshot wounds sustained months earlier in Connecticut, his stamina was not as strong as it had been before the shooting. Despite feeling run down after the first unsuccessful day of searching, Paul pushed through the second day as he and his team overcame every obstacle thrown their way. In the air above them, Bobby Ray and Regan had it far easier as the helicopter effortlessly scanned the same search grid. At the end of the second exhausting day, after a simple dinner with his friends Paul hit the sheets hours earlier than normal.

The following morning, despite their bumps, assorted bruises, and sore muscles, Paul's team continued their search for the elusive set of caves. For several hours they searched unsuccessfully. In the air above them, despite their ability to search a larger area in far less time, Bobby Ray and Regan experienced similar frustration.

Later that afternoon, as Paul checked on the injuries Chick and Peter sustained the previous day his cell phone announced an incoming call from Regan. "I'm kind of busy right now, so make it quick." Paul said, answering the call after several rings. While interested in hearing the results of Regan's end of the search, he was more concerned over the welfare of his two friends than he was in the unexpected phone call. Kneeling down on the side of a steep incline his team had just ruled out as being the site of any caves, sweat poured off Paul's face as he dressed Peter's injury with a clean bandage.

Standing on the tarmac at a nearby regional airport, Regan briefly watched as the helicopter pilot and a member of the ground crew worked to refuel the chopper. "How long are you planning on keeping this search going? We only have the chopper for two more days. It's scheduled for some mandatory maintenance, so it has to be at the maintenance facility by either Thursday afternoon or early the following morning. I can have it back here next week, but it has to be serviced so we don't run into any problems with the feds in the event something happens when it's in the air." As expected, Regan was fully aware of the project's growing costs.

"I'm not sure yet," Paul said, placing a second sterile gauze pad over the cut Peter had sustained. Bending and twisting his elbow over the course of the day's search had caused the partially closed cut to reopen. Drops of fresh blood stained the large boulder Peter was sitting on as his injury was being treated. "I take it you guys didn't see anything that looked promising while you were up there?"

"No, not really," Regan replied. "Bobby Ray pointed out one possible location, but we really couldn't see too much due to the tree cover. We have the GPS coordinates, so you may want to consider that as your jumping off point tomorrow morning."

"Alright, sounds like a plan. I'll talk to Bobby Ray when I see him later. Are you joining us for dinner?" Paul asked, taking a sip of cold water from his canteen after treating Peter's injury.

"No can do," Regan said, hollering over the noise being made by another helicopter coming in for fuel. "I'm hooking up with an old friend that I haven't seen in years. He's the commanding officer of the South Carolina Air National Guard. Years ago, he and I went to the Air Force Academy together. In the day, he was one of the best pilots I ever flew with. He's in Columbia for a couple of days of meetings, so I'm looking forward to seeing him. It will probably turn out to be a late night, but it'll be worth it."

"Sounds like a good time," Paul replied, learning something about Regan's past that he had previously not been told. "I'm impressed by that little tidbit you just tossed out there. The Air Force Academy isn't in the habit of graduating dummies, so I'm sure your degree had something to do with Mr. Church hiring you."

"It helped." Regan admitted, lowering his voice as the background noise caused by the second helicopter slowly subsided.

"Alright, we'll talk at breakfast or whenever I see you about the location Bobby Ray noticed. Have a good night."

Hearing the news that Bobby Ray had identified a promising piece of ground for them to search the following morning made the aches and pains Paul was feeling seem far better than they actually were.

The following morning was something Paul was already looking forward to.

41

As Paul and two of his friends planned out their day the following morning over a light breakfast, he filled them in on the exact location where their search was going to commence. It was, he told them, the same spot Bobby Ray had identified the previous afternoon. With Bobby Ray already at the airport addressing several logistical needs with Regan and the pilot, Paul advised Chick and Peter how the morning was about to unfold. Part of what he told them was that after clearing the helipad Simon Church's helicopter pilot would make a solo three minute flight to a local athletic field. After picking up Paul and Chick, the pilot would ferry them to the site identified by the GPS coordinates. After returning to the airport to pick up Bobby Ray, the pilot would make one last stop at the athletic field to pick up Peter before returning to the same location where Paul and Chick had been dropped off. As had been the case for much of the time he was in town, Regan chose to return to the hotel to work on other business issues.

Exploring the area around the landing zone as they waited for the helicopter to return, Paul took note of several distinctive features located in the landscape not far from where he was walking. The steep, rocky hillside had many of the same features described in Howard's journal. While double-checking the GPS coordinates, Paul asked Chick to start documenting the area with one of the cameras he was carrying. Pointing at the hillside, he said, "When you take your photographs, make sure you get a few of that opening on the right side of the hill. That's the spot which first attracted my attention." With the drone they had planned on using still grounded by both mechanical and software issues, this was the first occasion Paul and Chick had seen the terrain up close.

As they moved closer to the rocky hillside, Paul commented further on the landscape around them. "Even though the GPS coordinates tell us we're in the right location, some of those trees growing on the hillside make it difficult to tell if we're in the right spot. If this turns out to be place we're hoping for, there's a pretty good chance some of those trees hadn't even started growing when Howard and his men were here." As he spoke, Paul pointed to the handful of trees and patches of chest-high grass growing on the rocky slope.

Carefully documenting the uneven terrain they had covered, Chick watched as Paul slowly made his way towards a small opening in the formation of rocks. Unlike some of the other areas they had explored, the small opening was nearly ten feet wide. After several days of searching, it was also the largest gap they had come across. Shouting to his friend as he lowered his camera, Chick asked the same question Paul had already begun to consider. "Do you think it's . . . ."

"Maybe, but it's hard to say." Paul replied, confirming his friend's suspicion. "The opening seems wide enough, but it's only about four feet deep. If this is it, the rest of the cave has been closed off. From what I can tell, there seems to be a large number of rocks that have fallen over the years; they've sealed off most of the cave's interior. If they're as heavy as they appear, we're going to need some help moving them. They're far too big for us to be dealing with."

"His journal never mentioned anything about the cave collapsing after he hid the gold and silver in there, so it had to have collapsed sometime after Howard left the area." Chick replied, confirming his friend's suspicion.

"It seems that way." After responding to Chick's last comment, Paul looked up after hearing the distinctive sound of the helicopter's rotor blades as it returned to drop off its last two passengers. Shielding his eyes, Paul ducked as he turned away from the bits of sand, dirt, and other debris sent flying by the strong vertical downwash generated by the rotor blades.

Moments later, as the helicopter left to return to the airport, Paul watched as Bobby Ray and Peter made their way to where he was standing. As they reached the opening, Peter stood pointing at the unusual formation of rocks that kept Paul from entering the cave any further. Taking note of the wide, but shallow opening, he asked, "Is this the place? If it is, these rocks I'm looking at are the result of the hillside collapsing at some point. They weren't put there by Howard or anyone else."

Nodding his head in agreement of Peter's assessment of how the large rocks had found their way inside the cave, Paul said, "While we're still not sure if this is the place Howard was writing about, Chick and I agree it's the best location we've come across. From the looks of it, we have a bunch of work in front of us before we'll know if this is where the assets were left. Because of that, I think its best we limit the amount of speculation on what may be in there." As he spoke, Paul's eyes scanned the area to the left of the small anomaly they had been staring at. "If this is it, where are the other two caves? This hillside, while it's fairly steep and full of rocks, it's not how I had it pictured. I . . . I thought it would be more impressive; far steeper, perhaps. I'm having trouble picturing three caves being here less than two hundred years ago." As Paul and the others looked down the length of the rocky hillside, they saw nothing to indicate that two other caves had once stood there.

"Maybe they were here and maybe they weren't, but look at those two beauties. If those are the ones Howard told us about, they aren't so little any more, are they?" Standing close to where they believed the entrance to the last cave had stood; Chick shielded his eyes from the bright sunlight as he pointed to two nearby oak trees. The mature trees were nearly ninety feet in height.

Pulling out his working copy of Howard's journal, Chick quickly located the sheet of paper containing the clues they had solved. Moments later, after moving to where the taller of the two trees stood, Chick slowly began walking in the direction of where the cave's small entrance was located. As he walked, the history professor counted his steps. Frustrated by the number of steps he had taken as he reached the cave's entrance, Chick walked back and forth from the cave to the tree three more times. Each trip resulted in the same number of steps being counted. Confused over his count, he again consulted the clue they had solved. He also questioned whether it had been solved correctly.

"These numbers . . . the number of paces we believe Howard was referring to, they . . . they don't add up to the number of steps I've taken. The number I keep getting is several paces less than either of the numbers contained inside his clue."

"Really? You're confused by that?" Paul asked, chuckling over the problem his friend was dealing with. "I'm afraid your count is off for several reasons. Two for sure, but even more than that, I suspect."

"Care to enlighten me?" Chick asked, watching as Bobby Ray shrugged his shoulders after realizing he could not come up with a logical explanation for the difference in the number of paces his friend had counted.

"Well, besides not knowing where Howard was standing when he paced off the distance from the cave to the trees, he did so when the entrance was still intact. When he was counting his steps, Howard was also walking from the entrance to two trees that were much smaller than they are now. Like I said, there may be another one or two reasons for why your count is off . . . like the length of his stride may have been different than yours, but, for now, I'll stick with the ones I've just mentioned."

"*Idiot!*" Chick muttered loud enough for the others to hear as his face turned red after realizing the diameter of the trees had grown significantly since the time Howard had stood next to them. Moments later, he let the others know what his second mistake had been. "When the cave collapsed, rocks tumbling down the hill likely extended the mouth of the cave from where it had been during Howard's time. We're standing several feet in front of where it actually existed near the end of the war. Those are the reasons why my count was off."

"Good boy!" Paul answered, his sarcasm causing Peter a good laugh.

******

With his sunglasses propped above his eyebrows, as Bobby Ray walked back towards the small opening in the side of the hill he squinted as he peered between several large rocks and boulders. Picking up two of the smaller rocks resting near the opening, he tossed them aside after briefly staring at the bigger obstacles lying in and around the cave's entrance. Pointing at the tons of debris blocking his path, he said, "How the heck are we going to deal with all of this? Especially these big bastards, there's no way we're moving those without some serious help." A number of the boulders Bobby Ray was pointing to were not only several feet in circumference, but weighed well over a thousand pounds each.

"I'll have to call Mr. Church and Regan after we have dinner tonight. I expect they'll be pleased to learn we've finally identified a place to start searching, but I'm not so sure how pleased they'll be when I tell them we're going to have to hire someone to move all of these rocks and the rest of this crap out of our way. Besides having to obtain the necessary permits so we can do some digging, they have no choice but to give us permission to hire a construction company so we can get to work. One thing's for sure; this is going to cost Mr. Church a fair amount of change." Having no experience in estimating costs for a project like this, Paul had little idea what the price tag would be for the work needed to excavate part of the hillside.

"I agree," Chick offered, standing off to Bobby Ray's left as they tried peering inside the collapsed cave. Moving a handful of smaller rocks out of the way, Chick hoped to see a bone or two or some other clue confirming they had found the correct location. Stopping his work after glancing at some of the larger rocks lying above the cave's entrance, he added, "If we tried excavating this area on our own, we'd likely bring a few tons of rocks and dirt down on top of us." It was not something Paul or anyone else cared to experience.

As Peter and Chick continued to document the area by drawing a detailed map, using a one hundred foot steel tape measure they took several measurements from a variety of fixed points. To support their map, they also took over one hundred photographs. As they worked on finishing their map, after motioning for Bobby Ray to follow him, Paul walked to where the two large oak trees stood.

"Good idea getting out of the damn sun," Bobby Ray said, loosening the cap of his canteen before downing a healthy swig of cold water. "This freakin' heat kind of snuck up on us today."

Staring at a small mound of dirt nearly four feet high and just as wide, Paul gently kicked at the pile of debris that had collected around its base. "I'm not standing here because I wanted us to get out of the sun, Bobby Ray. We're standing here because of this." As he pointed at the mound of dirt, Paul called for Chick and Peter to join them.

"Better take a few more photos before we get started, Peter." Paul said, gently kicking the debris for a second time before speaking to one of his other friends. "Chick, you seem to have assumed the role as our cartographer, so make sure you plot this mound of dirt on the map you've been working on. I'd like to do some digging here, but we'll wait until all the photographs have been taken and you tell me you're done with your measurements. If I'm right, this mound is going to tell us if we're in the correct spot or not." As Bobby Ray had done a few moments earlier, Paul quenched his thirst with a long drink of water from his canteen.

Grasping the importance of what Paul had been pointing to, Peter and the others quickly got to work. As his friends performed their necessary tasks, leaning on the only shovel they had at their disposal, Paul waited patiently until they were done.

Thirty minutes later, as Paul sunk the shovel in the leaf and twig covered mound for the first time it struck something hard. Tossing the shovel aside, as he knelt down Paul began using his hands to move away more of the dirt, leaves, and twigs obscuring the pile of rocks Howard had piled up years earlier. Barely having time to move four mid-sized rocks off the top of the mound, Paul quickly found what he had expected to find. Staring down at a section of rocks and dirt that sat undisturbed since the time Howard had last seen it, Paul saw two bones; both appeared as if they had been crudely severed. Next to them, several smaller bones and what Paul and Chick soon took to be the remnants of at least three pairs of leather boots lie mixed amongst the dirt and rocks still in place. Turning to look back at the rocky hillside, with a wisp of emotion clearly in his voice, Paul said, "I guess we know where the rest of the remains are located."

Severed in half many years earlier as their remains were being pulled from the collapsing cave, the heads, arms, and upper torsos of three Union soldiers had been buried under tons of falling rock and dirt. At war with those soldiers fighting for the Confederacy, their remains had rested alongside those of Howard's men. Fighting against each other for reasons they never fully understood, the soldiers who had worn two different colored uniforms had slept in peace next to each other.

Their rest was finally about to be disturbed.

42

After returning to their hotel later that day, Paul contacted Regan and Simon Church to advise them that he believed the location his team was searching for had finally been located. As he spoke with the person financing this part of the search for the missing Confederate treasury, around a small circular table on the other side of his hotel room, Bobby Ray, Chick, and Peter stood celebrating with after-dinner drinks. In their hands, cold bottles of beer helped kick off the modest celebration.

"Paul, that's great news!" Simon Church roared from the comfort of his wood paneled office inside his Texas mansion. "I knew you were the right person to find this treasure. I can't tell you how pleased I am by this wonderful news. Well done, my friend!"

Moments later, while travelling back to Texas on one of his employer's private jets, Regan echoed the same sentiments. "Like Mr. Church just said, that's great news. I wish I could have been there, but Mr. Church directed me to fly back for an important meeting he has scheduled for tomorrow morning."

After several minutes of lavishing praise on Paul for the remarkable discovery he and his team had made, Church, as was his style with most people he did business with, hit his newest employee with a series of questions. Blessed with an uncanny memory, one nearly as flawless as Paul's, Church ignored the opportunity to take notes as the conversation continued. However, high in the sky above southern Arkansas, Regan scribbled away as he kept track of the discussion taking place. In a cup holder next to his seat, several ice cubes gently rocked against each other inside a glass of expensive bourbon. With others being paid to worry over the details of his flight, the former Air Force pilot enjoyed his beverage as he travelled home.

"So, what's your plan for getting to what we both know is buried under all that rubble? And, if you would, answer my next question first. What else did you find buried under that small pile of rocks? Was there anything interesting?" Picking up his glass, Regan took a long sip of bourbon as he waited to hear Paul's answer.

"Well, to start with, you both need to remember that all we've found so far is a very interesting location for us to explore. We haven't found any treasure yet; at least, not the kind I've been hired to find."

"We're aware of that, Paul. Mr. Church and I are just caught up in the moment, that's all." Regan replied before polishing off his drink. On the other end of the three-way conversation, Simon Church quickly concurred with Regan's statement.

"In that case, I can appreciate your excitement. The best news I can give you is under that pile of rocks and dirt we managed to find a few bones and the remnants of what we believe were three pairs of boots. Being buried for as long as they have has caused what little material is left to be in pretty rough shape, but it's given some credence to the clue we've solved. We're pretty confident the boots belonged to those Union soldiers who were murdered, but we'll have to do some testing before we know for sure."

"Paul, not to sound too morbid, but what about any skulls. What kind of condition were they in?" Church asked from where he sat inside his office.

"I can't help you there as we didn't find any. It's just something I've started to think about, but I believe those Union soldiers were likely being dragged out of the cave feet first when it collapsed. The fact that we found pieces of their boots seems to support my theory of how they were dragged out of the cave. From how badly damaged a few of the bones are, I suspect . . . and I hope this doesn't offend you, but it may be the bodies were severed in half when the ceiling of the cave gave way. If I'm correct, the skulls, like the soldiers' upper torsos, were probably crushed under the weight of the debris. Just before that happened, someone . . . or even someone's horse had likely begun the process of pulling the soldiers' remains from the cave. Sadly, because of the damage done to their bodies, only their boots and parts of their severed legs ended up being pulled from the cave. Whoever that person was that was left, and it's probably a safe bet to believe it was Captain Howard himself, he buried the boots and what was left of the soldiers' legs under that pile of dirt."

Shocked by what he was told, Church was at a loss for what to say. "You're telling me their skulls . . . were crushed when the cave gave way?"

"I'm afraid so, but I expected that to be the case after reading Howard's description of how his men had perished. I didn't expect to find much of anything in that pile of rocks; certainly not any intact skulls."

Realizing the point being made and somewhat embarrassed by how Paul phrased his response, Church qualified the question Regan had asked. "You know what Robert meant when he asked that question, Paul. Were there any signs of the missing treasury?"

"No, nothing like that."

Disappointed to learn his dreams of recovering part of the treasury would have to wait, Church took a moment to revisit one of his previous questions. Becoming irritated after learning Paul had only found a few bones and some scraps of old leather, the tone in his voice reflected the frustration which had settled in his mind. "So where do we go from here? I've hired you to find something for me, and you haven't done that as yet."

Quiet for several moments as Bobby Ray and the others suddenly halted their celebration after seeing the color drain from their friend's face, Paul immediately began questioning his employer's motive for wanting to recover the gold and silver Howard had been responsible for. Unlike their recent conversations, Church had suddenly become abrupt, almost rude and condescending, as he questioned what Paul's plan was to move the tons of rocks separating him from his dream.

"I'm working on it. I'll call one of you around nine your time tomorrow morning." Paul said tersely, calculating the time difference between South Carolina and Texas as he gave the watch around his left wrist a quick glance. Upset over how he had been spoken to, Paul ignored Simon Church with his next comment. "Does that sound reasonable, Robert?" Not waiting for a response, Paul abruptly ended the call.

*****

Regan's cell phone rang at precisely nine the following morning. Aware of his caller's reputation for adhering to the deadlines he set for himself, Regan smiled as he answered his phone.

"Good morning, Paul. Are you in a better mood this morning?" Regan's smile stayed fixed as he recalled the abrupt manner in which Paul had hung up on Simon Church. It was not something most people did to one of the world's richest men. Nor was it something Simon Church ever tolerated.

"I am," Paul admitted, less than pleased with himself for how he had responded to Church's rude tone. "I admit I was tired and upset, but I don't care how much money your boss has he shouldn't have talked to me like he did. If he talks to me like that again, I'm gone. And, if he wants to fire me for how our call ended last night, well, that's his prerogative."

"I doubt that's going to happen," Regan replied, unsure of what Church had planned for Paul. "I'm not making excuses for him, but he hasn't been feeling very well over the past few days. I'd like to believe it was nothing more than him being overly excited from what you had just told him about finding some of those remains. I'll have a talk with him this morning, but Mr. Church is incapable of holding a grudge against someone he respects as much as you. You may not be his favorite person this morning, but once he realizes how much you and your team have accomplished he'll probably call you to apologize. Like I said, I'll talk to him."

"Sounds fair." Committed to finding the next part of the Confederate treasury, Paul had little interest in allowing a momentary lapse of faith on Simon Church's part to interfere with his plans.

"Now that we've addressed the unpleasant exchange which occurred during last night's phone call, tell me what your game plan is so I can tell the old man. He's anxious to learn how you're planning to recover that gold he's so interested in finding?"

For the next fifteen minutes Paul carefully laid out his plan. It was one he spent hours working on after speaking with Regan and his boss the previous evening. As he spoke, the retired state trooper discussed the three main obstacles confronting him. "First, we need to obtain the land owner's permission so we can start digging. Then we need to determine if we're going to have to obtain any permits from either the county or the state of South Carolina."

"I've already asked two of Mr. Church's attorneys to start looking into what's required by the state of South Carolina when people like us are interested in searching for Civil War artifacts. There's likely a few hoops we'll have to jump through, but the fact that we'll be digging on private property and not on federal or state-owned land should make it far less complicated."

While pleased by the steps Regan had taken, Paul believed his team would soon have a few new members to help address a variety of issues, both expected and those they had no way of anticipating. "I'm not going to be surprised if they tell us we have to have the Office of the State Archeologist tagging along with us when we do our work. The more I've thought about that possibility, the more I believe it will be a mandatory condition they impose upon us. I guess that's to be expected as South Carolina is very protective of her heritage and of the role her sons played during the Civil War. After all of this legal business involving the permits gets squared away, I'll need to hire a contractor with some heavy equipment to do the work for us. All of this is going to cost Mr. Church a bunch of money, but we need an experienced contractor or even a road builder to shore up the hillside before we start any digging. We can't afford to have anyone get hurt, so whoever we hire is going to have to make sure the area is stable enough for us to start work."

"Anything else?" Regan asked.

"One thing. My team and I have enough work on our hands already. If those attorneys you've mentioned can obtain whatever permits we need, that would be a huge help. I'll take care of talking to the property owner, but if you can handle the permits and the rest of that legal nonsense that's a big weight off my shoulders."

"Understood. Consider it done. I'll call you once the permits have been obtained. Do the same for me after you speak with whoever owns the property. Mr. Church will be interested in knowing that detail has been addressed. Besides those issues, is there anything else?" Regan asked, visually picturing the work that needed to be done before the search for the missing treasury could commence.

"Unless you already have a plan in place for how we're going to move several large pieces of equipment up to the site, I guess that's it." Unlike Regan, Paul had spent time trying to figure out the best way to move several large backhoes, bulldozers, dump trucks, and other earth moving equipment to where the caves had once stood. With the area around the collapsed caves roughly five miles away from the nearest road, like the permit process, the task of cutting down a few hundred pine trees and building a road suitable enough for the heavy construction equipment to travel over was a project that would take several days to complete.

"OK, I see your point." Regan said, finally realizing that locating the gold was not going to be as easy as he and Simon Church had thought. "I'll talk to Mr. Church and let him know your thoughts on what we've discussed. In the meantime, do what you can to get started. You and I will talk later today."

43

Sitting on her front porch in a wicker rocking chair that had seen better days, Mary DeWolfe saw the steady trail of dust being kicked up by an unfamiliar pickup truck as it approached her home. Close to three miles long, the rough dirt driveway had been in the same condition ever since her family first settled the secluded piece of property in the early 1800s. Close to ninety-three years of age, she had outlived her husband and three sons by many years. Her two hundred acre farm, one that had been passed down through several generations, was now being leased by a family who grew soybeans and corn as their principal crops. Like several of her nearby barns, Mary's weather-beaten farmhouse was in poor condition. It had seen little care since her husband's passing ten years earlier. Spending most of her time sitting in her rocking chair when the weather permitted, Mary knew what to expect when she saw the dust being kicked up like it was.

Watching as the pickup came to an abrupt stop amidst a large cloud of thick choking dust, with her eyesight not as strong as it once was, DeWolfe fought to identify the three strangers walking towards her.

"You fellas need something or are ya just lost?" DeWolfe asked warily. Unaccustomed to strangers driving up unannounced, the elderly homeowner anxiously wondered what her unexpected guests were looking for. Too frail and far too old, she made no effort to fetch the shotgun her late husband had left hanging on the wall inside her house.

"Mrs. DeWolfe . . . Mrs. Mary DeWolfe?" Paul asked, his New England accent immediately giving away the fact that he had not been raised in the South. Standing on a sidewalk that had been set in place years earlier with fieldstones Mary's husband had harvested while plowing his fields, Paul waited for his question to be answered. As he waited, three flags hanging limply atop a weather-beaten flagpole suddenly snapped to life as a gust of wind brought them to attention. Nearest the top, an American flag was in far better condition than the tattered Stars and Bars flying directly underneath it. Further down, a faded South Carolina state flag was in the worst condition of the three.

Seeing Paul staring at the flags, Bobby Ray turned to look at DeWolfe. "That's an interesting set of flags you have displayed there, ma'am."

Pointing a long bony finger in the direction of her visitors, DeWolfe directed her first comment at Bobby Ray. "My eyes ain't what they used to be, but my hearing works just fine. I can tell you ain't one of them, but that fella with ya is a Yankee. The other fella ain't spoke yet, so I don't know whose side he's on, ours or theirs."

Chuckling at what DeWolfe had said, Paul responded by saying, "I'm the only Yankee standing here, ma'am. My two friends protecting my flanks were born and raised in South Carolina." As he continued to chuckle, Paul's eyes briefly focused on the elderly woman before taking in the home's dilapidated condition. Seated under a small broken window located above the porch, several broken boards and pieces of weathered trim reflected the lack of care the home had received over the past several years. Like the condition of her home, DeWolfe's old cotton dress was in similar shape.

"If them fellas is from South Carolina like ya say they is, I would have thought they'd have more sense than to be riding around in a fancy truck with a damn Yankee." DeWolfe glared at Bobby Ray and Chick before focusing her attention back on Paul.

Pointing to his friend, Bobby Ray let out a brief laugh before introducing himself. "Morning, Mrs. DeWolfe. My name is Bobby Ray Jenkins; I'm the undersheriff of Georgetown County. This fella standing next to me is a true Yankee, but he's a good Yankee. In fact, he may be the only good one they have left. He's not like some of them carpetbaggers we've had to deal with."

"What's the law want with me? Better yet, what's this damn Yankee doing here? Y'all don't see no *For Sale* signs do ya? My farm ain't for sale to no one." DeWolfe said suspiciously, not trusting what Bobby Ray had told her to be the truth. Having spent every day of her life on a farm that had never been owned by anyone outside of her family, DeWolfe's dislike for those living north of the Mason – Dixon line was forged from stories handed down by her ancestors. Among them were a few who had somehow managed to survive Mr. Lincoln's War. Her intense feelings had been exacerbated by two personal run-ins with Northerners years earlier.

"Would you mind if we talk with you on the porch for a spell, Mrs. DeWolfe? I'm not speaking for my friends, but I'd much rather be sitting in the shade than standing here in the hot sun." Reaching inside one of his pockets, Bobby Ray held up his badge so DeWolfe could see he was who he had said he was.

"Suppose not. Who's this other fella with ya?" DeWolfe asked, pointing the same bony finger she had used earlier in Chick's direction. "Does he know how to talk?"

"He's a school teacher. You know how they are . . . he only talks when he's hollering at one of his students." Bobby Ray said, laughing at his own joke while failing to give his friend credit for the advanced degrees he held from three different universities.

Years earlier, with their children already deceased and no other family members staying in touch with them, Mary and her late husband had donated their farmhouse and all of their land to the University of South Carolina. Far more interested in having their rural farmland kept in the same condition it had always been in, the DeWolfe's made the decision to donate their property to the state's flagship university rather than having it fall into the hands of a greedy real estate developer. As the Mary and Charles DeWolfe Irrevocable Land Trust was being created by a team of lawyers, the only stipulations Mary and her husband had demanded was that the land could never be developed, and they would no longer be required to pay property taxes as long as one of them was still living there. One of the stipulations also included a similar demand. The DeWolfe family would have exclusive rights to the property for the rest of their lives. They were conditions USC and the state of South Carolina had readily agreed to.

Dragging a dusty wooden picnic table closer to where Mary sat, Paul motioned for Bobby Ray to sit in the only other chair available. Moments after getting settled, Chick helped Paul unfurl a large map he had obtained from Berkeley County. Pointing out the boundaries of the DeWolfe property, with occasional comments from Bobby Ray and Chick, Paul explained the reason behind their visit. It was an explanation Mary, at first, did not totally grasp.

After explaining for the third time how Simon Church had found Captain Howard's handwritten journal inside an old chest, Mary finally began to connect the details carefully being explained to her. One part, however, was especially troubling for her to accept.

"You fellas are telling me these three Yankee soldiers . . . at least parts of them, have been buried on my property since the end of the war?" Like always, Mary did little to hide her disdain for anyone connected to the North; including soldiers who had died years before her birth. "What about the rest of their body parts, where are they buried?"

"That's why we're here, Mrs. DeWolfe. As we've already mentioned, not only is there a good chance those soldiers were murdered on your property, but we believe the rest of their remains were buried when the hillside collapsed. Along with the gold and silver that was hidden in another cave, the partial remains of those Union soldiers are in one of those other caves. We also believe the remains of three Confederate soldiers have also been interred with them since the hillside gave way. That part of the story is even more tragic than the part involving the Union soldiers as the information we've come across tells us the Confederate soldiers were alive when the hillside collapsed." With far more patience than Paul and Bobby Ray, Chick had carefully gone over the details Mary was having difficulty comprehending.

"Interred? What's that word mean?" Mary asked, the deep furrows displayed across her forehead gave every indication that she had never heard the word used before.

"It means those soldiers have been buried under the tons of rocks and dirt that fell on them when the hillside collapsed." Chick carefully explained, doing his best not to upset their elderly host.

"Oh my!"

"Mrs. DeWolfe, my friends and I would like your permission to excavate a section of the hillside where the bodies of those soldiers have been buried for far too long. Not only is that hillside hiding what many people would consider a national treasure, but it's also the location where several Civil War soldiers tragically lost their lives. If it's possible, we'd like to recover their remains and give them a proper burial." As he had spoken, Paul noticed a sudden change in Mary's attitude towards the Northern invaders who had perished on her property.

While interested in knowing more about the gold and silver hidden in a section of her property that she and her husband had never farmed due to the unfriendly terrain, Mary soon gave permission for the rocky hillside to be excavated. As she signed a form Paul had set in front of her, Mary peppered Chick with a variety of questions regarding the gold and silver. Satisfied by the answers she was given, she replied by saying, "I ain't real pleased to learn about them Yankees being buried on my property for as long as they have, but I want them boys to receive a proper burial. No one should have to die the way any of them soldiers did." Realizing she had just insulted Paul, without offering much of an apology Mary looked at the person who had done the most talking. "Ya seem like a nice fella, but, as my pa would say, you're still a no-good Yankee. I meant no harm by what I just said, but some of my kin was hurt real bad by what Sherman's boys did to South Carolina years back. My family, well . . . we just ain't the forgivin' kind."

"None taken, Mrs. DeWolfe," Paul said as he folded the piece of paper Mary had signed. "Once we know what's been buried on your property, we'll come back for another visit. How's that sound?"

"Sounds fine, Billy Yank, I'll be looking forward to it." Mary said as a playful smile graced her worn and tired face.

44

Pulling up to the curb outside of Lilly's, a fashionable, but overpriced restaurant catering to those Dallas residents who were more interested in being seen than enjoying a fine dining experience, the left rear door of the Mercedes Benz was slowly opened by a young parking attendant. Wearing a bright red sport coat, a pair of freshly pressed black pants, and polished dress shoes, the attendant's attire designated what his duties involved. Discreetly placed on the attire worn by those employees interacting with their customers, the attendant's sport coat displayed the restaurant's stylish logo on the left front pocket. Displaying a friendly smile, the attendant politely welcomed the vehicle's rear seat passenger; addressing her in a professional manner as he had been trained. As he had done on previous occasions, the young attendant took notice of the passenger's alluring figure.

Carefully being watched by two members of her security team, the attendant smiled as he helped the attractive wife of one of the restaurant's silent owners from her vehicle. Doing so allowed him to steal a second brief look at her scantily clad figure. From past visits, he knew the brief amount of time it would take to walk her inside the front door was good for at least a twenty dollar tip. Like previous gratuities she had given him, it was one the cash-strapped college-aged attendant would slip inside his pocket without giving a thought to sharing it with the other attendant working that afternoon.

Sitting down at her usual table next to two of her friends, Genevieve Church exchanged friendly, but insincere greetings with her lunch guests before acknowledging Martin Matern, her favorite waiter. Unlike the women she would soon be sharing a meal with, Genevieve thought highly of Matern. Occasionally in need of a discreet favor, she had sometimes slipped the middle-aged waiter a few dollars to fulfill her needs. Satisfying one of Genevieve's most recent requests had involved making a trip to a nearby hardware store to obtain a household need. The small amount of time it took to complete this transaction had garnered Matern a fifty dollar tip.

"The usual, Martin, please." Genevieve said politely, referring to her choice of an early afternoon martini. A fan of most types of martinis, when she visited Lilly's for lunch Genevieve always requested a vodka martini. Made of Grey Goose vodka, Noilly Prat dry vermouth, a dash of orange bitters, and garnished with two cocktail olives; it was one of her favorite drinks. Spying the drink glasses already sitting in front of her friends, she added, "I guess these ladies were either thirsty or too impolite to wait." Like always, whenever she felt slighted Genevieve sarcastically let the others with her know how she felt. Along with her poor manners, her inappropriate comments had caused her to lose a number of friends over the years.

Sitting between her guests at a small, but highly visible table in the middle of the dining room, after taking note of the other diners who were present Genevieve studied the expensive outfits being worn by her lunch companions. Wearing the latest fashions recently released by one of the country's most influential designers, she somehow managed to find fault with the outfits being worn. To their credit, her companions quietly ignored Genevieve's pithy comments. For one of them, it would be the last time she would ever allow herself to be insulted by Simon Church's wife.

"How's Simon feeling, Genevieve? I understand he told my husband he's been having problems with his throat?" Wendy Cleary asked rather casually before taking her next sip of wine. Four years younger than Genevieve, Cleary was neither jealous nor envious of her lunch companion's wealth or good looks. Blessed with a faithful husband who made more money each year than most men his age, and with a figure which still turned nearly as many heads as Genevieve's, Cleary was far more comfortable with her position in life than her friend. Like the Church mansion, the Cleary estate was far more spacious than what she and her husband needed.

Their other lunch companion, a woman in her late fifties by the name of Victoria Hegman, was just as attractive as her friends. Unlike Genevieve whose figure had been enhanced by silicone and several elective procedures, Hegman's stunning appearance was the result of grueling early morning workouts her private trainer put her through on a daily basis. Addicted to physical training as a means of keeping herself in shape, Hegman had only missed three workouts over the past four years. Divorced on two occasions from successful Dallas area bankers, she was currently engaged in an on-again, off-again relationship with a local architect. Ten-years younger than his girlfriend, Dennis

Pullman, a lifelong area resident, was well-known for the large modern estates he built for those who could afford his exorbitant fees. Fond of rich, older women, over the past several months he had discreetly spent a handful of long romantic weekends alone with Genevieve Church.

Growing tired of her elderly, but extremely wealthy husband, Genevieve found pleasure in not only seducing the boyfriend of one of her closest friends, but in getting back at Hegman for a disparaging comment she had made during a local fundraiser held at the Church estate. Fueled by a large donation made by Genevieve and her husband, the early afternoon fundraiser had raised over two hundred thousand dollars to rehabilitate a local park inside a depressed neighborhood in east Dallas.

From an early age, Genevieve had never been satisfied with the social status her family held in the community where they lived outside of Cincinnati, Ohio. Nor had she liked any of the schools she attended. Raised by parents who seldom denied their only child of anything she needed, Genevieve had been bullied in school for years by a group of girls who never accepted her for being different. Self-conscious about her thin, clumsy frame during her early teens, Genevieve, a loner with few friends and no siblings, had endured years of taunts and long bus rides. Frustrated by the lack of attention paid to her tears and complaints, she gradually withdrew into her own little world.

Ending her education after her sophomore year of college, Genevieve relocated to Dallas after her slim, bony looks had gained the attention of an unscrupulous modeling agency. Unlike other more prominent agencies, the one that signed up the immature teenager from Ohio promised her far too much to be able to deliver on. While certain promises had never materialized, what she soon perceived to be a successful summer of modeling outside of Dallas convinced the once shy teen that her looks could take her farther than she had ever hoped. In addition to her few modeling assignments, Genevieve landed two non-speaking roles in films which had been shot inside the city; neither had made it to the big screen. Over the next two years, several elective surgeries caused Genevieve's appearance, and her outlook, to improve. It did not, however, improve her relationship with her parents. Over the course of the following year she ceased all communications with her heartbroken mother and father. Within three years of her move to Dallas, both were dead. Their only child made no attempt to return home for either of their funerals.

Along with her growing confidence, Genevieve used her toned body to her advantage whenever it was required. As these occasions grew in frequency, the aspiring actress went through lover after lover as she learned to collect the toys and social status she so desperately sought. Less than six years after moving to the Lone Star state, she had used her skills to snare her current husband. First meeting at a social gathering inside Texas Stadium for some of the state's wealthiest residents, she and Simon Church had quickly grown very close.

While her marriage to Simon Church allowed Genevieve to attain the social and financial status she desperately sought, she soon grew tired of her husband and of his various business obligations. Heavily invested in the gas and oil industry across the globe, her husband's career caused him to be away from home for long periods of time. Within months of marrying a man several years older than her, she grew tired of everything about him. As they slowly drew apart, Genevieve, at first, gave serious consideration to making Pullman her next conquest. Then, after setting her plan in motion to rid herself of her billionaire husband, she suddenly lost interest in her newest lover. While continuing to have fun in every imaginable way with one of Dallas' most eligible bachelors, she realized Pullman had far too many faults; among them were an expensive lifestyle he often had trouble affording and, most importantly, his attraction to far too many other women.

"Genevieve, you've hardly said a word . . . are we boring you?" Cleary asked, interrupting her friend's thoughts while ignoring a friendly wave from across the room from someone she disliked a great deal. Sounding like a popular movie star from the 1960s, Cleary followed up with another meaningless question. "Is everything alright, darling?"

"Yes, I'm fine, thank you." Genevieve replied, rolling her eyes as she forced a smile. Nervously, her right hand began toying with the stem of her martini glass.

As her two friends carried on with their conversation, Genevieve's thoughts focused on an incident that had taken place inside the Church mansion the night before. After weeks of spending time conducting research on the Internet, she had recently put her plan in motion to do away with her husband. In doing so, she came up with several different ways of eliminating the biggest source of irritation in her life before deciding on the one she believed to be the most efficient, the most deadly, and the hardest to detect.

Then, with her plan underway for less than a week, Genevieve made one huge mistake; she had been caught red-handed by one of her staff members. It was someone she not only had little use for, but someone she despised. While often rude and condescending to most members of the household staff, those born outside the United States who struggled with the English language routinely incurred her wrath more than others. Pleased that her husband could afford to pay others to cook and clean for them, Genevieve had little appreciation for the hard work put forth each day by those who were just happy to be employed.

Now, as she sat inside one of her husband's restaurants, Genevieve thoughts were on Isabella Vasquez, and what she had witnessed. "How could I have been that stupid to allow that bitch to see what I was doing? She not only saw me mixing the ingredients, but she caught me holding *the damn bottle!*" Consumed by her thoughts, Genevieve's hands began to tremble as she took the last sip of her martini.

It was now time for her to decide how she would deal with the only person who could stand in her way of accomplishing what she had set out to do. With an already lengthy list of people she despised, including those who had made her life miserable while attending school back home, Genevieve Church now hated one of her maids more than anyone else.

45

Situated on a large tract of what had once been nothing more than barren wasteland, the dusty and tumbleweed-covered surface which still remained had been scarred years earlier by a steady stream of travelers seeking a better life further west. Like hundreds of others before them, most yearned of striking it rich in the California gold fields. Now the site of Simon Church's sizeable estate, years earlier as the property was being developed workers had unearthed a variety of discarded relics. Tossed out of their wagons as they travelled across the hot, arid Texas plains in the decades following the American Civil War, travelers had sought to lighten the loads by reducing the number of possessions they were travelling with. More often than not, those belongings had included a host of family heirlooms. For someone whose growing interest in the nation's history was becoming more than just a passing interest, those relics served to fuel Church's interest in becoming a collector of Civil War artifacts.

As the number of his successful business ventures increased over the years, so did Simon Church's wealth. Pouring a significant amount of money into his principal residence caused the wealthy billionaire to hire a small army of workers to maintain his estate. Among them was a part-time housekeeper by the name of Isabella Vasquez. Over time, the improvements to Church's estate included the addition of several large bedrooms, two luxurious swimming pools, a four-bedroom guest house, three barns, and a number of smaller outbuildings. Many of the artifacts Church began to collect were housed inside his mansion and a handful of small outbuildings. To protect his valuable and growing collection, the mansion and all of the outbuildings were equipped with a state of the art air conditioning system and an elaborate alarm system. Behind one of the buildings, a large industrial generator sat ready to provide power in the event of a natural disaster or the failure of the local power grid.

Arriving at the Church estate after standing next to a cash register at her second job inside a small grocery store, with the help of another housekeeper Isabella went to work cleaning the rooms located on the mansion's second floor. Among them were the separate sleeping quarters used by Simon and Genevieve Church. Elaborately decorated by a high-priced interior decorating firm Simon Church had hired several years earlier, the two suites, like the mansion's main hallway, had recently been updated by Church's younger wife, and the billionaire's checkbook.

With his busy schedule often filled with business meetings across the globe, and his wife's own schedule filled with social and humanitarian causes her husband seldom understood, Simon and Genevieve Church not only slept apart from each other for nights on end, but often did so in different parts of the world. While away from home for long stretches, they both insisted on the mansion being thoroughly cleaned at least four times a week. This was particularly true for each of their sleeping quarters. Doing so often meant washing sheets and towels that had never been used.

With the doors to the two separate sleeping quarters closed tightly after being cleaned for the second time in three days, after swapping out the sheets and towels inside a large guest room at the far end of the hall, Isabella finished her duties by dusting a large credenza. On the other side of the expansive suite, Susan Lopez stood next to an ornate window frame as she finished wrapping the power cord to her vacuum cleaner back in place. A second-generation Mexican-American, Lopez had started working at the Church estate less than a month after Isabella was hired. Working together at least twice a week had caused the two housekeepers to become fast friends. So had poverty and the need to keep their children fed.

"Don't look now, but it appears as if the bitch has returned home." Lopez said, staring out the window as Genevieve Church climbed out of the backseat of a shiny Mercedes Benz SUV her husband had recently purchased. Next to her door, one of the members of her three-man security team scanned the grounds for any unwanted guests. While concerned more about his wealth being targeted than he was in his wife being kidnapped, Simon Church had hired five highly-trained ex-military members to protect his interests. Impeccably dressed in a fashionable white pants suit which served to accentuate her slender, but well-endowed figure, Genevieve watched impatiently as two of the other members of her on-duty security team unloaded shopping bags filled with new outfits and shoes from her late afternoon shopping excursion in Dallas. Watching as Genevieve and her security team made their way towards one of the mansion's side doors, Lopez said, "I don't know who I feel more sorry for, the good-looking guy who is walking next to her or the two morons who have been reduced to being her servants."

"Are you referring to us?" Isabella asked, laughing at her own joke.

"*Freaking bitch!* She's living a life of luxury because of her big tits and good looks while hard-working *putas* like us are breaking our asses just to put food on the table." Having been treated rudely on two recent occasions, Lopez had little respect for the person she was staring at.

"*Susan, please don't call her that!* You don't know who might be listening. And don't call me a puta. I may not have much money, but I'll be damned if I ever start selling my body just to put food on the table." As she finished speaking, Isabella, fearful their conversation was being listened to, glanced at the security camera posted outside the room they were cleaning.

"I don't care if anyone hears me. No one who works here has any use for her, so she'll never know what names I call her. Like I said, if it wasn't for these I doubt Mr. Church would have any use for her." As she watched Genevieve Church disappear inside the mansion, Lopez mimicked the size of her employer's augmented breasts by placing her hands under her own breasts. Doing so allowed her friend to enjoy a good laugh.

Recovering from her moment of laughter, Isabella smiled as she looked at Lopez. "By the number of bags those guys unloaded from the back of that fancy car, it looks as if Mrs. Church did some serious damage to her husband's checkbook." A prolific shopper who often returned home with clothes and shoes she seldom wore, the spending habits of Simon Church's young wife were often a topic of discussion between the two impoverished housekeepers.

Moments later, as Isabella and her friend gathered their housekeeping supplies in order to move on to the last room they were responsible for cleaning, the unmistakable sound of a familiar voice came over the small portable radio clipped to the waistband of Isabella's uniform. One of twenty radios handed out to staff members as they reported for work; they were ones Simon Church required his staff to wear in the event he or his wife needed their assistance. Along with a number of other household supplies, the radios were stored inside a small first-floor room which served as the mansion's security office and mailroom. Earlier, when she and Isabella had clocked in, Lopez begged off on wearing the radio.

"Good evening, Isabella! Can you please meet me in the kitchen in about five minutes?"

Surprised by what she heard, Lopez stared suspiciously at the radio clipped to her friend's uniform. "That sounded rather friendly, Isabella. What was that all about? Are . . . are you and that bitch friends now?" Lopez suddenly became concerned over the name she had directed at Genevieve Church moments earlier.

"Are you crazy!" Isabella replied as she and her friend exchanged frightened stares. "Just as badly as she treats you and everyone else who works here, Mrs. Church barely acknowledges me whenever she sees me. I have an idea on why she wants to see me, but it certainly isn't because we're friends." Knowing what had occurred between them the previous evening; Isabella immediately dreaded the thought of any additional interaction with Simon Church's wife. Panicked over having to report to the kitchen, Isabella sensed her heart beating faster than normal.

"Isabella, did you hear me?"

Nodding at the portable radio, Lopez asked, "Are . . . are you going to answer her?"

Holding the radio in her trembling left hand, Isabella replied to Genevieve Church's request. As she did, Lopez noticed the pale look that had settled on her friend's face. "Isabella, are you okay? You . . . you look like you've just seen a ghost."

Unsure of what she was about to see and hear, Isabella's hands continued to shake as she returned the portable radio to where it had sat on her waist. Looking at her friend, she said, "She probably wants to see me about . . . what I . . ."

"About what?" Lopez demanded, growing worried over the pale look which continued to linger on her friend's normally cheery face.

"I have to go. I'll . . . I'll tell you all about it later." Isabella replied as she thought back to her last encounter with Genevieve Church. Seconds later, she turned and hurried towards the kitchen.

* * * * * *

Slowly pushing open the set of double-doors leading from the mansion's large opulent dining room to its equally spacious main kitchen, Isabella's fingers felt for the bank of light switches located off to her right. Glancing over her right shoulder, she stared at the row of cabinets inside the dimly lit butler's pantry. Each contained an assortment of fine china, expensive silverware, and many other items used during fancy dinner parties hosted by Simon Church and his wife. Walking inside the kitchen as several florescent lights came to life; her eyes anxiously scanned the large workspace for the person who had summoned her. Forcing herself to calm down after realizing Mrs. Church had not yet arrived, Isabella marveled at how well the kitchen and its sea of stainless steel appliances had been laid out. Like most members of the household staff whose duties did not require them to be there, Isabella had only briefly visited the kitchen on two other occasions. Much to her regret, one of those occasions had taken place the previous evening.

Briefly giving the kitchen's Terra Cotta floor a quick inspection, Isabella's attention then focused on the stainless steel appliances lining two adjoining walls. On one of the walls, a large stainless steel exhaust hood hung suspended over two identical gas stoves. Making her way around the fanciest kitchen she had ever seen, one which included a work area at least fifteen times bigger than her own small kitchen, Isabella marveled at how clean everything was kept. From the ovens and stoves and all across the shiny tile floor, not a scrap of paper or a morsel of food could be found. The large kitchen was often the scene of organized chaos as Simon Church's personal chef and her assistants worked to prepare meals for the variety of events held inside the mansion.

"Do you like what you see, Isabella?" Genevieve Church asked from where she stood watching her housekeeper hover over a fryer often used by the kitchen staff to cook one of her husband's most-requested treats, Pommes frites. As she often did when trying to surprise the kitchen staff with a quick inspection, Genevieve had quietly slithered into the kitchen.

"I'm a woman who likes to cook, Mrs. Church. How could I not dream about someday having a kitchen as nice as this one in my very own home? It's one I'll likely never be able to afford, but it's still nice to dream about things. Besides being the largest one I've even seen, it's also the cleanest kitchen I've ever been in." Pointing to a small pile of rubber floor mats and several large industrial-sized garbage cans lined up near one of the exterior doors, Isabella did her best to delay the real reason she and her employer were there to speak to each other. "Even the mats and garbage cans which have likely been used a thousand times appear to be as clean as the day they were purchased."

Forcing herself to acknowledge the observation made by a member of her staff who she seldom paid attention to, Genevieve Church reluctantly nodded her head. What followed was another example of the type of lies she often told. "I appreciate you noticing the attention the kitchen staff gives to making sure everything is thoroughly cleaned before they leave. But that's part of your job, isn't it?"

"I'm sorry. I'm not sure what you mean, Mrs. Church?" Isabella replied, stepping away from the fryer to look at her employer.

"Isabella, you're a housekeeper. My husband and I pay you to keep things clean around here. Part of your job is noticing when bathrooms or bedrooms or even a kitchen floor needs cleaning, correct?"

"Yes, ma'am." Isabella replied, ignoring her employer's condescending tone.

Walking across the kitchen, Genevieve paused next to a long stainless steel prep table sitting in the middle of the expansive space. Often used by the kitchen staff for a variety of different needs, it was where trays of appetizers, salads, desserts, and other decadent delights were prepared when parties of well over two hundred guests were in attendance. Turning to face the person standing on the other side of the table, Genevieve smiled after noticing the anxiety displayed on her housekeeper's face. Gesturing with her hands as she leaned against the prep table's shiny clean surface, she did her best at making sure her next few comments sounded as sincere as possible. "Thank you for taking the time to meet with me, Isabella. I know how busy you are, so I'll get right to the point. I asked you here as I felt it was necessary to clear up any misgivings you might have about seeing me mixing that drink for my husband last evening. It's important for me to know that you didn't misinterpret what you saw."

Casting her eyes downward towards the kitchen's elaborate tiled floor, Isabella refused to look at her employer as she followed the lead that had been set moments earlier. While not accustomed to lying, she prepared to do so in an attempt to keep Genevieve Church talking. "Mrs. Church, this is your home. You don't have to explain anything to me. I've cleaned enough homes to know what takes place between a husband and his wife are issues that don't involve me. I'm just here to do my job so I can provide for my family."

"I appreciate you feeling that way. That's why my husband and I value people like you." Genevieve offered, insulting her housekeeper for the second time in the span of a few minutes. "With that being said, it's important that you and everyone else who works here knows no matter how much we may argue with each other over simple and ordinary differences, my husband and I love each other very much."

Realizing she had just been insulted and lied to for the second time, Isabella, still refusing to lock eyes with the person standing on the other side of the table, outwitted her employer by remaining calm. "I know you love your husband, Mrs. Church. So do many others who work here."

Taking a moment to clear a thought that had just entered her mind, Genevieve adjusted her stance as she continued to lean against the prep table. "There are many reasons why Mr. Church and I insist on our house being kept so clean, but, for now, the most important is that neither of us has any interest in being exposed to this terrible virus that's causing so much turmoil across the world. Just like everyone else, we cherish our health." As she finished addressing her thought, Genevieve did her best at playing a role she often assumed when trying to gain a sympathetic ear. It was an act Isabella easily took for what it was, pure bullshit.

"I give thanks every day for the excellent health I've been blessed with." Poised to tell Genevieve about her husband's recent health issues, Isabella suddenly realized the less her employer knew about her family the better.

"I'm sure you do, Isabella. That's something I always seem to hear about Mexicans like you. Your people always seem to be praying about one thing or another; more people, including me, should pray more often than we do."

"I'm from Guatemala, Mrs. Church, not Mexico." Isabella replied, taking pleasure in correcting Mrs. Church's latest gaffe.

Turning a light shade of red after being corrected by someone she had little use for, Genevieve turned the conversation back to why they were meeting. "I want you to know that lately Mr. Church has not been feeling well. Besides a slight temperature and a sore throat that he's been dealing with for the past few weeks, he's recently developed a nasty cough. We're both afraid he's exhibiting some of the signs associated with this terrible virus."

Not sure if she was being told another lie or not, Isabella simply offered the response she believed her employer expected her to say. "I'll pray for him, Mrs. Church."

Except for a very brief smile and a quick nod of her head, Genevieve Church paid little attention to her housekeeper's comment. "That's why you saw me with that red and white plastic bottle last night. I was mixing a drink for Mr. Church to take to bed. He's often thirsty during the night, so having something to sip on helps ease his dry throat."

"The bottle with the bad markings on it?" Isabella asked, recalling the plastic bottle she had seen Genevieve holding.

"Bad markings?"

"Yes, ma'am, you know, the kind they put on containers containing household cleaners and poisons. Those markings are a warning not to let anyone drink whatever's inside those containers. Besides all of the words they put on those containers they sometimes put the pirate flag there as another kind of a warning. At least, that's what I always call it. You know . . . the skull and crossbones." While her command of the English language was better than most of her co-workers, her nervousness in being alone with someone she disliked caused Isabella to struggle while describing the warnings she had seen.

While realizing her housekeeper was smarter than she had given her credit for, Genevieve stayed with the story she was feeding her. "Yes, you're correct, Isabella, those warnings are put there for the reason you just mentioned. But just like the president mentioned the other night when he was on television talking about the virus, small doses of products like the one you saw me using are an acceptable way of ridding one's body of unhealthy bacteria. I was simply following his suggestion so I could make my husband feel better."

"So, you were trying to help Mr. Church, not hurt him, is that correct?" Isabella asked, making it sound as if she was naïve enough to believe the lie she was being fed.

"That's exactly what I was doing." Genevieve excitedly replied, believing her housekeeper was beginning to believe her twisted story.

"I'm glad to hear that Mrs. Church. I hope those drinks help to ease the discomfort Mr. Church has been experiencing." As much as she disliked meeting her employer inside the kitchen without anyone else being present, Isabella could not wait to get as far away from Genevieve Church as possible. "Susan was right," she thought, "this bitch is nothing more than a puta who is planning to kill her husband."

Making her way around the large free-standing prep table, Genevieve smiled as she wrapped her arms around Isabella. It was an embrace her housekeeper did not return.

Then, as they endured a brief awkward moment, Genevieve, for the second time in less than two days, slipped a one hundred dollar bill inside Isabella's left hand. "There may be times when I ask you to bring one of these drinks up to my husband's bedroom before he goes to bed. If I do, just set it on the nightstand closest to his bathroom. We often go to bed at different times, so if you can save me a couple of extra trips to the second floor I would appreciate that assistance. This little bit of extra money is just to show my appreciation."

Without giving it any thought, Isabella let the large bill fall out of her hand. As it landed on the prep table, she said, "I don't know about this, Mrs. Church. I . . . I don't want to get in any trouble if something happens to your husband." Having been alone with her employer for far too long, Isabella's eyes started to tear as she thought about what she was being asked to do. "I don't want this money. It's . . ."

"It's nothing more than a way for me to show you my appreciation for lending me some help when I'm too tired to make that extra trip upstairs, Isabella. Besides, someone recently told me about your husband being out of work due to a terrible injury he sustained. I'm sure this little bit of extra money will help you buy some groceries for your children, won't it?" As she finished speaking, Genevieve placed the one hundred dollar bill back inside Isabella's hand. Then, much to her housekeeper's surprise, Genevieve took her by the hand and walked her over to the large stainless steel sink. Bending down, she removed a red and white plastic container from a cabinet under the sink. It was the same container Isabella had seen her use the previous evening.

Making sure her housekeeper was paying attention to what she was doing, Genevieve slowly filled a tall crystal glass with water, being careful to leave just enough room near the top of the glass. Uncapping the plastic container, she then poured a small amount of liquid into the glass. Withdrawing a spoon from one of the nearby drawers, Genevieve carefully stirred the contents of the drink. Smiling as she glanced at Isabella as a way of making sure she was watching her every move, Genevieve held up the plastic container after mixing the drink. "This is the same one you saw me using last night, correct?"

"Yes . . . I think so." Isabella nervously replied, her large round eyes studying the container being held in Genevieve's left hand.

Setting the plastic container on the granite countertop next to the sink, Genevieve said, "Just for the record, it's the same container, Isabella. And, just so you feel more comfortable helping me with my husband's drinks, watch this." With no wasted motions, in front of her housekeeper Genevieve Church drank the contents of the drink she had just prepared. Wiping her mouth with a paper napkin after finishing her drink, she added, "If it's good enough for my husband, it's good enough for me."

"Yes, ma'am, I guess it is." Isabella mumbled as she continued to stare at the glass her employer had just set down.

"So, you'll help me then?"

Fingering the hundred dollar bill she tightly held in her left hand, Isabella waited a moment before responding. Expecting to see her employer grab her throat in panic after downing the drink which was laced with something she would have never considered drinking; Isabella surprisingly witnessed Genevieve experiencing no side effects. Moments later, she softly responded to the question she had been asked.

"I'll be glad to help you, Mrs. Church." Holding up her left hand, she mumbled, "My family and I thank you for the few extra dollars. It's much appreciated."

While pleased by the answer she heard, Genevieve remained standing next to the sink as she pondered her next move. Realizing her housekeeper had not returned her previous embrace, Genevieve decided against overacting the role she was playing.

"Thank you, Isabella. I'll look forward to your help. As you know, Mr. Church's business activities require him to travel a great deal. In fact, he'll be gone for the next four nights. We'll just leave it that whenever I need your help, I'll come find you. On nights you're not working, I'll bring the drinks upstairs myself. How's that sound?" As she finished speaking, Genevieve flashed her trademark smile. On most occasions, it meant she had pulled the wool over someone's eyes.

"That sounds fine, Mrs. Church." Isabella replied as she watched the red and white container being placed back under the sink.

Turning to leave, Isabella suddenly froze before reaching the same set of doors she had used earlier to enter the kitchen. Turning to look back at her employer, she watched as Genevieve rinsed out the glass she had mixed her drink in. The clean drinking glass now caused Isabella to break out in a cold sweat as she thought about what she had seen. "It's the same kind of glass from last night and the same plastic container, but it's not the same . . . "

Her next thought suddenly made Isabella feel sick to her stomach. Moments later, inside a bathroom reserved for household staff, the diminutive housekeeper puked her guts out.

46

Ten days after meeting with Mary DeWolfe and receiving her permission to excavate the hillside where the caves had once stood, with all of the necessary permits in hand work began on the construction of a rough five-mile road. Once finished, the winding dirt and gravel road would allow access to the site for the heavy construction equipment needed to excavate the rocky hillside. Among the items buried inside that hillside for several decades was a small fortune in gold and silver coins.

With access to the site nearing completion after a small army of loggers, road builders, and workers from several sub-contractors spent eight long days of double shifts carving out a road along the southern end of the DeWolfe property, a variety of construction equipment was moved into position not far from where Paul planned on digging. Among the equipment were three large dump trucks, a rock crusher, two front-end loaders, and three bulldozers. Parked nearby were two portable construction trailers; one of which would serve as the project's field office. As work commenced around the base of the hillside, members of the road crew continued to harvest the trees they had felled. While many of the larger trees would be sent to two nearby paper mills, others would be reduced to wood chips before being sold to local garden centers. It was the most activity the DeWolfe property had seen in years.

Inside the crowded field office owned by the construction company Paul had hired, a meeting took place between Paul's team, Phillip Groski, the owner of the construction company, and three forensic recovery experts. Each of the forensic experts was employed by the state's Office of the State Archaeologist. Invited to be there, but noticeably absent were Simon Church and Robert Regan.

As part of their assigned duties, the members of the forensic recovery team were present to make sure the recovery of any human remains, primarily bones and other historical artifacts, were recovered in accordance with state statutes and the policies of their office.

The owner of a large construction company which specialized in building interstate highways and other complex public works projects, Groski had been enticed to assist in the recovery project after receiving assurance from Simon Church that he would receive a significant bonus if the project was completed in less than one hundred days. Nearing retirement, the former Navy Seabee looked much younger than his actual age. Nearly six feet six inches in height, the powerfully built construction owner had spent a considerable amount of time studying the detailed plans his engineers had drafted after surveying the rocky hillside. As his surveyors and engineers had done, Groski and his foreman had also spent several hours probing the hillside with a variety of high-tech optics. Among them were two types of fiber optic cameras similar to those that had been successfully used in different parts of the world to rescue trapped miners.

After moving their meeting from the construction trailer to the base of the hillside where the gold and silver was believed to have been hidden, Paul and his crew, including the members of the forensic recovery team, saw the prep work Groski's crew had already completed. Close to where they stood, nearly two hundred and fifty wooden stakes displayed a series of handwritten elevation markings in black lettering. Others helped to outline the probable locations of the entrances to the three caves. They had been placed in these areas after the survey crew spent the better part of three days analyzing seismic data and other information in an attempt to pinpoint the exact locations of where the caves had stood. While one was still partially exposed, the other two were now completely hidden; closed off by layers of fallen rock. Like several others that had placed in the ground not far away, the ends of the stakes had been spray painted with bright orange fluorescent paint. This had been done to make them easier for the construction crews involved in the next phase of the project to spot.

"Do you want me to start or do you want to get this meeting going," Groski asked Paul as he kicked a small rock in the direction of where days of work would soon begin. "I've read all the reports my engineers have prepared and I've already walked this hill a bunch of times, so I'm kind of anxious to have my men start working."

"Don't let me hold you up. Let's hear what you have to say," Paul said, eyeing the bright orange stakes lining the rocky hillside. "I'm curious to know what your engineers had to say about the stability of this hillside. We don't need anyone getting hurt if that should give way."

"Well, that's an important point I'd like to address. The answer to your question isn't what I expected to learn from all of these reports I've read. The simple fact is this hillside is not as stable as we had hoped, so I'm asking all of you to stay away from it as much as possible. I know each of you wants to be in the middle of all this work that's about to commence, but I can't afford to have any of you getting hurt. I take my job seriously, so whether it's down here or up on the hill I'm going to chew each of you a new ass if I see you walking around without your hard hat and safety vest being worn. Those two items are to be worn at all times when you're on this work site; there are no exceptions when it comes to safety. I take pride in the fact that no one in my crew has ever been seriously injured at any of the sites we've worked." As he finished speaking, Groski paused to look each member of Paul's team in the eye. It was his way of reinforcing the safety talk he had just delivered.

"Any chance you or your crew has seen anything that indicates the gold and silver is actually buried in one of those caves?" Bobby Ray asked, doing his best to contain his excitement.

"One of the probes we conducted with some of our high-tech equipment showed an anomaly in that area over there, but at this point we have no idea what it is." As he answered Bobby Ray's question, Groski pointed to where a series of survey stakes outlined the possible entrance to the cave fitting Howard's description of where some of the Confederacy's precious assets had been hidden. "While we haven't found signs of any valuables, we did find what appeared to be a badly shattered bone. My guess is that it's human; probably a leg bone from one of those soldiers you've told me about. Here, take a look." Opening a green folder he was holding, Groski handed Paul two black and white photographs. They both had been taken by one of Groski's sophisticated optical cameras.

Peering over Paul's shoulder, Wayne Keller, the supervisor in charge of the forensic recovery team, stepped back after studying the photographs for a few seconds. Holding up a photo of one of the bones Paul's team had discovered several days earlier, he said, "Take a look at this. As you study it, hold it up to the ones Mr. Groski has just showed us. The bone appears to be very similar to the one in Mr. Groski's photos, especially the spot where it was shattered. Each of the photos seems to indicate it was broken rather violently. It's definitely human; it's too large to belong to any animal living in these parts. My team and I believe it was someone's tibia."

Listening to what Keller had said, Paul compared the bone in Groski's photograph to the one Keller had taken during his first examination. "I have to admit they're very similar, but we'll have to have someone take a closer look. That's if we're fortunate enough to recover the other half." After speaking with Keller for several minutes, Paul's eyes focused on a stake that had been placed in the ground within the outline of the middle cave. Turning to Groski, he said, "What's the purpose of that stake over there?"

"That's a reminder for my men. It marks the rough location of this bone we're talking about. From the data I've looked at, it's lying under about ten to twelve feet of debris. We'll find it, but it won't be today." Groski's comment served to reinforce that Paul's team had likely found the ground described in Howard's journal.

After several minutes of speculation regarding the images captured in the photographs, Groski finished outlining his plan to excavate two of the collapsed caves. While his engineers and survey crew had staked out the location of the cave that had stood to the left of the other two, Groski's contract stated this section of the hillside would not be excavated unless Paul determined there was a need to do so. While thought to be the smallest of the three caves, Howard had only briefly mentioned it in two of his entries.

Thirty minutes later, after Groski had thoroughly explained his plan to excavate the caves, he received the go-ahead for work to commence.

47

With another long day of being out in the hot sun under their belt, Paul and his friends sat at a picnic table cooling off inside a small municipal park not far from their hotel. Set back from the park's main entrance, the wooden picnic table was one of five placed beneath a long single row of mature maple trees. Like the others, the picnic table was completely covered in late afternoon shade. Afraid of succumbing to the cool temperatures and inviting beds inside their hotel rooms if they had gone back there to clean up, Paul and Bobby Ray had picked up enough food at a local Piggly Wiggly grocery store to feed a small army. It was the first time Paul's team had not cleaned up before eating their evening meal. It was also their first time relaxing outside after putting in a long day. On orders from Peter, two bottles of wine, a case of cold beer, and a large bag of ice had also been procured.

With the picnic table moved even further inside the large patch of shade, Paul sat at one end drinking a cold beer as he watched Chick and Bobby Ray spread out the cold cuts, chips, rolls, and

condiments that would soon comprise their evening meal. Next
to the cold cuts, two large plastic tubs of coleslaw and potato
salad sat waiting to be devoured. Close to where their picnic table
was located, near the right field foul line of one of two baseball
fields occupying most of the space inside the park, a small group
of parents shouted encouragement to a baserunner rounding
second base. Their loud cheers momentarily distracted Paul's
attention from the activity taking place around the picnic table.
Raising his bottle of beer as the teenager slid safely slid into third,
Paul softly uttered, "Nice hustle, young man!"

With sandwiches stuffed full of fresh meats and cheeses, and
lathered with a variety of condiments that would soon go to
waste, talk around the table grew quiet as Paul's crew satisfied
their hungry stomachs. With their long hot day leaving them
just enough time to enjoy a few sips of water and an energy bar
as they addressed a variety of needs, they were eager to enjoy a
good meal. The park's casual setting did little to dampen their
appetites.

Making a second sandwich as the others sat drinking their cold
beverages and polishing off a large bag of potato chips, Bobby
Ray raised the question of what would happen to any gold and
silver they recovered. While he was present weeks earlier when
Regan mentioned his employer only expected a small number
of coins in return for the money he spent financing this project,
Bobby Ray had never accepted Simon Church's statement as
being truthful. With too many other thoughts keeping them busy
over the past few days, Church's statement was one no one had
spent much time thinking about.

"I'm not sure what everyone else thinks, but if we find any
additional remains they need to be properly buried in a Civil War

cemetery. I'm sure those archeologists we're working with will have some say over where the remains are buried, but just like the ones we found on Duke Johnson's property they deserve a proper burial." As he sipped on a plastic cup filled with his favorite wine, Peter reminded his friends of the remains they had found several years earlier on Duke Johnson's hog farm just outside of Maple Hill, North Carolina. Weeks after finding the remains of several Confederate soldiers, including those of their commanding officer, Captain Judiah Francis, the remains had been buried in a touching ceremony at Arlington National Cemetery.

"Dang right, they do." With his mouth stuffed full of the first bite of his second sandwich, Bobby Ray somehow managed to offer his support of the recommendation that had just been made.

Under a fading sky, Paul listened as his friends discussed whether Mary DeWolfe, Simon Church, the state of South Carolina, or even the federal government was the rightful owner of any historical artifacts that might be found. While most of the conversation focused on the gold and silver coins described in Howard's journal, the discussion also included the crates of rifles that had supposedly been left inside the same cave.

"We're a long way from having to decide who owns what or who gets what, but we'll figure it out. In fact, we may not have any say in how it's dispersed. For now, the best we can hope for is an amicable settlement between the parties involved. If that doesn't happen, then I'm afraid it may come down to an expensive legal battle where only the attorneys come out on top." As someone who had always been far more interested in solving the complex investigations he was assigned than he was in the details of a negotiated settlement, Paul had little interest in getting caught up in a protracted legal battle.

Helping to police the area around the picnic table, Chick, who had little to say up till now, offered up a possible solution to the matter being discussed. "What about Judge Morgan? The hearing he presided over in Charleston after we found the first pot of money led to a fair settlement that pleased everyone. If we find what we're looking for, it might be a good idea for you to reach out to him again, Paul."

"Funny you should mention the good Judge. I was just thinking of him earlier today." Tying the end of a full bag of garbage, Paul added, "Let's see how this all plays out over the next few days, but I'll keep that thought in mind. If I have to, I'll have Steve reach out to him."

Years earlier, Paul's friend, Steve Alcott, invited one of his closest friends, Judge Howard Nathan Morgan, to a meeting Paul had orchestrated. It was a meeting that had taken place in the mayor's office in Charleston, South Carolina. Assigned to the United States Court of Appeals for the Fourth Circuit, Morgan, a passionate Civil War buff like Paul and the members of his team, had been present when a large portion of the Confederate treasury was discovered hidden inside several old cannons. Later, after presiding over a two-day hearing in which representatives from each of the former states of the Confederacy had presented their thoughts on what should happen to the recovered assets, Morgan carefully crafted a series of disbursements which were later approved by the United States District Court for the Eastern District of North Carolina. Those disbursements included several recommendations Paul had offered during the hearing.

Finished doing his part to clean up from the casual dinner they had all enjoyed, Paul said, "I'm too tired to give this anymore thought tonight. Let's get packed up so we can get back to the hotel and get cleaned up. I need a shower and a few minutes to clear my head before I hit the sheets."

Paul's suggestion was one no one disagreed with.

48

Outside his hotel room, an intense wind-driven rain drummed steadily against the large window situated above a faux leather couch. Beating against the glass for the past three hours, the rain did little to disturb Paul's restful sleep. With the room's inexpensive set of drapes pulled tight to prevent any unwanted intrusions from interrupting one of his favorite activities, the small amount of light managing to pierce the dark confines came from the digital numbers displayed on an alarm clock. Sitting to the left of the bed on the only night stand present, the clock's bright red numbers showed the time to be 4:29 a.m.

As the clock made its next time adjustment, the ringtone on Paul's cell phone announced an incoming call. No matter the reason, it was far too early for anyone to be woken from a peaceful, sound sleep. Knocking over the alarm clock as he fumbled for his phone, Paul barely opened his eyes as he squinted at the number being displayed.

"Do you ever sleep?" Paul mumbled, using his right hand to return the alarm clock to its original position after verifying the ungodly hour he had been woken. Less than pleased at being disturbed, he suddenly became even more irritated after realizing how early it was. "For crying out loud, it's not even five a.m. What the hell time is it where you are?" As he asked his question, Paul realized phone calls in the middle of the night seldom brought good news.

"It's 3:30 in the morning. I'm sorry to have to call you so early, but the time of day is irrelevant right now." Regan answered, glancing quickly at the expensive timepiece on his left wrist. Working late into the evening on a presentation drafted by one of Simon Church's employees, Regan had planned on spending the night at his employer's mansion instead of making the long drive home. "For what it's worth, I haven't been to bed yet and I doubt that's going to happen anytime soon."

"Something wrong?" Paul asked, his sore muscles telling him it was way too early to be even thinking about climbing out of bed. Ignoring the light switch next to his bed, he anxiously waited for Regan's answer.

"Simon Church is dead."

"*What!*" Paul said, startled by the unexpected news as he fought to free himself from the warm blankets tangled around his legs. Moments later, as he sat on the edge of the bed, he tried comprehending the disturbing news Regan was telling him.

"One of his servants found him. Part of his duties included checking on Mr. Church once or twice during the night. He found him on the floor next to his bed just after midnight. I'm thinking he must have had a heart attack on his way to use the bathroom."

Cutting Regan off, Paul asked, "What makes you think he was making his way to the bathroom and not returning to his bed after taking care of business?"

"I . . . I don't know, maybe because the bathroom light was turned off when he was found."

"I don't profess to know what Mr. Church's bathroom habits were, but the light being off would likely have been the case whether he was coming or going. From the bathroom, I mean. What I'm trying to say is either way the light would have been in the off position, correct?" Paul's investigative mind was already hard at work despite being woken from a sound sleep.

"I . . . I suppose, but what's that matter? The police have been here for the past three hours, they didn't seem to care if the light was on or off. Neither they nor the medical examiner believe it's anything more than a heart attack. Mr. Church's bedroom has been thoroughly examined, and the detective heading the investigation spent fifteen or twenty minutes interviewing me and the servant who found Mr. Church. So far, he doesn't seem to believe there's anything suspicious about Mr. Church's death; it looks as if he died of natural causes. The cops and the ME are downstairs packing up."

"Robert, people who die at home of natural causes generally aren't found on the floor next to their bed; they're found in bed or in a chair reading a book. I think you need to tell them Mr. Church hadn't been feeling well over the past few weeks. The cause of death may very well prove to be a heart attack, but stranger things have happened inside a bedroom. Where's Mr. Church right now?"

"His body is on the way to the ME's office. The ME isn't sure if there's going to be an autopsy or not later today, but that's where his body is being taken. Fifteen minutes ago, Mr. Church's wife was nearly pleading with the ME for that not to happen. I guess we'll find out who wins that fight later, won't we? Either way,

I assume I'll be dealing with the funeral home at some point. Mr. Church had already planned out his funeral, so I'm hoping I'll only have to address a few unexpected details. That probably sounds pretty strange, but he wanted it kept simple; that's why he took care of most of the details himself." Looking at the time displayed on his watch, Regan knew his long day was far from ending.

As he listened to what Regan was telling him, one comment stuck in Paul's head. "I can't say I saw this coming, but if I were you, and you're a better judge of this because you know her better than I do, I'd be concerned over Mrs. Church's request. Most people are squeamish over the thought of their loved one being cut open during an autopsy, but in this case I would err on the side of caution if she was that vocal about one not being performed. I have no idea if Mr. Church was dealing with any significant health issues, but I can't help thinking about the last time I saw him. Besides that minor throat issue, I thought he looked pretty good for a man his age. If I were you, I'd make sure an autopsy was conducted. If he had been under a doctor's care, my opinion might be different but for now something is telling me there's more to his death than a simple heart attack."

"Her request . . . actually it was more of a demand that an autopsy not be performed, shocked the hell out of me." Regan admitted.

"Then make sure an autopsy takes place. Something's telling me someone might be more interested in inheriting her late husband's pile of money than she is in learning how he died. That's, of course, unless she already knows the reason behind his death."

With his head already spinning from the number of details needing his attention in the wake of his employer's sudden passing, Regan said, "I hate to go against her wishes as I believe it was nothing more than a heart attack, but I'll give your suggestion some serious consideration. Right now I can't promise that I'll act on it, but I will spend some time thinking it over. I know how good your reputation is, but even good cops make mistakes every so often."

"Maybe, but not me."

For several minutes Paul and Regan consoled each other as they spoke about the passing of one of the world's richest men. For Regan, it was not only the passing of someone who had given him a job, but of an individual who had been one of the best mentors possible.

"Paul, I'm afraid Mr. Church's death may cause some problems for this project he's hired you to oversee."

"How so?" Paul asked as he pulled open the drapes to determine how hard the rain was falling. Looking outside, he managed to gauge the storm's intensity against the backdrop of light being discharged from several lights situated in the hotel parking lot. Across the parking lot, steady streams of water had begun to pool in several locations before plummeting deep inside a series of connecting storm drains.

"I know this isn't going to surprise you, but on orders from Mr. Church I've been tracking the expenses you've incurred since this project started. Through no fault of yours, this project has become more expensive than we anticipated. Most of the cost is due to the road we had to build. The costs associated with the use of the helicopter and the construction equipment have also contributed significantly to what's been spent, but those we had anticipated. Don't get me wrong, there's still plenty of money that's been set aside, but it's shrinking each time you send in your weekly expenses. My biggest fear is Mrs. Church and her attorneys may pull the plug on us once they find out about this little pet project her husband was underwriting. As you might expect, she's not the Civil War enthusiast her husband was. She has her own causes to support, and I'm pretty sure the one we're involved with isn't one of them." As he spoke, Regan did his best at estimating how much money was left in the special account only he and Simon Church had access to. Whatever the amount was, he was sure it was less than what Paul would need to complete the project he had barely had time to start.

"You really think she would pull the plug on us?" Paul asked, running Regan's concerns through his mind. "I mean, we're pretty close to finding what Mr. Church hired me to find. Would she really want to close us down when we're so close to achieving her husband's dream?"

"I can't say for sure, but I don't have a good feeling about this. I'm meeting with her later this morning, so we'll see what happens. For the time being, I'm grabbing some shut eye while I can. I'll call you later today after I've had a chance to meet with Mrs. Church."

"Go get some rest. I'm sure you can use an hour or two of sleep. I'll be waiting to hear from you. Just so you know, the weather here is pretty lousy right now. I'm not so sure what we'll accomplish today. I'll fill you in when I hear from you." Then Paul added one last comment. "I don't know where you're going to get the money from if Mrs. Church pulls the plug, but as long as the weather cooperates and my team feels we're making progress I intend to see this thing through to the end. We've come too far for us not to finish."

"I understand. We'll talk later." Regan said, ending the conversation as he walked to a nearby couch in Simon Church's bedroom. Minutes later, he fell fast asleep.

******

Too upset by the news of Simon Church's unexpected death, Paul knew there was little chance of falling back to sleep. While the dark, rainy morning made it an ideal day to grab an extra hour or two of some much-needed sleep, the thought of Simon Church's wife pulling the plug on a project he and his team had dedicated so much time to pushed thoughts of crawling back into bed from his mind. Making his way to where a small coffeemaker sat on top of a credenza on the other side of his room, Paul placed a coffee pod inside the machine as he waited for the water to heat up.

Already upset as a result of Regan's phone call, Paul grew even more upset moments later over the bitter taste of the warm, brown liquid dispensed by his coffeemaker.

It was not the only bitter taste he would experience on this gloomy morning.

49

Having showered and shaved, Paul made his way downstairs to the hotel restaurant just as the doors were being unlocked. Ordering a small pot of coffee, he made his way to the same booth where he and his friends had recently shared several meals during their two stays. Several minutes later, as he stirred his coffee for the umpteenth time, Paul took note of the fact that the ground floor restaurant was nearly as deserted as the nearby lobby.

Outside of two United States Air Force officers enjoying an early morning breakfast on the other side of the dining room before reporting to Joint Base Charleston, Paul was the only other customer present. Wearing their dress blue uniforms, their insignias clearly identified both officers as holding the rank of major. After attracting the attention of his waitress, as she stood at the end of his booth Paul softly whispered a request. Pointing in the direction of where the two officers were sitting, he said, "Please don't make a big deal over this, but I'd like to pick up the cost of their meals. Just add it to my tab, please."

Thirty minutes and three cups of coffee later, Paul looked up to see Bobby Ray making his way across the dining room floor. Not far behind him, Chick and Peter quietly followed the path their friend had taken as they approached Paul's booth. Dressed for another day of hard work, the restaurant's decorative industrial strength carpeting muffled the noise being made by their heavy work boots.

"Yankee Boy, you're looking even glummer than I'm feeling on this wet rainy morning. Did ya manage to get any sleep?" Bobby Ray asked while sliding into the booth next to his friend. Never accused of being overly quiet or shy, Bobby Ray's question had been asked loud enough for the cashier on the other side of the room to hear.

"You feeling OK, Paul?" Peter asked, doing so far quieter than Bobby Ray had done.

"Simon Church is dead."

"What!" Bobby Ray uttered just as loudly as he had asked his question.

"From what I was told it appears as if he may have suffered a massive heart attack. He was found last night on the floor of his bedroom."

"Wow! That's a shocker!" Chick said, letting out a loud whistle as he leaned against the back of the booth. "Don't take this the wrong way as I'm sorry he's no longer with us, but what's that mean for this project we've been working on?"

"Well, to start with, I really don't know. I do know that Regan hasn't painted a very bright picture. He's told me there's still money left from the recent advance Mr. Church set aside for us, but after that's gone, who knows. He's meeting with Mrs. Church and her lawyers later today. He said he'd call me once he knows more, but he told me he's not going to be surprised if the spigot gets turned off. It sounds as if Mrs. Church has her own interests to support. I wouldn't be surprised to learn that one or two of them are ones Regan isn't aware of." Based on some of the comments made by the billionaire's younger wife, Paul's suspicions were growing at an alarming rate.

The shock of their benefactor's death, coupled with the rainy morning blanketing most of South Carolina, allowed Paul and his team to spend close to two hours sitting in the restaurant discussing the possible repercussions of Simon Church's untimely passing. Continuing their conversation as they travelled to the work site later that morning, Paul resisted the urge to contact Regan for an update. Putting his cell phone back inside his pocket, he thought, "He'll call me when he knows more. For now, I'll let him sleep."

Climbing out of his truck after arriving at the scene of the collapsed caves, Paul was greeted with the smell of burnt diesel fuel and a variety of different noises. Several large construction vehicles and other heavy equipment being used around the work site contributed to the smell of exhaust fumes lingering in the air. Closer to where the survey stakes marked the possible entrances to three different caves, Groski and his crew had begun the process of stabilizing the hillside. Using a Pile Buck machine, commonly referred to as a pile driver, Groski's crew had already set four steel trench sheets in place near one of the entrances. Nearly thirteen inches wide and close to three-quarters of an inch thick, each sheet had been driven nearly thirty feet into the rocky hillside. Each was coupled together with the one next to it. Starting to the left of the cave where the remains of Howard's men were thought to be, the metal trench sheets were being set in place directly on top of a thick line of fluorescent orange paint that had been spray-painted on the rocky ground. Once in place they would form protective barriers around the entrances to each of the caves. Once finished, a similar number would then be placed around the area where Howard was thought to have hidden the assets he had been travelling with. Similar to the kind used to hold back water when forming a coffer dam, the trench sheets would prevent rocks and other debris from injuring any of Groski's crew as work was being conducted in and around the caves. After setting the trench sheets in place, Groski's crew planned on securing them with a series of heavy cables. Fastened to anchors drilled deep in the thick bedrock, the cables would add an additional layer of support in the event of an unexpected collapse or implosion. Later, after the mouths of the two main caves were opened, a series of T-shaped steel beams would be set in place inside each cave in an attempt to shore up the areas where work was being conducted. Doing so would make both environments safer places to work.

"Looks like you got an early start," Paul said, waving to Groski as the construction foreman walked away from the loud and dangerous work his crew had begun. Noticing how much the sky had cleared since the morning deluge, Paul then addressed a concern. He did so by asking a question he gave Groski little time to answer. "How's it going so far? By the looks of it, it appears you didn't let the storm stop you from working." Close to where they were talking, a large pile of nearly one hundred and fifty rusty trench sheets waited to be hammered into the ground around the two caves. Once set in place, they would form U-shaped protective barriers around both locations.

As he started to address the concern that had been raised, Groski noticed a large scar exposed under Paul's loose-fitting work shirt.

His next comment reminded Paul of how close he had recently come to losing his life. Pointing to the scar, Groski said, "That nasty-looking thing right there must have hurt. Bobby Ray told me about that Mexican drug-running son of a bitch who shot you."

Looking down, Paul noticed one of the scars on his chest had become visible through his partially unbuttoned shirt. Buttoning his shirt, he said, "Bobby Ray told you about that, huh?" Staring across the tight confines of the gravel parking lot where several equipment operators were doing their best to avoid running into each other as they steered their large, unwieldly vehicles in different directions, as he focused on his friend standing several yards away Paul wished Bobby Ray respected his privacy more than he sometimes did. Like most cops who had been shot in the line of duty, each time he undressed Paul was forced to look at the physical reminders of what had proved to be a deadly afternoon. As he did on most occasions, as he finished with his shirt Paul tried repressing his thoughts of the near-death experience.

Realizing he should not have raised the issue surrounding Paul's recent injury, Groski quickly changed the subject. "We started just after six this morning. It was raining pretty hard, but the report my engineers submitted didn't address any concerns about the ground being that unstable, so we went to work. If it had rained hard for two or three days I might have held off until the ground dried a bit, but the amount of rain we received overnight wasn't that significant. Like the amount of rain we received, the other concern I didn't have to worry about is the amount of noise this equipment makes. Outside of Mrs. DeWolfe's home, there's no one else living in the area; it's nothing but woods. It's nice when we don't have to worry about disturbing an entire neighborhood." As he spoke, Groski watched as the pile driver operator moved the large piece of equipment further up the hillside. Unlike most of the other equipment present, the pile driver was set on large metal tracks similar to the type used on army tanks. They not only allowed the heavy piece of equipment to travel over uneven terrain, but allowed for the operator to level the machine with each trench sheet being set in place.

Responding to Paul's other question; Groski outlined a few minor problems he and his men had encountered. One was extremely obvious. "The main problem we're having is moving some of those large surface rocks out of the way. They have to be moved before we start setting the trench sheets in place. The ground needs to be clear of any significant obstacles before we start butting these sheets together. It's not just the steel that gives them their strength; it's being able to couple them together. Other than that, we ran across a few places with some ledge, but we're doing okay. We've managed to bust that up fairly easily."

"How long do you think it's going to take to hammer all of these trench sheets in place?" Paul asked, shouting over the noise being made by the pile driver.

"Five days . . . maybe six, but that's if we don't hit too much ledge, and nothing breaks down. That's a tough call to make because of how steep the terrain is, but I think that's a pretty safe guess. Let's pray this doesn't happen, but if any equipment breaks down we'll have to add another day or two to our schedule."

On the heels of the other bad news he learned that morning, Groski's estimate of how long it was going to take to set the rest of the trench sheets in place was not what Paul had hoped to hear.

<u>50</u>

Five days after first learning of Simon Church's death, Paul received his third update from Regan. Climbing out of his vehicle back at the hotel after spending most of the day watching the progress Groski's crew was making, Paul slowly strode across the parking lot as he answered Regan's call. As he walked, the smell of freshly cut grass filled his nostrils. Looking towards the far end of the parking lot after noticing the hotel's grounds had been neatly trimmed, Paul briefly paid attention as several lawn mowers were loaded onto a small utility trailer.

"Paul, you're not going to believe what I'm about to tell you, so I hope you're ready for this." Regan said, almost whispering his words so others conducting business inside the Church mansion could not hear him.

"Why . . . why are you talking so softly?" Paul asked, straining to hear what Regan was telling him.

"I'm inside Mr. Church's home. There are quite a few people here, including some staff, cops, attorneys representing both Mr.

and Mrs. Church, and a few others I haven't been introduced to as yet, so I'm trying to avoid any unwanted attention. I just moved to the other side of the room so I could talk to you with some degree of privacy. I'm simply being careful about what people hear me saying."

"What's going on there? Is there some sort of a problem?" Paul was now alarmed over the steps Regan was taking to avoid being overheard.

After taking a cursory glance at the others standing nearby, Regan explained the latest developments surrounding Church's death. "Late last night a couple of detectives and a bunch of uniformed cops showed up. A few hours later they were joined by three investigators from the state's attorneys' office; they've had the house and grounds locked down ever since. They arrived with a couple of search warrants, and then went to work searching the mansion. I can't say they searched the entire place, but they were in and out of the kitchen on several occasions, all of the bathrooms, and each of the sleeping quarters used by Mr. and Mrs. Church. No one's been allowed in or out, and the staff has been told not to touch anything. I wasn't sure what was going on until about an hour ago, that's when the cops walked Mrs. Church out of the house in handcuffs. Now I'm being told that I'm the next person the detectives want to speak with, so that's why I'm being careful. I'm not sure if I should be telling you this or not, but I felt the need to call you." Regan's voice reflected the concern he was experiencing after witnessing Mrs. Church being arrested. While not responsible in any manner for his employer's death, his upcoming interview caused Regan to become very anxious.

"Telling me what?" Paul asked, his ears straining to hear every word Regan was saying.

"Mr. Church was supposedly being poisoned. His heart attack was likely brought on by the poison he was being fed." Regan said, making sure no one was listening to the conversation he was engaged in. "I don't have any problem telling you that my mind is freaking racing. I can't help thinking the problems he was experiencing with his throat were somehow related to the poison he had ingested."

"And they think Mrs. Church was responsible for poisoning him?" Paul asked rather incredulously. "I thought you told me you didn't believe a Post was going to be conducted?" As he asked his last question, the retired state trooper used a term most cops used when referring to an autopsy.

"Early on there wasn't one planned, but the doctor who made the official pronouncement of death apparently saw something he didn't like. I'm not sure what that was, but he ended up overriding the call the local medical examiner had made. From what I've been told, because of Mr. Church's status . . . meaning his wealth and prominence, whatever concerns this doctor had caused him to call a friend in the Attorney General's office. So, here we are."

"So, if an autopsy was done," Paul said, falling back on the many autopsies he had witnessed, "it's apparent that some sort of poison was found. I wouldn't be surprised if that doctor you just referred to found some damage to Mr. Church's throat. That's what probably caused the Post to be conducted. The cops are likely there as a result of further damage being found to his stomach and to a few of his organs from whatever he's ingested. Was Mrs. Church actually arrested or did they just take away to be interviewed?"

"I watched as one of the detectives advised her of her rights before placing the cuffs around her wrists, so, yes, she was arrested.

I'm not sure how much she heard as she was screaming like I've never heard anyone scream, but she left wearing handcuffs. They also took one of her assistants out of here in cuffs a few minutes later. Her assistant . . . a young woman who hails from either Mexico or El Salvador, was pretty upset, but she was a lot calmer than Mrs. Church. I hate to admit this, but I don't know that woman's name as I normally don't interact with members of the household staff. But getting back to Mrs. Church, just like you see on television she was threatening to sue every cop from here to the Rio Grande."

"Even though I've had my suspicions about her, I have to admit this news has caught me by surprise. Despite the favorable impressions they often made on people, I guess Mrs. Church and her husband weren't the ideal couple after all."

"Until the cops release more information regarding Mrs. Church's arrest, I'm keeping my opinions to myself." Regan replied, doing his best to remain loyal to those he worked for.

"You said they grabbed a maid as well?" Paul asked, doing his best to comprehend the events taking place inside the Church mansion.

"She wasn't a maid; I believe she was one of Mrs. Church's personal assistants." Regan replied, staring at a small group of cops and investigators speaking in hushed tones on the other side of the room.

"You know more about her than I do, but I'll bet you one or two of those gold coins we're about to find that when push comes to shove this personal assistant is the gal who cleans Mrs. Church's bathroom. She may be paid more than what some of the other staff members are paid, but no matter what fancy job title she has that gal's a maid."

"Are you saying that because she's from Mexico or El Salvador or some other depressed third world country?" Regan asked, too upset to be arguing over the job title held by one of Mrs. Church's employees.

"Has Mr. or Mrs. Church hired any other men or women from Mexico or El Salvador or, for that matter, any other Central American countries to serve as their personal assistants?" Paul asked, trying to make his point regarding the position Mrs. Church's employee held.

"No . . . not that I'm aware of, but what's that have to do with this gal's background?"

"It doesn't have a thing to do with her background, but it sure in hell has a lot to do with the type of job she was hired for. How many Caucasians . . . men, women, kids, currently clean the Church mansion? I'll bet the answer is none."

"That sounds about right. Now that you've brought this up, I'm afraid to admit I've never seen anyone cleaning the mansion except people like this lady who works for Mrs. Church. The same holds true for the property surrounding the mansion; it's taken care of by people who are different than you and I." Regan weakly replied.

"By that, you mean by people of color, likely Mexicans and others who have come to the United States from Central America, correct?"

"Correct." Regan's response was even weaker than before.

"So it sounds like Mr. and Mrs. Church haven't hired any white people to clean their mansion or cut their grass. Why's that?" Paul asked, pressing the point he was trying to make.

"I . . . I have no idea. You'd have to ask them." Regan replied, somewhat embarrassed by having to defend the hiring practices of his employers.

"So, like I said, the cops took one of the maids with them when they left with Mrs. Church."

"Yes, I suppose that's correct."

"If Mrs. Church left kicking and screaming like you've said, then it sounds as if the cops not only placed her in handcuffs for their protection, but for hers as well."

"Whatever . . . I just want this day to end. I'm already stressed out over everything that's taken place over the past few hours." On the other end of the phone conversation, Paul could tell Regan had been surprised by the sudden turn of events; including Mrs. Church's arrest.

"Do you have any information on what she had been feeding her husband or how it was being administered?" Paul asked, curious over the type of poison Simon Church had unknowingly ingested, and how it had been delivered.

"I'm not sure of all of the details, but earlier I overheard two cops talking about a few of the items they had seized from the kitchen and two bedrooms. One of them was telling the other about a substance known as Pequa being added to the drinks Mr. Church had sitting on his nightstand. Those drinks were originally placed there as a means of helping him deal with a dry throat in the middle of the night, but who would have thought they actually had another purpose. While I've always known him to have a glass of water handy, apparently he's been fed this poison for some time now. Even still, I can't believe she was poisoning him. I . . . I haven't even had the chance to find out what Pequa is used for. Whatever its use, I'm sure it wasn't meant for human consumption." Regan offered.

"It's very toxic," Paul replied, "even when it's been diluted or mixed in a drink of some kind. The reason it's often used to kill people is because when it's mixed correctly it doesn't leave an aftertaste in the victim's mouth. In most cases, by the time someone whose been fed this for a period of time realizes there's a problem, the damage to their system is pretty pronounced; it's also irreversible. Someone like Mr. Church could have easily ingested this over an extended period of time and they wouldn't know they had a problem until their organs started shutting down. By then, it would be too late to reverse any of the damage that's been caused. Pequa is one of the best drain cleaners on the market, but like other household cleaners when it's used inappropriately it can have deadly results. Products like the one we're discussing weren't designed for human consumption. From the few occasions I've used it at the house when my wife and I have had a minor plumbing problem or two; I seem to recall the plastic container it comes in has a warning label that mentions it can cause severe burns if it's been ingested."

"And, you know this how, Paul?" Regan asked, suspicious of his friend's knowledge of Pequa's deadly consequences.

"In my past life I was present on several occasions when someone died after ingesting, or should I say was forced to ingest, a deadly chemical. I personally investigated at least three cases which involved one spouse feeding the other small doses of a drain cleaner over an extended period of time. In each of those cases, all of the victims succumbed to being poisoned. I've lost count of how many times an original cause of death was changed to murder after it was ruled someone's death had been manipulated by the involuntary consumption of a toxic substance."

"I guess that does happen, doesn't it?" Regan replied, recalling Paul's previous line of work.

"It happens more times than most people know. I'm thinking Mrs. Church's arrest clouds things up for us even more than they already were. I'm also thinking you need a couple of minutes to yourself before your interview takes place. Keep me posted on any new developments."

"Will do, but I need I quick favor before you go. Do you have any tips for me before the cops start working me over?" Regan asked, exaggerating the reception he was about to receive from some of Dallas' finest.

Laughing at Regan's question, Paul responded rather bluntly. "I always find that telling the truth never hurts. I suggest you do that."

<u>51</u>

Five days later, with work held up for two days due to equipment problems, Groski's crew finally finished installing the protective trench sheets around the collapsed caves. Later that same morning, work began on excavating the caves mentioned in Howard's journal.

"Which one do you want us to concentrate on, Paul?" Groski asked as he used his hard hat to point to where the two caves were located along the rocky hillside. As his men finished installing the last few trench sheets around the mouths of the caves, several loads of rocks and debris had already been removed so other pieces of equipment could be set in place. Removing that limited amount of material had helped define both entrances.

"Let's start with the one on the left."

Paul's comment caught the veteran construction worker by complete surprise. "I would have bet all the money in the world you would have picked the one on the right. That's where you told me the gold and silver was supposedly hidden."

Realizing Groski's comment was one many people would have offered, Paul gently shook his head as he explained his position. "This may sound like a load of you know what, but I care more about the remains of those soldiers than I do about the coins and rifles we've been told about. The money that's in there is not mine to keep, so unlike some other people I know I have no intention of filing any claims against it. I've been hired to find what's been hidden inside these caves for all these years, but I'm much more interested in recovering the rest of those remains. One of my goals is to make sure those soldiers are given a proper burial."

Smiling over Paul's explanation, an impressed Groski said, "I guess that means you're not one of those money-grubbing whores we all hear about, right?"

"Guess not."

Turning to leave so his crew could start the process of excavating yards and yards of rocks, boulders, dirt, and other debris blanketing the remains of several long-forgotten Civil War soldiers, Groski paused to look back at Paul. "Those fellows over there in the yellow hats, the boys from the state of South Carolina, are they gonna be a pain in my ass?"

"If you mean are they going to watch every stone that's being moved and every ounce of dirt being scooped up by your bucket loaders as we look for the remains of those soldiers; yep, that's just what they're going to be. They're here to do their jobs, so you and I will just have to learn to be patient when they ask us to stop working from time to time." Laughing at what he had just said, Paul added, "As my friends will tell you, being patient isn't one of my best qualities."

* * * * * *

Early the following morning, as one of Groski's front end loaders backed out of the small opening his men had begun to clear inside one of the caves, a member of the forensic recovery team observed the first piece of evidence Paul and his crew had been hired to find. Holding up his hands as a way of stopping the work taking place, the forensic technician then pointed to a set of bones protruding from beneath several mid-sized rocks. *"We've . . . we've got something here! I found something!"*

As others around him motioned for the front end loader and two other large noisy construction vehicles to be turned off, Paul scrambled up the rocky hillside. On his heels were Chick, Bobby Ray, and Groski. Moments after entering the partially hollowed out cave, they realized the importance of the artifacts that had been found. After spending several minutes consulting with the forensic specialists, Paul started issuing orders. As was the case when he had been assigned a particularly heinous crime to investigate, his orders were issued in a clear and concise manner.

Nodding at two forensic specialists kneeling next to a pile of rocks, Paul started by speaking to Bobby Ray. Just as experienced in preserving crime scenes, Paul knew his friend had a good handle on what needed to be done. "Let these folks finish what they have to do, then I want you and Chick to prepare a detailed map of the inside of this cave. There's still a lot of debris to be removed, but let's get a jump on our map while work has been halted. Make sure you include every bone, fragment, piece of clothing, or whatever else we find on that map. We may never use it, but we'll never be able to document the scene as we've found it if we don't take the time to do it now." Then Paul told Peter what his assignment involved. "You're our photographer, so start taking as many photographs as you can. Bobby Ray and Chick are documenting the scene with their map; we need you to do the same with your photographs. Get started before *anything* gets moved." As he finished speaking, Paul moved closer to where the bones were lying. Awed by this discovery, in a hushed tone he mumbled, "And what was your name, soldier?"

"Got it, boss," Chick replied after watching Paul kneel down next to the soldiers' remains. Moments later, he and the others turned to retrieve the equipment needed to complete their assignments. As the members of his team got to work, Paul and Groski exchanged excited smiles and handshakes.

******

Over the next three days, Groski's crew diligently assisted the forensic experts as they worked to exhume the remains of those soldiers who had perished inside the small cave. Each had been crushed to death under the weight of several tons of rocks, boulders, and other debris.

As the collective crew of laborers, forensic recovery specialists, and those in Paul's team painstakingly spent hours clearing what had once been a cave roughly eight feet wide by seven feet high, they finally located the cave's rear wall. A massive thick sheet of impenetrable ledge told them they had come to the end of the forty-foot deep cave. As they had worked at clearing the cave, some of Groski's other men struggled to place a handful of massive vertical beams in different locations in an attempt to prevent the cave's ceiling from collapsing.

During the three long days it took to complete their work, they had toiled in the cave's dusty confines as a relentless hot sun pushed the humidity to record levels. Standing in loose rock and ankle-deep debris for much of the time, Paul personally directed the recovery efforts as each piece of cloth, leather, and bone fragments were collected, photographed, and recorded on Bobby Ray's map.

Halfway through their third day, Groski approached Paul as he was speaking with Chick. Their discussion centered on the type of artifacts the search had already recovered. As their conversation ended, Groski offered a comment while wiping his sweaty forehead with a small towel he often carried in one of his rear pockets. "Seeing this is only my second time working at a site where human remains have been found, I really didn't know what to expect but I'm kind of disappointed by what little we've managed to recover."

"Why's that?" Chick asked, folding a piece of paper he and Paul had been referring to.

"That's the part that really bugs me; I'm not sure why I'm so disappointed. Perhaps I thought we'd find the bodies of those poor soldiers more intact than we have. I also thought we'd find more in the way of uniforms and other personal effects, but that hasn't proven to be the case. I'm not even sure how big it is, but the biggest piece of cloth we've found can't be more than four inches in size. Maybe my expectations were thrown off from having watched too many movies where people have found piles of treasures and other riches."

"Phil, you have to remember these soldiers died nearly one hundred and sixty years ago. Not only were they crushed to death when the hillside gave way, but Mother Nature has had all that time to do even more damage to whatever was left. Heat, rain, rodents, that's all had time to inflict even more damage to uniforms that had likely

404 | PETER WARREN

seen better days even before they were ripped apart by all of those rocks we've been removing." Thinking about what Groski had said about being disappointed by what little they found, Paul added one other comment. "The other reason we haven't found much in the way of any personal items is because there wasn't much to start with. The entries in Howard's journal described how his men were sent inside the cave to recover the remains of those Union soldiers he had been told about. Those soldiers he sent in there didn't bring their horses with them; they were likely tied up outside someplace. Any personal items they may have had were either in their saddlebags or in the wagons they were travelling with."

"Yeah, I suppose so," Groski admitted, wiping his face again with the same dirty towel. Dressed in protective clothing, including steel toe boots and a hard hat, the construction foreman was soaked in sweat. While barely two p.m., the excessive humidity made it feel even hotter than it was.

"The few good things we've found are the partial skulls and jawbones of at least three soldiers. While we've found some other loose teeth, those jaw bones, like some of the bigger bones that were lying near them, lend some hope to the DNA testing the forensic examiners intend on conducting. I'm also going to reach out to a friend so she can run some tests on the teeth we've found. This friend of mine, Martha Mannion, is an expert in the field of forensic dentistry. She's never going to find dental records for any of those soldiers, but it won't hurt for her to take a look at what we've found. Knowing her as well as I do, I expect she'll come up with a suggestion or two for us to consider."

"You're kidding me, right?" The skeptical look on Groski's face told Paul and Chick he was not as confident as they were about being able to establish the soldiers' identities.

While well-aware of the slim chances of identifying any of the remains through DNA testing, Paul sought to remove some of Groski's skepticism. "This is probably a poor comparison due to the advances in medicine and the way patient information has been kept since the end of the Civil War, but if DNA technicians can identify the remains of some of those sailors who went down with their ships at Pearl Harbor nearly eighty years ago then maybe we can identify these soldiers the same way. Granted, we'd have to have an idea on who they were, and then try and determine who their living relatives might be, but it's a possibility. I'm not ready to close the door on that taking place." As the discussion continued, Paul spoke about the recent identification of a sailor who had been killed during World War II. Nearly eighty years after his tragic death, DNA testing had positively identified his remains from samples taken from family members living in New Jersey.

"Well, I hope that happens, but I won't bet on it." Groski offered as he waved to attract the attention of one of his workers.

"The way I look at it, we're on track to find what's been placed here for us to find," Paul said, watching as the work site started to come alive after shutting down for a mid-afternoon break. "We're nearly done with the first cave, Phil. What's the plan for the next one? We starting today or tomorrow?"

"I'm not good at sitting around when there's work to be done. We've still got plenty of daylight left, so I plan on starting today. Besides, the longer my men and I are here, the more it's costing someone."

As Groski's words sunk in, Paul realized Regan had promised he would call with an update regarding Simon Church's death. Concerned about missing his call, Paul checked his phone for any new messages as he walked away from where the loud noisy work had resumed around the first cave. Hoping to see that he had not missed any calls, he was disappointed when he saw his phone had one voicemail message.

The call had come from Robert Regan.

52

I could use some good news, Paul, so before I tell you what's been going on down here tell me that you've found something. Please tell me you've found the gold coins Mr. Church was so anxious for you to find." Having dealt with a host of attorneys, reporters, bankers, cops, household staff, and others in the wake of Simon Church's death, Regan was hoping for some good news after finally hearing from Paul. Like the person he was speaking with, Paul had worked several long days over the course of the past week. While interested in learning as much as possible regarding the circumstances surrounding Simon Church's death, updating Regan after returning to his hotel room each night had not been one of his priorities.

"Not yet, we haven't," Paul replied, hearing a loud sigh on the other end of the call after delivering his answer concerning the valuable assets. "But the good news is we're just about finished excavating the first cave. As you can imagine, it was slow going until we made our way inside, but despite the never-ending heat we managed to collect some of the remains we were looking for. We also found some bits of clothing, but nothing we can really identify."

"Such as?"

"As expected, we managed to find a variety of different bones in all types of condition. From their shapes and sizes, we all believe the bones are human, and not from animals. While many were badly damaged from the weight of the material that fell on top of them, we found parts of three skulls clustered around two large boulders. It's just speculation on our part, but we're thinking whoever they were they must have been standing fairly close to each other when the cave collapsed. We've also discussed the possibility of those skulls belonging to those three Union soldiers Howard's men had been tasked with recovering. No matter whose they were, they were badly damaged. Some of the other bones we found were in far worse condition. A couple of jawbones and some loose teeth were in the best condition, but that's not saying much."

"Wow, that's freaking amazing." Regan offered, picturing what it must have been like inside the cave as chaos erupted all around the soldiers. "Those forensic examiners you're working with, have you had any discussions with them about conducting some sort of DNA testing? It's probably a long shot, but that would be amazing if the soldiers' identities could be established."

"Earlier today DNA testing was discussed ad nauseam. It seems like that's the only thought on everyone's mind. I'm all in favor of that taking place, but it's way too early to be thinking of that. For now, we need to focus our attention on excavating the other cave before we start thinking about conducting any types of tests." Just as he had done earlier with Chick and Groski, Paul had also discussed the possibility of conducting DNA testing with the forensic specialists.

"What about any personal items the soldiers may have been carrying? Have you found anything like that?" Regan asked, regretting the fact that he had not been present when the first cave was being excavated.

"Like I said, we found some bits of clothing, but most of what the soldiers had been wearing has been lost to time, weather, and whatever creatures have been living in those rocks for all of these years. As I've already explained to Phil Groski, any personal effects the soldiers owned had likely been left outside the cave. There was no reason for any of those items to have been in either cave." As he answered Regan's question, Paul suddenly remembered one of the last discoveries his team had made. "We did manage to find one piece of fabric that appears to have been part of a uniform worn by one of the Union soldiers. Like everything else we've found, it needs to be looked at under a microscope before anyone can say with any certainty that it was part of a uniform worn by a Union soldier."

"That's it?" Regan asked.

"No, we found a few other artifacts, things like small pieces of leather that were probably from belts the soldiers had been wearing. We've also found some pieces of metal that may have been parts of a belt buckle. Chick believes we found part of an old canteen and parts of a small knife, but I'm not so sure about the canteen. Most of the knife's wooden handle is missing, but when you consider how long it's been buried under all of that debris the blade is still in decent shape. Perhaps our two best finds were a small wooden bowl that somehow survived being smashed to bits when the hill gave way, and some shreds of paper.

The bowl is not the kind anyone would have eaten from; it was part of someone's pipe. I try not to guess about things like this, but there's a good chance it was being carried inside someone's pocket when the hill gave way. When we were examining it, we could still see some of the features that had been carved into the bowl. The bits of paper we found are rather fragile, so out of fear of inflicting any more damage we've pretty much left them alone. Our best guess is they may have been part of a letter one of the soldiers had either written or received from home. We really didn't find any one piece that we considered special, but we're pleased by what we've managed to find."

"That sounds pretty neat," Regan said, nearly gushing over the few personal effects Paul and his team had located inside the small cave.

After spending the next several minutes describing how the recovery operation had gone, Paul addressed the issue Regan had been waiting to hear about. It concerned the process of excavating the next cave; the one containing the missing gold and silver.

******

"OK, your turn, Robert." Paul said as he concluded his remarks about the second cave. "What's new on your end? I'm anxious to learn of any new developments surrounding Mr. Church's death."

"There have been several, I'm afraid." Regan said, setting the tone for the rest of the conversation. "To start with, I don't have any good news to report. While the medical examiner's office is still waiting on the pathology report, the results of the autopsy aren't good. I guess the best way to put it is if you're one of those people in Mrs. Church's camp, you would have hoped for a better outcome."

"That bad, huh?" Paul asked.

"That bad."

"I have to tell you, from everything you've told me and from the few newspaper articles I've read about Mr. Church's death, I'm impressed by how fast things get done in Texas. That autopsy report would not have surfaced for at least another two weeks or so in Connecticut. Those results you're telling me about came out very quick."

"Paul, if you haven't already realized this, Texas is unlike any other state in the country. If someone commits a murder down here and they get caught, no matter who you are there's gonna be a noose hanging from a tree with your name on it pretty darn quick. Folks like to brag about three things down here, the first being how much they still believe in God. The next two can be put in any order you want. As you likely know us Texans like our barbeque; so don't go messing with any of our recipes. They're far better than anything North Carolina can put on the table. And, finally, we believe in justice. We're still old school when it comes to an eye for an eye, especially when it comes to killing someone most folks adore. After all of the facts came out about his cause of death, folks down here are livid. They haven't forgotten how generous Mr. Church was to a lot of causes, especially those involving children in need of medical care. Spouse or no spouse, your goose is cooked if the evidence is stacked against you."

"If Mr. Church died like it seems he did, I'm guessing Mrs. Church . . . or maybe her maid had been feeding the old gent this deadly elixir for a good period of time. Once Pequa reaches a certain level of toxicity inside someone's body, it's as deadly as they come. Anyone, meaning the maid or Mrs. Church, start singing yet?" Familiar with how offers were often made in homicide investigations, Paul was curious to know if either of the two suspects had sought to distance themselves from the death penalty.

"In the vernacular often used by cops in old black and white movies, the maid folded like a cheap suit. It sounds like either the pressure she was under or her conscience got to her. I was told the state's attorneys' office offered a deal to the first one who decided to cooperate. While no formal charges have been filed against her, the maid and her attorneys didn't blink when that offer was put on the table. Mrs. Church's attorneys are doing their best to pin Simon's death on the maid, but the investigators I've been dealing with are telling me her attorneys now realize they screwed up by not taking the deal they were offered. They're doing their best at performing damage control, but, like I just said, even when it's being offered up by a team of high-priced attorneys folks down here can sense when someone's feeding them bullshit."

"So, why'd she do it, any idea?" Paul asked, referring to Mrs. Church and not her maid. "I know there was a fairly good age difference between them, but it had to have been more about money than anything else. More often than not, when it comes to one spouse killing the other, it's always about money."

"I would have thought the number one cause would have involved infidelity." Regan replied.

"So do most people, but money rules everything, especially in a marriage that's spinning out of control."

"If that's the case, I suspect that's the reason behind what happened down here. Like I told you a few weeks ago, I noticed a slight disconnect between Mr. and Mrs. Church over the past few months. Based on what's occurred, I guess whatever problems they were having were worse than it appeared. Despite their differences, I never thought it would come to this," Regan offered, accepting Paul's explanation for why most murders occurred between spouses. "She still spends far too much, but a year ago Mr. Church put an end to what he called his wife's lavish spending habits. I know they had some nasty arguments over her allowance being cut, so that may have added some stress to their relationship. But . . . "

"So, basically it's the same old story," Paul said, interrupting Regan before he could finish. "Rich guy marries an attractive younger woman as his second or third or fourth wife, she ticks him off for some reason or another, they have a fight, and later she kills him after believing no one will suspect her after her husband turns up dead."

"Pretty much." Regan admitted.

"Pushing his wife's spending habits to the side for now, let's go back to one of the questions I asked you the night you told me Mr. Church was dead. What's all of this mean for the project we've been working on? Are we still following the mandate Mr. Church gave us, or are we up the proverbial creek without a paddle?"

After doing his best to sidestep the question he had been asked, Regan, still doing his best at performing damage control, said what had to be said. "I'm afraid we're dead in the water. That holds true for all of us; the pipeline has definitely been shut off." As he had spoken, Regan lightly touched on the fact that his tenure as an employee of Church Industries would soon be ending.

"I was afraid of that," Paul replied, his analytical mind already hard at work trying to figure out how the remaining amount of work could be funded before hearing the rest of what Regan had to say. "The small pot of money Mr. Church gave me for incidentals is nearly gone, so that's no help."

"Both sets of attorneys, the ones on our side and the ones against us, and there's too many of them to count, have already petitioned the court to appoint an overseer to manage the acquired wealth of the Church estate. That request was approved early this morning. So, in a nutshell, we're done. Fortunately, because of the way Mr. Church funded this project, Mrs. Church's attorneys will never know about the cost of this operation. Mr. Church had deposited those funds into a special account, a so-called slush fund only he and I had access to. Just like the account you opened, there's not much left that I can put my hands on. The good news is at least her attorneys can't raise any problems about what's been spent."

"That's good, I guess," Paul muttered as he listened to the bad news being delivered. "It's really none of my business, but what's this mean for you?"

"Paul, you're not the only one who's been kicked in the teeth. I was told last night my duties are about to change. I was also told I'll need to start looking for a new job in another year or so. Mr. Church treated me very well, so financially I'll be in good shape for a few years. After that, I'll need to find some type of work to keep me busy. I've kept all of my ratings current, so maybe I'll go back to flying planes again." Shaking his head as he thought about his time working for Simon Church, Regan added one last comment. "This has been a great job. I'm pretty sure I'll never find anything like it, or anything that pays as well."

After speaking for several minutes on a variety of issues, including the merits of the case against Mrs. Church, Paul advised Regan that unless he was told otherwise he would assume responsibility for the balance of the excavation costs.

While unsure of how he was going to raise the funds needed to complete the project he had undertaken, Paul knew he was not the type of person to abandon something he had started. More importantly, he was not about to abandon something he believed in as much as this project. For the immediate future, he was committed to solving the story Captain Howard had detailed inside his journal.

Like his previous search for another portion of the missing Confederate treasury, one which proved to be even more demanding and just as costly, Paul was intrigued by more than just the search for the gold and silver.

It was more than money that drove Paul Waring.

53

The following morning, after leaving Bobby Ray and Chick to manage the issues and problems associated with the excavation of the last cave, Paul headed back to his hotel room just before noon to clean up before making the drive back to Murrells Inlet. Before doing so, he urged his friends to trust Groski's instincts. "Besides being a decent guy, he knows a heck of a lot more about the work being done than we do. We have to trust his judgement on what it's going to take to get that cave cleaned out. Do us all a favor while I'm gone, don't piss the guy off."

Two hours later, while driving through McClellanville on his way to Murrells Inlet, Paul's already overworked mind was busy trying to find a solution to his newly created woes. Far more interested in solving old historical clues that were both obscure and directly connected to the bigger picture he was working on, he had little interest in how the bills were going to be paid from this point on. Now, with this latest problem to cope with, he would have to rely on his wife's astute financial experience to come up with a way for Groski's growing bill to be paid. As he had always done with his and Donna's personal expenses, Paul was again relying on her to solve his newest dilemma.

Climbing out of his truck outside the Dead Dog Saloon, a popular eatery located along the MarshWalk in Murrells Inlet, Paul saw Donna waving from where she was sitting on the restaurant's large outdoor deck. One of several shops and restaurants located along the expansive tourist destination, she was seated at a picnic table facing the inlet's constantly changing tide. Sitting under a large umbrella adorned with the logo of a popular regional beer, Donna smiled as she sat protected from the sun.

While it was somewhat unusual for Paul to display much affection while out in public, he paused to kiss his wife before sitting down in the chair next to her. They had barely had time to discuss the proceedings of the past few days when a college-aged waitress approached their table.

"Afternoon, folks!" The young waitress cheerfully offered as she smiled at her newest customers. With only a few tables on the spacious deck occupied by a small number of customers and her prospect of experiencing a decent day of tips growing more unlikely as the hours passed, the blonde haired college student was pleased to have two other guests to wait on. "What can I get you to drink?"

Eyeing the blue and white nametag clipped to the polo shirt their waitress was wearing, Paul ordered their first round of drinks. "Thank you, Wendy. I'll have a Bud Light draft and my wife will have a glass of Chardonnay; J. Lohr, if you have it. She would also like a glass of ice on the side."

"Coming up!" Wendy politely replied, not bothering to write the drink order down after setting two menus on the table.

After a few minutes of catching up after not seeing each other for the past few days, Donna brought up the issue involving her husband's newest problem. "When we were talking on the phone the other night I could sense the frustration you were feeling after learning of Mr. Church's death. But something else must have happened to cause you to drive all the way back here. You're so close to finding the gold and silver, so why are we having lunch together when you should be back there with Bobby Ray and the others?"

"I came back to see you." Paul said, a warm smile crossing his face as he prepared to take his first sip of beer.

"Yeah, right!" Donna scoffed as Wendy stood ready to take their lunch orders. "I'll have a large tossed salad with Ranch dressing, please. Just one thing, the last time I was here my salad nearly drowned in all the dressing someone put on it. This time, I'd like it on the side. My husband, well, he doesn't eat as healthy as he should, so he'll have the Cheeseburger Special . . . with fries and everything else that comes with it."

As their waitress moved away from where they were seated, Paul clarified his previous answer. "Actually I did drive back here to see you, but I'm also here to pick your brain."

Disappointed by the news of Paul's funding being shut off before his latest search had concluded, Donna offered up several suggestions on how he might be able to obtain some additional, yet expensive, funding. While most of her ideas were fairly creative, her recommendations were ones Paul quickly dismissed for a variety of reasons.

As they sat eating their lunch while enjoying the constantly changing views provided by the warm sunny environment around them, Donna suddenly turned and looked at her husband. Stunned by a thought neither of them had come up with as a means of addressing Paul's most pressing problem, the color in Donna's face soon revealed the excitement her thought had generated. Moments later, the color in her husband's face reflected the same degree of excitement.

"We're both dummies, you know," Donna said, setting down her fork as she stared at her husband. "I'm not sure how you're going to feel about this, but who's the one person we know with the kind of money you need to fund this project?"

Sitting still for a few moments, in a raised voice Paul suddenly responded to Donna's question after realizing who she had been referring to. *"Steve! Steve Alcott!"* Paul's loud response briefly drew the attention of others seated nearby.

"He loved every minute of being involved in your first search, so why not ask him to fund the rest of the work that needs to be completed?" Donna said, referring to their wealthy, but elderly friend. "Call him and tell him what you need. I'm sure he'd help you, especially when he knows there's some money to be made on the back end. He may not fund the entire amount, but he'll manage to get you the support you need."

Within weeks of moving to Murrells Inlet, Paul helped an elderly motorist change a flat tire along Highway 17 during a heavy rainstorm. That motorist had been Steve Alcott. In the days and weeks that followed, the two had become fast friends. The last surviving member of one of the first European families to settle the area around Murrells Inlet, Steve's family, along with his own business acumen, had helped the elderly businessman become very wealthy.

Years earlier, as Paul and his friends prepared to search for several million dollars of gold and silver inside the city of Charleston, two of Steve's contacts had helped to make that discovery take place. While his involvement in recovering the gold and silver had been minimal, Steve's friendships with the city's mayor and a federal judge proved instrumental in the final outcome.

"I can't believe I hadn't thought of him," Paul said, excitedly contemplating his wife's suggestion as he pushed aside what little remained of his lunch.

"Just be careful . . . and don't get too excited, it's just a thought. You're setting yourself up for a huge letdown if Steve turns you down." Donna said, cautioning her husband about the possibility of becoming disappointed.

******

Knowing where his friend hung out on most afternoons around five p.m., Paul smiled as soon as he saw Steve Alcott's Mercedes Benz parked in its usual spot outside *The Grumpy Sailor*. Like several other pieces of real estate along the Grand Strand, the popular restaurant was owned by his elderly friend. Known for its generous cuts of Prime Rib and heaping portions of fresh seafood, even in the off-season it was not uncommon for patrons to have to wait at least two hours for a table. With a steady clientele and a large circle of friends who routinely stopped in for dinner, Steve had never felt the need to accept reservations.

Walking inside, Paul found his friend seated in a comfortable chair at the head of the bar. It was a chair most people knew never to sit in. Making his way to where Steve was holding court with three of his regular customers, Paul smiled after realizing his presence had been detected.

"Paul! What the heck are you doing here? I thought you and Bobby Ray were down in Moncks Corner on some wild-goose chase?" Steve said in a loud, but warm tone as he excused himself from the customers he had been speaking with. In seconds, he was shaking hands with his friend after climbing down off his chair. Similar to the kind often used by movie directors as they watched a scene being played out, the wooden chair sat higher than the others situated around the large U-shaped bar.

"I was there this morning. I drove back a few hours ago to see Donna." Paul said in response to his friend's comment about Moncks Corner.

"Anything wrong?" Steve asked. While close to Paul and his wife, Donna had earned a special place in Steve's heart. Having never married, he often referred to her as being the daughter he had never been blessed with.

"No, not really. I just stopped to say hello, that's all. I had lunch with Donna earlier and your name came up, so I thought I'd stop in to see how you're doing."

"Hogwash!"

Draining the remaining liquid from the afternoon's first martini, Steve politely excused himself from where he had been sitting. Grabbing Paul by the left arm, he steered his friend in the direction of the empty dining room. As he did, Steve motioned for the bartender to bring them a round of drinks. Entering the spacious room, one that would soon be filled with a host of hungry guests, Paul followed Steve to his favorite table near the rear of the large dining area.

"You've never just dropped in to see how I was doing, so let's cut the bullshit, OK? In the past, we've either made plans to have a drink or to enjoy a meal with your lovely wife. Forgive me for saying this, but you're not the kind of person who operates on the fly." Seeing through Paul's feeble excuse for being there, Steve waved his right index finger in his friend's face as a means of letting him know he was not buying the story he was being told. "So, now that that's settled, what's the problem? Are you sure Donna's OK?"

After assuring his friend for the second time that Donna was not the reason he had come to see him, Paul spelled out the purpose for his visit. As he spoke, he explained the facts surrounding Simon Church's death.

"Damn fool!" Steve said, shaking his head after learning Church's attractive young wife had been arrested for orchestrating his murder. "That's what happens when fellas my age marry a younger woman with good looks. It *always* seems to turn out this way." Sipping his second martini, Steve continued to shake his head in disgust over the story he was being told.

"Simon's death is the reason I'm back here. And, while I hate to admit this, I'm here because Donna suggested I should stop to see if you can help me."

"How much?" Steve asked, not giving Paul time to discuss the actual reason behind his visit.

"What?" Paul replied, startled by the forcefulness of his friend's question.

"*What* nothing. I asked you how much you needed. If the person who's been funding this project of yours has been murdered, I'm guessing his or his wife's attorneys have cut you off, correct? I know you well-enough that if you're close to finding what you had set out to find, you're not walking away without finishing what you've started. So, how much? Cut the bullshit . . . just tell me how much you need." Finished speaking, Steve took a healthy swig of his late afternoon libation. It would not be the last one he would enjoy.

"Somewhere in the area of two hundred thousand." While well-aware of his friend's business savvy, Paul was still impressed by how quickly Steve had identified the problem he was facing.

"You sure?"

"At least that, maybe a bit more."

"I don't mean to sound greedy, but just like those investors I watch on *Shark Tank* I expect something in return for letting you use my money." As he had spoken, there was not the slightest bit of embarrassment in Steve's voice. An intelligent businessman, Paul's friend was not shy when it came to expecting some form of a return on his investment.

"I'm not sure if that's possible, but I'll do my best to see you get something. There are too many variables that have recently come into play for me to say how this project is going to play out. For all I know, Mrs. Church, or even her husband's attorneys, could drag this mess out for years before it's settled. If they do, there's no way to predict what the outcome will be. Whatever it is, it will be influenced by how much we find and who some of the new players might be. For now, all I can do is to ask you to trust me." Pausing a few moments, Paul then advised Steve of a thought he had been wrestling with. "Perhaps you could call our friend to determine if he can help us navigate our way through this recent turmoil that's been caused by Simon's death."

"Judge Morgan?"

"Why not? He would be the perfect person to put an end to any shenanigans Mrs. Church's attorneys might attempt."

"Maybe. We'll see."

Thirty minutes later, after discussing Paul's needs over two more rounds of drinks, Steve Alcott agreed to fund the balance of his friend's search for the gold and silver Captain Howard had hidden inside a cave outside of Moncks Corner.

"I'll have a talk with two of my partners. But don't worry, we'll come up with the money you need. You get back to work so you can find what you've been looking for."

* * * * * *

The following morning, in a far better mood than he had experienced the day before, Paul made the trip back to Moncks Corner. With Donna and Steve's assistance, Paul had received the help he desperately needed.

Now it would take another friend to see that Steve was properly compensated.

54

Find anything?" Paul asked, donning his hard hat after arriving back at the site of the two caves. Standing next to Bobby Ray as several construction vehicles weaved their way across the roughly graded parking lot, the two friends watched and listened as the heavy pieces of equipment belched thick black smoke and made a series of loud noises as their operators constantly shifted gears to keep the excavation process moving forward.

"Not yet, Yankee Boy, but it ain't because we haven't been trying. We've cleaned out most of the first twenty feet or so of the cave's entrance," Bobby Ray replied, pointing at the hillside where the entrance to the second cave was defined more than when Paul last saw it. The hours spent excavating the entrance had transformed the area from simply being outlined with a large number of survey stakes to one that now resembled an opening seen in hundreds of books and movies. "After you left yesterday, Groski's fellas experienced a few problems with some of their equipment, so that set us back a bit. To make up for the time they lost, we all stayed a few hours longer than we normally do. So far this morning it seems like we're running on all cylinders."

"No other surprises or setbacks, then?"

"Nope, just a bunch of rocks and some thick ledge that needs busting up, but we're doing OK. You find anyone with some deep pockets to help us?" Bobby Ray asked as a front end loader was slowly backed out of the cave's entrance. As it had on several previous occasions, the loader's large bucket was filled to near capacity with rocks and other debris that had carefully been picked through. A short distance away, a handful of workers stood with two archeologists near a large heavy-duty metal screen that had been set on four concrete blocks. Unlike others working inside the cave, their job was to screen the contents of each bucket one last time making sure nothing of historical significance had been missed. Once satisfied the contents had been thoroughly searched, a front end loader transported the rocks and debris to where another larger piece of equipment was busy separating the different material. Further away, an aging rock crusher spewed clouds of dust into the air as it turned many of the larger rocks into smaller pieces so they could be used for needs on future projects or sold as fill. An experienced negotiator, Groski had worked out a separate deal with Mrs. DeWolfe to purchase as much of the fill as he could haul. Doing so had given him access to hundreds of yards of crushed stone. A savvy businessman, Groski knew there was a huge market for the gravel his rock crusher was turning out on a daily basis.

"Sort of. Donna actually solved our problem for us." Paul replied as he answered his friend's question regarding their money problems.

"Her bank is going to bankroll us?" Bobby Ray asked, confused by his friend's response.

"No, it's not her bank that's come through for us; it's someone she thought of. In fact, it's someone you know. He even asked about you yesterday during our meeting." As he finished speaking, a small smile curled in the corner of Paul's mouth.

"Who's that?" Far more interested in the skill being demonstrated by the operator of one of the front end loaders than he was in hearing his friend's answer, Bobby Ray watched as the large piece of equipment was slowly maneuvered back inside the cave.

"Our friend, Steve Alcott."

"I never would of thought of him." Hearing his friend admit that he would not have thought of Steve as someone to resolve their financial problems made Paul feel better.

"Have you talked to Regan again?"

"We spoke about an hour ago. According to what he's told me, things aren't looking too good for Mrs. Church. Her lawyers seem to be doing her more harm than good. First, they responded too slowly to an offer the state's attorney's office had put on the table, and now they won't let her speak with the investigators working the case. Her attorneys were told if Mrs. Church cooperated there would still be some kind of consideration applied if she pled guilty, but for some reason they're not interested."

"It sounds as if her attorneys are willing to take her case to trial. Perhaps they know something, like some mitigating factor that no one else knows about. Seeing she's the one who's going to take the brunt of an unfavorable decision, I wonder how much Genevieve supports that strategy?"

428 | PETER WARREN

"Good question." Paul replied.

"As far as I'm concerned, her attorneys are a bunch of dumb asses. Taking her case to trial doesn't surprise me, but the case against her seems to be pretty strong. Even if she's found guilty, her cooperation would likely have an impact on whether the death penalty stays on the table. If it was me, and I was living in a state which doesn't have a problem executing its most vicious killers, I'd be telling those prosecutors whatever they wanted to know. If her attorneys are advising her not to cooperate because they're confident she's going to be found not guilty . . . well, they're bigger fools than I think they are." Shaking his head over what he perceived to be bad advice on the part of Genevieve Church's attorneys, Bobby Ray added, "As Old Bill himself once wrote 'Let's kill all the lawyers.' " While never a fan of William Shakespeare's work, Bobby Ray was familiar with a line from one of the playwright's plays.

"From what he's heard, Regan told me Mrs. Church's alleged co-conspirator has given the investigators a bunch of damaging evidence against her. It supposedly includes how many times her boss had asked her to feed Mr. Church those deadly cocktails. According to the maid's signed statement, Mrs. Church had allegedly paid her a few hundred dollars for her assistance. Not to anyone's surprise, these payments started after this maid apparently caught her mixing one of the deadly cocktails. Like I said, this maid has given the investigators a written statement stating she wanted no part of what she was being asked to do."

"Have they given her a polygraph test to determine her veracity?" Bobby Ray asked.

"It's supposedly in the works, but get this. With the exception of the first one hundred dollar bill she was given, this maid handed over all of the other money she had been paid; including notes which captured the dates and times she received this money. The dates and times are important as they identify the occasions when this maid was asked to deliver those poisonous drinks. Then, as a final dagger to any defense Mrs. Church's attorneys might raise, she took the cops to where Mrs. Church had stored several bottles of her favorite poison. Two of the bottles came back with at least two sets of prints on them; not surprisingly, one of the sets belongs to Mrs. Church. Care to guess who the other set belongs to?"

"No idea, but I'm sure you're going to tell me."

"They belong to a waiter who works at a restaurant where Mrs. Church likes to be seen having lunch once or twice each week. Along with three or four other dining establishments located in the greater Dallas area, her husband was a silent partner in this restaurant with a few of his friends. At this exact moment, his name escapes me, but this waiter has a rap sheet which includes some pending narcotic charges. To save his own ass, he's admitted to buying the poison at Mrs. Church's request."

"That's an interesting bit of news, isn't it?" Bobby Ray asked, his focus now shifting from the operations around the caves to the news Paul was telling him.

"Besides all of this evidence, it appears as if President Trump was not the only one who liked to send tweets and text messages. To use one of Regan's recent metaphors, it seems as if Mrs. Church's goose might be cooked."

"So why isn't the maid being charged as a co-conspirator if she had been the one delivering the deadly cocktails to Mr. Church's bedside?" Bobby Ray asked, more interested in the details surrounding Simon Church's murder than he was in Paul's comment regarding President Trump.

"Because she really hadn't delivered any of those drinks; at least not the ones Mrs. Church had made. After being handed the drinks, the maid had figured out a way to hustle up to a bathroom on the mansion's second floor. Once there, she swapped each drink for a simple glass of water. Each night she worked when Mr. Church was home, she expected Mrs. Church to ask her to deliver one of those deadly cocktails to his bedroom. To be prepared, she staged a similar-looking drink in that same bathroom. I have to give her credit as she had the wits to swipe the same type of glass from the kitchen so Mrs. Church wouldn't be suspicious if she checked her husband's bedroom."

"Smart gal, this maid."

"She knew Mrs. Church could easily track her movements by way of the security cameras inside the mansion, but the maid outsmarted her by holding up the glass when she passed under the three cameras on her way to Mr. Church's sleeping quarters. Fortunately, a small section of the upstairs hallway just outside the bathroom in question had a blind spot, so she was able to swap the drinks without being seen. She even paused on a few occasions outside of Mr. Church's suite so Mrs. Church could clearly see the drink being delivered."

"Not bad," Bobby Ray offered, trying to follow the story he was being told. "I thought you said the autopsy had found a bunch of poison in the old guy's system. How'd that get there if the drinks were being swapped for plain old tap water?"

"First of all, before the end of her shifts the maid would return to the bathroom and pour the deadly cocktails she had been handed down the sink. Later, when Mrs. Church was in another section of the mansion or had gone to bed, the washed out glass was returned to the kitchen so it wasn't missed. To answer your question, the maid didn't work every night. When she was off on those nights Mr. Church slept at the mansion, Mrs. Church delivered the drinks herself. That's why the poison was found in his system during the autopsy."

"Do the cops have any idea what caused that bitch to poison the old man with Pequa? I mean, where'd she come up with that idea?" Bobby Ray asked, thinking of a variety of other ways Genevieve Church could have killed her husband.

"Once they started looking at her for this murder, the investigators assigned to this case apparently put Mrs. Church under round-the-clock surveillance. On two or three occasions they followed her to this fancy restaurant; that's when they saw her meeting with this waiter. According to what I've been told, these investigators described those meetings as being suspicious as they also included a few hand-to-hand transactions between Mrs. Church and this waiter. Turns out this guy, who was also under surveillance for several days, has admitted to being the owner of a small, but lucrative cocaine business. He's identified some of the restaurant's biggest spenders as being some of his best customers. The part that nobody expected was that Simon Church and a few of his friends were silent owners of this eating establishment."

While the news caught Bobby Ray by surprise, the fact that Genevieve Church was involved with drugs was hardly a shock to the veteran cop. "From the sounds of it, Genevieve's not only a cold-blooded killer, but she's also a coke freak. So, what'd they do, put some pressure on this waiter to get him to spill the beans on who was responsible for Simon Church's death?"

"Yep, just like you and I would have done. Because of the charges that are pending against him, as a convicted felon he had no choice but to cooperate. The fact that the cops told him he was close to being arrested as an accessory in Mr. Church's death, didn't hurt. Nor did the surveillance video which showed him selling to a few of his customers."

"He's a smart guy; a whole lot smarter than Genevieve. It's always best to save your own ass than it is to protect someone else's."

"Besides a few other favors he's done for her, this waiter fessed up to being the one who purchased the Pequa. He claimed it was purchased at a local hardware store not far from the restaurant, and that he paid for it with cash supplied to him by Mrs. Church. There's one last thing that I'll know you'll find amusing."

"What's that?" Bobby Ray asked.

"He claimed he wouldn't have purchased this deadly household cleaner if he knew Genevieve was planning on using it to kill her husband. Like everyone else who's been caught red-handed, we know that's not the case."

Smirking over what Paul had told him, Bobby Ray said, "That's what everyone expects a drug dealing scumbag to say. I hope he was paid well, because he's probably looking at spending a fair amount of time in prison for being involved with her. At this point, he's probably wishing he had never met the bitch."

Laughing at his friend's response, Paul added one last comment about the waiter's role. "He claimed she had tipped him fifty bucks for purchasing the Pequa. The cops are in the process of verifying his story with the owner of the hardware store, so we'll just have to sit back and see how the rest of this story plays out."

Thinking for a moment, Bobby Ray offered up a comment only a seasoned investigator would offer. "If I was working that case, I'd be yanking that bathroom drain apart so the lab could test for the presence of any harmful chemicals, especially Pequa. While any smart defense attorney could easily argue that chemicals like the one in question could have been poured down any number of drains . . . by either the household staff or others, to some degree the presence of Pequa would at least confirm the maid's story. Interviews with the rest of the staff, including any outside contractors, could easily blow any postulations made by Church's defense attorneys out of the water."

"Nice word," Paul said, smiling over the fancy word his friend had used. Having worked close to two hundred crime scenes during his career, Bobby Ray's comment regarding the contents of the bathroom drain being analyzed had been spot-on.

"Thanks. I like to sneak them in every once in a while to keep you on your toes."

"Sounds like you haven't lost your touch, Mr. Undersheriff," Paul replied, complimenting his friend. "Just so you know that course of action you suggested has already been addressed. Regan told me the cops showed up the other day with a search warrant so they could take apart the drains in three different bathrooms and the kitchen. Just as you have mentioned, they were looking for the presence of any harmful chemicals, including Pequa."

Addressing one of Paul's previous comments, Bobby Ray sought a clarification. "You mean that dumb bitch was sending her maid tweets and text messages while they were poisoning the old man?"

"Yep. My understanding is there was something in the area of fifty-eight messages between the two of them; according to Regan, most had been sent by Mrs. Church. Pretty stupid, huh?" Paul asked, rolling his eyes over Mrs. Church's alleged transgressions.

******

The following afternoon under a hot, but fading sun Groski's crew pushed deeper inside the collapsed cave. Confronted with rocks and boulders far bigger than those near the cave's entrance, and fearful of triggering another collapse, their progress soon drew slower. Forced to hammer away at several large boulders with chipping hammers and jack hammers, they worked cautiously as they turned the boulders into manageable pieces the front end loaders could handle. Close to where they were working, two large exhaust fans recently bolted to the rock walls worked at removing the thick choking dust from deep inside the cave. Even with the amount of dust being vented out of the cave, men and equipment were coated in a layer of fine white powder.

Halting work shortly after six p.m. to allow his men time to rest after working inside the cramped hot conditions for over five hours, with Paul and Bobby Ray's assistance Groski adjusted the positions of the large industrial fans in an attempt to push more dust outside the cave. Powered by a large portable generator situated not far from the cave's entrance, the fans worked at clearing the remaining dust particles lingering inside the tight quarters.

Thirty minutes later, with Groski's tired crew still enjoying their late afternoon break, Paul ventured back inside the cave to inspect the progress being made. Dust-covered work lights strung along both sides of the narrowing cave quickly revealed how much the air quality had improved since the fans were repositioned. Wearing a hard hat and safety glasses, as well as a bulky respirator which protected his lungs from breathing in any of the remaining dust particles, Paul easily noticed the amount of work that had been completed.

Venturing further inside as he continued with his inspection, a thin wall of rocks near the rear of the cave suddenly collapsed. Weakened by the jack hammers incessant pounding, the wall collapsed without warning. Fearful of another and, perhaps, more dangerous collapse occurring, Paul moved quickly towards the cave's entrance as a way of protecting himself. As he moved, the cave suddenly grew silent.

With the newest dust cloud soon cleared by the powerful fans, gathering his courage Paul slowly made his way towards the rear of the cave. Focusing the small tactical headlamp attached to his hard hat on the newest pile of rocks, he saw something Groski's crew had not yet encountered.

Joined by Bobby Ray, who entered the cave in search of his friend after seeing the latest surge of dust being expelled, Paul bent down and picked up what remained of a burnt piece of wood. Pulling off his respirator as he began inspecting the object, Paul moved it closer to his nose. As he did, Bobby Ray pulled a similar, but slightly larger piece from underneath two rocks.

"From the looks and smell of them, I'm guessing this is all that remains of a few torches our Confederate friend must have been using when he was working in here." Looking back towards the cave's entrance as they shut their headlamps off caused Bobby Ray and Paul to realize how little natural light was present. "It's too dark to be working this far back without any type of light. He probably wrapped some dried grass or bits of cloth around the ends of a few sticks and placed them every few feet so he could see. Once they were lit, they likely gave off enough light so he could see what he was doing."

"Did I hear you say something about torches, Bobby Ray?" Groski asked, moving closer to where Paul and Bobby Ray were standing. Walking along one of the cave's jagged walls; Groski's silhouette had been hidden from view. The unexpected sound of his voice startled both men as they finished inspecting the burnt pieces of wood.

"Damn, Phil, make some noise when you're sneaking up on folks. You scared the crap out of me!" Bobby Ray said, nearly dropping the piece of wood he was holding. Deep inside the hillside, the sound of an unfamiliar noise had already caused Paul and Bobby Ray to be on edge.

After showing Groski the burnt ends of the wood they found, pieces Paul concluded were once tree branches, the three men gingerly moved towards the pile of rubble that had yet to be inspected by the crew working inside the cave. Picking through the rocks, Paul realized they were now coming across what had been a large pile of tree branches.

"These branches are probably the ones Howard wrote about in his journal. After he moved the gold and silver to the rear of the cave, he used the branches to hide what he had carried in here." Bending down, Paul pulled several additional pieces of burnt and decayed wood from the pile he was sifting through.

"Why'd he do that?" Groski asked.

"Back then it was still a cave. When the hillside first collapsed and buried his men in the adjoining cave, this one still had an entrance. He didn't want anyone finding the assets he had hidden in here, so he covered everything with tree branches. When they were first put down, they were probably full of pine needles or leaves, so they covered everything up."

Finished with their discussion on what the tree branches had been used for, Paul instructed Bobby Ray to locate the members of the forensic recovery team so the findings inside the cave could be properly documented. "Bring Chick and Peter back with you. And make sure Peter has a couple of his cameras with him."

Three hours later, after the area around the rear of the cave had been properly documented; including the locations where splintered pieces of several wooden barrels had been found, the large pile of rubble was cautiously removed. In what was now a well-lit cave illuminated from front to back by two long strings of clear white bulbs and four portable work lights, Paul and his crew, along with the members of the forensic recovery team, stared at several old wooden crates. Roughly five feet in length, each crate contained ten of the most effective rifles the Union and Confederate armies had available to them during the war. Manufactured close to one hundred and seventy years earlier, outside of a few test rounds fired at the time they had been made, the rifles had never been fired in anger. To the right of where they stood, a large pile of coins sat just as Howard had left them. Blanketed in rock dust, dirt, and years of cobwebs, most of what was sitting there was no longer hidden from view. To Groski and three of his men who stood off to the side taking in this remarkable sight, it was an event they had never expected to witness.

Pushing aside one of the wooden lids that had been badly damaged years earlier, after moving a handful of rocks and several pieces of decaying wood, Paul carefully untied a small cloth bag resting on top of the pile. Moments later, as Peter clicked away with his camera Paul slowly placed his right hand inside the old bag. With his headlamp illuminating the small opening, he gently pushed his hand deeper inside the bag. With the headlamps worn by Bobby

Ray and Chick shining on their friend's hand as it was pulled from the bag's dark confines, they saw what it held. Inside Paul's hand was a remarkable collection of fifteen dusty gold coins; each had been worth ten federal dollars at the time of the war.

"Those real?" Groski asked, stepping closer to get a better look.

"They're as real as they can be," Chick answered, gently rubbing the dust off an 1861 Liberty Head gold coin. Moving the coin closer to the beam cast by his headlamp, he added, "This one I'm holding was minted in 1861 . . . the same year the Civil War started. It's worth a helluva lot more these days than the ten-dollars it was worth back then. While the gold alone makes it valuable, numismatic collectibles with a story like ours behind it are worth a bunch of money these days."

As he looked through a partially torn bag of coins that had been damaged from a number of rocks falling on it, Bobby Ray's attention was drawn to the pile of crates sitting nearby. Pointing in their direction after gaining Paul's attention, he asked, "What's the plan for all of this stuff? Are you thinking of opening any of them to see what kind of condition the rifles are in?" Bending down to see if he could make out any of the faint markings displayed on the top and sides of the crates, Bobby Ray realized whatever information had been stenciled there had been lost to the human eye. The owner of a variety of different firearms, he was anxious to see how the rifles had stood up after being hidden inside the cave for as long as they had.

"Not today I'm not," Paul replied, watching as Bobby Ray continued with his efforts to decipher several of the faded markings on two of the crates. "For now, the plan is to remove everything that's here so we can move the artifacts to a safer location. After Peter finishes taking whatever photographs he needs, we're going to load all of these bags and crates in two of Phil's front end loaders. Once that's done, we'll spend some time inspecting what we've found. When we're finished, we'll load everything in the back of my truck."

As Wayne Keller, the senior member of the forensic recovery team angrily protested the plan Paul had laid out, the loud voice of one of the two men walking towards the rear of the cave suddenly echoed against the rocky interior. Silhouetted against the backdrop of the bright work lights, for a few brief moments the features displayed on the men's faces were not discernable.

"I'll decide on where the artifacts end up!" One of the voices boomed.

Shielding their eyes from the bright light cast in their direction, Bobby Ray, Chick, and the others tried figuring out the identities of the men approaching them. Unlike Paul, they had no idea who the men were.

"It's not your responsibility to make such a decision, it's mine," the loud voice said sternly as the person behind it cast a glance in Keller's direction. *"That's what I get paid to do, isn't that right, Mr. Waring?"*

"Yes, Your Honor, that's correct." Paul replied, easily recognizing the distinct sound of Judge Howard C. Morgan's voice. "Nice to see you, sir. Your timing is . . . well, it's rather timely, to say the least. I see you brought our friend with you." Walking to where Judge Morgan and Steve Alcott had halted their progress, Paul shot Steve a quick wink as the three exchanged handshakes. Moments later, Groski handed their two visitors yellow hard hats and safety glasses.

"Just to be safe, Your Honor." Groski added, shocked by the unexpected presence of a federal judge standing inside a somewhat unstable cave.

As he had done years earlier when Paul arranged for Steve Alcott to bring Judge Morgan to a meeting he had orchestrated in Charleston, Chick stood off to the side shaking his head as Paul's guests donned their safety equipment. Muttering to himself, he said, "The son of a bitch has done it again. He's brought the Judge here to show the forensic boys who's still calling the shots. *Freakin' amazing!*"

After briefly introducing Judge Morgan and Steve Alcott to everyone present, Paul showed his guests the artifacts he and the others had just found. After answering a few of Morgan's questions, Paul filled his visitors in on some of the details related to their latest search for the missing Confederate treasury. While briefly explaining how they had come to search this section of the cave after finding the remains of several Civil War soldiers in an adjacent cave, for the time being Paul chose not to mention any of the newest details surrounding Simon Church's death. Minutes later, after noticing how uneasy his guests had become while standing inside the cave's tight confines, Paul, in an indirect manner, suggested their conversation should be moved to a safer location outside.

Several minutes later, as they stood close to where the first few bones had been located under a small pile of rocks and dirt, Paul continued to answer a few additional questions the jurist asked. At the same time, Steve Alcott took in everything being discussed.

"Are you confident this map you've shown me is valid? By that, I mean are you sure there have been no other claims filed against this property?" As he asked his questions, one of Judge Morgan's fingers traced the boundaries of the DeWolfe property on a map Paul had obtained from Berkeley County.

"We're as confident as we can be based on the information supplied to us by the folks in charge of updating the county's property records. We were given this information when we obtained our permits. As an added precaution, one of Mr. Groski's engineers verified all was in order before we put the first shovel in the ground. If there are any claims or liens against this property, then the county has some explaining to do because this map we're looking at was certified as being accurate when it was issued to us." As he addressed Morgan's concern, Paul pointed at the official date and time stamp a county employee had placed in a corner of the map.

Nodding his head as a means of showing he was satisfied by Paul's explanation, Morgan then asked his next question. As he formed his question, the jurist, who had developed a great deal of respect for Paul over the past few years, pretty much knew what his friend's answer was going to be.

"Paul, this property owner, this elderly woman . . . Mrs. DeWolfe I believe you called her earlier, have you or any of your associates or, for that matter, even Mr. Groski, made this gal any promises as it relates to the sharing of any artifacts in return for being granted access to her property?" As he finished speaking, Morgan scanned the faces of those standing in front of him. Expecting to see a grimace or some form of a facial expression indicating that such a promise had been made, to his surprise Morgan saw nothing but blank faces staring back at him.

"We have not made any such promises, Your Honor," Paul said confidently. "The only promise we made was to stop and see her when we were finished with our work. We believed we owed her that. I did make one other promise, but that was nothing more than to return her property to the condition we found it in. I . . .

I wanted her to know what we found, that's why we told her we'd give her an update before we left."

"I see." Morgan replied, lightly rubbing his jaw with his right hand.

"Your Honor, there's one more thing about Mrs. DeWolfe I'd like to mention. I'm not sure if you're the one who will be issuing a ruling on how these artifacts are going to be handled, by that I mean are they going to stay together as a possible collection or are they going to be disbursed to some degree like the others we found several years ago. For what my opinion matters, Mrs. DeWolfe deserves something. From speaking with her, it's easy to see that she doesn't have much. She's certainly not in the best of health, she has no real family left, her house is falling apart, and without her permission none of these artifacts would have ever been found." Chuckling out loud, Paul added, "Hell, we haven't even had time to inspect anything that's been found, but whatever it proves to be, she deserves something."

"We'll see," Morgan replied, his voice immediately trailing off as he processed Paul's recommendation. "I . . . I suppose she does, but that decision will be made at a later time. For now, I'd like to hear what your immediate plans are for these bags of gold and silver coins. While you're at it, take a moment or two to include your thoughts on those crates of rifles I saw earlier. But first, let's take a look at those artifacts being unloaded by Mr. Groski's men. I need to have a mental picture of everything we're about to discuss." Using his right index finger, Morgan pointed at the wooden crates being unloaded from one of Groski's front end loaders. As they were being unloaded, the fragile crates were gently stacked on two large pallets.

A passionate Civil War buff like Paul and Bobby Ray, as Morgan inspected the valuable coins he paused to reflect back on the ones he witnessed being recovered in Charleston several years earlier. Looking at Paul, he said, "I can't help thinking about the coins you recovered from those cannons. Just like this discovery, that was another remarkable find."

"I had the same thought earlier, Your Honor. From the few I've had a chance to look at, they appear to be the same denominations and in nearly the same condition. I expect they'll likely prove to be just as valuable as the others we've found." As he reflected back on his previous discovery, Paul pointed at the caves Groski's crew had opened up in the steep, rocky hillside. "But for me, I have to say solving the mystery of those markings we found on the cannons in Charleston was a lot more satisfying than cleaning out those two holes over there; that was definitely more of a challenge."

After patiently listening to another challenge raised by the forensic examiners regarding whose control the valuable artifacts should be placed under, Morgan used his authority to temporarily put an end to the growing tension between Paul and his counterpart, Wayne Keller.

"We're all here because Mr. Waring was hired to find this part of the Confederate treasury. While we all know who the money belonged to when it left Richmond, some of us, including you, Mr. Keller, seem to have forgotten that some of this money may have been stolen from the federal government. It was stolen shortly after the war began when the Confederacy raided the United States Mint that was located in New Orleans. Until it's proven otherwise, I'm considering these coins and rifles federal property; so seeing that I'm a federal judge that makes me the only one present with authority over federal property." Looking at Keller, Morgan added, "While the estate of the late Mr. Church may disagree with me, for now I'm placing these valuables in Mr. Waring's custody. However, these coins, just like the crates of rifles we've been looking at, are not leaving in the back of anyone's pick-up truck."

Raising his hand as a means of warding off another challenge from Keller and his partners, Morgan looked in Groski's direction. "Mr. Groski, for no other reason than to protect them from being stolen, I would be foolish to ignore the fact that these artifacts need to be properly secured." Pointing to the other side of the parking lot, Morgan asked, "That large storage container of yours sitting there packed with an assortment of tools and equipment, do you have the means of bringing another one just like it to this site?"

Turning to look at the storage container Morgan was pointing to, one slightly larger than the type used by most major moving companies, Groski answered the jurist's question. "Yes, sir. If that's what you're thinking of storing the artifacts in, I can probably have one here in about three hours. Someone's going to have to pay for it, but I can get it here. Give me the word, and I'll get on the horn with my yard boss."

"Make it happen, Mr. Groski." Morgan said in a tone normally reserved for his courtroom. While issuing an order as a means of securing the artifacts so they were not lost or misappropriated, the jurist gave little thought to the expense involved in not only transporting the large storage container to and from the work site, but to the cost involved in guarding the artifacts. Morgan's plan included having the artifacts guarded until the court had time to determine their fate.

Aware of Bobby Ray's position within the South Carolina law enforcement community, as he turned toward him Morgan instructed the Undersheriff of Georgetown County to draft a security plan for protecting the assets once they left the DeWolfe property. "Put together a team of state troopers, deputies, local police officers, and whomever else you deem necessary, to guard this container. This team will be responsible for guarding it around the clock for several days. One more thing, I want this container guarded by law enforcement personnel with full police powers, not security guards. Understand?"

"Yes, sir."

"And, while you're at it, I want another team assigned to the property here. It's to be staffed 24/7. Each shift will need three deputies or state troopers assigned to this detail; one here at the site of the two caves, one in front of Mrs. DeWolfe's residence, and the other at the beginning of her driveway. I don't want anyone bothering her once word of this discovery becomes public."

"Yes, sir."

"If anyone raises Cain about assigning some of their personnel to this detail, feel free to use my name. If they continue to be a pain in the ass, tell them to come visit me in my chambers tomorrow morning. That should bring them around."

"Yes, sir." Bobby Ray replied, hoping someone would challenge Morgan's authority. It had been a long time since he had seen anyone have their heads handed to them by a federal judge.

Then, turning to the forensic examiners, Morgan said, "Gentlemen, I completely understand and respect your role in all of this, but, for now, my decision stands. The remains of those soldiers who were killed inside that cave over there are your responsibility. I'll expect you to protect their remains as much as I expect Mr. Waring will do with the other artifacts."

Still irritated by the position Morgan had taken, Keller tried one last time to change the jurist's thinking. "Your Honor, by state statute our office is . . ."

Unaccustomed to his instructions being challenged, the glare Morgan directed at the senior member of the forensic recovery team told him it was not a wise idea to contest his decision any further. Seconds later, Keller dropped his protest.

******

Moments after Paul and the others had finished their inspection of the artifacts packed inside the cloth bags, one of Groski's front end loaders backed out of the cave with the balance of the precious cargo Howard had hidden there. Barely having time to move away from the rocky entrance, the operator of the front end loader and his co-workers were greeted with two loud moans coming from deep inside the hillside. Both were loud enough to cause Paul and the others to stop what they were doing. Turning to look in the direction of the caves, they watched as the metal trench sheets that had been holding back the rocks and dirt around the caves instantly crumbled under the weight of the collapsing hillside. The quickness of how fast the strong metal sheets gave way stunned everyone who was watching. Moments later, thick clouds of choking dust and chunks of rocks bigger than bowling bowls spewed from the entrances Groski's men had recently excavated. As he and his team sought cover behind several pieces of heavy equipment, Paul watched as a large rock flew through the air before bouncing off the front of one of Groski's trucks.

"Charlie! Joe! Gard!" Groski screamed in horror, dropping the shovel he was holding as he watched his men run for cover before disappearing behind a dark, impenetrable wall of dust. Fueled by a single, but massive shock wave, the expanding cloud of dust quickly made it difficult for even the largest features on the nearby hillside to be recognizable. With little regard for his own safety, as Groski raced towards the caves and the unstable ground around them he frantically tried accounting for his men as the dust enveloped his panicked crew. Most had been part of the crew checking the caves to make sure all of the artifacts had been removed. Unable to see or hear much of anything for nearly five minutes, with the help of two of his foremen Groski did what he could to account for his men.

Several minutes later, as the dust slowly dissipated, Charlie Sturges and Joe Sullivan, badly bruised and having sustained several cuts and lacerations after being struck by chunks of flying debris, stumbled in the direction of Groski's cries. Like their sweaty matted hair, their faces, arms, and clothing were caked in dust.

"We're OK! We're OK!" Sturges yelled, holding onto Sullivan as they collapsed to the ground after briefly fearing for their lives. Seeking safety next to one of Groski's vehicles, both had done what they could to avoid being struck by the large pieces of debris sent flying by the collapse.

"Where's Gard?" Groski anxiously asked, breathing heavily from the distance he had covered as the hillside continued to give way in front of him. Caked in dust, he had somehow managed to avoid being struck by any rocks or other debris. The panic of nearly losing at least three of his men contributed significantly to the stress the construction owner was now experiencing.

"He's OK, but you know him," Sturges said, spitting a mouthful of dirt and dust onto the ground after surviving an experience he hoped he would never see the likes of again. "The three of us just managed to make it away from the freakin' hillside when all hell broke loose. Gard's machine took a couple of good hits from a few of those boulders tumbling down the hill, but he's OK. Knowing him, he's probably back there trying to get that machine of his running. You know how he is; he treats that thing better than he treats his kids."

Sturges' comment made Groski breathe easier even as dust continued to collect on everything it encountered. Near the entrances to the two caves, groans from deep inside the hillside could still be heard. Soon feeling better after confirming his crew was safe, Groski ignored the eerie noises as he went to check on Gardner Banks. One of the first men he had hired after starting his own construction business, Banks was also one of Groski's favorite employees.

55

With the panic of the moment and the thick cloud of dust having dissipated, Paul and Judge Morgan helped to triage the injuries caused by the rocks, shards of metal, and other debris that had been sent flying by energy released from deep inside the hillside. All around them rocks of all sizes littered the parking area where several damaged construction vehicles stood quiet. The once busy construction site was now awash with a variety of different activities. For the moment, none were related to the recovery of any precious artifacts.

Less than thirty feet away from where a large boulder had crushed the cab of one of Groski's trucks, Bobby Ray, Chick, and Peter assisted those who had barely escaped a horrible death. While no one had suffered any fatal or traumatic injuries, a small pile of bloody gauze pads grew in size as Paul's friends frantically worked at stemming the flow of blood from a variety of wounds. Off in the distance, the loud wail of sirens could be heard as three area ambulances struggled to make their way up the rough access road.

With the injured soon being cared for by a small contingent of emergency medical technicians and two members of the forensic recovery team who served their respective communities as volunteer firemen, Chick began taking photographs of the collapsed hillside. Working with Bobby Ray and Peter, they pulled bits and pieces of crushed work lights, hand tools, and other construction equipment from the rubble around the front of the two caves.

"Are your men doing OK?" Sweating profusely from the assistance he had lent to the chaotic scene around him, Judge Morgan wiped his brow as he handed Groski a cold bottle of water. Near the jurist's left wrist, a small laceration allowed a steady trickle of blood to flow from the wound. "That was too damn close! I'm grateful the good Lord spared us from being hurt worse than we were." While a passionate Civil War buff, Morgan was a firm believer in the ways of his church. Like most Southerners who went to church each Sunday, he readily accepted Jesus Christ as his savior.

Caked in sweat and dust, after taking two healthy swigs of the cool water Groski poured what little was left on his face as a way of flushing some of the dust from his eyes and nose. "Not as much as I am, Your Honor. I lost some fairly expensive equipment when the hill gave way, but that can always be replaced. I'm not sure how I would have reacted if any of my men had been killed. Most of them are like family; they've been with me for years." Still shaking over what had taken place, Groski used a wad of damp paper towels to wipe away the dust and sweat the water had missed. "My men and I are road builders, not miners. After living through this, we're done with any more jobs like this one. No matter what it pays, no job is worth getting my men hurt over."

After making sure the EMTs had all of the injuries under control, Paul spoke with Groski for several minutes as he sought his assurance that the large metal container Judge Morgan had asked about would soon arrive. Regaining his composure after being advised that all of his men had been accounted for, Groski walked off to finalize the remaining details regarding the container's arrival. Moments earlier, the construction foreman advised Paul that his men had managed to remove all of the artifacts just before the hillside had given way.

"Seeing what's happened here today has that changed your thoughts on where this gold and silver should end up? And, if I might be so bold to ask, do you still believe Simon Church's estate is entitled to any of these artifacts?" Morgan asked, watching as a damaged, but valuable bag of roughly eight hundred coins was carefully set inside a large plastic tub. Sitting exposed inside the bucket of a front end loader with several others when rocks and other material were sent flying, the bag had been severely damaged after being struck by a missile in the shape of a two-pound piece of rock. Struck on its left side, the bag's gaping hole had allowed a steady flow of coins to empty into the loader's metal bucket before being placed inside the plastic tub.

"No, it hasn't, Your Honor," Paul replied. "To be honest, shortly after his death I stopped believing Mr. Church's estate had any right to file a claim against these artifacts."

While Paul's response caught Morgan by surprise, it also pleased him. "I'm not disagreeing with you, but he's the one who hired you. His financial support, along with the journal he found, is what enabled you to find this treasure. You have to expect his attorneys are going to do everything in their power to file a hundred different claims against the treasures you've found."

"Let them. The old man is dead, his wife has been arrested for murder, and Mr. and Mrs. Church, during their marriage or in any other relationships they were involved in, never produced any children. From what Regan has told me, the attorneys representing Mr. Church's estate are only looking to be compensated for the amount of money that had been shelled out before he died. Those attorneys are also the ones who cut Mr. Church's supply of money off to us. His money may have got us started, but shortly after he died our friend over there has become our banker. We found this part of the treasury on his dime, not Simon Church's." As he spoke, Paul pointed in the direction of the project's newest benefactor. It was his and Morgan's close friend, Steve Alcott.

"Sounds like those attorneys might be looking for a quick settlement."

"I hope my next comment doesn't offend you, Your Honor, but it has nothing to do with a quick settlement. It's more about them making a few quick bucks for themselves than anything else. They'll put whatever money we give them back into the old man's estate, sell off his homes and the rest of his holdings, then they'll take their cut and move on to their next set of clients."

Ignoring Paul's comments about the attorneys he had taken a disliking to, Morgan said, "What about his collection of Civil War artifacts? From how you've described it, I'm sure it's worth a tidy sum."

"Maybe, but that's another chapter in this saga that we'll have to discuss at another time. Rest assured, when I know more, you'll know more."

Paul's last comment caused Morgan to become very quiet. It also caused him to become even more suspicious of the circumstances surrounding Simon Church's death.

56

Later that evening, with the valuable assets safely secured inside a large metal construction trailer fastened with more locks than anyone thought was possible, Paul enjoyed a leisurely dinner with his team at a local restaurant. Hours earlier, Bobby Ray had followed the construction trailer as it was towed to the South Carolina Highway Patrol's Troop Six Headquarters in Goose Creek. Parked in the rear parking lot, the trailer and its precious cargo sat guarded by two heavily armed state troopers. It would remain there until one of Judge Morgan's fellow jurists decided where the assets would be moved to.

After enjoying a couple of after-dinner drinks with his friends as a means of celebrating their successful find, Paul excused himself. Walking the short distance back to the hotel, he found a quiet place to sit on one of the benches usually occupied by those in need of a smoke. Enjoying the pleasant evening as the last vestiges of the day's bright sky slowly gave way to darkness; Paul could not help feeling disgusted at the number of cigarette butts, half-smoked cigars, and burnt matches littering the ground around his feet. "This is just as bad as some of those intersections I've been stopped at. It's amazing how lazy and disrespectful people have become." Having never been a smoker, Paul had always been turned off by the disgusting, harmful habits of most smokers.

Refusing to allow the poor habits of others to ruin his evening, Paul placed a call to the person he had planned on speaking with earlier that afternoon. His call was answered on its third ring.

"Hello, Paul! How are things going?" Regan asked in a cordial tone as he answered his friend's call while seated in a comfortable chair inside his deceased employer's residence. Even with Simon Church and his wife no longer residing inside their Texas mansion, Regan was still putting in long days addressing a variety of business needs.

"Well, except for the hillside suddenly giving way today, things are going OK. We just had an enjoyable dinner . . . a small celebration of sorts, at a local restaurant. Everyone else is still enjoying another drink or two, but I hoofed it back to the hotel so we could have a talk." Paul said, updating his friend on the recent proceedings that had taken place.

"Please tell me no one was hurt." Regan replied, growing alarmed after learning of the injuries and damage that had taken place hours earlier.

"A few of Groski's men got banged up pretty badly, but they'll be OK. They've been sent home after being treated and released from the hospital. Several others were treated at the scene by some very dedicated EMTs and First Responders. Thank goodness for those people who still enjoy helping others when the need arises." Paul said, grateful for the timely response and care the local volunteer ambulance service and others had given to the injured workers. "Groski lost a bunch of equipment that was being used inside the caves, but stuff like that can be replaced. He's already contacted his insurance company to file a claim, but, for now, that's all I know about that issue."

"I'm already dealing with a host of other issues that's attracted the attention of far too many reporters. Please tell me this incident hasn't caused us to have to deal with any more attention."

"So far, so good. No one's contacted me." Paul replied.

Breathing a sigh of relief, Regan sought to learn the reason behind what had taken place. "I'm pleased to hear that. Any idea how this happened? Was this something we caused?"

"No . . . not at all," Paul replied, reassuring Regan the work being done had nothing to do with the day's near disaster. "Other than Mother Nature deciding it was time for another collapse to occur, I'm not sure what caused it. It's obvious there's been a collapse or two in the past, so I have to suspect it's a geological issue of some kind that keeps causing them to occur. I will tell you all of us, especially Groski, were scared to death for several minutes, but once everyone was accounted for we all felt much better. What we recovered inside the cave was certainly discussed over dinner, but not as much as what we endured during those terrifying few minutes while dodging rocks and other debris. I've witnessed some scary stuff during my career, but nothing beats what happened today."

"That must have been scary." Regan said, picturing the frantic few minutes Paul and the others had endured.

"Rest assured, it was all of that."

"What about the assets inside the cave? Were you able to save any of them?"

"Fortunately, the collapse took place roughly three hours after we located the bags of money and the crates of rifles Howard had hidden there. Unless you saw the collapse take place, you wouldn't believe how lucky we were to have just removed the last load of artifacts from the cave. I mean, it was literally that close. The men who had been removing everything had to run for the lives when the hill gave way. A few of them sustained some pretty serious cuts and bruises, but the only other casualties were a few pieces of equipment that were badly damaged; if not totally destroyed. Two of the crates and a bag of coins were also damaged, but not in the way that would reduce the value of any of their contents. They had been sitting inside the buckets of two front end loaders when they were hit by rocks. The crates were pretty-much destroyed after they were struck."

"*Wow!* That sounds like you folks had a rather interesting afternoon. I'm glad no one was hurt worse than they were."

For several minutes, Paul filled Regan in with the rest of the details that had taken place, including telling him of the current whereabouts of the precious artifacts. As they spoke, he also answered several questions Regan posed regarding the status of the project. Finished answering every question he was asked, Paul sought confirmation on the position Church's attorneys had taken regarding any artifacts his team recovered.

"Quite strangely, their position hasn't changed. They're just insistent that Mr. Church's estate be compensated for the entire cost of this operation. Of course, things may change once they learn what you've found, but they won't hear about it from me." Having been one of Simon Church's most loyal employees for several years, Regan knew the steps needed to minimize the number of people who knew about this particular project his employer had funded.

"Do they realize how valuable these artifacts are? They're likely worth millions." Paul said, still shocked by the position Simon Church's attorneys had taken, and by the manner in which Regan planned on keeping them in the dark.

"Early on they were adamant about seizing every last coin, rifle, and whatever else you found, but some recent events have caused them to lose interest in this project. From what little I've told them, I think they feel there's more to be made on settling Mr. Church's estate than there is in dealing with a few old coins and some outdated rifles. Mrs. Church's arrest has likely had something to do with this new position they've taken, but I can't speak with any certainty on that."

"So, you're not going to tell them about what we've found today?"

"Not unless I'm asked. Listen, I have plenty of friends who are attorneys, but most of the time I treat them like mushrooms when they ask questions concerning Mr. Church's business dealings. I'll be doing the same with his attorneys. Unless they come looking for answers, I'll keep them in the dark for as long as I can. If I have to, I'll feed them as much bullshit as I feel is necessary. Mr. Church would have wanted it handled that way."

"I'm sure you can be pretty persuasive when you want." Paul said, chuckling over Regan's comments regarding Simon Church's attorneys. "But if they were so hot to seize whatever we found, something must have caused them to change the position they had taken. Was it the negative publicity surrounding Mr. Church's murder or was it because of the talks you've had with them? Or was it something else? I find it hard to believe they're going to walk away before knowing how much money is likely going to be on the table once the artifacts have been appraised."

"I'd like to think they changed their position after I raised a few points for them to consider, especially the long expensive legal fight that might occur if they didn't focus all of their attention on settling his estate. Mrs. Church's arrest and the fact that Mr. Church had never owned any of the assets may have had something to do with it, but I also believe they decided there was little chance of winning a protracted court battle when the artifacts were found on property owned by someone else. The fact that the property owner has already deeded her land to someone as powerful as the state of South Carolina likely influenced their decision as well. In this case, it's an elderly woman who has deeded her property to not only the state where the Civil War first started, but to a respected university."

"I'm sure the fact that Mr. Church had never laid eyes on these artifacts played a huge role in the position they have taken." Paul added, knowing how some courts had previously ruled that historical treasures found on property owned by someone other than those either locating the artifacts or financing a search were the legal owners.

"It's safe to say that played a huge role in the reversal that's taken place."

"Even with that being said, I'm still shocked these piranhas aren't coming after these valuable artifacts. Don't get me wrong, I'm happy they're not, but I'm very surprised by the turn of events that have taken place." Paul said, knowing Simon Church's vast financial empire could have easily sustained a prolonged legal battle for several years.

"Paul, a few minutes ago you asked if something else had caused Mr. Church's attorneys to change their position. What did you mean by that?" Regan asked.

Not sure if this was the proper time to bring this up or not, Paul hesitated a few moments before answering Regan's question. "I just wanted to know if some other outside influence caused them to change their position on who the rightful owner was."

"What other influences would there be?" Regan asked, trying his best to hide the latest troubles facing Simon Church's estate. As he planned on doing with the attorneys he was dealing with, Regan had been less than forthcoming with some of the issues and problems surrounding his late employer's wife.

"Maybe a writer by the name of Greg Masterson and a retired cop turned private investigator by the name of Martha Kowalski."

Hearing the names Paul mentioned caused Regan to gasp as hard as he would have if he had been punched in the stomach. With the wind knocked out of him, for a few brief moments he struggled to catch his breath. "I'm not sure who those people are," Regan said, his voice thrown off as he fought to regain his composure. Gasping for air, Regan realized he had underestimated Paul's abilities.

Snickering over Regan's last comment, Paul told the person Simon Church had trusted even more than his own wife bits of what he knew. He started by setting Regan straight.

"Robert, let's agree to one thing. From the day we first met I've considered you to be a pretty straight shooter, so let's cut the bullshit. First of all, you know who both of those people are. Masterson is a writer based in North Carolina. Some of his articles about the Civil War have graced the covers of a number of influential magazines and newspapers. What you need to realize is he's someone who excels at digging at the facts when he believes something stinks. He's someone you'd rather have on your side, not the other way around. Got it?"

"Yes. I got it." Regan said, embarrassed over the conversation now taking place. He now realized the project Paul had been hired for had taken on a whole new twist; it was becoming more than just a search for Civil War treasure.

"As far as Kowalski goes, I'm fairly certain you know her as well. From what she's told me, I'm pretty sure you two have shared at least two phone conversations. In fact, both of those conversations took place over the past few days. If I have to, I can tell you the exact times they occurred."

"You've talked to her?" Regan asked, bewildered by the fact that Paul not only knew Kowalski, but also knew about their recent conversations.

"Yes, and so have you. Martha's a former cop from Albuquerque, New Mexico. We got to know each other last year when we worked a case together. The people who worked for her at APD tagged her with a special nickname. That nickname, Special K, should be a warning to you that she's not someone you want to piss off. After she retired, I referred her to a friend of mine who owns one of the largest security firms in the country. When he hired her, it wasn't to fill any quotas for how many minorities . . . or females, he has working for him. Special K was hired because she's a relentless SOB who doesn't leave any stones unturned when she's working an investigation. If she's contacted you, then she's working on something fairly significant."

"Not that this matters, but how is someone with the last name of Kowalski considered a minority?" Regan asked, believing the person he had spoken with was of Polish ancestry. It was not a heritage he associated as having a minority designation.

"Her father settled in Albuquerque after moving to the United States from Poland. Along with a few family members, he arrived here in the early 1940s just as the problems in Europe were beginning to intensify. A few years later he married this gal he had gotten to know at work. Martha's mother was born in Mexico, but came to the states when she was an infant. I've met her parents on a few occasions, they're great folks."

"I'm sure they are." Regan acknowledged, his voice reflecting the anguish he was feeling over the issues confronting him, and for being less than honest with someone he had come to trust.

"Would you like my help?" Paul asked, sensing not only the stress his friend was experiencing, but the new problem he was dealing with. It was one that involved a whole new set of legal implications.

"I'm sorry about trying to bullshit you when I said I didn't know who Masterson and Kowalski were. I'm just caught in the middle of a huge shitstorm and didn't know how to respond. I'm worried about Mr. Church's reputation taking another big hit."

"The hell with Mr. Church. He's turned out to be someone totally different than the person you thought he was, so he doesn't deserve your loyalty. He's dead. Who cares what people say about him. What you need to worry about is keeping Kowalski from twisting your ass in a vise any more than she already has."

"Yeah, I suppose you're right."

Ignoring Regan's naïve response, Paul told his troubled friend how it was going to be. "Let me ask you one question, but before you give me your answer I want you to know one thing. If I think you're lying, you can forget I exist. Tell me the truth, and I'll do my best to keep you out of trouble."

"What's the question?" Regan asked, realizing he needed Paul's help due to the increasing number of issues he was being confronted with. What he did not realize was that those issues were about to become even bigger.

"Did you know about any of this? By that I mean, did you know Simon Church, one of the richest people in the country, if not the world, was paying people to steal historical artifacts from private collections here in the United States?"

"I . . . I had my suspicions, but I could never prove he was directly involved in anything like that." Regan's voice quivered as he answered Paul's questions.

"Tell me about these suspicions?" Paul demanded, frustrated over Regan's weak response. "I thought you were the one who helped him acquire most of the artifacts in his collection. Didn't you tell me you were the one who saw the invoices and paid the bills whenever he acquired something new?"

"Yes, that was one of my responsibilities. I thought I was on top of everything, but four or five years ago Mr. Church showed me this Gatling gun we've been talking about. Like I've told you, I first saw it a few days after he took possession of it. He told me he obtained this weapon after verifying it had actually been used by the Union Army. Based on its serial number, and likely from information given to him by one of his contacts, he determined it had been used during the last two years of the war. Later, when I asked him about the invoice so I could document the method of payment and then log the Gatling gun into our inventory, he told me it had been paid for from an account that only he had access to. The strange thing was, I never knew about that account. That's one of the things which caused me to become suspicious of his dealings. I mean, if he trusted me to monitor all of his other accounts, then why wasn't I told about this one? Based on some later conversations between us, I had a pretty-good feeling the gun came with no paperwork vouching for its authenticity. I've tried on several occasions to locate any documents related to this purchase, but I've never been able to find any."

"You didn't think that was unusual?"

"Of course I did, but he was my boss. He was one of the world's richest men, so I knew he had the funds to pay for it. Before this, I had no reason to question any of his purchases. At least I didn't until I read an article several months later about a Gatling gun being stolen from a private collection in Ohio."

Regan's comment caused Paul to realize he had read the same article. As he tried recalling some of the details contained inside the article, Paul asked an important question. "What caused you to think Church may have had a hand in stealing the gun?"

"You're going to think this is very weird, but the owner of this Gatling gun was someone Mr. Church knew fairly well. He has a collection of Civil War artifacts that rivals the one Mr. Church has put together. Both collections are very impressive."

"*Wait* . . . your boss stole this gun from someone he knew?" Paul asked, stunned by this latest revelation.

"Wealthy collectors like Mr. Church are often invited to parties which serve as fundraisers for a variety of needs related to the Civil War . . . one is so historic battlefield property can be saved from being plowed under by real estate developers. Mr. Church would generally attend four or five of these fundraisers every year. At each one he would always make a generous donation to whatever cause was seeking his help. After returning home from one of these events, Mr. Church told me in no uncertain terms how jealous he was that this acquaintance owned a Gatling gun and he didn't."

Hearing that, Paul asked his next question. It was very similar to the one he had already asked. "Do you want my help or are you going to handle this problem on your own?"

"What do you propose?" Regan asked, afraid of being dragged even further into the controversy surrounding his late employer's death.

"Answer two more questions for me and I'll let you know if I'm coming down there to help you. Is Mr. Church's private collection, including the Gatling gun, still intact?"

"Yes, it is."

"Do you have any suspicions about Captain Howard's wooden chest being among the artifacts Mr. Church has obtained by ill-gotten gains?"

"No, not at all," Regan answered confidently. "That piece I know he purchased fair and square as I have the invoice from the auction house on file here at the house. I was the signer on the check as well. I know for sure that piece was paid for fair and square."

"One last question. Once the Gatling gun arrived at his house, how did Mr. Church not think that any of his fellow collectors wouldn't put two and two together? If these wealthy Civil War friends of his are collectors of rare pieces like it seems your late employer was, once they saw it wouldn't they have asked a bunch of questions about where it had come from? Pieces that rare just don't show up; they're either purchased from an auction house specializing in military goods or, like in this case, they've been stolen. If these friends are as passionate about their collections as Mr. Church was, they would have inspected the Gatling gun for a serial number or any unusual markings. How would a respected businessman like Mr. Church have explained a stolen Gatling gun being found in his collection?"

"That's the other issue which raised my suspicions. Unlike almost every other object he's purchased, the Gatling gun was never put on display inside the mansion. It's one of the best pieces in his collection and outside of me and his wife, I don't believe anyone else has ever seen it."

"Do you know if Mrs. Church has any idea how her husband obtained the Gatling gun?" Paul asked, trying to gauge the level of detail Mrs. Church knew about her husband's collection.

On the other end of the phone, Regan broke out laughing. "Mrs. Church wouldn't know the difference between a Gatling gun and a bazooka. The only names she cares about are Christian Dior, Giorgio Armani, Gucci, and several others. She's never shown any interest in her husband's collection. I'm quite confident she's also had no interest in learning where any of the pieces had come from."

"Where was the Gatling gun being kept then? Was it kept in some private study or office that only your boss had access to?"

"Good guess. Mr. Church has a private study that's off-limits to almost everyone. In the time I've been working for him, I've only been inside this particular study on two or three occasions. The rest of the staff, especially the maids and others who do the housecleaning, has never set foot in there. That's where the Gatling gun is right now. By placing it inside his study, he knew he had control over who saw it and who didn't."

"As I've told you before, I don't guess on matters like this. It was just a logical response as I knew your boss wouldn't allow his staff or anyone else to see the gun without his consent. If I'm as good as some people believe, I'll also tell you it was probably delivered in the middle of the night when there weren't many people around to see what was taking place."

"From a conversation I had with Mr. Church several days after the gun arrived, he told me it had been delivered around two a.m. on a Sunday morning." Regan replied, confirming Paul's suspicions. "Outside of Mr. Church, the driver and his helper were the only ones around. I can't prove this, but they're probably the same ones who stole it. As for me, I knew very little about this purchase until I spoke to Mr. Church about that invoice I've already mentioned."

"Any idea on who they were?" Paul asked, referring to the men responsible for stealing the Gatling gun.

"No idea whatsoever. When I asked how it had been delivered, Mr. Church explained that he had paid a couple of guys to have it delivered and set up in his study. He never identified them by name; he simply told me they were friends of a friend who had done odd jobs for him in the past. He also told me he had paid them in cash as they had done him a favor. I could tell he didn't want me asking too many questions, so I didn't pursue the matter any further."

"Had your boss ever paid cash for any other artifacts?" Paul asked, growing even more suspicious of how Church had conducted this purchase.

"No, never. He always insisted on having a paper trail for every artifact he purchased."

"What about hiring some guys to deliver one of his purchases during the middle of the night? Did he ever pay them or anyone else in cash?"

"Never. That's why this purchase stood out. He never did business that way as it was his policy that either he or the person who sold him an artifact would always arrange for a reputable moving firm to deliver the goods. Like I just said, there's a paper trail for almost every other purchase; especially for the more expensive artifacts in his collection."

"Any idea what the Gatling gun cost him?"

"Mr. Church told me he spent fifty thousand dollars, but I think he paid a lot more than that. These antique guns are not only very rare, but in the condition this one's in I believe he paid close to one hundred thousand dollars. That's not for the gun, mind you; that's what he paid those guys to steal it and to buy their silence. Whoever he paid, I'm guessing they were compensated very well for fulfilling one of his needs."

After taking in what Regan had told him, Paul told his friend what he wanted done. "Send a plane to pick me up tomorrow morning at Charleston International. You can text me the particulars once you've worked them out. In the meantime, I'll call Masterson and Kowalski to do some damage control. Set aside some time to meet with me after I arrive. I'll be staying at the mansion, so find a comfortable place for me to sleep."

"OK, thanks for the help. I appreciate you taking the time to help me out. I'll see you when your flight arrives as it will give us some time to talk." Regan replied warily. "Are you planning on conducting an inventory of the artifacts in Mr. Church's collection?"

"Absolutely, that's the first thing we'll be addressing. We're doing that tomorrow, so find someone to help us. The day after I'm feeding you to that SOB I mentioned before, but before I do I expect you to have all the documentation ready for this inventory we'll be conducting. Kowalski doesn't like it when someone's story can't be supported by either eyewitnesses or the proper documentation, so if you can provide her with the necessary paperwork for the artifacts in Mr. Church's collection that's going to reduce the number of bites she's going to be taking out of your ass. Invoices, copies of checks, Bills of Sale . . . have it all ready. If we can't prove you weren't involved in any of these shenanigans like your boss was, she's going to make you wish you had never met Simon Church."

"Shit!"

After telling Regan it was in his best interest to meet with him and Kowalski without any attorneys being present, Paul went back to join his friends for one last drink.

It would be the last drink he would enjoy for several days.

57

Four hours after being delivered to Dallas/Fort Worth International Airport in one of Simon Church's private jets, with Regan's assistance Paul started the process of identifying what artifacts inside the elaborate estate had been rightfully purchased.

With the help of one of Regan's assistants, a young female in her late twenties who two days earlier had updated a series of spreadsheets related to the artifacts in her late employer's collection, the tedious task of locating, identifying, and tagging each object began. Armed with separate spreadsheets which not only cross-referenced much of the same information, such as where, when, and whom the artifacts had been purchased from, their plan was to assign each piece a sequential number and to identify its current location. While most were on display inside the Church mansion, some of the lesser expensive pieces were either stored or displayed inside the nearby outbuildings. As Paul had hoped, the spreadsheets also listed the amount each artifact had been purchased for and its current market value.

Using the spreadsheets as they methodically moved from room to room and floor to floor inside the main house, while slow and tedious, the process went as smoothly as expected. After finishing inside the mansion, including Simon Church's private study, the inventory continued inside the handful of outbuildings.

Three hours later, while pleased by what they had accomplished, as they finished jotting down their last few notes Paul made one comment about the amount of time it had taken to complete the inventory. While the process of marrying each artifact in Church's collection to the proper documents had been completed without encountering any significant difficulties, his comment reflected how much time the process would have taken without the detailed spreadsheets.

"Robert, whose idea was it to create these spreadsheets," Paul asked, holding onto his copy as he carefully inspected the wooden chest Captain Howard had once owned. It was the same artifact that caused Regan to come meet with him two months earlier. Exquisitely crafted shortly after the start of the war, the chest was the one object in Church's collection that Paul appreciated the most. It was something Regan took notice of.

"I have to give credit where credit is due," Regan replied, smiling at his assistant, Rory Culhane. Sitting on a simple wooden bench which had been purchased at an auction several years earlier, Culhane's light complexion quickly turned as red as her shoulder length hair. Quiet, reserved, and overly shy, Culhane, while appreciating the recognition she was being given, preferred the anonymity her position usually afforded. A member of a large Irish-American family, she had been Regan's assistant for the past three years.

Impressed by her organizational skills, Paul smiled as he turned to face Culhane. Pointing to where Regan was sitting, he said,

"As this guy will vouch for, I usually don't guess when it comes to important matters I'm working on. However, for this particular occasion I'll make an exception. I'm guessing either library science or information management; possibly a combination of both. Am I right?"

"Actually it's both, Mr. Waring." Culhane answered, somewhat surprised by Paul's question. Having known the stranger standing next to her for less than an afternoon, she was amazed he had correctly guessed what her field of study had been at the University of Texas. "My degree is from the University of Texas at Austin. I'm not sure why, but someone supplied Mr. Church with my name just before I received my master's degree. Much to my surprise, a week after I graduated I started working here. Later, when Mr. Regan's duties were expanded to include every aspect of Mr. Church's remarkable collection, I started working for him. To say I'm blessed, well, that's an understatement, for sure."

"Are you familiar with the work of Shiyali Ramamrita Ranganathan?" Paul asked, testing Culhane's knowledge.

"You know about him?" Culhane asked, sliding forward on the bench she was sitting on as Regan shot his guest a surprised look.

"Not every cop sits around drinking coffee and eating donuts all day." Paul replied, joking about the stereotypical meal many police officers are accused of eating on a daily basis.

"He's passed away, but Ranganathan is considered one of the giants in library science. His contributions not only occurred in India, but across the entire world. I hate to admit this, but I'm . . . I'm not sure if I'm more impressed by the fact that you've heard of him or that you pronounced his name correctly." As she sat there, a wide smile broke out on Culhane's face.

As they compared notes on the inventory they had just completed, Culhane quickly figured out that of the three hundred and fourteen Civil War artifacts Simon Church had acquired, only eleven were found to have no traces of any form of documentation. After checking all of their records, as well as each of the laptops they were working with, neither Culhane nor Regan could locate any form of documentation of how or where the eleven pieces had been purchased. Much to Regan's surprise, four were ones he had never seen. Like the Gatling gun, each had been located in Church's private study.

Of the eleven unique artifacts, seven had been stamped or engraved with markings from either the Confederate or Union armies. Several, including the Gatling gun, were firearms. Obsessed with his collection, Church had even gone as far as having brass plates made up for the artifacts found inside his private study. Placed on rich black walnut frames, the plaques identified where the firearms and other objects had been made, what battle they had been used in, and, for three of the artifacts, they identified the names of their original owners. Among those found with no paperwork were two diaries owned by soldiers who had served in General Robert E. Lee's Army of Northern Virginia, a badly torn uniform once worn by an unknown Union sergeant during the fighting that had taken place at Gettysburg, a canteen still stained with its owner's blood after being pierced by two Minie balls, and a telegram bearing the handwritten initials of President Abraham Lincoln. It was one of several sent by Lincoln to General Ulysses S. Grant in the days leading up to Grant's meeting with Lee at Appomattox Court House.

"Are you sure you've never seen these artifacts before?" Paul asked, watching intently as Regan and his assistant checked their records for at least the third time.

"No, I haven't. With the exception of the Gatling gun and maybe one or two others, I have *never* seen those artifacts; nor can I ever recall Mr. Church even mentioning them during the course of our many conversations. The record keeping system I had in place before Miss Culhane computerized them was pretty darn good, so if my files don't have any notes or records of those artifacts ever being purchased then only Mr. Church would have known how much he paid for them and where they had been purchased. We've checked the files several times today, so I'm confident I've *never* received any receipts, invoices, letters, or cancelled checks for those artifacts you're referring to. The same holds true for all eleven pieces; if there are no records of them being purchased, then only Mr. Church would have known the answers to how and when they arrived here." As a way of convincing Paul he had not received any form of documentation for the artifacts in question, Regan had put a strong emphasis on one word he had spoken. That same word had been used twice.

"So what's that suggest?" Paul asked, anxiously waiting to see the type of expressions that appeared on the faces of the two people sitting less than six feet away.

Fumbling for the right words while staring at Culhane for some form of support, Regan, at first, tried remaining loyal to his former employer. "I guess it means Mr. Church must have handled those transactions by himself, or he must have . . ."

"Must have what?" Paul demanded.

"Obtained them by some other means." Culhane tearfully uttered, saying the words Regan could not bring himself to say.

"That sound about right?" Knowing the intense grilling Regan would have to endure the next day, Paul wanted him to acknowledge the words Culhane had just spoken.

"I guess so. These artifacts we're struggling to find the paperwork for, they're all pretty unique in one way or another. I doubt anyone gave them to Mr. Church. When it came to gifts or trinkets related to the Civil War, he liked to say some of those gifts were ones he never considered valuable enough to be included in his collection as no one gave away anything Lincoln, Lee, or Grant ever touched. The kinds of gifts he often declined were objects the everyday soldier would have used; like minie balls and bayonets. He already has a number of those objects in his collection, so he stopped accepting gifts the everyday soldier would have used. Most people would cherish any kind of gift given to them from the war, but not Mr. Church. He only purchased those that were unique or expensive; mostly because someone famous had used them . . . or, in some cases, because of the person who had invented them. They were the artifacts that piqued his interest."

"Or stole." Paul said, taking exception to one of the ways Regan described how his employer had taken ownership of several artifacts.

"Correct; or stole," conceded Regan.

<u>58</u>

Electing to meet with Martha Kowalski privately the following afternoon in a small second floor conference room inside an outbuilding next to the Church mansion, Paul sought to find the answers to several questions. While doing so, he hoped to do his best at performing damage control on Regan's behalf.

Sitting down next to a small glass table after exchanging a friendly greeting with someone he had not seen in several months, Paul began the conversation by speaking to her about her new job. "Martha, I'm pleased to hear your new career is going well. I spoke to Roland not too long ago, and he's very pleased by your performance so far. I wish you the best." The owner of Road Dog Services, Roland Farrell, was someone Paul had become friendly with after meeting him during a previous investigation. It was an investigation they both had vested interests in. Highly rated by several companies similar to the Better Business Bureau, Farrell's security firm was one of the most respected privately-owned firms in the United States.

"I had a nice talk with Mr. Farrell yesterday myself. In fact, he mentioned the two of you had recently enjoyed a couple of long-distance talks with each other." Having only recently started working for Farrell, Kowalski was reluctant to address him by his first name. "I'm still in shock over how quickly I left my job in Albuquerque, but I couldn't pass up his offer. The salary and benefit package I was presented with was not only extremely generous and more than I ever would have expected, but coupled with my retirement package from APD I should be able to retire for good after a few more years of hard work. As you know, opportunities like this don't come along too often for people like you and me." Kowalski smiled as she thought of the generous three-year contract she had recently signed with Road Dog Services. Besides a salary increase that was close to three times what she had been making with the Albuquerque Police Department, her contract included several incentives that were easily obtainable. Meeting them would add a small five-figure bonus to her annual salary.

"So how did you end up in the middle of this mess involving stolen Civil War artifacts?" Paul asked, anxious to learn if what Kowalski was about to tell him would match the news Farrell had recently told him.

"The collectors of some of these missing artifacts are all people with expensive homes, rich lifestyles, and more money in the bank than you and I could count. After being disappointed by the efforts of their local police departments in recovering their stolen property, they reached out to Mr. Farrell. They did so as they each believed their alarm systems had failed to prevent the thefts from occurring. Soon after that, I was asked to look into these alleged thefts. As you probably expect, I conducted the same due diligence every investigator would have conducted; well, at least the good ones like you and me." Kowalski joked, before adding another comment. "I have to admit, these victims are some pretty heavy hitters in both the business and political communities. Mr. Farrell asked me to look into these thefts as a good part of his business involves keeping his clients satisfied. These particular clients, people you and I would have referred to as victims in our past lives, are folks whose business he doesn't want to lose. He's stressed to me several times how important it is to keep them happy."

"That was nice of you to refer to them as *alleged* thefts."

"I only used that word out of respect to you, Paul. It was not directed towards any activities Simon Church or Robert Regan may have participated in."

"Thank you." Paul said, raising a glass of water he poured for himself as a sign of appreciation. "Whether this is on or off-the-record doesn't really matter, but my opinion of Simon Church has changed dramatically since I've learned about his role in these alleged thefts. With that being said, there's one thing you need to know; while Simon Church may be guilty, Regan never had a hand in any of these artifacts being stolen."

"You sure about that?" Kowalski asked, removing a yellow legal pad and a folder stuffed full of notes from her valise. Based on an earlier comment about having known Regan for only a short amount of time, she was surprised Paul had that much faith in someone he barely knew.

"You know me well enough to know that I wouldn't be telling you something like that if I hadn't conducted my own due diligence." Over the next few minutes, Paul explained the steps he had taken to investigate the backgrounds of the two men he was working for. What he told Kowalski excluded several key points.

While anticipating Paul had spent time looking into the allegations that had been raised, his comments caused Kowalski to stiffen for a brief moment after learning of the steps he had taken. Knowing how Paul operated, she knew his past career would not allow him to have offered such a strong supportive statement without thoroughly investigating the backgrounds of her two suspects. As she processed the information she was told, and how it was directly connected to the complex investigation she was conducting, it was clear Paul had looked into much of the same information, and maybe even more. It caused Kowalski to wonder what else her friend knew about the other players caught up in her investigation.

"I'm sure you didn't tell me about these rich clients of yours for any other reason than to mention this due diligence you've conducted. In case you've forgotten, let me remind you of one thing. I really don't care how rich these people are that you're representing. That means nothing to me. I'm more interested in hearing why you believe Regan is caught up in all of this, so when you explain your theory on his *alleged* involvement I hope you have more to offer than some weak *guilt through association* connection." Paul said defensively, emphasizing several words as he began to defend Regan against Kowalski's implied allegations.

Ignoring the sudden change in her friend's voice, Kowalski teased Paul with bits of information she had uncovered. "The first two thefts occurred in Ohio and Illinois. Besides being homes whose owners had hosted elaborate fundraisers attended by Simon Church in the recent past, they were homes protected by expensive state-of-the-art alarm systems."

"Ones designed and installed by computer-savvy people employed by your new boss, no doubt."

"No doubt." Kowalski admitted.

"And?"

"After the thefts occurred, as part of my investigation I've made sure these systems were inspected for any problems. Malfunctions may be a better word, but the end result showed both had been compromised electronically."

"Had the cops checked to see if these systems had been functioning correctly?" Paul asked, hoping the responding detectives had been experienced enough to have seen to it that the alarm systems had been tested for signs of being compromised.

"Outside of a couple of visual inspections of each of the alarm panels, I'm afraid nothing else was done. I'm not defending these cops, but these alarm systems are pretty sophisticated; they wouldn't have had a clue if the systems were functioning correctly or not. However, if it had been me investigating any of these thefts, I would have had the owner test the system on his end and then I would have had the alarm company run a systems check to make sure everything was working like it had been designed. That's a pretty basic step any cop should have taken when initiating an investigation like the ones I'm referring to."

"Good answer," Paul said before moving on to his next question. "How had the systems been compromised?"

"When the first two thefts occurred both owners had been away on business, but being techies they periodically checked their alarm systems using their smartphones. Each time they checked, their systems showed no signs of trouble. None, that is, until the last time one of the owners checked his system. By then, the thefts had already occurred."

"I'm sure it was something to do with the motion detectors and cameras that were tied into those systems." Paul said in response to the problems that had been detected.

"Correct." Kowalski replied, not surprised Paul had correctly identified one of the problems she was looking into. "Each of these thefts occurred late at night when the homeowners' children were sleeping. Quite conveniently, they also occurred when the homeowners were either away on business or, on one occasion, away on some fancy vacation at a place I can't even spell. It appears whoever stole these pricey artifacts, and in one situation a rather heavy one, remotely disabled the motion detectors and the cameras before even stepping foot on any of the properties. It wasn't until Mr. Farrell's engineers tested the systems for the third time that they figured out how each of them had been compromised."

"How could those kids not . . ."

Replying to Paul's comment, Kowalski cut him off before he was able to ask how it had been possible for the heavy Gatling gun to be stolen without the homeowner's children being woken up. "The Gatling gun, just like the other missing artifacts, wasn't on display inside this particular home. Just like this place that's owned by Mr. and Mrs. Church . . . well, I guess it's just Mrs. Church now," Kowalski said, correcting herself due to Simon Church's recent death. "The estates owned by these victims I'm working with all have outbuildings like the one we're sitting in. In the case involving the Gatling gun, it was on display in a building roughly fifty yards away from where the victim's children were sleeping. Next to their heated swimming pool is a pretty fancy structure the owner and his family refer to as their pool house. Just in case you're interested, besides being equipped with a kitchen that's far nicer than anything you and your wife have ever owned, this pool house also has a recreation room that's furnished with every toy you'd expect some rich SOB and his wife would have to keep their guests entertained. It also includes two full baths and a couple of bedrooms; both of which are only slightly smaller than your average convenience store. That's where this Gatling gun was stolen from. On the second floor of this *smaller* four thousand square foot pool house the owner has several of his Civil War artifacts on display inside his so-called man cave. You should see this place; it's a lot swankier than almost every other home I've been in."

"Gatling guns aren't the lightest things to steal, so I'm thinking this so-called pool house must have been built into the side of a hill." Paul said, visualizing the possible layouts of where this heavy weapon had been stolen from. "That would have allowed whoever stole it to push it out a set of wide doors instead of having to move it down a flight or two of stairs. If they had done it that way, this house . . . and maybe the Gatling gun itself, would have likely sustained a fair amount of damage."

"That's exactly how they moved it out of the house. Because it was designed to accommodate the surrounding terrain, the pool house is tiered. Each floor not only has its own separate entrance, but its own driveway. Both tie into the main driveway at different spots. The entrance on the first floor is near the pool and patio area. The entrance to the second floor is located near the rear of the house. Just inside that entrance is a rather fancy elevator; it services the two main floors, as well as the basement. The security system inside this pool house is just as sophisticated as the one inside the main house. Recessed sensors, digital cameras supported by infrared lights, a separate connection from the main system that's tied into one of Mr. Farrell's monitoring stations . . . you name it, each system has it."

"What about the property around these estates? Did you find anything unusual?"

"In the case involving the stolen Gatling gun, as you might expect the victim had spent a ton of money having the grounds professionally landscaped. Even if his children had been awake, it's doubtful they would have seen anyone stealing anything due to the extensive plantings between the main house and the pool house. The grounds are stunning; they're straight out of *Better Homes & Gardens*."

"Were there any signs of forced entry or attempts to compromise the locks at these locations?" Paul asked, believing he already knew the answer to his question.

"Only amateurs smash windows and doors to gain entry; whoever was involved in these thefts were professionals. As you've just hinted, all of the exterior doors were tied into the security systems. The homes had been entered after the alarm systems had been compromised electronically."

"Sounds like whoever's behind these thefts knew what they were doing."

"They certainly did." Kowalski admitted.

"Is there anything else you think I should know?" Paul asked, more impressed by how the security systems had been compromised than he was in Kowalski's description of the property owned by one of her clients.

"At one of the other homes, the cops found a set of tire tracks but the impressions weren't deep enough for them to cast. I have copies of the photos that were taken, but I suspect the truck or van that was used was either stolen or rented; either way the vague description the cops came up with could fit a thousand different vehicles. At this point, no one's positive what kind of vehicle the bad guys used to haul the loot away in."

"Go figure." Paul said sarcastically. "I'm waiting for you to tell me more about these security systems, but seeing that each of these thefts involves at least two components being defeated it sounds like you're dealing with someone on the inside. Whoever it is, I wouldn't be surprised to learn that he or she has likely received a thick envelope stuffed full of dead presidents for their help in arranging these thefts. It's also quite possible this person is someone who feels their talents aren't being recognized enough."

"You are freaking amazing!" Kowalski said, setting down her pad and pen after listening to her friend discuss a few of the issues she and her associates had spent several days piecing together regarding the recent thefts. "Do you have anything else you care to share with me? Like maybe the bad guys' names?"

"I'm waiting for you to tell me who the bad guys are." Paul replied, smiling over Kowalski's comment. "I expect you're operating under the premise that someone other than Simon Church committed the actual thefts and the rest of the dirty work. Has anyone come up with any suspects as yet?"

"I'm working on that as we speak." Kowalski's vague response told Paul she and the detectives working the investigations had not yet identified any of the individuals responsible for committing the thefts.

"In layman's terms, tell me about these alarm systems."

"There's not much to tell. As I've already mentioned, a couple of the systems were very sophisticated. They both had all the bells and whistles that come with a system than complex. The others were regular run-of-the-mill types found in many expensive homes across the country. Don't get me wrong, none of them are cheap; they're all far better the ones advertised on television. All of them were designed by Mr. Farrell's engineers. They were built to meet the specific needs of each of his clients."

"When you say a couple of systems, just how many do you mean? The way you described it on the phone I was under the assumption that you were only working with three victims."

"Actually, it's seven. We've determined that our victims have had a total of eleven artifacts stolen from their homes." Kowalski replied as she briefly scanned a list containing the victims she was working with and the artifacts they were missing. While remaining quiet, the number of stolen artifacts immediately attracted Paul's attention.

"Sounds like one of Roland's employees may have started a side business by selling some of the company's secrets. Are you looking into that possibility?" Paul asked, detecting an obvious connection between the recent thefts and the security problems that had been encountered.

"Three of the cops I'm working with are addressing that concern as we speak. They've already started focusing their attention on two particular individuals after LexisNexis checks revealed some concerns with their bank accounts." Kowalski replied, referring to an electronic search she had conducted based on information supplied by a private provider.

Before addressing the findings of the unofficial inventory he, Regan, and Rory Culhane had conducted, Paul asked one last question. "Have you heard of a similar investigation, if that's the right word to use, being conducted by a writer by the name of Greg Masterson?"

"Yes, I've heard of him. In fact, he's called me twice over the past few days. Do you know him?" Kowalski asked as she jotted down a thought which needed to be followed up on.

"Not well, but I know him. We've talked, mostly on the phone, regarding several issues of mutual interest." Paul replied, thinking back to the first time he and Masterson had met. "We met a few years ago when I was searching for another part of the Confederate treasury. He's a damn good writer. From reading a few of his articles, I'm convinced he's pretty good at getting to the bottom of any historical controversy he's researching. You might give a thought to staying in touch with him, especially when it concerns some of these stolen artifacts. Once you get to know him, he's a very good source of information."

"I'll do that," Kowalski said, gesturing to show her appreciation for the point Paul had raised.

"Do you have any idea how much Simon Church paid these people to steal the Gatling gun or any of the other artifacts?" Paul asked, knowing this was a figure Regan had only guessed at and not identified.

"No, I don't. I was hoping you or Regan could provide me with that information."

"Let's make sure we ask him that question." Paul said, deciding against telling Kowalski the amount of money Regan believed his boss had paid for the services of those who had stolen the Gatling gun.

As the two seasoned investigators discussed the results of Paul's inspection of Simon Church's collection, Kowalski scribbled several notes down in her notebook. Then, knowing how Paul valued his integrity, she began to accept what he had told her regarding Regan's lack of involvement in any of the thefts. Believing what her friend had told her to be the truth, she thought, "I'll just spot check a few of the artifacts in Church's collection to make sure everything jives with what he's told me. He wouldn't dare lie to me; it would ruin his reputation."

After a few brief moments of silence, Kowalski asked her next set of questions. They were ones Paul had anticipated being asked. "So, what you're telling me is Regan and this assistant of his . . . this Rory lady you keep referring to, they're claiming they never saw those artifacts you discovered in Church's study? The ones with no paperwork, correct?"

"Besides the Gatling gun which Regan has seen on only three or four occasions, that's what they're telling me. I can't speak for Ms. Culhane . . . who has likely never told a lie in her entire life, but I'm confident Regan is telling the truth. If he was lying, I would have figured that out by now. If you feel you have to interview them, then go do it. I expect you to cover all the bases; so does your boss. Doing your job is not going to upset me. Drag them both over the coals if you have to."

As she searched through her folder for two photographs she wanted Paul to see, Kowalski smiled over her friend's suggestion. "I'll do what I have to do to make sure I'm comfortable with their version of the events, but I'll be gentle. However, if I determine Regan's taking me down the wrong path, his ass is mine. I'll drag his sorry ass over the coals more than once."

"I'll enjoy watching that." Paul said, well-aware of his friend's propensity for treating suspects very harshly. As he spoke, Paul looked at the first photograph he had been handed.

"Ever see that?" Kowalski asked.

"Maybe, but I can't see any markings on it to confirm it's the one in Simon's collection."

"Here, look at this photograph. You can easily see the identification markings the manufacturer put on the Gatling gun. If you take an even closer look, you can see someone scratched their initials on this piece right here. My guess is they likely belonged to a Union soldier who had been assigned to the crew responsible for this gun." As Kowalski spoke, she pointed to a section of the weapon's carriage where the initials were located.

While the identification markings he was looking at meant little to Paul as he had not memorized the ones on the Gatling gun inside Church's study, the initials N.W. were ones he noticed during the inventory process. The same two initials were distinctly visible on the antique weapon sitting inside Church's private study.

"Martha, at the moment some of these markings mean nothing to me. They may or may not be the ones on the Gatling gun inside Simon Church's study. We'll look at them when I show you this piece later today. While this is hardly enough evidence to prove he's responsible for what's taken place, I'll admit it's pretty convincing."

"Are these same initials on the Gatling gun we're going to be looking at? If they are, are they located in the same place as the ones in the photo?"

"Yes and yes."

As the two friends wound down their meeting, briefly referring to her notes Kowalski asked Paul what he knew about two other valuable artifacts that had been stolen prior to the recent thefts. Both had been owned by a prominent Civil War reenactor residing in Georgia. "What about a pair of binoculars and a rather elaborate Civil War-era sword. Do you recall seeing either of those artifacts when you were conducting your inventory?" As she finished asking her question, Kowalski handed Paul a set of photographs containing the two artifacts in question.

Studying the photographs, Paul recalled seeing the stolen binoculars featured in a magazine article a Civil War magazine had run nearly a year earlier. "These binoculars . . . are they the same ones Admiral David Farragut supposedly wore during the Battle of Mobile Bay? If they're the ones he was wearing, he likely had them hanging around his neck when he uttered his famous order, *'Damn the torpedoes, full speed ahead!'* This is going back a year or so, but I believe they were featured in a magazine article I enjoyed reading. If these are the ones I'm referring to, I seem to recall they had been appraised for a great deal of money."

"Those are the ones Farragut was supposedly wearing." Kowalski replied, confirming the name of one of the United States Navy's earliest heroes. As she had been on more than one occasion, Kowalski was again stunned by Paul's recollection of the details contained inside an article he had read months earlier.

After studying the photographs, Paul advised Kowalski that neither artifact had been among those in Church's collection. "Feel free to ask Regan about them, but as far as I know they're not here. As for the sword, I've never seen it."

As Paul escorted Kowalski towards the Church residence, she paused to ask him one important question. "If Simon Church is as wealthy as everyone says he is, why didn't he simply purchase the Gatling gun and the other items in question? Why pay someone to steal them for you?"

"I guess you're not the investigator I thought you were." Paul said, staring emotionless at his friend.

"What's that mean?"

"Tell me what you've learned about Simon Church."

"Well, besides what everyone else knows about one of the world's richest men, I can tell you there's one thing that troubles me. When I started digging into his background, I learned he's never been arrested or even accused of doing anything wrong. The issue that's confusing to me is that I know nothing about his younger years. I've found a wealth of information about him from the time he was in his mid-twenties to the time of his death, but before that I couldn't find hide nor hare of him; nada, nothing. I've looked everywhere for information on Mr. Church, but I haven't been able to find his birth certificate, the place where he was born, where he went to high school, if he had any service time, or anything like that."

"Shouldn't that suggest something to you?"

"Like what?"

"That maybe Simon Church wasn't always known as Simon Church."

"What!" Kowalski shrieked, stunned by what Paul had suggested.

"Everything I've learned about my late employer still needs to be corroborated, but I'm fairly certain what I'm about to tell you is pretty accurate. Just before he died, I began to have some concerns over a few comments Church had made. Those were comments I either overheard when he was speaking with Regan or ones he made to me during two phone conversations. I grew even more suspicious after I learned he had been murdered; that's what caused me to start digging into his past. To do so, I called in some favors from a few friends."

"I . . . I never expected anything like this." Kowalski said, her eyes growing wider as she waited for Paul to continue.

"Me either."

"What friends are you referring to?" Kowalski asked, ready to jot down the names of those who had supplied Paul with information.

"Most of them are personal and professional friends; some are ex-military and some are contacts I was lucky enough to have made during my law enforcement career. Three others are cops I've recently spoken with. You can give it your best, but you won't learn any of their names from me."

"So, if you won't reveal their identities, what did they tell you about Mr. Church's background? Was it anything mysterious?"

"Around the time he was seventeen, Church's father passed away unexpectedly. That forced him to quit school to help put food on the table for him and his mother. From what I've been able to learn, that's when he started working in the oil business doing whatever job was available. What I also learned was Simon apparently fell in with a bunch of roughnecks who were a few years older than some of his other friends. One of my sources told me these young men apparently weren't the perfect role models for someone trying to find his way in life."

"You're kidding me, right? Please tell me that you're making this tale of BS up as you go?" Kowalski pleaded, unsure if Paul was telling her the truth or not.

"I'm not fabricating any of this. Like I said, this information still needs to be corroborated, but I believe it's all true. Most of this information has come from friends who I've relied on in the past. Every piece of information they've ever supplied me with has always been spot on."

"I'm still not sure about all of this, but go ahead, I'm all ears."

"Well, without going into everything I've learned about him, Simon apparently became a pretty good thief. It's a pretty safe bet those roughnecks he was hanging around with taught him more than just the oil business. That's how he developed the taste for some of the finer things in life, things he couldn't afford on the money he was making."

"So, what you're telling me is that Mr. Church has a checkered past?"

"Yes, and that's being very polite. From the people I've spoken with, Simon apparently was quite the con artist in his early twenties. From a variety of different means, including a series of thefts he allegedly committed, Simon separated cars, large amounts of cash, jewelry, and much more from their rightful owners. Some of what he stole was fenced in order to put food on the table, but I was also told he kept a lot of cash for himself. Some of that cash that kept coming in was later used to buy his first oil rig." Pausing for a brief moment, Paul added, "You've heard the story about his first oil rig, right?"

"Uh, no . . ."

"Maybe it was beginner's luck, but Simon's first oil rig struck a vein that produced so much liquid gold that he and his partner were millionaires in less than a month. From that point on, he just kept striking it rich wherever he planted his next few rigs. After a steady flow of cash had been coming in for a few years, that's when he started investing in everything else he thought he could make a few bucks on."

"Was he ever arrested for any of those alleged crimes?" Kowalski asked as she jotted down the information Paul was telling her.

"Not that I was told, but supposedly the cops had suspected he and his friends were responsible for a series of unsolved crimes. Their suspicions grew when the guys Simon had been hanging around with started robbing paymasters every couple of weeks. You have to remember this all occurred when Texas was still considered the Old West. At that time the oil business was just starting to hit it big in this part of the country. There were a few people making some big money back then, but times were still pretty rough."

"I'm still having a hard time believing all of this." Kowalski admitted. "Is one of your sources that partner Simon started out with?"

"Maybe," Paul replied, neither denying nor confirming Kowalski's suspicion. "The reason you're having a hard time believing all of this is based on the type of person Simon Church was at the time of his death. Your feelings are understandable, and I might have felt the same way if our roles were reversed, but you have to start thinking outside the box. These days everyone who knew this rich old man thought of him as a pretty generous and charitable individual, but that's not who he was during his younger days. In some ways, like the matter involving the Gatling gun, he hadn't shaken parts of his past."

"So what caused him to change his name? That's if he really did."

"During a rather long drunken spree where several robberies were committed over the course of ten days or so, two of the people Simon had been running with shot and killed a paymaster after he refused to give up the payroll he was carrying. From what I was told, Simon had nothing to do with the actual murder except for being in the wrong place at the wrong time."

"Wow!" Kowalski uttered, growing more and more surprised by what she was hearing.

"Well, that must have scared Simon a great deal as he supposedly cut ties with these buddies of his and disappeared for a few years. When he resurfaced back in Texas, he had already changed his name from Simon Bucknell to what it was at the time of his death. During the time of his disappearance from the Texas oil fields, his mother passed away. Shortly after her death, Simon got the urge to get back into the oil business so he resurfaced with a new identity in a different part of the state."

"So that's why I wasn't able to learn anything about him during his younger years."

"The other reason you haven't been able to learn much is because Simon was born out of wedlock. Back then kids born to single mothers weren't usually born in a hospital. I'm not sure where he was born, but it wasn't in a hospital where his birth would have been recorded as a matter of record. Shortly after his birth, his mother and father finally married. Even though their marriage was now official, his father was in and out of his life for long periods. While he resented his father for not being there while he was growing up, by all accounts Simon and his mother were very close."

"Freaking amazing!" Kowalski said, scribbling away in her notebook.

"Yep. Weird story, huh?"

"Think so?" The sarcasm in her voice was obvious as Kowalski shook her head over the information she had learned. "But why was he never arrested for any of those crimes?"

"For a variety of reasons, I guess. As time passed some people disappeared, some died, evidence was lost, and, as you might expect, he probably paid a few people off. The system back then wasn't as sophisticated as it is today. Relocating in a different part of the state under a new name also helped to conceal his identity. When you have time, start digging into the story about that paymaster who was murdered by Simon's friends. Years later, his wife received a rather large check from an anonymous source. I think you're smart enough to figure out who sent her that check."

Realizing who Paul had been referring to, Kowalski's next comment let him know how she felt about Simon Church. "I'm guessing it came from someone with a guilty conscience. That same bastard likely used some of his profits from his oil business to try and fill the void her husband's death had caused. I'm sure he felt obligated to try and make up for his past mistakes, and for never telling the authorities who was responsible for the paymaster's death."

"Sounds about right." Paul replied, agreeing with Kowalski's summation.

"So, despite a few missteps along the way, Simon Bucknell quietly became a highly successful businessman. Successful, that is, under the name of Simon Church."

"Yep."

"Even though he became richer than he ever expected, it sounds as if the troubled side of Simon Bucknell still existed. Despite his billions, his former lifestyle caused him to orchestrate the thefts of these expensive Civil War artifacts."

"According to what Regan and a few others have told me, if Simon Church could get something for free he was a happy guy. So, yes, I would say that's why he was still involved in some shady deals. Whether it was a meal that someone else paid for or a priceless artifact dating back to the Civil War, that's just how he was wired. If he could get something for free, he took it; no questions asked. But, on the other hand, he was also the type of person who would routinely give away a sizeable amount of money to some charity to help fund whatever project they were working on." Talking about some of Church's deep-seated personality concerns caused Paul to think of one other person with even more problems. They were ones he would soon discuss with Robert Regan.

"Does anyone else know about this?" Kowalski asked.

"Not yet, but once I'm able to corroborate the details I've shared with you, I'll probably sit down with Greg Masterson so he can write a story about the complex life of the person the world had come to know as Simon Church."

"That's a good thought, but not until I finish my investigation, OK?"

"You let me know when the time is right." Paul said, nodding his head as a way of showing Kowalski he would honor her request.

As they resumed their walk towards the Church residence, Paul and Kowalski continued to chat about Simon Church's checkered past.

59

After being shown a sampling of the artifacts in Simon Church's collection, Kowalski prepared to interview Robert Regan and his assistant, Rory Culhane. An experienced investigator with years of conducting interviews with those accused of murder, drug smuggling, sexual assaults, and a host of other heinous crimes, the time she was planning on spending with Regan and his assistant would be far less stressful than those occasions she had spent with some of New Mexico's most-hardened criminals. While Regan was still considered a person of interest in the theft of several expensive artifacts, with her powers of arrest no longer part of her current job Kowalski had little concern about violating any of his rights or legal protections.

For close to two hours, armed with photographs and paperwork related to each of the thefts, Kowalski grilled Regan, and later Culhane, on how Church had managed to obtain the stolen artifacts for his collection. As she conducted her interviews, Paul sat off to the side quietly taking in the proceedings. As the give-and-take took place during Regan's interview, Paul found it difficult to decide which of his friends he was pulling for. While he admired Kowalski's interview and interrogation skills, and her tenacity in trying to get to the bottom of who had helped Simon Church fulfill his need for a Gatling gun, he also appreciated how Regan conducted himself during this intense grilling.

As his interview wound to a close, Kowalski felt satisfied Regan had answered her questions truthfully and to the best of his ability. However, being the suspicious ex-cop she was, Kowalski finished the interview by asking the one question most suspects dreaded being asked. Guilty or innocent, the inference that went with it was terrifying.

"Mr. Regan, would you be willing to submit to a polygraph examination?"

"A lie detector test?" Regan asked, briefly casting a glance in Paul's direction before returning his attention to the person who had asked the question.

"Yes." Kowalski replied, her voice showing little emotion. "I feel the need to address a few points that we discussed this afternoon."

"So, you're telling me you don't believe me?" Regan asked rather defensively, his face turning red from the anger he was feeling. The position he took pleased the person who had sat through his interview. "I . . . I friggin' answered every one of your questions as honestly as I could. I'm not an investigator like you and Paul, but I could tell from your facial expressions that some of the information I was telling you were things you hadn't heard before. If there's anything amiss here as it relates to Mr. Church's collection, I knew nothing about it. He's dead, but if anyone's guilty it's him . . . not me."

"Robert, do Martha a favor, take the test. You'll be doing yourself a favor as well, especially when the polygraph operator lets her know you've been telling the truth. Passing the test will prove you've had nothing to do with any of this." Paul explained, doing his best to calm Regan down.

"How's that going to help me? I know I'm innocent, but even if I pass this test is that going to satisfy this friend of yours or, for that matter, the courts or anyone else investigating these thefts?" The disturbing tone of his voice reflected the anger Regan felt in still being thought of as one of Simon Church's accomplices.

Understanding Regan's concern, after thinking of the responses he had given to the many questions she had asked, Kowalski attempted to reduce the amount of stress her suspect was dealing with. "If you agree to take this examination, I'll agree to eliminate you as a person of interest. That's, of course, as long as the polygraph examiner tells me you haven't been deceptive in any of your responses."

"What about the other investigators looking into these thefts? Are they still going to be looking at me as a suspect?"

"If I eliminate you, I'll make sure they know that. I can't promise they'll do the same, but I expect they will. There's no sense chasing someone who's not guilty, right?"

After several minutes of some additional give-and-take between Regan and Kowalski, as the last few issues were ironed out between them on the other side of the room Regan watched as Paul carefully inspected one of Simon Church's favorite pieces.

Bending over as he studied the artifact from several different angles, Paul marveled at the excellent condition it had remained in since the time of the Civil War. The object he was fascinated with was the wooden chest that had once been owned by Captain Howard.

60

Walking Kowalski to her vehicle as the sun slowly sank out of sight behind the Church estate; Paul asked his friend what her gut feelings were as to how Regan had answered her questions. With plenty of experience under her belt and a host of other work already completed regarding the stolen artifacts, he knew she had already started to form her opinion on whether Regan had been telling the truth.

"As of right now, I'm comfortable clearing Culhane of any wrongdoing. It's obvious she was never directly involved in any of the purchases or thefts. Her role simply involved some record-keeping and research; she's clean. My instincts are also telling me your buddy Regan was being truthful on all accounts. The concern I still have has nothing to do with his veracity; it has to do with how Church took possession of those stolen artifacts without Regan knowing about them. That's why I raised the issue about the polygraph."

"I thought I was pretty clear when I addressed those concerns earlier. You do remember us discussing the issues involving the Gatling gun, don't you?" Paul asked, wondering if Kowalski had lost track of that part of the day's proceedings.

"Of course I do."

"If that's the case, then you should understand Simon Church had apparently arranged for the Gatling gun and the other objects to be delivered here when Regan was away from the mansion. Those stolen artifacts we've located were all found in his private study. Regan testified . . . sorry, Regan explained that he seldom visited Church's private study. So, if you accept what I'm telling you, you should have your polygraph examiner ask Regan a question or two about his whereabouts on certain dates. That should clear up any lingering concerns you still have."

"Maybe, but . . ."

"Martha, does your boss know everything you do? Or, for that matter, do you know everything your boss does?" Paul's eyebrows arched slightly as he asked his two questions.

"No, but I don't . . ."

"You've already answered my question, Martha." Paul said abruptly, cutting off his friend's response. "Just as your boss, or even your boyfriend, doesn't know what you're doing every minute of the day, the same holds true for Regan. You can't hold him responsible for any criminal activity his boss was engaged in; nor can you hold him responsible if his boss decided to place a few artifacts, stolen or otherwise, inside his own home. No matter how those artifacts were obtained, it wasn't Regan's responsibility to inspect Church's home for stolen property."

"I suppose you're right," Kowalski replied, sighing as she acknowledged the points Paul had raised. "But I'm still scheduling that polygraph. For his sake, he had better not be lying to either of us because I'll fry his ass if he has."

Kowalski's comments caused Paul to enjoy a good laugh.

"As you like to say, I've done my due diligence for now. All that's left for me to do is to look into Simon *Bucknell's* background and somehow connect him to these thefts that have taken place. For what it's worth, I appreciate you asking Regan to look into that special account Church used to purchase those stolen artifacts. I seem to think you agree with me on this, but it galls me to see these artifacts on display here."

"No problem, I'm happy to help. If Regan told you he'd get back to you, he will. He's a very honest guy. When it comes to Mr. Church displaying those artifacts inside his mansion; you're correct, that's pretty arrogant."

"I doubt any of the victims will ever read the report I'll be submitting as they'll just be happy to get their expensive toys back. The only people who will give a damn about it are the cops and insurance investigators I've been working with." Still unsure of what name Simon Church had actually gone by when he was younger, Kowalski had put a heavy emphasis on the name Bucknell when she pronounced it moments earlier.

"I'm sure your boss will want to read it. The more details you mention, the more he'll charge his clients for the work you've performed."

"After I email it to the cops I've been working with, I'll let them decide on how they want to proceed. Even though Simon Church is dead, I'm sure you'll see a handful of departments or, for that matter, the Texas Rangers show up here with a few pieces of paper giving them the authority to search this big-ass mansion that Church called home."

"I guess I should tell Regan to be expecting them." Paul said, not wanting his friend to be caught off guard by the next wave of investigators arriving at his doorstep.

"That's probably a good idea. While you're doing that, you might warn him about doing anything stupid. He seems like a decent guy, so I have no interest in hearing about him getting into any trouble. You and I both know what we saw inside the mansion." While not a Civil War buff, Kowalski knew the artifacts in Simon Church's collection, from both their age and their place in the American Civil War, were close to being priceless.

"Don't worry, Martha, nothing is going to disappear. I can't speak for any of the attorneys he's been dealing with, but Regan isn't that dumb."

******

Three days later, four Texas Rangers, accompanied by a small team of evidence technicians, quietly executed two search warrants at the Church mansion and the nearby outbuildings. Unlike a host of other warrants they had executed at the homes and cribs of suspected drug dealers, there had been no need for battering rams or flash bang grenades. Robert Regan simply opened the front door and allowed the Rangers access to the palatial home of his deceased boss.

Several hours later, with the stolen artifacts secured in the rear of a large box truck, the Rangers and their staff left the Church home. Unlike others they had searched for narcotics, weapons, and other forms of contraband, they left the Church residence in the same condition they found it. As they left, the Rangers thanked Regan for his cooperation.

It was just as Paul had advised his friend to act.

61

Over the course of the following six months, with the gold and silver coins and other artifacts now in the possession of the United States Marshal's Service, Paul patiently waited to learn their fate. As he and his friends waited for the court's decision to be released, Paul learned the crates of unused, but badly rusted rifles had been quietly transported to Quantico, Virginia.

Realizing the historical significance of these weapons, Judge Morgan had used his influence to make arrangements for the forensic examiners and firearm specialists employed by the Federal Bureau of Investigation to document the condition of each of the Civil War rifles.

Two months later, with each rifle photographed from several different angles, and with each serial number captured and entered into a database of historical weapons, the rifles were sent to one of the nation's largest gun manufacturers in an attempt to restore them to their original condition.

As the rifles were being restored, the United States District Court for the Eastern District of South Carolina held hearings to decide who the legal owner of the gold and silver now was. They were hearings Paul attended on several occasions.

While called upon on two occasions to offer testimony on how he had come to be involved with the remarkable discovery of the lost artifacts, Paul spent much of his free time enjoying his boat or playing golf with Bobby Ray and Chick. It was how retirement life was supposed to be spent.

Fascinated by the rich antebellum way of life lingering in the shells of old plantations still visible along the banks of the Waccamaw River, Paul's boat, the *Donna Lynn*, allowed him the escape he needed from the long hours spent searching for part of the Confederate treasury. With his friends joining him whenever Donna was at work or back home visiting their grandchildren, Paul did his best at pushing aside thoughts of his latest adventure.

But then, as the long hot days of summer slowly turned cooler with each passing month, the court finally reached a decision on how the assets would be disbursed. It was a decision which included several recommendations Paul had offered during his testimony. Unbeknownst to him, a good friend had lent his own support to those thoughts and recommendations.

As he waited for the details of the disbursement to be made public, Paul received an invitation to have lunch with Steve Alcott at his restaurant, *The Grumpy Sailor*. Not letting on what he had planned, Steve extended a similar invitation to a mutual friend.

"Hello, Steve," Paul said warmly as he unzipped the wet windbreaker he was wearing. Thirty minutes earlier, the day's pleasant start had been interrupted by several short bursts of heavy rain. While the midday weather report had mentioned the inconvenient interruptions were expected to move out of the area by late afternoon, Paul's jacket managed to become soaking wet during his brief walk across the restaurant's parking lot. As the two friends shook hands, Paul smiled after noticing Steve's other guest. "If I had known we were going to be having company, I would have dressed for the occasion. Afternoon, Your Honor, it's good to see you."

Standing up from where he was seated, Judge Howard Nathan Morgan returned his friend's smile with one of his own as they shook hands. Like Paul, Morgan had followed Steve's orders by dressing casually for the afternoon.

"What brings you up here, Judge? Perhaps some good news?" Paul asked, noticing the brief smile Morgan exchanged with the person who had invited them to lunch.

"Steve called the other day and suggested we have lunch together sometime this week. I initially declined his generous offer as I no longer enjoy driving significant distances, but then I learned one of my law clerks was coming up this way to visit her mother for the day. Once I learned she was planning on returning home after her visit, I hitched a ride with her. So, here we are."

Noticing Steve's table had been set for four guests, Paul scanned the area around the dining room for signs of Morgan's clerk. While two decorative columns and a portable lattice partition blocked part of his view, Paul saw no one he believed to be Morgan's clerk.

"She's not here, Paul." Morgan said after noticing his friend's visual hunt for their missing lunch companion. "Steve was kind enough to extend an invitation for her to join us, but at the last minute she elected to have lunch with her mother at the nursing home where she's staying. Her mother is receiving some physical therapy for a few weeks; the poor gal fell recently and broke her hip." Clutching Steve's wrist, Morgan winked at Paul before tossing a friendly insult in the direction of their host. "I guess the Salisbury steak that's being served at that facility must be better than anything we're about to eat."

"Maybe you'll still have time to join them!" Steve replied, quickly responding to his friend's good-humored insult as he raised the day's first cocktail. While never one to drink to excess, on most afternoons Steve spread out three or four martinis over the course of several hours. Today would be no different.

"Touché!" Morgan said, clinking glasses with his friend. Not having to worry about driving later that afternoon, the jurist had ordered a double Jack and Coke to enjoy over lunch. Believing that if it was good enough for a federal judge it was good enough for him, Paul ordered the same drink. Outside of an occasional beer or two, the drink was one of Paul's favorites.

"So, that's why you're here, Your Honor. You found someone to drive you to and from this lunch we're about to share." Paul joked, trying to pry some additional information from Morgan.

"No, not entirely." Morgan replied, doing his best to suppress a smile that was already breaking out across the jurist's face. "I thought I'd come up here so I could share some good news with you. I've already shared some of it with Steve earlier in the week, but once he insisted on arranging lunch for the three of us I thought you should hear the details surrounding the disbursement before reading about it the newspaper. Two of the newspapers which service the greater Charleston area are running stories tomorrow regarding the court's decision."

Turning in his chair, Paul looked at Morgan for a few brief moments before setting down his drink. Sliding forward in his chair, he was anxious to hear how the court had decided to disburse the artifacts. Then, as he briefly glanced at Steve, he said, "I was told some type of a decision had been reached, but I wasn't sure if the disbursement part had been finalized."

"It has," Morgan replied, nodding his head affirmatively. "I received a call late yesterday afternoon advising me that the final few details had just been worked out. I believe the end result is a very favorable one which reflects several of your suggestions."

As Paul sat back in his chair after learning the court had finalized the various disbursements, a wide smile broke out across his face.

"Paul, before our friend here tells you what's been decided, you need to know Judge Morgan worked hard to make sure the appropriate people gave serious thought to your suggestions. He certainly didn't do anything unethical, at least that's my opinion, but he did meet with the judge who had the ultimate say in how those artifacts would be disbursed. In doing so, he made sure your concerns were addressed regarding any potential claims that might be filed on behalf of Simon Church's estate. I just thought you needed to know that." Finished speaking, Steve acknowledged Morgan's efforts by raising his glass as a sign of appreciation. Moments later, he drained the remaining cool liquid before ordering another round for the table.

"We all appreciate your help, Your Honor. Many Civil War enthusiasts will never know what you've done, but I'm confident they appreciate your efforts."

A brief smile crossed Morgan's face as he thanked Steve and Paul for their comments. "While so many states, and even the court system, seem to be in the midst of a quandary over what Civil War monuments are or are not offensive, the artifacts you have recently found have little involvement in that convoluted controversy. Just as I felt when I had the opportunity of witnessing the coins being recovered during your previous adventure, this newest find, of both the historical coins and rifles, was just as amazing. However, what really touched me was the recovery of the remains of several Civil War soldiers. I . . . I was deeply moved when I witnessed those bones from yesteryear being unearthed."

"I believe we all felt that way, Your Honor." Paul said, recalling the few pieces of human remains Morgan had seen recovered from the cave where Howard's men had perished.

Nodding his head, Morgan then continued. As he did, the jurist directed his remarks in Paul's direction. "In a war in which both sides were so diametrically opposed on a variety of different issues, your team found the remains of a small group of soldiers who had been led by someone that was a brave and compassionate person. Whether they volunteered for this assignment or not makes little difference, but those Confederate soldiers risked their lives to recover the remains of adversaries who had been brutally murdered. Sadly, that brave act ended up costing those young soldiers their lives. That, my friends, is what caused me to intervene in this matter. My interest is simply seeing those soldiers being laid to rest like so many others who fought in that terrible war."

Recalling how he and his team had worked to get the remains of other Civil War soldiers laid to rest in Arlington National Cemetery, Paul, genuinely touched by Morgan's comments, sought to reassure the jurist. "Your Honor, I believe we can make that happen for these soldiers. Just like Captain Francis and some of his men who perished during that same brutal war, my team and I will find a way to make sure Captain Howard's soldiers are buried with their brothers-in-arms." Unlike what had been done for Francis and his men, Howard would not be joining his men at Arlington National Cemetery. While his remains had been found shortly after he committed suicide, no one had taken the time to record the location where Howard's body had been buried.

For a few moments, the three friends sat quiet, lost in their own thoughts about how the Civil War had claimed so many lives as the nation came close to imploding. The quiet was soon broken when Steve brought up the issue they were meeting over. "So, tell us the specifics of the court's decision, Your Honor."

Waiting until their waitress finished setting down their meals, Judge Morgan then spoke on the various issues and disbursements the court had decided upon.

"Well, seeing that we were just speaking about the soldiers' remains, let's address that issue first." Glancing down at his plate of fried oysters, clams, and shrimp, one garnished with a heaping pile of French fries, Morgan dipped one of the fries in a small container of the restaurant's homemade ketchup before continuing. As before, the jurist directed most of his comments in Paul's direction. "The court has ordered you to work with the state archeologist to make sure the remains are properly buried. When you read the court's decision, you will see the court has no objection to anyone, whether it's by way of DNA testing or other means, trying to identify who these soldiers were. As long as this testing is done with reverence and within the next two years, the court has made it clear that outside of one other condition they will not be issuing any other directives regarding those remains."

"What's the other condition?" Paul asked before taking a sip of his drink.

"This condition involves how and where the remains are to be interred. Basically the decision states that unless one or more sets of remains are identified through some sort of testing or research, they are to be buried together in a military cemetery alongside other Confederate war veterans."

Ignoring his own lunch, Paul responded to Morgan's comments. "My team and I will be honored to be a part of that process, Your Honor."

While interested in what Morgan was telling them about the court's decision, Steve, whose own interest in the Civil War was dwarfed by that of his two friends, sat quietly enjoying his lunch. For Paul and Judge Morgan, the court's decision regarding this historic find took precedence over a meal they could enjoy at a later time. For now, both men paid little attention to the food sitting in front of them.

"I'll address the rifles next," Morgan said, refocusing his attention after slipping another French fry in his mouth. "In this matter, the court has followed, to some degree, one of Paul's previous recommendations. It was one made during the hearing I conducted in Charleston after your first discovery of part of the Confederate treasury. If you recall, you had suggested sharing the gold and silver you and your team found in North and South Carolina between several public entities; meaning most of the states that had banded together to form the Confederate States of America. That suggestion also included a recommendation for sharing some of it with the federal government; more specifically, with the National Park Service. Do you recall that presentation?"

"I do, Your Honor." Paul replied as he took the first bite of his steak sandwich. "I was very pleased the court agreed with my logic. I may have been the one who presented the thoughts my team and I came up with, but I'm smart enough to know that you had a hand in those disbursements taking place like they did."

Slipping another French fry in his mouth, Morgan said, "Well, I was thoroughly impressed by the logic behind your suggestions, and felt I couldn't ignore the opportunity there was to share some of that money with everyone involved. The same held true in this recent hearing I sat through. You presented a sound argument for each of the points that were being discussed; I just felt the need to follow up on your recommendations. That simply involved me taking the liberty of having a conversation with one of my colleagues. He's the one who was assigned this case, and who ultimately wrote the decision we're speaking about."

"And?" Paul asked.

"Based on the disbursements the court has ordered, it seems as if my skills as an arbitrator are still intact. This colleague of mine not only agreed with my recommendations on how the rifles should be dispersed and protected after they've been restored, but it seems he's closely followed the decision that was handed down from your previous adventure."

"I'm pleased to hear that, but I'm anxious to hear the specifics," Paul said, politely encouraging Judge Morgan to get to the gist of the court's ruling.

"Of the fifty-eight rifles that have been recovered, the court has ordered that each of the states, with Hawaii being the exception for some unknown reason, is to receive one rifle from this collection. The court has also ordered each of these rifles to be displayed in either a Civil War museum or one that honors the sacrifices made by the men and women who have served in the Armed Forces."

"What happens to them in the event any of these museums fail or go out of business? Would the rifles be sold or auctioned off?" Paul asked, concerned over the future of these historical artifacts.

"That's an excellent question. I'm pleased to say it's one the court had already taken into consideration. The simple answer is none of those rifles may be dealt with in such a manner. If such an occasion occurs as you have mentioned, the rifle that's been loaned to that museum would revert to the National Park Service. That branch of the federal government remains as the custodian of these weapons for perpetuity; the rifles are simply on loan to those museums." Morgan replied, addressing Paul's concern.

"So far, so good," Paul said, pleased by the conditions set by the court. "What about the others?"

"The others?" For a brief moment, this question confused the jurist as he believed Paul had been asking about a few additional public entities he had not been told about. Quickly recovering, Morgan said, "The remaining nine rifles are being given to the National Park Service, the FBI, the National Civil War Museum in Dauphin County, Pennsylvania, and the American Civil War Museum in Richmond. One of the rifles is still in pretty bad condition from sitting inside that cave for so many years. That's also going to the National Park Service for some additional TLC."

Nodding his head after learning how the court had ordered the rifles to be disbursed, Paul smiled as he glanced across the table at Steve. While not having any proof, he believed his friend had exerted some influence upon Judge Morgan. Shooting Steve a friendly wink, one Morgan failed to notice as he was too busy using his fork to spear two oysters, Paul said, "I believe the court has rendered a very sensible decision concerning those rifles." As always, even when it came to commenting on a decision reached by a United States District Court, Paul was not bashful about sharing his opinion.

Well ahead of his friends in how much of his lunch he had eaten, Steve paused for a moment to ask what the court had decided to do with the precious and valuable coins that had been found alongside the rifles.

"This decision pretty much follows the previous decision I've been referring to. Once the three court-appointed numismatists finished appraising the coins, they documented their findings in a report submitted to the court. As I believe many had hoped, the court elected to distribute equal shares of the coins to those states who had once been members of the Confederacy. The only real difference is that unlike the previous decision Texas was included in this disbursement." As he finished answering Steve's question, Morgan somehow managed to take the last bite of his lunch.

"Is the National Park Service included in this disbursement?" Paul asked. A huge supporter of the woefully underfunded park service, as well as an annual visitor to several national military parks, Paul hoped that branch of the federal government had been awarded a portion of the recovered funds.

"Yes, the National Park Service was awarded a generous portion." Morgan noted, apologizing for not mentioning the park service in his previous comments. Sitting at the table with his friends, the jurist recalled the passionate plea Paul had made years earlier on behalf of the National Park Service when a much larger pot of money was in the process of being disbursed.

Waiting until the wait staff had finished clearing the table; Steve asked a question regarding an issue involving the gold and silver coins. Like Paul, he expected Morgan to have offered much more information concerning the report submitted by the numismatists. Already excited by the good news they had learned, the two friends were anxious to hear what the coins had been appraised for. Turning in his chair to get a better look at Morgan, Steve asked, "What where the coins finally appraised for?"

Quiet for several moments, Morgan tried recalling the exact figure the numismatists had assigned to the coins. Deep in thought, his eyes nearly disappeared from view as they unconsciously rolled upwards inside his eyelids. Seeing this occur, Paul realized what was taking place. While never professing to be an expert in reading a person's body language, he knew enough to recognize Morgan's eye movements for what they were. The jurist was now trying to recall the exact amount mentioned in the court's ruling.

"I'm trying to recall what the figure was, but I . . . I just can't remember the exact amount. It was somewhere in the area of just over ten point three or ten point five, but . . ." Morgan's words drifted off as tried recalling what the appraisal had come in at.

"As in millions?" Steve asked, somewhat surprised by the amount he heard.

"I'm sorry, yes, that's correct. That's millions." Morgan replied, his focus still on trying to recall the exact amount of the appraisal. "As you might expect, the court is allocating most of the money to those states which once comprised the Confederacy. With Texas now in the mix, they'll be divvying up a few million dollars. Most of what's left has been designated for the National Park Service." While not completely sure of the amount of money being split between the states and the National Park Service, Morgan knew his breakdown was fairly close to what the court had ordered. For the sake of their conversation, it was close enough.

"Did the court order the coins to be sold, or are the states receiving the actual coins?" Paul asked.

"They're receiving the coins. The court is leaving it up to the states as to whether they retain them or sell them off. I have nothing to base this on, but with the economy in the shape it's in I wouldn't be surprised to see a number of states banding together and selling the coins off. While I'm totally against them being sold or auctioned off, if you think about it I guess this could be considered another form of a stimulus package for the states to enjoy." Then Morgan surprised his two lunch companions with one last statement. "For the most part, the balance of this money is being shared by the woman who owns the property where the caves were located and Mr. Groski, the person you hired to do the excavation work. The suggestion you made about him being compensated for the loss of some of his equipment was one the court heeded. For me personally, I was very pleased to learn Mr. Groski was not being overlooked when all of this money was being doled out."

"I'm very pleased to hear Phil is being taken care of. The settlement he reached with his insurance company didn't cover all of the costs associated with either repairing or replacing the equipment he lost, so whatever he receives should help make up the difference." Paul said, growing even happier over the disbursements the court had awarded. Jerking his thumb in Steve's direction as he looked at Morgan, Paul added, "What about this guy right here?"

"There's nothing to be concerned with, Paul, the court has compensated Steve for the money he contributed to your operation. It probably wasn't as much as he would have liked, but it was fair."

Patting his friend's hand, Steve thanked Morgan for looking out for him.

"Thanks for being so gracious, Steve." Morgan said, smiling at his longtime friend before addressing his other lunch companion. "Well, aren't you going to ask me?"

Caught by surprise, Paul's mind momentarily went blank. "I'm sorry, Your Honor. I'm missing the meaning behind your question."

Realizing Paul was at a loss, the jurist simply replied by stating, "About the gold and silver bars."

Pleased by how the court had addressed the disbursement of the rifles and the valuable coins, Paul had forgotten about the twenty-five gold and silver bars he and his team had recovered. Years earlier, Captain Howard had neatly stacked them inside the cave near the other artifacts. Somewhat embarrassed by his momentary lapse, Paul smiled as he addressed Morgan's earlier question. "OK, Your Honor, I'm asking. What about those bars?" The question caused Morgan and Steve to enjoy a good laugh. In moments, Paul joined them.

"That's the one issue that hasn't been completely resolved. The tentative plan is to distribute those items just as the other artifacts have been disbursed, but the final appraisal hasn't been completed. That process has not been as simple as it was with the other artifacts. Once it's complete, I'll have a better handle on how they're being disbursed. I expect to know more in another week to ten days."

"That sounds fair." Paul replied, still slightly embarrassed over forgetting about the valuable gold and silver bars.

Moving on, Steve raised a concern he and Paul had discussed days earlier. "It sounds as if the court wrote off Simon Church's estate when they were figuring out who should get what. My guess is the court wanted no part of that mess that's still taking place down in Texas." Steve's comment caused Paul to realize he had not thought of Church or, for that matter, his right-hand man, Robert Regan, for several days.

"A wise move, if you ask me." Morgan replied, watching as Steve took another sip of his martini. "But I'm pleased to let you know the court did award a small number of coins to someone else. It's nothing more than a token gesture, but it's one that's richly deserved."

"Who's that?" Paul asked, believing he had forgotten about something else besides the gold and silver bars.

"You, Mr. Waring." Morgan replied as a smile broke out across his face. "It took a little convincing, but when I had the opportunity to interject some of my thoughts on how the disbursement should take place I suggested you should receive some form of compensation for your time and expertise. After all, you're the one who is directly responsible for this discovery taking place. In the very near future, you'll be receiving a letter directing you to pick up this small allocation at the federal courthouse in Charleston. You're free to do anything you would like with them."

"Wow!" Paul said quietly, doing his best to suppress his emotions. "I didn't see this coming. I'm not expecting that my friends and I are ever going to be paid the fee Simon Church promised us, so this will help to ease that pain."

Hearing what Paul said about not expecting to be paid the balance of the money he had been promised, Morgan's legal skills kicked in as he settled back in his chair. "Paul, I recall you telling me you and your colleagues had each signed a Professional Services Agreement, isn't that correct?"

"Yes, sir. We each signed one. Mr. Church also signed every one of them. He even went as far as having one of his assistants sign each PSA as a witness. When that was done, Regan personally notarized them in front of us. Each agreement broke down Mr. Church's expectations, how long the agreement was valid for, the amount we were to be paid, and what our individual bonuses would be if we located the artifacts he believed had been hidden inside one of those caves. It also included a few other details, such as what expenses Mr. Church would be paying; things like hotel costs, meals, and so on."

"Did you and your friends receive a copy of these agreements?"

"Yes. In fact, and I don't recall why we did this, but we put them all in a large envelope after they had been signed. The envelope is under lock and key inside my safety deposit box. It hasn't been touched since I placed the agreements inside the box."

"While I would have to read these agreements in order to determine if they are enforceable or not, but from the sounds of it I would say they likely are. If you would like, I'll be happy to review them. I would also be pleased to contact a couple of lawyer friends who live in Texas if you and your friends are unable to convince Mr. Church's estate to compensate you for your efforts. The recovery of these valuable artifacts certainly makes it sound like you have honored the conditions set forth in those agreements."

With a great deal of information being presented to him in such a short amount of time, as someone who always liked settling issues at the lowest level, for the moment, Paul declined Morgan's offer of assistance. "Your Honor, I know I speak for my friends when I say we appreciate your generous offer. For now, let me see if I can convince Regan to honor those agreements without you or anyone else becoming involved. I've found him to be a pretty reasonable individual, so I'm sure he'll come through for us. He's been dealing with a bunch of issues related to Mr. Church's death and Mrs. Church's arrest, but I'll speak to him in a day or two about this matter. If I need your help, I know where to find you." Leaning to his right, Paul shook hands with someone he had come to respect a great deal.

"Paul, do you have any idea on what you're going to do with your share of the coins?" Steve asked before taking his first sip of coffee. Moments earlier, the wait staff had set down cups of hot coffee and a small tray of pastries in front of Steve and his guests.

"I'll probably share them with Bobby Ray, Chick, and Peter. They deserve something for all of their hard work."

"What about Regan? Do you plan on giving him a cut?"

"Maybe . . . maybe not. I'll give it some thought, but he's about to receive a healthy severance package from Church's attorneys. Maybe I'll slip him a coin or two, but we'll see. I'm more interested in seeing if he's going to honor the Personal Services

Agreements we signed. I'm anxious for Bobby Ray, Chick, and Peter to be compensated for the time and effort they invested in this project."

"What about you?" Steve asked.

"I'm doing okay, so I'm not so concerned about myself. Simon Church told me when I brought on the members of my team he would take care of them, so I expect Regan to honor that promise."

Smiling as he took his first bite of the mini-cheesecake he selected from the dessert tray, Paul savored its creamy taste. Made in the back of Steve's restaurant, the luscious dessert was good enough to be served in any fine New York City restaurant. Moments later, finished with the desserts he had sampled, Morgan added one last comment to the discussion taking place. "From what I've read in the papers the last two days, I doubt Regan needs a gold or silver coin to remind him of what's taken place. The story about Church's death seems to take on a new twist every time I pick up a newspaper."

62

Two days after meeting with Steve and Judge Morgan, Paul made the trip back to Moncks Corner. Unlike several of his recent trips to the small community, there was another purpose behind this visit.

Making his way up the long rough driveway, the thick cloud of dust stirred up by his truck gave notice to the property owner that she was about to have company. Two days of rain earlier in the week did little to keep the dirt driveway from announcing the pending arrival of visitors, both welcomed and those who were not.

"Morning, Mrs. DeWolfe," Paul said, waving to the person he had come to see. "It's a nice day for you to be sitting outside." Thirty minutes shy of the day's halfway point, the bright sunny morning was devoid of the recent humidity and high temperatures that had blanketed the area for the past few weeks.

"That it is," Mary DeWolfe replied, carefully watching her unexpected guest as he placed a small black bag on the floor of her porch next to the seat he was about to take. Nodding at the small rusty table next to her chair, Mary said, "Help yourself to some fresh lemonade. I made it this morning. It's just water, a little sugar, and some freshly squeezed lemons. It's not like that crap they sell in stores. Besides being overpriced, that store-bought stuff is far too sugary. Most of them drinks they sell cause my sugar to go haywire. The doc who's treating my diabetes doesn't like me drinking stuff produced in factories; that's why I make my own. Besides, mine's better for ya." As she finished bragging about her lemonade, Mary took a healthy swig from the glass sitting next to her.

"Thanks, I think I will," Paul said, pouring himself a tall glass of the cold beverage. Packed full of ice, the pitcher's cool contents immediately caused his glass to be covered in a thin layer of condensation. Moments later, as he raised his glass after taking his first sip, Paul paid his host a well-deserved compliment. "Tastes pretty good after a long ride."

"My lemonade tastes pretty good all the time." Mary said sternly, correcting her visitor's opinion of when her lemonade tasted good.

"I'm sure it does." Paul said, smiling over Mary's comment.

While she would never be accused of softening her opinion when it came to dealing with those who had been born north of the Mason – Dixon line, after several recent visits Mary had softened her stance when it came to Paul. Occasionally stopping in with updates as the caves were being excavated, the retired state trooper had made a favorable impression on the elderly woman. Despite his friendly visits, he had not completely won her over. At least, not until now, he hadn't.

"The last time ya come to see me ya told me your work at the caves was done. So, whatcha doing back here then? Did ya come back for one more look?" As she finished speaking, Mary fished two large chunks of lemon from her drink. A moment later, her normally sunken cheeks were puffed out from the sour fruit she had placed inside her mouth. The sight of her sitting there sucking on the chunks of lemon nearly caused Paul to burst out laughing.

"I'll probably make a quick stop over at the caves after I leave here, but the main reason I'm here is to see you."

"I doubt that! I don't have too many visitors these days, and I doubt you drove all the way down here to see me." To Paul's amazement, Mary had expressed her opinion regarding his visit while still sucking on the sour chunks of lemon. It was something he found quite amusing.

Pulling a single sheet of paper from his small bag, Paul handed it to Mary. "This is an email I received late yesterday afternoon. I thought you might like to read it. When you're done, read this article on the front page of the newspaper. It's right here, just below the fold." As he handed Mary the email, Paul pointed to the news article he wanted her to read. It was one of three articles prominently displayed on the front page of Charleston's daily newspaper, *The Post and Courier.*

Sipping her drink as she slowly read the email; Mary glanced suspiciously at her visitor as she set her glass down. "This really true?" She asked, leery of what she had just read.

"Keep reading, it gets even better." Paul replied as he nodded at the newspaper.

Ten minutes later and after several reads of the news article Paul had pointed out, Mary sat back in her chair as she whistled out loud. "This your doing, Yankee Boy?"

"Does it matter?"

"To me it does. I wouldn't have asked if it didn't." Finished sucking on the chunks of lemon, Mary fished them out of her mouth before tossing them off the side of her porch. Much to Paul's surprise, they landed next to several others Mary had previously disposed of in the same manner.

"A little, perhaps. Judge Morgan had more to do with it than I did, but I spoke my piece. I'm glad the court thought enough of my suggestion to add your name to the disbursement list." Sliding forward in his chair, Paul gently patted Mary on her left knee. "You deserve this and much more for allowing us to excavate those caves."

Bowing her head, Mary did her best at hiding the tears that were slowly streaming down her cheeks. It was as if years of hate were slowly dissipating. "I . . . I can't ever recall anyone doing something so thoughtful for me, especially some Yankee like you. I'm . . . I'm very grateful."

"You're welcome, Mrs. DeWolfe. Those coins the court awarded you should be delivered here in the very near future. Who knows, if it'll get me another glass of lemonade maybe I'll deliver them myself."

"I'd like that." Mary said, drying her eyes with the worn apron she always wore.

"Once they're delivered, you're free to keep them, give them away, or even sell them. They're pretty valuable considering their age and because of the two precious metals they're made from, but it's up to you to do what you want with them."

Wiping away her few lingering tears, Mary dismissed any thoughts of selling the precious coins. "The remains of them boys you found in one of the caves, some of them died protecting those coins y'all found. A couple of them died trying to do the right thing for them Yankee soldiers that had been murdered. Because of what them soldiers died for, I'd be insulting them if I tried selling those coins I'm about to get. Maybe I'll give a few to some museum, but I ain't selling what's left. That wouldn't be right."

"I suppose not," Paul replied, agreeing with the position Mary had taken.

Born and raised during a time when an education was not deemed to be as important as it is these days, Mary's values more than made up for the manner in which she spoke. Those same values reflected the proper upbringing she had received at an early age.

<u>63</u>

After leaving Mary's house and making a brief stop to inspect the area around the caves, Paul called Regan later that afternoon to advise him of the decision the court had handed down.

"That's good news, Paul. Based on what you've told me, that's a pretty equitable disbursement. I'm glad you called as I've been so busy down here I haven't had a moment to think about what you've been dealing with."

"Lawyers keeping you busy?" Paul asked as he thought about the host of issues Regan was likely dealing with since Simon Church had been found murdered.

"It's not just the attorneys; it's dealing with your friend, Martha Kowalski, and trying to accommodate all of her questions. I lost the entire afternoon yesterday going over the results of that freaking polygraph test. I'm glad it went as well as it did, but my afternoon could have been spent addressing a variety of other needs. I passed that test months ago, so when is all of this nonsense going to end?"

"Are you sure the polygraph examiner advised Kowalski that you had passed?" Paul asked.

"Yes, that took place weeks ago. Shortly after learning the results, Kowalski told me the examiner had determined that my answers were truthful. He told her there wasn't the slightest bit of deception in any of my responses."

"Good. I'm glad to hear that. She's probably just tying up a few loose ends involving her investigation. I'll give her a call and ask her to put an end to this."

"I'd appreciate you doing that. The other reason I'm so busy is because I'm still receiving ten to twelve calls a day from cops, insurance agents, private investigators, and auction houses asking about missing artifacts they're trying to locate. The number of emails I have to deal with on a daily basis is just as painful. I'm doing my best to limit the amount of time I spend on each of these interruptions, but many of them are chewing up significant amounts of my day."

"There aren't many things that try my patience more than having to spend time answering a host of meaningless questions that I've already answered far too many times. Believe me, I share your pain." From his efforts in recovering two significant portions of the missing Confederate treasury, Paul had spent many hours speaking with a growing number of reporters on the telephone. Most had asked the same series of questions several different ways.

"I can't prove this, but many of those emails I've been dealing with are probably from scam artists phishing for information. It seems the whole world believes Mr. Church was responsible for every artifact that's ever gone missing. I've even fielded a number of calls from a private investigator in Boston who's been trying to track down some missing artwork for the past ten years. I told him a week or two ago that Mr. Church wasn't an art collector, but the son of a bitch hasn't left me alone. In the past two days, he's called me three more times. Just before I hung up on him, I told him I'd be driving up there to kick his ass if he called me again."

"Tell me more about the scam artists." Paul said, not the least bit surprised that the situation Regan was dealing with had sunk to the level it had. "Are they threatening to expose Mr. Church's involvement in these thefts or are they threatening to create new problems unless you send a sizable check to some post office box in Nigeria?"

"Both, but you pretty much nailed it. They're a bunch of slimy no-good bastards." Regan answered, laughing over how Paul had phrased his last question.

"So, do you have any idea of how much money Mrs. Church had siphoned off before she killed him?"

Not anticipating any questions being brought up concerning Simon Church's finances caused Regan to be stunned by his friend's question. The investigation being conducted by the Texas Rangers had only recently determined that funds from several of Simon Church's accounts had been tampered with. "How did you . . ."

"Do you always answer a question with another question?" Paul asked, giving Regan little time to answer the question before asking his next one. "How much had she stolen?"

Still loyal to the person who had treated him like a son, Regan felt his anger towards Genevieve Church rising as he tried answering

Paul's question. While he had always been respectful in his dealings with Mrs. Church, he now hated her for what she had done.

"We're still working on the exact amount, but it's several million, at least. So far we've determined she's made several cash withdrawals from at least two accounts over the last two years. She's also written a number of checks for repairs or upgrades allegedly performed at each of their homes."

"As the saying goes, let me guess," Paul said, his voice going quiet for a few seconds before making his next statement. "I'll bet she even tried covering those checks by having someone write up a few bogus receipts. I'll even go a step further by saying those contractors probably never existed; nor did the repairs or upgrades."

"I know you like to brag that you don't guess when it comes to matters like this, but good guess. That's just what she had done. The newest problem Mrs. Church is facing is that every receipt or work order we've looked at had the same handwriting. When we compared them to the handwriting of one of Mrs. Church's closest friends, they all matched. As you might expect, when the Texas Rangers threatened to arrest her as one of Mrs. Church's accomplices, this so-called friend couldn't distance herself enough from the circumstances surrounding Mr. Church's murder. Because of what we've found, Mr. Church's attorneys have hired a team of forensic accountants to try and determine if she has hidden any of this money in accounts we aren't aware of. That's going to take some time, but it's being worked on."

"Good luck with that." The tone of Paul's sarcastic comment meant he realized Mrs. Church had likely hidden a considerable amount of her ill-gotten gains in offshore accounts or bit coins. "I'm assuming they had a prenup, correct?"

"Yes, they did. The majority of Mr. Church's assets had already been designated to assist several charities and other humanitarian causes by the time he and Mrs. Church were married, but with no children or grandchildren to take care of she stood to inherit the remainder of his estate. I know better than most people what the value of his estate was worth, so I'm comfortable saying she would have inherited a significant amount of cash, as well as his business holdings across the globe, stocks and bonds, and much more. Even if she had only converted half of it to cash, she still would have had trouble spending that amount of money, and that's taking into account her lavish lifestyle. Simply put, Mr. Church's holdings were not only diverse, they were huge."

"So what's the reason for poisoning him? Was it because she couldn't wait for him to die from natural causes or was it because she had other plans involving a younger lover?"

"It could have been for any number of reasons," Regan admitted, unaware of what the true motive had been behind Simon Church's murder. "If someone is lurking in the shadows, he hasn't surfaced. But that doesn't surprise me as Mrs. Church, well . . . let's just say she kept her private life private. She was pretty adept at ditching her security team for hours on end, so who knows where she went or who she was seeing. Those occasions pissed Mr. Church off for obvious reasons, and while he never said too much I know he was concerned over his wife's antics when she was out of contact with her security team."

"Remind me to never hire any of those guys," Paul said, shaking his head over the number of times Genevieve Church had successfully eluded her security team. "Most of the times she ditched her security detail, she was either shopping or out to lunch with her friends. How difficult could it have been to keep a set of eyes on her?"

"I'm with you on that. I suggested they be fired on more than one occasion, but Mr. Church wouldn't pull the trigger. He wanted her protected as much as possible."

Regan's brief description of Genevieve Church was somewhat similar to the opinion Paul had formed. "You know her far better than I do, but the couple of times I met her I wasn't impressed. I can't tell you what made me feel that way, but I thought she was a phony or a gold digger or something else along those lines. Maybe it was due to her age, but I was convinced there was another side of her than what she was letting people see. I know my wife felt the same way about Mrs. Church. She had a really bad feeling about her."

"Wow. That surprises me as Mrs. Church always did her best at leaving a favorable impression with everyone she met. It may have been contrived at times, but I've always thought she tried being sociable with most people she met. I know she sometimes irritated those close to her, but I can't say that was the case when she was meeting someone for the first time. In most cases, I believe she succeeded in being friendly, but with you and your wife I guess the impression wasn't as good." Regan said, surprised by the negative feelings Paul and Donna Waring had felt about Genevieve Church.

"She may have stood to inherit her husband's fortune, but I doubt she was sitting around as innocently as she led others to believe. Mr. Church had every right to be concerned about those occasions when she ditched her security team as someone her age and with her good looks wasn't going to be content lounging around the pool all day, especially when her husband was travelling as much as you say he did. I'm sure she belonged to several social groups frequented by some pretty rich people from across Texas. Even if she took part in those groups just to socialize, I'm sure she was tempted on several occasions to violate her wedding vows. And, I'm pretty confident her taste for nice clothes and fancy cars set her husband back a few dollars over the years. Who knows, maybe she murdered the old gent because she had already identified who her next husband was going to be. Out of curiosity, how much was Mr. Church giving her every month?"

"You seem to know quite a bit about Mrs. Church, Paul. What's caused you to make these assumptions?"

"I don't make assumptions, Robert. My previous career trained me to ask questions, and to look into *every* aspect of an investigation I was working. In this case, due to the fact that Mrs. Church had made me feel so uneasy when I first met her, I asked several of my former colleagues to obtain some answers to a few of my concerns. Because of those concerns, they've supplied me with some information from databases most cops can't access. I also reached out to them in an attempt to separate you from all of this nonsense. You may not realize this, but Mrs. Church has caused you to become tangled up in quite a mess."

"Thanks. I . . . appreciate the help." Regan mumbled, surprised over how much Paul had managed to learn about Genevieve Church in such a short period of time.

"After you told me she had been arrested, I had my friends start digging into her past. Were you aware, or better yet was Mr. Church aware that his wife had once gone by the name of Genevieve Ho?"

"What!" Regan said loudly, standing up from the comfortable chair he had been sitting in.

The tone of Regan's response told Paul his friend had never known that just like her rich husband, Genevieve Church had tried covering up her checkered past by assuming a different name.

"It took some doing, but these friends I have are paid to dig up as much information as they can on any issue thrown at them. Sometimes this information has been hidden behind some sophisticated firewalls that most folks can't crack, but these friends are some pretty savvy computer specialists. Just like the government and some of those Silicon Valley tech companies, these folks I reached out to can see and read everything there is on anyone's computer at any moment they want. Fortunately for us, Genevieve wasn't that sophisticated when it came to computers. What she was good at was documenting some of her past and current transgressions on a small laptop. One of the first interesting bits of information my friends came across were several suspicious entries she had saved. Each were related to the deaths of a former boyfriend and her first husband. By the way, if you're already thinking of her as a Black Widow, you're not too far off."

"This is all a bad dream, right?" Regan said, shocked over the news he was hearing.

"Afraid not. The fact that she wasn't prosecuted for her boyfriend's death or that the case involving the death of her first husband suddenly collapsed because some Texas judge was far more interested in seeing the balance of his bank account grow than he was in conducting a fair trial, doesn't mean she's not guilty. Each of those matters also involved two inexperienced prosecutors who were in over their heads. In case you haven't figured this out, the presiding judge in charge of the murder trial involving her first husband had been paid a bunch of money to dismiss the charges against her." After watching Regan's eye movements as his friend processed the information regarding the corrupt judge, Paul added another comment. "I'm sure you noticed I didn't use the word *allegedly* when I was referring to the payments that judge received."

"I did notice that. That must mean the bastard was paid off like you said. I'm guessing the money he received went a long way in influencing the outcome of Genevieve's trial."

Ignoring Regan's comment regarding the outcome of one of Genevieve's earlier trials, Paul's next statement identified the amount of money the judge had quietly accepted. "Seems to me that if I accepted a bribe to make sure the outcome of a trial went the way someone wanted it to, I'd be expecting a lot more than the eighty thousand dollars this judge took. I wouldn't risk ruining my career for that kind of money."

"Anything being done about this information you've learned?"

"The Texas Rangers have already started looking into this issue. My understanding is this judge is going to be greeted first thing tomorrow morning by members of the Office of the Attorney General and by three or four Texas Rangers. I'm pretty sure it won't be how he expected his day to start."

"Is this shit really true?" Regan asked, stunned by Paul's accusations.

"It's as true as it gets. However, the other matter involving Genevieve isn't much better. I've recently spoken to some friends in Utah where her boyfriend died in a skiing accident several years back. These friends include some cops and a couple of prosecutors I got to know while we were working an interstate drug smuggling case a year or so before I retired. Once I told them about Mrs.

Church being charged with her husband's death, they told me they would revisit the circumstances surrounding her boyfriend's death. I've already sent them copies of her computer records, but that raises another obstacle they'll likely have to overcome as the court may frown on how those records were obtained. To their credit, the folks I've contacted acknowledged the fact that the initial investigation had been improperly influenced by a report filed by an inexperienced medical examiner. From what they've told me about the case involving the deceased boyfriend, the doctor's medical degree, like his faulty report, carried more weight with the jury than the evidence against Genevieve."

"How did you . . ."

"I told you, I ask questions, but it's also helpful to have a lot of friends who are good at what they do." Paul replied, aware that what he was telling Regan was more than enough to base a good movie on. "This is off the record, and I'll deny ever telling you this, but I've also had a copy of that entire case report, including the reports filed by the medical examiner's office, sent to me so I could take a look at what took place. Based on what I've read it's pretty clear, at least to me it is, that the person identified in the report as being Genevieve Ho is responsible for her boyfriend's death. He may have blacked out while skiing due to a medical emergency, but I have no doubt it was brought on because he was being poisoned. I hate to criticize the work conducted by another police department, but the lead investigator and the medical examiner's office bungled that investigation from the beginning. One of the biggest mistakes they made was not conducting a thorough search of the condo where Genevieve and her boyfriend had been staying. If that had been done, who knows what the cops would have found."

"Sounds like some serious mistakes were made by the investigator and that doctor, but I'm not sure I'm getting this. Did she benefit in any way from her boyfriend's death?" Regan asked, learning of a suspicious incident from Genevieve Church's past for the first time.

"Bobby Ray has been helping me by looking into different facets of Genevieve's past. By using some of the information my intelligence officer friends have developed, we determined that six months after the investigation into her boyfriend's death had been closed she purchased a Porsche Boxster GTS. That purchase alone set her back eighty-seven thousand big ones, and it wasn't one she financed."

"How'd she pull that off?" Regan asked, running his fingers through his hair as he realized how little he really knew about Genevieve's past.

"Apparently she had convinced her boyfriend to open two joint accounts in both their names. Their savings account didn't have much in it, but the checking account they shared had a substantial balance at the time of the boyfriend's death. She was also the sole beneficiary of a significant life insurance policy her boyfriend purchased only months before his death. The details of this policy, meaning the who, what, why, and when, are being scrutinized very closely due to Genevieve's current problems. This is still being looked into, but after he died she simply gave the dealership a certified check and drove off with the car."

"*No good bitch!*" Regan yelled, furious over being duped by someone he had trusted.

"That's not all she did. A week later, she placed a hefty down-payment on a three-bedroom condo in a fashionable high-rise in downtown Dallas. Two years later, that's where she met her first husband. Who, quite ironically, was not only richer than her dead boyfriend, but as it turns out he was someone who occasionally did business with one of her future victims."

"Her first husband did business with Mr. Church?" Regan asked incredulously.

"Sure did."

"What was his name, and how did he die?"

"Samuel Hettrick . . . and he didn't die. He was murdered; there's a big difference."

"Wait . . . 'Slamming' Sammy Hettrick was married to Genevieve Church . . . I mean Genevieve Ho . . . or whatever her name was. They . . . they were married to each other?"

"Seems like it." While interested in knowing how Hettrick had gotten his nickname, Paul decided against complicating the discussion any further than it already was. "By the sounds of it, I take it you knew him?" As he waited for Regan's response, Paul studied a copy of the marriage license that had been issued years earlier to Genevieve Ho and Samuel Hettrick by the state of Texas. Like several other documents, the marriage license had been faxed to him by one of his law enforcement contacts.

"I never actually met Mr. Hettrick, but I've heard many stories about him. Like you said, he and Mr. Church had done some business together but he died shortly after I started working for Mr. Church."

"Robert, I never said he died; I said he was murdered." Paul replied, correcting Regan for a second time. "At the time of his death, due to his age and a pre-existing medical condition that was fairly serious, his cause of death was ruled a heart attack.

Just like the investigation into the boyfriend's death, there wasn't much done when Mr. Hettrick's body was found. From what little I've been able to read about this investigation, his family, including our Black Widow friend, accepted the coroner's ruling regarding the cause of death. The good news is one of the reports I read indicated that an assistant coroner thought Hettrick's death was suspicious enough to warrant taking a few blood and tissue samples before he was cremated. Now all we have to do is to locate the toxicology report associated with those samples. If the report documents the fact that Slamming Sammy had been poisoned, then we'll raise enough hell until we find out why the findings were never followed up on. We may already know that answer, but we're still going to raise some hell over it."

"Think it still exists?" Regan asked, concerned how a case could be made against Mrs. Church if the toxicology report no longer existed.

"Let's hope so. The paper copy in the case file no longer exists for some unexplained reason. It's quite possible that someone was paid a sum of money to make it disappear. However, medical records, especially those related to an unattended death, are retained for however long the state mandates the medical examiner's office to retain them. In this case, it's probably for a minimum of twenty-five years, so we should be good. We may have to do some digging, but we'll find it." Having done his share of digging for outdated reports while employed by the Connecticut State Police Department, Paul was confident the report still existed.

"What do you think happened to the copy of the Toxicology Report that was included in the police report?" Regan asked rather naively, not grasping what Paul had implied moments early.

"Is that really a question that needs answering?" Paul replied, believing like several of his contacts that Genevieve Church had arranged for the report to never be seen again.

"Holy crap!" Stunned by the news Paul had told him, Regan was amazed by the similarities in each of the three deaths connected to Genevieve Church. Sitting alone on one of three expensive couches inside a large spacious room Simon Church had often retreated to during hectic periods; Regan quickly drained the remaining liquid inside a glass etched with a large single letter. Personalized with the first letter of his employer's last name, the glass was from a set neatly arranged on a nearby bar. Minutes earlier, just as his phone announced his friend's incoming call, Regan had taken his first two sips of the generous dose of bourbon he had poured for himself.

"Just like my contacts in Utah, the Texas Rangers and Dallas PD are going to be taking a second look into the circumstances surrounding 'Slamming' Sammy Hettrick's death." Paul said, unable to mention Hettrick's name without using the nickname Simon Church had tagged him with many years earlier. "They'll be comparing those tissue samples to the ones taken from Mr. Church. Obviously, that's something that needs to be done, but I believe we already know what they're going to find."

"This story . . . this is just friggin' amazing! I've worked for Mr. Church for years and I've never heard him speak a word about either of those two deaths." Regan said as he refilled his glass with another healthy amount of what had been Simon Church's favorite bourbon. The large glass decanter sitting next to him, like several others perched on the long wooden bar on the opposite side of the room, was something Regan knew Simon Church had occasionally checked; often accusing staff members of taking a nip or two each time they cleaned the room. The thought of one of the world's richest men periodically checking the liquor levels inside a few decanters made Regan laugh at the absurdity of Church's actions.

"Why would you?" Paul asked, referring to the lack of communication on the part of Simon Church concerning the suspicious deaths of two people Regan never knew.

"Why . . . why wouldn't I? I would have thought Mr. Church would have said *something* about his friend's death at some point or that I would have made the connection between Mrs. Church and her former husband. At times I handled some of her affairs, so I should have been able to put two and two together."

"You didn't learn anything about her former husband's death because unfortunately for Mr. Church, despite her spending habits he loved his wife more than she loved him. He likely trusted what she had told him regarding the circumstances surrounding his friend's death, and then used his influence, meaning his money, to see to it the media never brought the issue up again. It's a pretty safe bet to say that his influence kept his pretty young wife from being embarrassed more than she already had."

"Doing so probably contributed to his own demise. Isn't that right, Paul?" In some strange way, the alcohol was slowly helping Regan connect the details of the three tragic deaths.

"It's more than probably. I'd say it was more than likely."

"Freakin' amazing! Does that bitch Kowalski know about this? She made me take a friggin' polygraph test after I had told her the truth about everything I knew, and now you're telling me Mrs. Church has been running around killing everyone. Those no-good . . ." Angrily expressing his feelings about Kowalski and Genevieve Church, as well as the

polygraph test he had been forced him to take, Regan suddenly realized he had insulted one of Paul's good friends. "I'm . . . I'm sorry. I didn't mean to refer to Kowalski as being a bitch, I . . . I just got caught up in the moment."

"I'm sure she's been called worse, so don't sweat it. But if I were you, I'd slow down on the booze. Don't let that stuff cause you any more problems than you already have. I'll be in touch in the near future." More interested in wrapping up his phone conversation than he was in prolonging it, Paul tried ending it with one last comment. "When I learn more about those two deaths we've been talking about, I'll be sure to fill you in."

"Sounds like a plan. Not as good of a plan as the one I have to finish off this bourbon I've been drinking, but it's a plan. There's nothing to worry about, I'm staying at the mansion tonight. I have everything I need right here. And, by the way, she was getting ten thousand every month."

"Was that part of the prenup?"

"Yes, a very big part. Mr. Church never understood how one person could spend that kind of money each month, but he saw to it she received her allowance on the first of every month. It was deposited into one of her accounts like clockwork. I'm not sure why he never did this, but he never asked for receipts or looked to see where the money had been spent."

"Maybe he already knew what she was doing with it," Paul offered. "On the other hand, maybe he didn't want to know where it was going. It could be she was using it to increase the amount of money she already had in a nest egg for the next chapter in her life. If I were you, I'd have those forensic accountants do some digging to see where that money was going."

"I'll mention that," Regan replied, taking another sip of his drink after realizing how cunning Genevieve Church had been.

"Have any of the investigators talked to you about those deadly cocktails Mrs. Church was sending up to her husband's bedroom?" Paul asked, hoping this would be the last time he would have to address this concern.

"I just know what the maid has told them. According to the cops, Mrs. Church had asked her to deliver these drinks on several occasions. If you can believe this, the maid has supposedly supplied the cops with the exact dates she was asked to deliver the cocktails."

"That's all they've told you? They haven't mentioned anything about the meeting that took place in the mansion's kitchen between Mrs. Church and this maid?"

"Uh . . . no, not that I recall." Regan replied, wondering where Paul was going with this line of questioning.

"The bare-bones version of this part of this very weird story is when the maid was leaving the kitchen after her meeting with Mrs. Church; she turned and saw her rinsing out the glass she had just used."

"She saw Mrs. Church rinsing out a glass? How is that weird?" Regan asked.

"It's weird because in her interview the maid told the investigators about seeing Mrs. Church allegedly pouring a small amount of Pequa into a glass of water."

"So?" Regan said, interrupting what Paul was telling him.

"Robert, I really hate it when people interrupt me before I have the chance to finish making my point. Just put the booze down and listen for a few minutes."

"OK, sorry."

"The maid told the investigators how she had watched Mrs. Church drink that cocktail she had made for herself, and how surprised she was when her employer suffered no side effects. But, as she paused when she was leaving the kitchen, that's when the maid saw the glass being rinsed out. She claimed Mrs. Church had tried pulling the wool over her eyes by drinking what was inside that glass."

"What wool?" Regan asked, growing bored with this part of the conversation.

"The night before this maid had caught Mrs. Church red-handed when she was pouring a small amount of Pequa in a drink she was making for her husband. The maid has said that she knew Mrs. Church had been lying to her when she claimed the drink contained no harmful side effects, but when she recalled the drink Mrs. C had made for herself as being crystal clear, that confirmed her suspicions."

"How so?" Regan asked, suddenly becoming more interested than he had been moments earlier.

"Because the night before the drink that had been made for Mr. Church wasn't nearly as clear as the one Mrs. Church drank. The maid has described it as being cloudy: almost murky-like."

"That's because whatever Mrs. Church poured into her glass of water wasn't Pequa or any other harmful chemical, it was just water being mixed with water."

"More than likely," Paul replied, pleased that Regan was finally catching on.

"My guess is Mrs. Church had already planned this out. At some point, she had likely spent a few minutes purging the bottle of any remaining chemicals. After pouring out what was left, she likely flushed the remaining residue with copious amounts of water. Once that was done, she filled the bottle with water and placed it back under the sink. When she felt it was safe, Genevieve summoned Isabella to this meeting inside the kitchen. When they met, she made it appear as if she had mixed the same drink as the night before." Much to his surprise, Regan had somehow recalled the maid's first name.

"It looks that way." Paul admitted.

"Freaking bitch!" It was not the first time Regan had used that term when referring to Simon Church's wife.

"Robert, there are two more things you need to know. Look for a package in the next couple of days. I'll FedEx it to the address you're at now. It will be addressed to your attention. The package contains a small gift from me and the others on my team. And don't forget to keep me posted on any new information that develops regarding Mrs. Church's spending habits. Besides those two issues, I expect you to do the right thing with those Personal Service Agreements my friends and I signed with Mr. Church. Don't let my friends down or I'm coming after you." While Paul was joking with Regan about coming after him, he was serious about the terms of each PSA being honored; terms Simon Church had agreed to.

"I'm guessing the package is either going to contain a life jacket so I don't drown in all of this bullshit I'm swimming in or a nail file to help me escape from my prison cell. With all of this crap that's rising to the surface, I'm sure I'll be convicted one way or another for some of this nonsense everyone else has caused." With the phone call already terminated on the other end, Regan's suspicions regarding the package Paul was sending him were never confirmed.

******

Four days later, Regan received the small cardboard package his friend had sent him. Inside were a couple of the artifacts Simon Church had paid Paul a great deal of money to find.

64

Six months after Paul's remarkable discovery came to an end, the court signed off on the disbursements that had taken place. Just as it had been when all of the assets had finally been disbursed from his first discovery, those benefitting from this latest disbursement showered Paul and his friends with a variety of unwanted tributes.

While aware of the disbursements that had taken place, Paul paid little attention as the process played out. With little interest in capitalizing on the riches he and his friends had recovered, with the exception of a few interviews granted to a select group of newspapers and magazines, Paul spent the bulk of his time meeting with members of the National Park Service. As the keepers of the national military parks, a small group of NPS staff members and one retired state trooper began planning a series of maintenance projects in parks along the east coast.

Officially retired from being a cop and with no plans of conducting any future searches for Civil War treasures, Paul looked forward to spending the majority of his time conducting the research that was needed for a book he was planning on writing. When he was not busy with his newest venture, Paul visited a number of Civil War battlefields he had yet to explore. When time allowed, and when he and Donna weren't out on the *Donna Lynn* exploring the many parts of the Waccamaw River they had yet to visit, he managed to play a few rounds of golf with Chick and Bobby Ray and some of his new neighbors.

But, like most people who spent a great deal of their lives working in a career they loved, Paul could not walk away while one particular investigation remained active. Staying in contact with Regan and Martha Kowalski, he followed, and occasionally offered his opinion on the ongoing investigation into Simon Church's murder. It was an investigation he closely followed for several months until Genevieve Church was found guilty by a jury of her peers. Comprised of twelve individuals from vastly different walks of life, including those who believed in the Lord Almighty and two who knew little about the commandments God had handed down, Genevieve Church was found guilty. Like many others across Texas, the jurors had easily seen through the excuses and lies she and her attorneys continued to promote. Devious and pitiless to the very end, on a bright sunny afternoon Church was turned over to the Texas Department of Justice to await the execution of her sentence at the Texas State Penitentiary in Huntsville, Texas. Confined to Death Row inside the Mountain View Unit with several other females, Church and her attorneys soon began filing a variety of baseless appeals. Like many of the others reviewed by the Texas courts each year, those filed on behalf of Genevieve Church garnered little sympathy.

******

Grabbing a beer from the refrigerator in his garage on the same afternoon Genevieve Church arrived in Huntsville, Paul watched as Mike Norris searched the back of his FedEx truck for the package he had been sent to deliver. A frequent visitor to Paul's neighborhood, Norris was an occasional golfing partner of Paul and Bobby Ray's. Friendly and outgoing, he had first become friends with Paul several months earlier after making several deliveries to the Waring residence.

"Afternoon, Mike," Paul said, raising his can of beer as Norris wheeled a hand truck closer to the front of the garage. Holding up his cold beverage, Paul asked Norris if he needed something to quench his thirst. "I know you'd rather have one of these, but can I offer you something else to drink? A soft drink, a bottle of water, or maybe an iced tea?"

"Thanks, Paul, but I'm good. I've got a couple of drinks on ice inside the truck. I'm not being rude, but I have another twenty stops to make this afternoon so I need to make this quick." As he finished speaking, Norris handed his friend the electronic reader he had used to scan Paul's package. "Just sign the usual spot, and I'm gone. I have to hustle if I'm going to make it all the way up to Little River tonight."

"No problem, here you go." Paul said, barely paying attention to the package resting near his feet. Handing the reader back to Norris after giving little thought to how he had scribbled his name to confirm his package had been delivered, Paul added, "That's right, tonight is Thursday. What course are you playing on this beautiful afternoon?"

Far more interested in the game of golf than Paul, Norris, a divorced father of two teenage boys, played golf religiously every Tuesday and Thursday evenings in a men's league with fifty other players. Unlike Norris, most of the members were retirees who cared more about what went on inside the 19th Hole than they did about their golf scores.

"We're playing at Eagle Creek; it's better than some we play, but it's not my favorite." Norris said, taking back his reader. "This league I'm playing in is filled with cheapskates. Most of them get upset if they have to pay more than forty bucks each time we play. Meanwhile, they're all walking around with more money in their pockets than you know who." Making his way back to his truck, Norris realized Paul had not been expecting a delivery. Pointing at the package sitting in his friend's driveway, Norris added one last comment. "I have no idea what's inside that box and from the look on your face neither do you. I just know it's a lot heavier than most of the others I deliver here."

As Norris drove away, Paul carefully placed the heavy package down on a table inside his garage. As this took place, Donna pulled into their driveway. At work all day, she had been gone since early that morning.

"I see Mike's been here. I just waved to him as I was coming up the street." Donna said, planting a warm kiss on her husband's cheek as he was about to open the large package. "Any idea what's inside?"

"Not sure," Paul said, barely paying attention to the information contained on the shipping label as he offered his wife a friendly smile. "Outside of it being heavy and containing something Regan has sent me, I have no idea what it is. He never told me he was sending me anything."

Pointing to an unusual handwritten warning located below the shipping label, Donna asked her husband what it meant. "Have you ever received a package marked like this?" Written with some type of a black felt marker, the warning read, *Do not open using any sharp instruments.* The first two words had been underlined with the same felt marker.

"No . . . no, I haven't." Paul admitted. Stopping what he was doing, Paul stared at the inscription.

"So why would he write that? That's if he was the person who actually sent you this package." Donna asked, referring to Regan. Always concerned about another attack on her husband's life, Donna had become much more vigilant of anything unusual taking place in their lives.

"Let's find out." Paul said, pulling his phone out of his back pocket as he backed away from the table. Moments later, he dialed Regan's phone number.

"What took so long? I've been waiting to hear from you for the past two days," Regan said, his voice full of excitement over the gift he had sent his friend. "Well, were you surprised?"

"I haven't opened it yet. I wanted to make sure it had come from you. Donna got me thinking that maybe Mrs. Church or one of her underlings may have sent me a bomb or some other type of special gift."

"Then you were wise to call me, weren't you?" Regan said, laughing over Paul's reason for calling.

"How long do I have to deactivate the timer?" Paul asked, joking with his friend after Regan assured him that he had sent the package. "And, what wire do I cut; the red, white, or black one? I've never really paid attention to those scenes in the movies where some hero saves the day at the very last second."

"Sorry, I can't tell you that." Regan said, adding to the humor being exchanged between them.

"I suppose not."

"Listen, I have another call coming in that I have to take. Call me in a day or two after you've had a chance to enjoy your gift. We'll talk more when we aren't dealing with any other issues. *Have fun!*" Regan said before moving on to his next call.

As he attempted to protest, Paul heard Regan's phone terminate their call. Confused by what his friend had just said, he turned and stared at the package.

"Well?" Donna asked.

Focusing his attention as intensely as he ever had on any one object, Paul had nothing to say in response to his wife's question.

"Paul, did you hear me? What did Regan send you?"

Still distracted over Regan's comment, Paul weakly answered Donna's question. "He didn't say."

After carefully opening the package, Paul noticed the care Regan had given to protecting the object inside. Wrapped in a thick protective layer of foam padding, the object was further protected on all four sides by an equally thick layer of Styrofoam peanuts. Above and below, thicker layers of foam padding had helped secure it from being damaged while in transit. While the anti-static version of the shipping peanuts had done their job, several annoying pieces of white Styrofoam clung to the foam padding as Paul carefully removed the object from its cardboard shipping container.

"I hate these things," Donna said as she picked up three large handfuls of peanuts that had tumbled out of the cardboard container. As he began to remove the protective wrapping from around the object, Paul paid little attention to the small trail of white peanuts his wife was attending to.

Carefully tearing away the Styrofoam padding, Paul realized what the object was that Regan had sent him. Stunned by the magnitude of his friend's gift, Paul was nearly speechless as he finished unwrapping the artifact.

"This . . . this is the same chest we saw at Simon Church's house. It's the same wooden chest that was owned by Captain Howard, isn't it?" As she asked her questions, Donna's eyes slowly studied the wooden chest her husband had spoken about on several occasions. While sustaining a handful of small nicks and scratches over the years, the chest was still in remarkable condition. A valuable artifact that somehow managed to survive the Civil War and several subsequent owners, its value had escalated significantly after a series of newspaper articles described the role the chest played in concealing Captain Howard's journal.

"It's the same one, Donna," Paul softly answered, gently wiping away several small bits of packing material that continued to adhere to the chest's wooden surface.

While the precious artifact had little in common with any of her furniture, Donna marveled at how the chest had been constructed. Pointing out how well the fan-shaped tenons fit inside each corresponding mortise and the craftsmanship that went into making each hinge, she commented on the visual absence of any nails or screws. "I'm very impressed by the detail that was given to constructing this chest. Whoever made it certainly knew what he was doing."

Nodding over the detail his wife had pointed out, as he opened the chest for a closer look Paul spoke to his wife. In doing so, he slowly ran a finger over the hidden compartment where Howard's journal had been hidden. As the hidden compartment slowly opened, Paul and Donna noticed the envelope that had been placed there. Pulling it from its hiding spot, they noticed Paul's full name had carefully been written in an elaborate cursive font.

"That's impressive," Donna said, briefly examining the fanciest and, by far, neatest version of her husband's name she had ever seen. "Were you expecting this?"

Looking at his wife, Paul nodded at the envelope before pointing to the artifact he had been examining. "I wasn't expecting the chest, so how could I have expected this?"

After speculating on what might be inside the envelope, Paul carefully opened it; deliberately making sure not to damage the elaborate style in which his name had been written. Among the several pieces of paper inside the envelope was a brief handwritten note from Regan. Like Paul's name, the note had been neatly written.

Paul,

From the first time I saw you admiring Captain Howard's chest, I knew you were the person Simon would have wanted to have this. For everything you have accomplished for him, and for me, please accept this gift as a token of our appreciation.

Unlike some of the other Civil War artifacts which recently came into Mr. Church's possession by inappropriate means, this gift comes with no worries. Besides the enclosed paperwork which shows this chest was legally purchased, I have worked out the necessary details with Mr. Church's attorneys to reflect this gift was donated to you as payment for services rendered to the Church estate. Please accept this for what it is, for it is simply a gift from the collection of a Civil War buff to a dear friend.

I hope you treasure it just as much as my good friend had.

Sincerely,

Robert Regan

P.S. – Maybe someday I'll show you the letter Mr. Church found inside Howard's journal. As far as I know, he and I are the only ones who have ever read it. The contents of this letter describe another adventure we should someday consider. In the event you don't believe me, I've included a photocopy of the envelope Howard had sealed. For now, enjoy your gift. We'll talk soon!

"What!" Paul screamed, expressing his disbelief over the letter Regan described in his note. It was something neither Simon Church nor Regan had hinted at over the past several months. Seconds later, his wife uttered a similar comment. Shocked by what he read, Paul carefully inspected the photocopy of the old envelope that had been included with the other paperwork.

"Do as he's suggesting, Paul, enjoy the gift he sent you." Donna said, nearly pleading with her husband to ignore Regan's comment regarding this next adventure. Like Paul, she had carefully read Regan's note several times as a way of absorbing every detail. "Take some time to relax and enjoy your latest find. This note Regan wrote you isn't going anywhere; nor is this adventure he's mentioned. He's not going to do anything without contacting you first. You and your friends have the rest of your lives to solve this next mystery."

Agreeing with everything Donna had said, Paul, on the verge of calling Regan to verify the letter actually existed, allowed his phone to gently slide back inside his pants pocket. Smiling at his wife, he promised her he would not contact Regan until he had spent some time relaxing and enjoying his newest gift.

Without breaking his promise, three days later Paul was already thinking of what he would tell Bobby Ray, Chick, and Peter the following morning. At the Waccamaw Diner, over a thick stack of his favorite blueberry pancakes, he would somehow find the right words to tell his friends about the next adventure Regan had in store for them.

It was an adventure he was already looking forward to.